'How do you supp[...] sudden feeling. 'I [...] about i[...]

'I couldn't face you, Jim. I felt so . . . dirty. I . . . I loved you. I really did. I couldn't face the future.' The small voice betrayed her sincerity. He hesitated, anger assuaged, but the enormity of what she'd done was too much.

'And your father!' he came back at her. 'He was broken up. Know that? Poor bastard had just got you back. And college! One more year! You could have had a career! You just blew it all! And for what?'

It was too much; too brutal. Her face turned red, then white, and she wished she hadn't come. She should never have come back. She'd known it really. They'd asked too much of her. She wasn't strong enough. She couldn't face it. But there was no escape . . .

THE GARDEN

VALERIE GEORGESON

WARNER BOOKS

A WARNER BOOK

First published in Great Britain in 1991
by Macdonald & Co
This edition published by Warner Books in 1993

A CIP catalogue record for this book is
available from the British Library.

ISBN 0 7515 0209 X

Printed in England by Clays Ltd, St Ives plc

Warner Books
A Division of
Little, Brown and Company (UK) Limited
165 Great Dover Street
London SE1 4YA

THE GARDEN

BEATTIE FAMILY

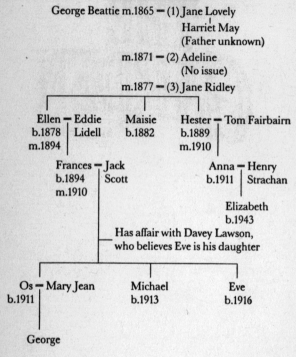

George Beattie m.1865 ━ (1) Jane Lovely

Harriet May
(Father unknown)

m.1871 ━ (2) Adeline
(No issue)

m.1877 ━ (3) Jane Ridley

Ellen ━ Eddie   Maisie   Hester ━ Tom Fairbairn
b.1878 Lidell   b.1882   b.1889
m.1894   m.1910

Frances ━ Jack   Anna ━ Henry
b.1894 Scott   b.1911 Strachan
m.1910

Elizabeth
b.1943

Has affair with Davey Lawson,
who believes Eve is his daughter

Os ━ Mary Jean   Michael   Eve
b.1911   b.1913   b.1916

George

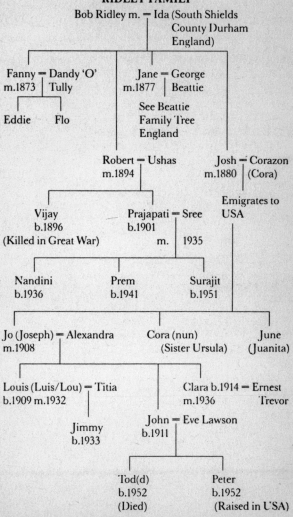

RIDLEY FAMILY

Bob Ridley m. = Ida (South Shields County Durham England)

Fanny = Dandy 'O' Tully
m.1873

Eddie   Flo

Jane = George Beattie
m.1877

See Beattie Family Tree England

Robert = Ushas
m.1894

Josh = Corazon (Cora)
m.1880

Emigrates to USA

Vijay
b.1896
(Killed in Great War)

Prajapati = Sree
b.1901
m. 1935

Nandini
b.1936

Prem
b.1941

Surajit
b.1951

Jo (Joseph) = Alexandra
m.1908

Cora (nun)
(Sister Ursula)

June
(Juanita)

Louis (Luis/Lou) = Titia
b.1909 m.1932

Clara b.1914 = Ernest
m.1936   Trevor

Jimmy
b.1933

John = Eve Lawson
b.1911

Tod(d)
b.1952
(Died)

Peter
b.1952
(Raised in USA)

PART ONE

At first she couldn't find the key. She stood in the doorway fumbling with the collection given her by the solicitor. Then when the right one slipped into the lock and turned at last, she froze on the threshold, listening. Hearing no sound, she pushed open the door and looked inside. Patches of light floated in the darkness. She watched them fearfully, then remembered the front door opened straight onto the dance studio with its mirrored walls. All she was seeing was the reflection of street lights filtering in through the windows. Reassured, Liz found the effect really rather beautiful. The house remembered her, she decided. The floating spaces were waiting for her, expecting her. She had come home.

She tip-toed to the edge of the pool, then passed through the membrane, into the light and felt herself lifted, like a feather, ready to dance across the floor. She smiled, looking up to admire the youthful Liz, the fairy in the mirror; but saw instead what she had become, a woman in her late forties, hair scraped back, uneasy in the oversized dirndl and fawn mac. She looked like a refugee, or, she smiled ironically at her ghostly shadow, a nun recently stepped out of a convent.

She dropped her travelling bag to the floor with a thud and wondered where the light switch was. By the door? But, hearing a rustle somewhere deep in the house, Liz paused, caught in the light. Was there family here? Or intruders? She turned to the back of the room, where the stairs rose and disappeared out of sight. Somewhere up there in the darkness was the door to the office. It had been her great grandfather's in the days when this studio was still a flower shop; before Liz's half cousin Eve had changed it all.

Eve was more like an aunt really; from an older generation; gone now, too. She had a child of her own. Why had she left Liz the house? Guilt? Liz closed her eyes, imagining the days when the room had been filled with flowers. She inhaled deeply. Her nose wrinkled with distaste. Damp. Eve had certainly let the place go before she died. But then, by all accounts she hadn't been well. Had she continued teaching up to the end, Liz wondered?

A loud bang made her jump. She looked at the ceiling, trembling. Footsteps crossed over head. Who was it? Looking round quickly Liz found Eve's old cane. She used to use it on the dancers' legs. 'Point your toes! Watch that turn out!' She picked it up and crept to the foot of the stairs then, step by step, fearing creaking boards, she made her way into the darkness.

The place was much bigger than she remembered. There were a lot of doors; more than before surely? She pushed one. A ghostly lavatory stared indignantly from the closet. She walked on, feeling her way along the wall; another door, bigger, glass panels; the office door. She paused. A draught blew from inside. The door must be open then. Was he, she, it in there? She pushed it a little further and slid inside. Reaching along the frame, she found the light switch and flicked it. A spotlight fell on a picture over the fireplace; an abstract in oils; her own work in another life. Abruptly, she extinguished the light and passed on. She was entering a corridor. Was there a step up to it? Her foot searched the floor. Then there was another bang, and a light came on in the empty corridor ahead. Someone was coming. She looked at the doors. There were so many of them. That was a room. That was a cupboard. The one she had determined for a cupboard opened and a man came out, walking towards

4

her, his still-youthful silhouette belied by the gleam of his thinning dome. So he *was* here. She'd hoped and feared to see him. She must not faint. She spoke in a stern voice.

'Where is everybody?'

His eyes scanned the ageing girl, and he wasn't pleased. 'They all left,' he told her. His voice was antagonistic in spite of the faint transatlantic twang. 'You're too late for the funeral.'

'I know. The solicitor told me.' She sounded defensive. She must not. 'What are *you* doing here?' she challenged.

'I'm a trustee. I'm surprised the solicitor didn't tell you *that*!'

Like children, each was determined to stare out the other.

'He told me there were two trustees,' Liz replied warily. 'I knew he was one of them but he didn't tell me you were the other.'

'Didn't you want to know who it was?'

'No.'

'*I* would have,' he sneered. Liz said nothing. No doubt he found her behaviour unusual. She must be prepared for that. 'You sound like a foreigner,' he observed. She was surprised and showed it. 'You sound like a foreigner, speaking English. I mean you've got an accent. Indian, Swiss, I don't know. You don't sound English any more.' Was it an accusation?

'That's funny.' She shrugged it off.

'Why?'

'You do. Well almost. I remember you as having a much stronger American accent.'

'Ah. So you do remember something.' And now there was bitterness. She made a sort of pass in front of her with her hands. Jim ignored it. 'I've been teaching in Cambridge for nearly eight years now,' he explained. 'The accent rubs off.' She smiled with polite interest. 'I

5

didn't think you'd come,' he added abruptly.

'I surprised myself,' she answered.

'I hardly recognise you.'

'You haven't changed much.'

Then he got angry. 'Why are you looking so superior?' he demanded.

'Me?'

'Yes, you! And what the hell were you doing there with your hands. Warding off the evil eye?' Her face closed. 'Is that what you think of me? Is that why you walked out on me?' She looked away. This wasn't getting them anywhere.

'You know why I left, Jim. Leave it alone now.'

'I can't leave it alone.'

'It was twenty years ago.'

'Seems like yesterday.' His voice grated on her conscience.

'*You* weren't evil, Jim. It was me.'

'Crap! So what was this ritual gesture, hah? No, don't tell me, it's all part of that stuff you got into, isn't it?'

'It isn't "stuff"! How dare you call it "stuff"!'

'It's cultish crap!'

'It saved my life!' The big black eyes glared at him. They hadn't changed. They were still lost looking, lost but defiant. Don't you dare rescue me, you bastard! they said. He almost laughed. But suddenly he found he didn't want to hurt her. He remembered the white-faced beatnik Eve had introduced him to, in this very house, that first time he'd come over from the States. She had amused him with her spiky lacquered hair and her pale lips. She was full of youthful love of life. Her energy had revived him. He had fallen in love with her restless soul. Too bloody restless! Those black eyes. Don't you dare rescue me!

'I didn't want this, you know,' he said testily. 'Eve dropped it on me from a great height. I didn't ask to be made a trustee. I guess she thought it would be some

6

kind of a joke!' His voice rang hollow through the house, as though searching for laughter.

'I see,' Liz said forgivingly. 'And I suppose we are sort of related, so it isn't so strange. Really it's a good thing we *didn't* marry. We are sort of cousins.'

'Sort of removed,' Jim nodded slowly. 'Sort of distantly removed. Like it no longer mattered.' His voice rose to a protest. Liz fidgeted unhappily. 'Got any luggage?' he asked wearily.

'Down there,' She glanced over the rail into the studio.

'Okay. I'll fetch it. I suppose you *are* stopping the night?'

'It is my house.'

'In trust,' he retorted. He shot off down the stairs and picked up the little bag, returning with it in seconds. He was panting. 'Got to get back in shape,' he said. 'Not as young as I was.' He looked down at the bag then held it out to her. 'Travelling light?' he asked.

'Possessions only weigh you down.'

'That sounded a little sanctimonious!'

'Sorry.'

But he wasn't finished picking her over yet. 'That how you look on your new home? Like a possession to get rid of? Or is it your old home?' She smiled, then laughed, relieved to be over the sticky bit and into the chat. She was gabbling on about the old days. Jim wasn't listening. He was remembering. He remembered Eve, the failed starlet, failed wife, failed mother, he'd known as a boy back in New Mexico. She'd been a rebel, too. Finally, she'd come home, tail between her legs and been a mother to Liz; little orphan Liz. Her own mother had been a neurotic mess and her dad ... he lived in London with his lady-friend and probably couldn't cope with his rebel daughter; still couldn't. She'd even gone to school here. Eve hadn't done so badly by her, until ... The memory of pain cut off the inner monologue. He started listening to Liz.

'You know what this place has always lacked?' she was saying, 'a garden!'

'Garden?' Jim was surprised. 'Why? Would you think of staying on here if it had?' She shook her head.

'No. Not really. I don't know why I said that really. I mean, what's there here for me? In Shields? I don't belong here any more.' So, he thought, it was just another big tease. She *was* going to sell. *If* the trustees let her!

'You'd better come upstairs,' he said. 'There's a room at the top that's pretty dry. I'll show you.'

She followed him up. The house was much bigger than she remembered; but so neglected. There were two flats. One on the first floor, one on the top, and under the studio was a basement. Eve had turned it into changing rooms. It all seemed so empty.

'When did she die?' she asked.

'Must be ten weeks now.'

'Feels more like ten years.' Liz shuddered. 'The place's got that deserted feel. You know?'

He looked at her, then opened the door into her room. Switching on the light, he flung the travel bag to the floor. 'Welcome home,' he said. He was about to leave.

'You going?' she asked, alarmed.

'Why? Want me to stay?' he jeered.

'I don't know.' Now she was flustered.

'Stop buggering me about, Liz.'

Her face burned. 'You haven't forgiven me, have you?' she asked. She was near to tears. Jim saw how fragile she was. She was thin; almost transparent. You had to pity her her lack of armour.

'Do you want anything?' he asked gently. She was puzzled.

'What can you possibly give me that I might want?' she asked in a superior tone. Jim gritted his teeth. She would try the patience of a saint.

'I meant tea, coffee,' he explained. 'There's some in the kitchen.'

She had the grace to blush. 'No. Thanks. But if *you* want some ...'

'Playing Lady Bountiful now, are we?' He was not a saint. 'What the hell *did* you run off for?' he shouted suddenly.

'But she told you! Didn't she?'

'Who?'

'Eve!'

'Eve gave me a cock and bull story about how your great-grandparents had committed incest and you were the long-term result and how, when you found out, when she told you, the bitch, you were so upset you ran off!'

'Well then! You know!'

'No! I *don't* know!'

Liz stared at him in shocked silence. It had been a long time since anyone had so much as mentioned the bald facts, and to hear them in so direct a manner and from him, of all people, was more than she could cope with. For years the truth had been veiled in merciful silence. And he had torn the veil asunder! It was shocking. How could he *be* so flippant? Was he punishing her for hurting him? She glared at him, but the hurt was all too clear in his eyes. She looked away. She supposed, after all, she did owe him an explanation.

'I couldn't marry you, Jim!' she pleaded. 'Not knowing what I was! Suppose we'd had children? What would their lives have been like? Look at my grandmother. Look at my mother. How they died? They went crazy. You know that. And I know it's all because ... because ... they were cursed!' Jim swallowed the drama without blinking. Behind the brittle, clichéd phrases primeval feelings lurked. He would have to choose his words carefully.

'*Who* cursed them?' he asked.

9

'My great-grandparents!' She spoke as though she thought him a fool. 'Jane and her brother Robert. You know what it says in the Bible, "The sins of the fathers shall be visited on the sons up until the fourth generation." Or something like that. What if we'd had kids? Jim, I couldn't do it to them! Or to you! And I felt ...'

'How do you suppose *I* felt?' He interrupted with sudden feeling. 'I mean, you didn't even tell me about it. You just took off!'

'I couldn't face you, Jim. I felt so ... dirty. I ... I loved you. I really did. I couldn't face the future.' The small voice betrayed her sincerity. He hesitated, anger assuaged, but the enormity of what she'd done was too much.

'And your father!' he came back at her. 'He was broken up. Know that? Poor bastard had just got you back. And college! One more year! You could have had a career! You just blew it all! And for what?'

It was too much; too brutal. Her face turned red, then white, and she wished she hadn't come. She should never have come back. She'd known it really. They'd asked too much of her. She wasn't strong enough. She couldn't face it. But there was no escape. She was here now. She sighed. Jim would never understand. Outsiders never did. He would never understand! Oh, what was the point in even trying to tell him? Unless ... unless he was some part of her, still unresolved? If so, he had to *be* resolved before life moved on! You have to travel light; jettison the baggage. Was this man still part of her baggage? She looked at him and knew he was. And she knew she wasn't equal to the task. But she would try. God she would try!

'You have to imagine how I was,' she began.

He frowned. Why was it he suddenly had this feeling like a snake was creeping up his back? No, he wouldn't dream of rescuing her. He wouldn't dare; didn't even want to. His face closed. So, she thought, he doesn't understand. She'd known he wouldn't. She slumped onto the bed and started crying, leaning over like a weeping tree. She repeated the words, like a mantra.

'You have to imagine how I was.'

And he saw the art student, beatnik turned into a girl in a flowered dress making wedding plans; rounding overnight; wisecracks turning into smiles.

And she saw a dark tunnel at either end, and herself between them on the platform. She felt the cold air that precedes the tube train coming down the tunnel. She was reading a poster, and it said: '"This life is not reality."'

Sitting on the bed now, she stared into space as though she could see it. '"Nor is death the gateway to paradise. Reality is here and now and yet beyond us and it alone is paradise. One step will take you there." Imagine what impact that poster had on me?' She turned to look at him directly. 'I mean my life had turned overnight into a nightmare. One minute I was writing wedding invitations, the next Eve was telling me I was damned. "One step will take you there," it said. And then it gave you the address of a meditation centre. It was the only way out.'

'I knew you'd gone to India,' he snorted. 'I couldn't believe you were still there. You were hard to find.'

'Eve wanted you to find me. Didn't she?' she said.

'Yes.' Jim spoke as though he could see Eve's point of view. 'I guess it was the one way she could think of to put matters right. She split us up! I guess she felt she owed it to us to bring us back together again.'

'And that's why she left me the house.' She looked at Jim. 'In trust.'

'Sure. Didn't leave her son much. Minor legacy, that's all. Still, he's alright. Over in Albuquerque. Likes it there. I'd looked after him for her and ... you and me ... we were just about the only thing left on her mind.'

'Interfering cow!' The intensity of her feeling astonished

11

Liz. She had thought she'd forgiven her.

'Yeah.' Jim's voice rang hollow in the empty house. 'Should have left well alone!'

'Did you marry?' Liz asked with some hesitation.

'Yup!' Jim thrust his chin out. 'Got a kid as well. They're back in Albuquerque, too. Popular place is Albuquerque. Haven't seen either of them in six years.'

Liz dropped her eyes to the floor.

'Oh,' she said. 'I hoped you'd be happy.'

'You hypocritical little bitch!'

'Sorry. I didn't mean to be.'

She wouldn't look at him. She felt he was dragging her in deeper and deeper and though she was letting it happen alright, she wasn't going to encourage him. His feet moved restlessly by the door. Sooner or later he'd ask her the same thing.

'How about you? You married?' he asked. She shrugged noncommittally.

'What the hell does that mean?' he shouted.

'Don't shout.'

'I'm not shouting.'

'You are.'

'I give up.'

'Don't go.' She stopped him as his foot crossed the threshold. He turned and looked at her. Her eyes showed terror. He registered this in a part of himself he thought defunct, long, long ago. There was a lot he didn't know.

'What're you scared of?' he asked, alarmed.

'Me? Scared?' Pure bravado. He said nothing. He waited. 'This empty house, I suppose. I don't know. *Am* I scared?' She was looking at him as though he contained the answer to her every question. But how could he? He waited. She started trembling; really trembling. Her teeth were chattering. 'I don't know where I am,' she said.

'18 Victoria Terrace, Fowler Street, South Shields,

Tyne and Wear, England. And it is the twentieth century,' he added, because it seemed important she should know.

'It could be any time,' she said.

'I see!' He nodded. 'You really *don't* know where you are, do you?' He sighed, then came to sit on the chair by the cupboard. '*Did* you marry?' he asked.

'Er ... yes.'

'Where is he?'

'India.'

'Figures.' Suddenly she resented him knowing all the answers. 'So. You fell in love again,' he said. 'When?'

'I didn't say I'd fallen in love,' she corrected him. 'I said I'd married.' Her face had a prudish expression which exasperated him.

'But you *do love* him,' he insisted tersely.

'I've grown fond of him already ...'

He stared at her, weighing her words, before he spoke. 'What are you telling me here?' he asked. Liz bit her lip and shook her head. She couldn't tell him; didn't want to try. 'Alright, when did you marry this ... Is he Indian by the way?' She shook her head. 'When did you get married?' He was shouting. She found him intimidating.

'A few days ago,' she answered, defensively.

'Hell!'

'It had all been arranged! Before the news about Eve! Plans had been made.'

'Arranged?' Jim decided to take a sideways approach to the question that had sprung so immediately to his mind. 'Is he ... does he do this meditation of yours?' he asked.

'Oh yes,' she replied with a mixture of pride and smugness, intended to close the subject.

'Well I won't ask if you've got any kids!' he laughed shortly.

'I can't have kids. I mustn't. You know that. And you know why,' she reminded him primly.

13

'Oh yeah!' He slapped his knee. 'Tainted genes!'

'Don't sneer!' she shouted. 'It's not funny. And I'm not making it up, either. Because I *have* got tainted genes. It's real.'

'You sure of that?'

The question threw her. 'What do you mean?' she asked.

'Are you sure about this incest thing?' He spoke slowly. There was a long silence.

'Why not?' she said finally. 'It makes sense. And I mean, I don't believe Eve was making it up. Why should she? She wouldn't do a thing like that. Would she? And ... well ... look at my mother and then look at *her* mother! Don't you think they inherited some sort of a problem? It came from somewhere. Something must have happened to cause it. It makes sense, or do you think I'm crazy?'

'You're not crazy,' he said. Then he snorted, 'No. I take that back.'

'Look at me, Jim!' He looked. 'I'm the one that got away! I found freedom from my family karma!'

'Oh, I see. Through spiritual means, I suppose.' He laughed.

'Yes! Actually, I'm working out the family problem for them too. For the whole family!'

'Great!' he smiled, but his eyes glinted with challenge. 'So you can have kids now!'

'No. I ... I didn't say that.' She looked away furtively. It was as he expected. Well, if she was acting, so would he.

'I'm sorry,' he said. 'I'm a little bit confused here. You said you'd found freedom from the family ... curse. But ... now you say you can't have kids, so how have you found freedom?'

'Well, I haven't found it yet.' She cringed at the lameness of her reply. She must do better. 'But I will! It's just I'm not a very good yogi. I have so much to learn first!'

He was near to tears. He could hardly bear to be in the room with her. He wanted to kill her; if only to put her out of her misery. 'It's difficult to explain to an outsider,' she wailed.

'Try me,' he said grimly. Her heart sank.

'I don't know where to start.' She shook her head as if to send him off. She was like a poor student, unable to defend her thesis. She needed encouragement.

'Tell me about this ... marriage,' he said with professional patience.

'It's difficult.' She was struggling. 'But I'll try.' She took a deep breath, thinking, 'in for a penny ...', and threw herself in at the deep end. 'You've obviously heard about "The Family",' she said, daring him to say anything bad about it. Jim stared at her, gauging his response.

'This cult you were in in India?' he asked, believing he had been restrained beyond all reproach. But she took offence even at that.

'It's not a cult!' she said angrily. 'And it's a worldwide organisation!'

'Alright. I'm sorry,' he soothed. 'Go on.'

With sinking heart, Liz continued: 'Well, the spiritual leader ... the man who started the movement ... actually, we call him "Father", I mean, you have to know who he is, I mean who he really is, to understand our relation to him.' Jim was still staring. She went on. 'Well, soon after I started meditating, there was a chance to go to India and meet him. And it seemed like a blessing from heaven. I mean, I thought he might be able to sort me out. So I went and, well, he was very kind to me. And I confessed my problem to him. I mean about the incest. And he told me ... don't look at me like that.'

'Sorry.'

'He told me I could work out my problems, through "The Way". That's what we call our meditation system.

15

So I stayed in India, working in the ashram, cooking, cleaning and so on, and I meditated a lot and, do you know, I started to be happy. I mean I really felt happy. I felt I belonged. I mean "The Family" was good to me. It took me in and fed and clothed me and gave me everything. And all this in spite of what I was!'

'A child of shame,' Jim mocked. But Liz was too absorbed in her memories to hear.

'Father'd told me I shouldn't get married or have children,' she went on, 'because the curse would pass on and . . .' She stopped, choking.

'Did you ever think about me?'

'Yes. At first. A lot. But he told me I should put all the past behind me.'

'Hah!'

'You see, when I was accepted into "The Family" and he baptised me, I was reborn. I was a new person. You can't let ghosts mar your happiness.'

'Thanks.'

'Nothing personal.'

'No. No. I can see that.' He turned his face to the wall, to hide his feelings.

'You see if I wanted to be free of my karma, I had to be free of everything else too. I had to give everything up. Including painting.' Clearly, Jim thought, this was a more painful memory still. 'And I was rewarded for my devotion. My meditation got deeper and I got more sensitive. Though I was always too inclined to go my own way. You know?' Jim stared sardonically at those rebellious black eyes and nodded slowly.

'Anyway,' Liz went on flustered, 'I was getting on fine really. Other people seemed to hit problems. But not me. I kept my nose clean and my head down and . . . I was alright. Or at least I thought I was getting away with it. Maybe I was just treading water. Maybe that's why things started happening. Perhaps I was getting . . . smug. I mean, I'd been in "The Family" for twenty odd

16

years. Other people became teachers; travelled the globe; influenced world events. They got all kinds of sidhis. I mean, they got spiritual powers. Like Jeanne. She was very high up. But not me. I just meditated, and cooked and washed up. And of course ... I tried not to think.' Liz gathered her strength. 'Well anyway, I was on the washing-up rota for the week, and up to my elbows in dirty water, when Jeanne came up behind me and whispered in my ear.

'"A word, dear." I looked round to say I'd be with her as soon as I'd finished, but her raised eyebrows were enough to stop me. She had the power to challenge the authority of even the kitchen rota. No-one would dare contradict her, or complain if I left the sink; not if Jeanne ordered it. The other women watched as I dried my hands and followed her, head down out of the kitchen. I could hear the sudden buzz of conversation as the door closed behind me and Jeanne led me into the meditation room. Together we did our ritual obeisance before Father's photograph, then sat cross-legged on the floor, staring at the everlasting light flickering in front of the picture. I watched it reflecting in the glass and wondered when Jeanne was going to speak. I had no idea what she was going to say, but I knew it must be important. I glanced at her, but her eyes were closed with an intense concentration. She drew in a deep, deep breath and let it out again very slowly. I thought I'd better follow her example and was drifting nicely into a timeless zone, when suddenly, Jeanne spoke.

'"This is all very nice, dear," she said, "but we need to talk." My eyes sprang open. My heart beat faster. "Talk" sounded ominous. I panicked. Had I done something wrong? Had I fallen short of Father's wishes? Worse, was I going to have to go on the teaching course! To be sent out into the world, like Jeanne, to teach "The Way" was, *is* my worst fear. I mean, I'm no missionary. Of course it's very selfish of me. I realise that. Everyone should benefit from Father's teachings. But, you see, I'm not really a very good yogi! As they'd find out for themselves, if they tried to train me.'

Seeing Jim smile, Liz faltered. 'Don't get me wrong,' she explained, 'I *want* to be a good yogi. It's just I've somehow never found it easy to carry on in the "received" way, I mean the received way of thinking and doing things; that's all. I mean, and at least I know it, I'm too idiosyncratic by half! What an example to set others, eh? I suppose I'd hoped I could just go on forever, humbly keeping my low profile, following my inner voyage, guided by little more than instinct and Father's promptings. It's amazing; they come so spontaneously during meditation! He really seems to speak to you! In your head, I mean. And I'd have liked to carry on like that. You know?' Liz sighed. 'Anyway I'd be a rotten teacher! I knew it. So, it was with fear that I turned to look at Jeanne. She saw it and she was amused. Jeanne's a strange creature. She's got short curly hair, and she's thin, elfinlike really, but strong as an ox. And her eyes bulge, glittering with a sharp light that always makes me wonder if she's "on" something. Though of course she isn't. Anyway, slowly, dramatically, she put her long fingers on my arm and spoke with a studied gentleness in that funny Swiss–American accent of hers.

'"Liz," she said, "you have been alone too long. You need to find your femininity again. You must become a woman." I suppose I must've frowned. I was very puzzled.

'"Father forbade me to have children," I reminded her. Jeanne nodded deliberately, as though suppressing great impatience.

'"True," she said, "but he did not forbid you to marry." I tell you, my heart stopped! My jaw dropped open. Jeanne chuckled. She was very pleased with herself. "Yes," she said, shaking her head, "a great honour has been done you, Elizabeth. Father has chosen you for one of his favourite sons." She looked at me as though she was expecting me to whoop with joy or something. But, I was puzzled. I had no idea who she was talking about, you see. He could have been one of the Indians, or a Swiss, or an Australian, anything. I tried hard to detach myself from any preference, and, I've got to admit it, especially from the preference of not getting married at all. Because, you know, Jim, I didn't want to. I hadn't asked for it. Anyway, then she said, with a somewhat forced jocularity, "Can you imagine who it is?"

'"No," I said, truthfully. Then, I made the mistake of saying something in pious competition with her. I'm sorry to talk like this about a sister, but ...' then she blurted out with real feeling, 'I've got to be honest with you, Jim, Jeanne really does get right up my nose!' Jim shrugged in an accepting kind of way. It was good to know Liz was still human. Blushing, she went on.

'I said, and I'm ashamed to admit it,' Liz chastised herself, 'I said, "I am unworthy." Well of course it was a cop out, I realise that, but actually I did believe it at the time. Anyway, she didn't even try to hide her impatience after that. She just hissed at me.

'"Then you must prove yourself worthy!" I said nothing. I looked away, searching for something safe to fix my eyes on. Then Jeanne threw down her ace. "You are to be married to Nathan Robson!" she said. I breathed in sharply. Was she joking? But her eyes had that greedy, jealous look. No. She wasn't joking. I didn't know what to say. The long fingers patted my arm. "Meditate on it, my dear," she instructed. So I closed my eyes. I suppose she felt a bit redundant after that. Anyway she just sighed, then stood up, saying, "Well, mission accomplished!" Then she bowed to the photograph and swished out of the room, leaving me, I might add, in total turmoil.'

The humour faded from Liz's face as she relived the moment, sitting cross-legged on the floor before the ever-lasting light, her security smashed to smithereens.

'I felt trapped. I remember hearing voices in the kitchen, chattering away, and the silence that fell when Jeanne graciously looked in. You have to watch your p's and q's when she's around! I think I was waiting for her to leave. I think everybody was. Because the moment she crossed the threshold, all the ladies broke out in a real old buzz of chatter, and I sank to the floor, in tears. Thank God, at least I was alone! Usually there's a minimum of two or maybe three devotees in there, meditating or reading or something. We don't get much privacy. Anyway, after I'd cried for a bit, I pulled myself together. I had to meditate. Because, well, you see, if Father wanted this marriage, and apparently he did, I had to do my best to harmonise my desire with his. You see, he only desires our good. We only get upset because we don't know what's best for us. We must be guided by him. Anyway, I straightened my meditation posture, took a deep breath and said my mantra several times. Somehow the word sounded hollow in the empty room. For some reason it wasn't working. So I just closed my eyes and rested, thinking about "love"; I mean,' she said, flushing, '"Divine Love." But it was a mistake. I started crying again; like a lonely child; like a deserted woman. I felt like Ophelia drifting downstream. And yet, I knew it was stupid. This was quite a different situation! I was no Ophelia! I had a man waiting for me! Only I didn't love him. I wondered, "Does he love me?"'

Liz stopped. She couldn't speak. She was in confusion, reliving the confusion of the moment, when she had summoned Nathan's image to her mind, considering him for the first time as her future husand. Would it work? He had always treated her with distant courtesy, but she would never have thought of him like *that.*

'Anyway why should he love me?' she blurted out. 'He was a world teacher of "The Way" and I was a mere devotee, and not a very good one at that. He was way out of my class. But I thought, if Father wants the marriage, it must be alright! So I tried again. I mean, I tried to harmonise my desire with Father's. But I only cried again and had to pull myself up short. I mean what on earth was I crying for, for heaven's sake? The word "love" seemed to be the trigger. It shot a hole right through my consciousness, letting out all the suppressed feelings of the past years. I'd wanted to marry originally. I'd wanted to have a child. And when Father'd said to me, "No, no children. Not now or ever!", I thought my heart would break. I couldn't bear to pick up the ashram babies. Not for ages. And even now, years later, the sight of a baby's shoe's enough to bring the tears welling up in my eyes.' She sobbed. 'Honestly, I'd no idea whether I wanted to marry Nathan or not! All I knew was that once I'd wanted to marry *you*!' She stopped again, struggling with the violence of suddenly exposed feeling and gulped down some tears.

Jim saw she didn't dare look at him, the hypocrite, rubbing his nose in the past, making out she was the grieved party. He took life with a pinch of salt. *She'd* taught him. He wouldn't be taken in.

No, she didn't dare look at him. But she felt him, sitting still, too still for comfort, within reach of her after all these years, warm and real ... and yet so distant. She hoped he would speak, say something. He cleared his throat. It was enough. She looked at him but he looked away to avoid eye contact and she felt humiliated. She had exposed herself by her reference to the past. She spoke bitterly:

'You knew that anyway!'

'I believed it at the time,' he said.

'It was true,' Liz said quietly. 'I did love you.' At least she had set the love she had spoken of safely in the past.

She had retained some dignity. But how could she go on? Did he want her to? She glanced at him again. He was sitting, arms folded, a sardonic smile on his face, waiting for her to continue. Why? He clearly didn't believe a word she said!

He was thinking, how could she be so gullible? To believe that love can be ordered by another? To actually try to erase one love and put another in its place? To tell him this? How could she believe a word this so-called guru said? Well, if she could do that, if she could love to order (if you could call it 'love'), she had never loved him. He was well out of it.

Was he punishing her now? she thought. If so, she couldn't blame him. He didn't understand. You had to know who Father was to do that, and he didn't. But she must help him to understand. Only through understanding could they resolve their relationship and, forgiving one another, be able at last to let one another go. She had to jettison the baggage and move on. So had he. Resolutely she began again:

'I thought I'd forgotten you. But I hadn't. The whole thing had brought the memories flooding back. I could see you so clearly. As I sat there in the meditation room, I let my mind dwell on your image for a while. I think I was testing myself. You know, to see if I still felt anything. I mean I couldn't honestly give myself to another man if I still loved you, could I?' Liz paused. Jim gritted his teeth and said nothing. She went on:

'Well, you'll be surprised to know that I felt a great ... compassion welling up inside me. For you, I mean.' She looked at him and saw the shock in his face. So she pitied him, did she? The patronising, stupid little ... She hurried on to explain, 'I mean I really wanted to know if you were happy. Alright. You know?' A smile flickered on his lips. What was that they said? 'If you don't laugh you'll cry?' She pressed on. 'And I *wanted* you to be. I began praying for it. I don't know who to. God

Almighty. Christ. Anyway, I prayed you were alright and had forgiven me. And I asked for guidance about this ... this arranged marriage. And ... suddenly I became aware of a perfume on the air ... lilies.' Liz's eyes were hazy. 'Away with the fairies', Jim thought.

'I opened my eyes,' she went on dreamily, 'There were flowers by the altar as there always were, but no lilies. Then I closed my eyes again and slowly the perfume disappeared, and so did your picture. I wondered what to make of it. Lilies are always associated with the Virgin, so I thought maybe it was a sign, you know, the guidance I'd asked for. Maybe God really did want me to marry Nathan. And then I began to feel flattered. Yes. I did. I admit it. After all, I'd been selected for a man very high up in the hierarchy. Though it scared me, too. Someone so high up meant trouble; trouble for me. I'd be watching my step from betrothal onwards. Whatever I did would be wrong! You see, whatever happens, the wife's always blamed for it. I suppose it goes back to Adam and Eve and how she was the one who listened to the serpent and got Adam into trouble. I mean the woman's the weaker vessel, isn't she?'

Except sometimes, Liz thought rebelliously, it *wasn't* the woman's fault when things went wrong; even in 'The Family'! Only she still got blamed. In some subtle way she was usually found to have caused the ill event. Some hidden evil lurking within her had triggered the situation and caused her husband to make his mistake. Oh yes, in 'The Family' the wives trod on eggs, no matter how lowly the husband. How much worse it would be to be married to someone prominent, like Nathan. If he caught a cold, it'd be her fault somehow. Jim watched her, unaware of him, chewing the inside of her cheek. He wished he could read her thoughts. But, remembering where she was, Liz looked up guiltily.

'And why should I be any different?' she said. 'And

then, and I can still hear Father's voice telling me, "Your giving birth would be like giving birth straight into the hands of the devil!" So he couldn't possibly mean Nathan and me to have children.

'So, I thought, did he mean this to be a loveless marriage? Loveless! Imagine! I mean is it possible? And yet, it'd be worse still if I ended up loving him. I mean, I need to love and to be loved. I really do. But if I loved Nathan as I wanted, I'd be sent away. You see, in "The Family" a woman's husband isn't so much her husband as Father's son. Nathan would have to be that first and foremost. Marriages are arranged entirely to serve the cause of "The Family", you see; to progress future world order; that brave new world we all long for; you know? Not at all for personal gratification.

'But would I come up to it? Could I really be that detached about Nathan if I married him? Well, one thing's for sure, I wasn't going to manage it by sitting there in a state, was I? So I tried to find my inner peace again. But if I found it, it didn't last long. There was a sudden bang; a door somewhere in the ashram. I opened my eyes and glanced over my shoulder to the archway that led to the lobby. There was another bang; upstairs. My eyes rose to the ceiling; Paula and Bhanamurti's room was right over my head. I could hear Paula sobbing. Then feet shuffled, came out of the room and started down the stairs. There was a funny atmosphere about. Was it me, or had something happened?

'I got to my feet as Paula's husband, Bhanamurti, pushed his wife into the frame of the door. Paula glanced into the meditation room with a look that was half ashamed, half despairing. I met her eyes, and immediately knew what was wrong. Paula was in disgrace. But why? Then she was led away, out of the house. I rose shakily to my feet and went into the kitchen. All the women were working in silence, eyes down, like the three wise monkeys, hearing, seeing and

24

saying nothing. I didn't ask, anyway. I went upstairs to Paula and Bhanamurti's room. The baby had gone. Suddenly a voice spoke from somewhere behind me, from the shadows.

'"Father wants you," it said.

'I gasped and turned. I saw the white kurta of Father's right-hand man, the American, Nathan Robson; my intended. I stared at him, paralysed. He didn't move. Then, without a word, I pulled my sari over my head and fled downstairs, out of the ashram and up the road to the house.

'There, I was ushered by a harassed Indian woman through the lobby. I had to pick my way through the crouching, cross-legged worshippers waiting there. The mixture of incense and curry turned my stomach. I was going up the stairs, flying almost. The door at the top was open. I hesitated a moment, adjusting my sari and composing myself, but Nathan was behind me and he gave me a sort of light shove, sending me into the ante-room, where more worshippers sat, stern-faced, staring at the flimsy silk which festooned and veiled the entrance to Father's room.

'"Wait," Nathan said. His voice had a kind of soft expectation, incongruous in the situation. It crossed my mind, at that moment, that perhaps he'd *asked* Father for me! Then, sliding past the petal-strewn floor, he edged behind the curtain into the sanctum.

'"Elizabeth's here," he said quietly. I recognised the familiar obsequious tone he always used when approaching the guru. My heart fluttered; not with love, but with fear and excitement, because I knew Father's attention was on me. I heard a low growl. Then, after a moment, Nathan's head reappeared and he beckoned to me.

'I edged past the petals and the silk into the room. It was smoky with incense. Nathan had taken his place on the dais, on Father's right. But I stood by the curtain uncertainly, waiting for my cue. Our guru was sprawled in his chair, Paula's baby at his feet. It was squirming and wriggling, its face red, and as it turned towards me, it screamed. Nathan looked down on it with what I can only describe as distaste. I was afraid I'd be blamed for the outburst. But Father turned on Paula.

'"See?" he said. "Your own child recognises you as a witch! Innocence speaks!" Paula choked on a sob. I didn't look at her, but I could feel her pain in my heart. I moved forward to pick up the child.

'"Stop!" Father glared at me. "Do you want to be contaminated?" he asked. He looked down on the squirming child in disgust. "Where can we send the children to be decontaminated?" I didn't know what to say. I was gaping like a fool. Who did he mean by "children"? Paula? Her baby? Or both? "This child is ruined!" Father spat in Paula's direction. "My child! How could you do it? Ruin MY CHILD?!"

'"I'm sorry," Paula whispered. "I'm sorry."

'"Hah!" he snorted victoriously. "She's sorry!" A strangled laugh issued from his throat and he looked round to see the effect. The assembled hierarchy laughed uncomfortably. I laughed too as his gaze passed over my face. To my amazement, his look softened. "Sit down, Elizabeth," he said. I obeyed and sat cross-legged, well at the back.

'"No. By me," he insisted. I rose and scurried over to his feet, to sit on the left of the dais, uncomfortably aware that Nathan and I looked like a pair of china dogs on a mantelpiece. The guru was making a subtle statement to the assembled dignitaries. Bending my head to avoid looking at them, I caught sight of Jeanne in the front row. She was staring hard at me. Had she known about this Paula business when she brought the news of the engagement? I mean, she knew Paula was my friend. Why didn't she say something? What was *really* going on here? I wondered, was this a test of some sort? Perhaps a test of detachment to see if I was worthy of Nathan? I tried to calm my thoughts, then suddenly I realised Father was speaking about me.

'"She works so hard," he purred, patting my head. I felt his hand grow heavier and he began stroking my hair. My heart jumped with joy. You have to realise that for Father to actually touch you is quite something. It's a real honour – a blessing. His touch can change your life! Everyone was looking at me. You could read their thoughts in their faces. They all knew my family history; the incest and so on. "What's going on?" they were thinking. "Why's Elizabeth suddenly in favour? Is she going to be married to Nathan?" In view of this amazing possibility they assumed a sudden look of reverence suitable to my exalted status. But it only thinly disguised their amazement and their contempt.

'"You should take your example from her!" Father shouted at Paula. (Her eyes were fixed on the rug.) "She has her problems, we know. But she is modest, she works hard, she is a good devotee." He patted my head again. I was gratified and I'm sorry, but I have to admit it, it took the sting out of what was happening to Paula.

'"Did you know," Father went on at her, "Did you know, Elizabeth was made ill by you?" Paula shook her head miserably. "You bring ill on everyone you come in contact with! I am sorry I married you to Bhanamurti!" Bhanamurti's face took on a pained, smug look. The flattery was working on him, too. "She's useless! She dominates you! Why do you let her? She makes a slave of you, working for her, babysitting!" He snorted and everyone laughed. Including me.

'Paula caught my eye and her eyes said, "You've betrayed me." I looked away. "I bet she makes you iron her saris, even!" More laughter. "You want to watch out! She'll have you wearing them next!" More laughter. Including mine. Nathan shook his head, wiping the tears of laughter from his eyes.

'Father turned to him. "It's a joke, yes?" Nathan nodded, laughing a little more and everyone but Paula laughed at him. Including me. Then Nathan caught my eye, and I looked away. Bedroom eyes, they were. A band tightened round my heart. "But I don't know how funny it is really!" the guru snapped. Everyone fell silent. Faces went pink. Eyes looked down and people shifted uncomfortably. I stole a glance at Nathan. He was staring at the wall, "detaching himself". After all, Father was playing games with all of us all the time, for our own good. This is how he teaches our souls to grow. It's what we all want. So I followed Nathan's example and tried to detach myself from Paula's suffering. Father paused, girding himself for the onslaught and Paula sat, trembling before him, waiting for the blow.

'"She thinks so much of herself!" he said. "She's got this sidhi, she's got that sidhi. She can talk with the animals. She can talk with the plants. She smells subtle perfumes." His eye strayed to me. And my heart jumped. He knew everything. He really did. He even knew about the lilies. "She hears voices." Suddenly, he leaned forward and darted his barb. "Can you fly yet?" he challenged. Paula looked up startled.

'"I can get nearly a metre off the ground," she volunteered hopefully.

'"See? Still showing off!" He laughed again. Everyone laughed. Including me. "She thinks she's got nothing to learn from me. Who am I?" he bawled at her. Paula swallowed hard.

'"God," she whispered. The guru smiled, satisfied.

'"Good." He started purring under his voice somewhere. "So you know that whatever I do is for your good?"

'"Yes," Paula whispered.

'"Hah! Let's put it to the test, shall we?" Another test on the spiritual road. It's hard if you want to be a yogi. "What would you say if I said I wanted you to give all your money to Bhanamurti?" he asked.

'"He can have it," Paula said quickly.

'"Fine!" The guru slapped his knee. "And afterwards he can divorce you!" Paula gasped and gave a quick look at her husband, who kept his eyes steadfastly fixed to the ground.

'"What about my baby?" Paula whimpered.

'"*Your* baby?" Father howled. Jeanne gasped at Paula's audacity. Father stared at her in disbelief, and a deathly hush descended on the throne room, on the anteroom behind, and crept downstairs to descend on the worshippers below. Paula's mouth was working. She was in a terrible state. She knew she'd done it now and there was nothing she could say in her defence. "Condemned from her own mouth!" the guru screamed. "This child is mine! What have you to do with it? Who gave you your husband?"

'"You did."

'"Who gave you your child?"

'"You did."

'"And why did I give you those joys and blessings?"

'"For ... for ..." Paula's voice faded. "The good of 'The Family'."

'"But what do you care for the 'Family'?"

'Some shred of protest must still have lurked under the broken spirit, because she cried out, "I do care! I do! Really! I've given everything!"

'"What can *you* give?" he sneered. "*I* give you everything. *You* have nothing at all. *I* only take what is mine in the first place. You live under an illusion, Paula, if you think you can give *me* anything!" He watched her for a second, considering her. Then he shouted again, "No! You only care for *your* family! Personal! Subjective!" The words hissed at her, like venomous snakes. Suddenly he sat back in his chair and looked from Nathan to me and back again. "She doesn't know who I am," he said, very casually. Nathan shook his head sadly. Then Jeanne shook her head, too. I looked down. But from the corner of my eye I saw Paula's face, looking wild. Then the guru spoke again. "She has plotted against us. You know that?" I was puzzled. I looked at Paula again. Evidently she was puzzled, too.

'"*I know,*" he said with meaning. Again he turned to me. I looked away, feeling very hot. Yes. He did know. He knew everything. He knew about the lilies. Paula tried to protest. She got as far as:

'"But ..." Then she closed her mouth again. It was useless. Judgement had been given. The guru snarled.

'"You have no sense of reverence. Your voices are the evil one inciting you to plot my overthrow! You are working with Satan!"

'Jeanne gasped and shifted from side to side as though in pain. Everyone else was silent. But their thoughts were racing. Then Father started to explain. "It is a great battle now. All the portents are there. We have to be very careful." Everyone but Paula nodded sagely. Including me. "She is a witch! Very clever no doubt. She appears to be nice. She's pretty." He turned to me. "You English have an expression about a pretty face, haven't you?" I nodded. "There you are then!" he said, victoriously. "She had you all in the palm of her hand!" His hand made a fist in front of them and everyone stared at it. Then the fist unclenched and dropped, lethargically to his side.

'Suddenly his eyes sharpened, and he looked straight into Paula's soul. "You have cheated us! You have been using 'Family' funds for your own purposes!" I looked at Paula, shocked. Had she really done this terrible thing? The guru fell back into his chair, exhausted. Then he said, "We should sue her, I think." No-one breathed a word. Suddenly he turned to Nathan. "I was about to proclaim your engagement, Nathan!" My heart sank to my toes and came up again, like seasickness.

'I felt very hot and I think I must've been blushing,

because Father said, misinterpreting, "See! The blushing bride!" He laughed. Everyone clapped and laughed and Nathan smiled. I hadn't said "yes" and already the thing was done. But I was saved by Paula. The guru turned on her bitterly, "You've spoiled it for them. You know that?" he said. And Paula turned to me, tears in her eyes and managed to get out the words:

'"I'm sorry." Then her eyes turned beseechingly to her guru. "Please, Father, I realise I don't deserve to know, but please tell me what is to happen to ... the baby?" The guru considered her humble appeal.

'"Do you love it?" he asked. Paula nodded. "Good. That's something anyway! There is something natural about you, I suppose! Alright, if you love it, you'll leave it to me! *I'll* look after it." He put his foot on the baby's stomach and it wriggled to be free. The guru shook his head. "See? I bless it with my foot and it doesn't want it. Clearly there is something wrong with this child. She has put a devil in it! See it wriggling! Watch the devil wriggling!"

'Paula gasped as she watched her baby, close to convulsions at the guru's feet. Her hands reached out to take it, but her husband pulled them back sharply.

'"Don't you know anything?" he growled at her.

'"Get her out of here!" Father threw his arm in the air and Paula was escorted from the room by Jeanne. "I'll want you later!" Father commanded. Jeanne bowed and went out with the miscreant. Then he motioned to Nathan and me. "You stay!" he ordered.

'I stood awkwardly, watching the screaming infant. And I wanted to pick it up and comfort it. But Father was bending down and his long fingers reached out to the baby. It stopped crying, staring up at the bright eyes that were fixed on it. The guru touched its forehead and it screamed suddenly. Then it seemed to collapse and everyone stared at it, thinking it had died or something until, after a few seconds, it opened its eyes, looked straight at Father and gurgled happily. Nathan let out a cry of praise for the guru, who smiled and handed the baby to me.

'I must say, I took the child unwillingly. I remember I glanced up from it to the guru, wondering what his game was now. He smiled at me, then at Nathan, amusement wrinkling his eyes.

'"See?" he said. "A ready-made family!" He might have added, "Aren't I clever?" but he was too clever for that. Only I didn't know that at the time. It's all very well judging things in retrospect ... but if you'd been there ...

'I don't know why I'm talking like this,' she said, glaring at Jim. His face was impassive. He was numb with shock. 'I'm saying terrible things here. To talk about Father in that way! I'll be damned for it. I will! I don't know ... it's being back here ...' She looked round the attic room, and at Jim, so still on his chair by the cupboard. 'Maybe I'm catching it from you!' Jim looked up, startled. 'I'm catching your critical aura and it's making me say terrible things!'

'I haven't said a word.'

'You don't have to!'

'You sold out your friend. You know you did. Only you don't want to admit it, so you're blaming me.'

'I didn't sell her out.'

'You damn well did.'

'Alright. In a way. But for the sake of her eternal soul!'

Jim laughed. 'That's what they said when they burned Joan of Arc. You're talking like the Inquisition!'

'You don't understand.'

'I understand alright,' Jim said wearily.

'You think you do but ... Look, I know it looks bad but, you see, Father doesn't care what people think about him. That's what's so wonderful really. His only concern is the health and well-being of our souls. He'll do

32

anything to help someone's spiritual growth. He was probably playing a sort of game with Paula; with me and Nathan, too. I don't know. I mean, he's so kind. I know he wants our good. Only from this distance it all looks so ... different.'

'Admit it, Liz. It's how you felt at the time,' Jim said. Fiercely honest, Liz examined his statement.

'Yes,' she agreed unwillingly. 'Even as I sat there at his feet, I was criticising him. I do admit it. Yes, I was. I told you I wasn't a very good yogi. There have always been things I haven't liked about "The Family".' Subdued by her own admission, Liz brooded, then she looked up, eyes dark, and she said, 'It's a relief to let it out really. Not fair on you, but a relief. I mean, you're not going to tell tales to Father are you?'

'I thought he knew everything anyway,' Jim reminded her with a wry smile. Liz paled so suddenly, Jim thought she was going to faint. Her eyes darted aimlessly, reflecting desperate thoughts. She must not blaspheme against Father! She must not! It was the utimate sin.

'Not that I believe it,' Jim said quickly, amazed at the effect of his words.

'Then you'd better!' Liz spat. 'Because I do! I have every reason to believe it!' Her face was grim. 'You'll see.' She nodded at him sternly. 'You'll see how powerful he is! Just listen!' Jim shrugged cynically and waited to hear.

She went on, 'Nathan was given the task of "talking to Paula". As her "elder brother" his task was to show her where she'd gone wrong so that, in isolation, she might transform and, as she certainly hoped, be welcomed back into "The Family" as the prodigal daughter. People did come back, you know, after they'd been thrown out, well ... sometimes. Anyway, Nathan came to me for help. I had been as close to Paula as anyone got in "The Family", and she'd talked to me a lot. He wanted a sort of psychiatric profile. I was desperately trying to coax her child into feeding from a bottle at the time. I was a bit upset and really harassed, because the baby kept wriggling and crying – with frustration, I suppose, because it didn't see why it couldn't have its mother's teats as usual. I told him:

'"Paula said something about the odd problem with her mother. But it wasn't anything to write home about. Just the usual generation gap sort of thing." That's all. But when I glanced up, I saw Nathan was staring at me with real admiration.

'"Look at you," he whispered. "Mother and child. It's beautiful." I smiled, pleased at the parallel with the holy family. I know it sounds blasphemous to you, but well, we'd all been told we'd been chosen by God for his special task of raising world consciousness. So, you see it wasn't really a blasphemy. Actually, the only real blasphemy is to blaspheme against Father and I wasn't likely to do that, was I? I mean, reflecting on my history and the dark burden of sin that stains my soul I realised that only Father could have raised me to this. So I said to him:

'"He is so kind to us." And Nathan nodded. He was genuinely too full to speak. He stroked the baby's head. But it was still crying. Finally, I dared to tell him the truth.

'"He wants his mother's milk."

'*He* said, "It's poison to him."

'"I know," I said. Then, I don't know why, perhaps I was trying to make some real contact with the man or something, but anyway I told him, "You know *I* wanted to have a baby ..." But he cut me short and said;

'"Father knows best. And now you have one, anyway!" I looked down at Paula's son. He wasn't mine. Never would be. It was Paula's breasts that ran with milk. Not mine. I sobbed:

'"But I can't feed it!"

'Nathan was silent. Then he sighed a long sigh. "I'll

speak to Father," he said and left me.

'As I waited in the ashram for Nathan's return, I knew I was warming to the idea of marriage. I shut my eyes to all memories of you and I tried to shut my eyes to the dangers of marriage in "The Family", too, which was difficult after seeing what had just happened to Paula! And yet, I told myself, what difference did it really make? If Paula was a witch then what had happened was for her own good. And if I proved to be evil, too, why, Father would punish and purge *me*. And would I have wanted it any other way? Weighed against the salvation of the eternal soul, a little heartache's nothing, is it? It does make sense, doesn't it? But well, if I'm honest, the real truth is ... I was lonely. And the soft husbandly voice had already worked its magic; so had the child. Before long I was thanking God for his blessings.

'Well I waited and Nathan came back. And at once I knew something was wrong.

'"Things are worse than I thought," he said. "Jeanne's been going through the accounts. I've seen some of the entries and Paula's been stealing money from the funds." It seemed incredible. This woman I thought I knew had stolen from "The Family"? From me, actually! I mean my money was in there, too. Everybody puts their earnings and savings into the fund. I asked:

'"Are you sure?" Nathan shrugged.

'"Well," he said, "I've seen the evidence in the books. And anyway Father says so. He says she has the soul of a thief and ..." his voice became hushed, "She's actually stolen Father's silver goblet!" I gasped. I remembered the goblet had gone missing in mysterious circumstances.

'"How do you know?" I asked. "Have they found it in her room?" Nathan shook his head.

'"Jeanne thinks she must have sold it," he said.

'"But what would she want with the money?" I asked.

35

'"Who knows? If she was plotting to overthrow 'The Family', she'll probably have an accomplice out there. She's very cunning."

'Suddenly I remembered the newspaper article. A few years before, Paula had got an article into a small-time paper in Louisiana. It had been about racism and how we are all brothers and should love one another, and how "The Family" was the only way of wiping the slate of hatred clean and that through "The Way" we could all evolve and there would be a new world. Father had praised the article at the time. But it had brought attention down on us, and "The Family" had been pursued by an antagonistic press ever after. Well, he said she was clever, didn't he?'

'"What is it?" Nathan asked. I shook my head. I couldn't bring down more trouble on Paula's head, even if she *had* deserved it.

'"Your loyalty's to 'The Family', not Paula," Nathan reminded me gently. I looked into his eyes. They were dark, concerned. I said:

'"Really. It was nothing. I ... it's just I felt her pain in there. She's really suffering." Nathan sounded pleased. He said:

'"You're very sensitive. I know. Father told me that. But you must learn to be more detached." Then I asked about the baby.

'"He said Paula had better breastfeed it for a few days more, with the bottle alongside. Then, when it's weaned ..." And he broke off, smiling at me. He meant that then the baby would be mine. I just said:

'"Fine. I'll feel better when he's got some milk inside him." And he nodded and told me to follow him.

I followed Nathan out of the ashram and up the street to a small house on the edge of the village. I'd never been there before. I asked who lived there. Nathan put his finger to his lips and eased open the gate. Immediately an agitated Indian woman appeared and started speaking Hindi at great speed, hands flying to express her distress. I was surprised to see her. I'd half expected to see Jeanne there. But of course she was with Father, going through the accounts. Nathan answered her in his halting Hindi. I asked him what was wrong as soon as I could get a word in and he told me. Paula had been caught trying to use the telephone. I wondered why she shouldn't use the telephone. After all, she was being thrown out of "The Family"! She had to make arrangements for herself. Somewhere to live and so on ... But Nathan explained:

'"Father's arranged everything. She had no need to contact anyone. She's just making trouble."

'"Oh," I said. Anyway, eventually Nathan calmed the woman down and left her on the verandah wringing the end of her sari, and we went in with the baby.

'Paula was sitting on the floor, legs to her chest. She didn't look up until Billy cried. Then she looked up alright, eyes alight, jumping to her feet to take him.

'"Does this mean they're giving my baby back to me?" she cried. She was thrilled to pieces!

'"Don't build your hopes up, Paula," Nathan chided. "He was hungry and wouldn't take the bottle. That's all."

'"I see," she said, then Paula's face fell into darkness. Without another word she turned her back and loosened the bodice of her sari. I glanced at Nathan, hoping he would leave, but,

'"I've *got* to stay," he said.

'"It's not kind, or proper," I told him. "Anyway *I'm* here. *I'll* keep an eye on her. I'll call you if there's anything wrong."

'Nathan sighed, then nodding abruptly he went out onto the verandah to join the woman, still wringing her sari.

'There was a long silence. I watched Paula's back, rounded to the baby at the breast. It was suckling hungrily and she had to take the breast away for a moment.

'"Slowly now. You'll give yourself wind," she said. Then she let him suck again. Her back was trembling. I asked her if she was alright. I know I sounded stupid. She sobbed suddenly, and cried out,

'"I'm frightened for Billy!"

'I tried to soothe her. I told her we'd take good care of him. But Paula wasn't satisfied. Apparently I'd got it wrong, and she explained,

'"No, I mean ... my milk. I wouldn't want him to be hurt by my milk." I said nothing. But after a moment I moved closer to her and laid my hand on the back of Paula's heart. I could feel her pain singing right through my arm.

'"Of course it's alright," I told her. "Father wouldn't let you do it if there was any danger for Billy." Paula was grateful for that crumb of comfort. I encouraged Paula to sit down so she'd be more comfortable feeding the baby. And slowly she turned to face me, glancing over my shoulder to the man through the window. I led her to a corner where we couldn't be seen.

'We sat together, leaning against the wall. Billy was still suckling, white froth at his lips. His eyes were closed in deep content.

'"So, you're marrying Nathan?" Paula whispered. I shrugged.

'"I was only told this morning."

'"You'll make a good wife," she said. "Better than me."

'"I'm no different from you, Paula," I whispered.

'"Don't say that," Paula hissed. "Look at what I've done!"

'"Can I ask you something?" I said. Paula looked straight at me and nodded, glancing furtively at the window. Nathan was peering in. I stood and waved, shouting to him.

'"It's alright. She's in the corner. More private." Nathan scowled but turned away.

'"What do you want to know?" Paula said when I'd sat down again.

'"Oh. Yes. The money, Paula. What did you want it for?"

'"What money?" Paula asked.

'"The money you stole from the funds," I said.

'"But I never ..." That's all she said. "But I never ..." Then her mouth dropped open and saliva oozed over the bottom lip. Tears welled up in her eyes and she shook her head. "Did Father say I'd stolen money?" she asked. I nodded and she said, "I'm going mad. I must be. I don't remember ..."

'"You didn't do it. Not really," I told her. I was trying to make Paula feel better. Somehow she was going to have to live with all this.

'"But if Father says I did ... then I must have!" she protested. I tried to explain.

'"No. It's not you. It's something in you, something in your subconscious that's using you."

'"I *am* mad then," she said.

'"Look at the article you did for that newspaper," I reminded her. Paula nodded. "You thought you were doing good for 'The Family', didn't you?" She nodded again. "But look what happened. It brought the attention of all the dirt-seeking media down on our heads, didn't it?"

'Then Paula started crying, but the baby stirred so she made an effort to calm down, suppressing her tears for his sake. I took advantage of the moment to explain things more. I told her, "No-one's saying you're consciously doing evil, but there *is* evil in you, and it's using you to harm 'The Family'." There was a long silence as Paula watched her baby suckle. When he'd finished, she handed him back.

'"Better take him away, Elizabeth," she said. "Poor

child. What's he ever done to be born to a mother like me?" She was so humble it hurt. I said nothing, but I was hugging the child too close and making him cry, so she told me:

'"Don't squeeze him." She was so loving and tender. She sighed, watching me adjust the pressure of my arms, and the baby settling, burping, then settling again. Then she asked the question I'd really been dreading:

'"Did you say, '*we'll* look after him'?"

'"Yes," I answered. "Nathan and I are to take him over."

'"Then don't tell him about his mother," Paula said. As Nathan's shadow fell across the room, a feeling of sudden urgency took hold of me. I knew I was sympathising with Paula. And I knew I shouldn't, but I was! I spoke quickly, incoherently really.

'"What happened, Paula?" I asked. "What triggered this ... this attack on you. I mean, why now?"

'"It was Bhanamurti," she told me. "He didn't have time for his work. The Bombay brothers and sisters keep him pretty busy you know, and when Father's here there's never any time for anything. He's at his beck and call all the time. Just like Nathan! And he wasn't feeling well. He needed a rest. And ... I needed him, too. It didn't feel like we were married. Not really. We'd had no time to settle down. I felt like ... like a whore!"

'"Shh," I glanced fearfully at the window, but Nathan was now practising his Hindi on the Indian woman and had momentarily forgotten about us.

'"I felt like a slave, a concubine," Paula went on, "not like a wife. You know?" I nodded. I could well imagine. "And just having had the baby and everything, I found the limelight, being Bhanamurti's wife, a bit much. It was such a strain! I was certain to crack sooner or later. And so I encouraged him when he wanted to ask Father for a break from his 'Family' duties. A rest, you know? Maybe for a year or so. He deserved it, God knows. He's worked harder than anyone for Father."

'"What happened?" I asked.

'"They blamed me," Paula answered. "They said I'd put him up to it. That I'd made him write to Father and it was an insult to him. I don't know. I'd thought ... well, he *is* our Father and so he'll understand. He'll be kind, but ... well, you were there. You heard what he said." Paula wiped her tears on her sari. "I suppose I never deserved to be married to Bhanamurti. I just wasn't good enough for him. I'm ... too American. Can't get rid of my Western conditioning." She looked at me plaintively. Never was there a more sincere devotee, hard-pressed and fallen on hard times, true, but sincere and honest. Yes, honest! But I banished the thought from my mind. She was *not* honest, I told myself. Father had said so. He had also said how clever Paula was. Well, she was being clever now alright. She had almost made me believe she wasn't a thief.

'"What did you do with the silver goblet?" I asked. Suddenly Paula laughed wildly, throwing her head back and yelling:

'"Don't ask me! Ask the devil who took it!"

'Then Nathan bounded into the room and ushered me out. Glancing back, I saw poor Paula distraught, sari falling from her shoulder, hair spilling over her face, struggling in the strong arms of the Indian woman.

'I couldn't speak on the way back to the ashram. I was trembling with fright.

'"I shouldn't have left you alone in there," Nathan said. "Better get to your room and meditate with Father's photograph as soon as you get back."

'I nodded obediently and, handing Billy to one of the women in the kitchen, I ran up to my room, closing the door behind me.

'But I wasn't alone. One of my three room-mates was in, a Danish girl called Meena. She was sitting on the floor, composing songs on the guitar in honour of our guru.

41

'"Hi!" she said.

'"Hi!" I answered. Then I turned my back to her and reached for the matches, lighting the candle and sitting cross-legged before the photograph. I took a deep breath and started chanting my mantra. Meena stopped strumming and I went on chanting. My forehead felt frozen and Paula's pain still bit into me. It was my own fault. I had let it in. I had sympathised with evil! I asked forgiveness of Father, then forgave Paula, and began to feel better, persuading myself that to take good care of her son was the best thing I could do for my friend. Then, staring into Father's eyes, I waited for the moment when his voice would speak in my mind and I would know what to do, what to believe, what to think.

'There was a sort of flash in front of my eyes. Lots of people get it. It's supposed to be a good thing. It means you've plugged in. Not that I get it very often. Usually I just sit with my eyes closed, thinking about the aspects of God: Ganesha, Christ ... and there's no flash.

'But, anyway, this time I was looking at the photograph and it happened. Then the voice spoke. "Give your troubles to me," it said. "I will look after you, dirt as you are." "Dirt", he'd said. Dirt crawled through my flesh like a creeping poison, invading the life, replacing it with sickness and exhaustion. I actually smelt of sick; I reeked of it. I wondered, was this me? Was I really such filth as this? Why? Because my ancestors broke a sexual taboo? What did I do to deserve it? Must be something. Must be. Nothing's without reason. If I thought things happened without reason, I'd go mad. So I sat, eyes closed, feeling as though someone had thrown a bowl of vomit over me. I think I must have sobbed. Anyway, Meena seemed to think I needed help and she began singing some song she'd made up:

Father your children cry out to be free.
Drugs and drink and sin won't fill their thirst for thee.

42

Despair and loneliness lead us into crime
And yet we are your children and all we need is time.
Time with you, father. Time to grow strong.
Time to see the light, time to know right from wrong.

'Her voice was so sickly sweet she made me want to puke. I've always hated those made-up sort of songs. They've got nothing to do with God or music or anything at all, if you ask me! And yet, Father likes them. I suppose he just tolerates them, out of kindness really. But I wasn't in the mood to be kind. I wanted peace and quiet so I could meditate. Anyway I yelled at her:

'"Shut up! Shut up!" And then of course I was sorry. Meena was very shocked. Senior devotees aren't supposed to behave like temperamental children and she was looking at me with frightened eyes as though I was a dangerous animal. She glanced furtively towards the open door. I wondered if she was going to make a dash for it, but in the end, she just got up and closed it.

'"Now you don't want people thinking you're 'ill' do you?" she said. I shook my head. "Ill" is a word used to cover anyone who isn't behaving according to "The Way".

'"I'm not ill. I'm just upset," I told her, "Paula ..."

'"I don't want to know," Meena answered quickly. "And you shouldn't think about it." I stared at her. She was right, I shouldn't. Thinking gets you into trouble. Thoughts well up from the ego or the subconscious and get in the way of the truth which speaks in the silent mind. "Father knows best," Meena said. Then she got up and left the room, as though distancing herself from some disease. And, you see, I *was* diseased; I knew that. The incest. "Filth" the voice said in the silence. Who was *I* to question anything?

'Anyway, after a while, remembering I was on the rota, I got up and went down to the kitchen to help prepare the next meal. I was very depressed and mechanical, physical work helped me to not think, so I didn't mind. The news about me and Nathan had got out and the women were going round with secret little smiles on their faces. It lightened the atmosphere and I must say I did enjoy it. It was a relief, you know. I mean it still felt all make believe to me and yet, after Paula, I really wanted, needed to get caught up in something nice, and everyone kept saying how lucky I was to be chosen for such a wonderful soul; how it was bound to help my spiritual evolution; how near I'd be to Father, and so on. And they all looked at me searchingly as though trying to see the amazing spiritual qualities they'd missed in me before. There had to be something special that qualified me for Nathan. No-one mentioned Paula. She was outcast. And I was raised up!

'The days continued like that. I saw Nathan from time to time, usually from a distance, scurrying about Father's business. And the other women in the room helped me with Billy, so I wasn't tied. I didn't see Paula again. Things had started going missing; money from purses, jewellery from suitcases, silver from the little altars in the rooms. It was all put down to Paula. Of course she wasn't actually around to physically do anything, but her evil spirit was abroad, causing these things to happen. Actually, I think ... I know I found it very hard to be with Billy.

'Contact with his mother was now considered to be too dangerous for the baby, and so the Indian woman up at the house milked Paula's breasts, then ran down the hill with the full bottle to give to her baby. But it was still her milk. It was still poison and he was drinking it. And I was supposed to be looking after him! It was dangerous for me, too! But gradually the women in the kitchen mixed the natural milk with powdered, till slowly Billy got used to the artificial product, and then, thank goodness, Paula's services could be dispensed with altogether.

'I wondered what was going to happen to her. But I hardly saw Nathan and when I did, I didn't get the chance to ask. Anyway, it was none of my business. Really I shouldn't be putting any attention on Paula at all. My mind must not be an open door to her evil. Especially now I was marrying Nathan. And the nearer the wedding came, the less I thought about Paula. I really didn't want to, you see. She was a can of worms ... however you looked at it.' Liz paused, then added, 'She still is.'

Jim noted the chink in Liz's armour but said nothing. He had heard nothing to persuade him of the enormous power of this 'Father' of hers. And she was, even now, deprogramming herself. All he had to do was sit back and let her ... and try not to laugh! She'd soon see sense. He smiled encouragingly and she went on:

'Then Nathan got into a bit of a "thing". I mean he got cold feet about the wedding. It scared me a bit. The first I knew about it was from Jeanne. She took me aside one day, slotting her arm through mine as we walked in the shade of the trees ...

'"Nathan's such a proper man," she said, nodding ponderously. I waited a long time for further enlightenment. But Jeanne was considering her words carefully. "You know of course about his wife," she said. God knows what my facial expression was, but her eagle eyes were watching every fleeting emotion. I cleared my throat, but my voice was still rather hoarse, when I said:

'"But ... he got divorced." Actually it was a question.

'"Not quite," Jeanne answered. "But even so, that wouldn't worry you, would it? Marriages in 'The Family' are genuinely made in heaven. We are so lucky!"

'"Yes," I agreed.

'"Well," she said, "about his wife. It was very sad. Actually she had reached a very high level of spiritual attainment, but, sadly, it seems her karma caught up with her."

' "What happened?" I asked. My throat was very dry. I was finding it hard to speak.

' "She, er ... started having fits," Jeanne said crisply. I looked at her. Clearly what she'd said was true. She expanded on the subject in subdued, compassionate tones. "Very sad. But of course, she's no use to Father now, poor thing. He says she won't get better in this life and we should all pray for her immediate death and rebirth." I said nothing. My mind was racing. I know I shouldn't have been thinking at all, but I needed to know a few things.

' "So, are they divorced or not?" I asked. Jeanne shook her head.

' "No, they're not," she answered.

' "So where is she?" I asked.

' "Who knows?" Jeanne sighed deeply. I think I was asking tedious questions that she really didn't think worth answering. "In some hospital or other," she said dismissively. "Of course, she'll have to be found to sign the papers for the divorce."

' "I see." I didn't know whether I felt relieved or disappointed. "So, the marriage has to wait," I said. I was grateful to her for breaking the news so gently. But I'd got it wrong. She was shocked at my supposition.

' "Of course not! What an extraordinary idea!" Jeanne let out a peal of laughter. "In God's eyes they're divorced already. Man's laws don't really matter, now do they?"

' "Of course not," I said apologetically. So Nathan was to marry first and divorce later. "But, I gather Nathan's not happy about it. Or is it the choice of bride he's not happy about? Me. I mean, I don't blame him if he's got cold feet ..." You see, I could still hear the voice, "you are filth". But Jeanne dismissed that one with a wave of the hand.

' "You?" she said. "Oh no! Why should he have any doubts about you? Father chose you for him. No, it's just the divorce he's worried about. But don't worry.

We'll talk him round. He'll go through with the wedding alright!" I smiled gratefully. Then Jeanne's tone became suddenly rather sharp. "Of course there won't just be you! You do realise that!" she rebuked. "We're not laying on the works just for you!" I came to earth with a bump. Suddenly I realised I'd been getting a little too egotistical about this wedding. *Of course* other couples would be getting married at the same time. I asked when the wedding would take place. Jeanne shrugged and answered:

'"Father will speak when the time is auspicious." I nodded. "You should go into Gulhapur and get fitted for your sari blouse and that sort of thing," she said encouragingly, "so you'll be ready."'

Jim's mouth was hanging open. The nerves in his arms and legs crept. Outside a foghorn blew. Liz didn't hear it. 'Away with the fairies.' Jim glanced at the darkened window, his sense of revulsion growing, wishing he could escape. But Liz had merely paused for breath.

'The preparations for the wedding kept my mind off Paula and Billy. Though every time I set my eyes on that baby my stomach turned over. You see, apart from whose son he was and everything, just taking on a "Family" child is an enormous responsibility. You have to vow to bring it up in "The Way" and God help the mother if anything goes wrong with it. It's bound to be your fault somehow.

'I mean, it's an impossible job to bring up the perfect child. Most mothers end up paranoid and the kids alternate between extremes of discipline – you know, getting up at five, meditation from four years old, learning mantras and sitting through hour upon hour of rituals – and being spoiled rotten. No wonder the poor kids never know where they are. And of course they're not supposed to get too attached to their parents. Their biological parents, I mean. They're Father's children actually, not ours, and they're all destined to great things

47

in the new world order. Mothers are mere vessels honoured by their children's birth, blessed by Father to bear his children and nurture them in his service.

'Before, I mean before Paula's problems, whenever I'd thought about having children, and how I couldn't, I used to console myself with the knowledge that at least *I* wouldn't have that terrible responsibility.' Liz laughed. 'I really had managed to keep my head down for a long, long time. But this was worse. Now, I had responsibility for another woman's child; and yet, I wasn't allowed to love it. Really I didn't know what I was supposed to be to that baby. Poor little beggar. At least it was young enough not to feel the terrible heartache of being parted from its mother.'

Jim couldn't take much more of this. Who was she kidding? Anyway, she wasn't the only one with memories. Somehow her reminiscences had stirred up old memories, old feelings, in *him*. Now he was in Korea and a child called Kim, dressed in a pair of seersucker pyjamas, was holding onto him for dear life. Didn't want to let him go. 'You get killed,' she kept on saying. 'You get killed.' But he hadn't got killed. What the hell had happened to that little girl? All those years ago! It'd taken a bomb to part *her* from *her* mother. He had taken her to Seoul. Thank God, at least Liz had stopped talking.

Something else had flooded through her more recent flow of memory. Liz was seeing another picture: a thin, middle-aged Indian woman, pulling her sari round her shoulders as though for protection. Her hair was loose, greying at the temples, and her face was drawn as her husband tore her eight-year-old daughter, her only child, away from her skirts. Liz could hear the child screaming as it was carted out of the ashram. It was after that the woman had committed suicide and left Bhanamurti alone. After that. Not before. Liz was hardly breathing as she realised the truth. *After* that. Not before.

48

She must not think.

Pushing Kim's face back into the dark cupboards of his mind, Jim watched Liz pondering in the shadows. Then, as though dredging herself from the depths, she spoke again.

'It had happened to other children, you know. I mean, being parted from their mothers. Of course it was for their own good. And before long they'd learnt to realise she'd been bad news. I remembered Bhanamurti's eldest. He'd been married before, you see. His first wife had committed suicide. She was a bad lot by all accounts and he was glad to be rid of her. And Father had married him to Paula to console him and provide a mother for little Sushena. I hadn't seen Sushena for ages. She went to school of course, a boarding school, but she usually came home to the ashram on weekends.

'Bhanamurti must have taken her away somewhere, to get over Paula. Anyway, it wasn't my business. Actually I didn't want to know. I just wanted to choose my wedding sari and order my wedding jewellery and all that. Of course I hadn't any money. I hadn't worked for years. "The Family" kept me. Actually they'd kept me ever since I came to India. But Nathan was generous and he gave me more than enough for my wedding gear. Yes, he was generous. I'll say that for him.

'Anyway, Father gave me permission for me to go into Gulhapur, and as soon as everyone heard where I was going, they flooded me with orders: soap, safety pins, incense, iodine, waist slips, rubber teats – you name it, it was on my list. And slowly I began to realise I was going out on my own. I felt a little bit scared. I hadn't been out alone for ... years.'

While Liz reflected on the word 'years', Jim shifted uneasily. He'd been sitting a long time. His cheeks were numb, his nerve-ends buzzed and Kim's face didn't want to fade.

'I'm sorry. Am I boring you?' Liz asked with genuine

concern. Jim laughed loudly. Then he looked at her and shook his head. She blushed.

'I know how it must sound. But if you'd been there ...' Her voice trailed off. 'Do you want me to stop?'

'Oh no! You aren't going to leave me high and dry again!' he snapped. He hadn't meant to. It just came out that way. And Liz closed up like a clam. 'I was teasing,' he explained. She dared to look at him, and saw his eyes were very dark. She wondered why he'd snapped at her. Was he punishing her for the past? Or did he still care? She *wanted* him to care. She wanted *somebody* to care. But you never know what's going on inside somebody else, do you?

'You hadn't been out for years,' Jim prompted in the weary tones of a man rehearsing a play. Elizabeth looked away. She fiddled with her cardigan. She was beginning to feel irritated. He watched her, half amused, knowing that at any minute she would dart a fiery glance at him. And she did. And he smiled. And she didn't know where to put herself.

'You're very easy to manipulate,' he said in a very matter-of-fact voice. 'You should try and take hold of yourself.' Elizabeth bridled at the insult.

'How can I? I don't even know who I am.'

'Stop the self-dramatising and get on with the story!'

'You're behaving just like ... Father!' she cried out. Then she laughed. And then she stopped laughing and her face betrayed a desolation that cut through all Jim's resistance. 'I know it sounds like I'm making it up ... a tall story,' Liz whispered. 'But it's true. Every word I'm telling you.' She looked at him beseechingly. 'It really happened. And it happened to me.' He looked away. He didn't want to be involved in her emotions. It wouldn't help her if he was.

'I believe you,' he said abruptly. 'You hadn't been out for years.' Slowly Elizabeth turned her face away and her mind into the past.

50

'I hadn't been out for years; on my own that is. Well, it wasn't really on my own, anyway. I was getting a lift with Bhanamurti. He was going into Gulhapur to see his daughter, Sushena. It was funny; very funny; weird. There were only the two of us. We were very tense. Everybody was all smiles as they waved us out of the compound, and Bhanamurti waved and the car skidded on its bald tyres in the dust, and then we were on the road.

'Neither of us spoke. Bhanamurti was a very senior devotee; a big teacher, the boss in Bombay! Oh ... I told you that, didn't I? I was just ... a woman for a start and, on top of that, an upstart who had never even taught "The Way" even though I'd been in the movement for twenty odd years! Imagine. Twenty years. I didn't know what Bhanamurti really felt about Paula or whether he wanted to talk about her or anything. Probably not. And I felt embarrassed because, well, Nathan and I were taking his child. Billy, I mean. And yet I couldn't think of anything else to say; at least, nothing that was safe.

'Well, it was hot. The car windows were open and I'd pulled my sari over my mouth to keep the dust out. I remember Bhanamurti glanced at me from time to time, but he wouldn't be able to see much of my face because of the sari, you see. I felt sorry for him. To lose two wives ...'

Elizabeth's laugh began as a gurgle in the back of the throat and spread and spread till there were tears falling down her cheeks. 'I kept ... I kept ...' She gasped, 'I kept thinking of that line from *The Importance of Being Ernest*: 'To lose one wife is a misfortune. To lose two is carelessness!' Elizabeth laughed till her sides ached. Hysterical, Jim thought. Then she dried her tears and started crying. 'I think we all lived in a permanent state of shock really,' she said.

'Shock is a form of heightened awareness,' Jim agreed. 'But not what one usually thinks of as particularly spiritual!' His voice was cold, arrogant. He spoke as from a great height and Liz was cowed by him. But how else could he distance himself from this description of the process of dehumanisation, a process which a woman he had once loved had willingly gone through? And after all, what was left of her? Had she become some form of subhuman being, incapable of love? Had she *ever* been capable of love? he thought bitterly.

The involuntary memory of his own wife and child back home in the States posed him the uncomfortable question: was he himself capable of love? But the matter was easily resolved. If he hadn't loved his wife, it was *her* fault! Liz's! She had done it to him. She had thrown him back on himself. He should be grateful in a way, for his career had prospered, driven by the keen mental objectivity that had come to him as a result. Yes, Jim prided himself on his intelligence. He was a man who lived through intellect alone. A rare breed, supremely suited to the habitat of Cambridge. Yes, he was known for his keen intelligence and he guarded his reputation as something precious. Cowed by his confidence, Liz took refuge in her story. She spoke as though she was telling it to herself.

'It did occur to me,' she said, 'that Bhanamurti himself might feel vulnerable. After all, it was beginning to look like something might be wrong with *him*! I mean, Paula had done her best, hadn't she? Though of course there was the stealing. But I stopped myself dwelling on any of that. And in the end I plucked up courage to ask about Sushena. Did she know? Bhanamurti shook his head.

'"I've got to tell her," he said. I wondered if I was supposed to offer to go with him, in support; to help, you know? But I didn't dare ask, in case he said yes, so I just said:

'"What will you say?"

'"I'll tell her her stepmother's ill," he said.

'"Which, of course, she is!" I put in. Bhanamurti nodded.

'"She will accept it if *I* tell her," he said. I thought, poor little Sushena. But I didn't say so. And neither of us mentioned Billy. Anyway, after that, we both lapsed into silence, but it was a very pregnant silence, and what with bracing myself against the bumps in the road, and the tension in the atmosphere, my whole body was aching by the time we drove into Gulhapur.

'Bhanamurti directed me to the main street where the haberdashers and sari houses were. And then he left me. He was going to be a long time, he said. He had business in Gulhapur besides the school. I wondered what it was. It crossed my mind he might be making contact with Paula's ... well, fence, I suppose! The silver goblet, you know. I mean, supposing he was involved? Supposing all the time, *he* was telling tales about the movement to some outsider? I shook myself and told him I'd be fine. But he hesitated before leaving me and said:

'"You could spend your afternoon somewhere uplifting." I nodded enthusiastically. Encouraged, he told me, "There's a shrine I know of. A swayambhu of Ganesha. It's not far from Gulhapur. You can get a bus." He waved in the direction of the bus depot. "They do excursions, I believe. Of course meditating on Father's better than anything. As we all know, you can't beat that. But sometimes I find it good to meditate on the aspects, the deities, you know?"

'"Yes," I confessed, "I still pray to Christ." He nodded, smiling away, rather glad he hadn't betrayed himself, I think. Then he said:

'"Sometimes Father seems too powerful for us to approach. And even though he is the apotheosis of all the religions, still ..." Bhanamurti paused. 'Anyway, it would be auspicious for you to visit this particular shrine before your marriage. You see, this Ganesha is the elephant-headed God who removes all obstacles. His name is Chintamani. His Innocence overcomes everything! All your problems dissolve away in His Love!"

'Poor Bhanamurti. It was so kind of him to think of me and my marriage, when ... well, you know? His generosity really opened my heart to him. This man, who was losing a second wife ... he could think about my good at a time like that. You know what I mean? He's a nice, decent man is Bhanamurti.

'Well, I finished my shopping in record speed and, taking a taxi – I say taxi but it was a rickshaw, actually – I got to the depot and waited for a couple of hours. A bus came and suddenly there were a lot of people all clambering onto it, and I got on it because suddenly I was desperate to go there. I don't know why. I just felt I couldn't get on with my life or do anything until I'd been there and got whatever it was I was supposed to get from it. I was at a sort of watershed, you see. I had this feeling my life was going to change. I didn't know how. But ... anyway, I got on the bus. I nearly got off again. But then the bus started so I didn't. I was on my way. And I knew it was sort of "mean", you know? It was as though Ganesha was waiting for me. He was there, had been there since forever, and the moment had come when I was to face Him and know Him. It was an extraordinary feeling. And after all, I knew about Ganesha. I didn't let on to Bhanamurti that I knew, but I did.

'Ganesha had come to mean a great deal to my family. I mean ... this family, here in England. My ... natural, I mean my biological family. Eve had that statue of Ganesha. I wonder where it is? It used to belong to my great-grandmother, Jane Beattie, years and years ago. And my great-grandfather, George, his dying words were something about "The shadow of the elephant". I mean, I knew my past, and present and future were somehow tied up in this image, this ancient, powerful God of Innocence. But did I dare to approach him? I remember I laughed at myself. After all, I dared to approach Father, didn't I? And I was scared of *him* alright. But this was something different. In Ganesha, I knew I was approaching ... well ... my fate. It felt that big, that powerful. It felt like the real thing. It felt different.'

Jim felt the hairs on the back of his neck prickle. Liz's voice had approached something near to a tone of sincerity. Recognising this danger, he shuffled uneasily and wondered if he should end all this here and now and escape. Anyway, he glanced at his watch. It was high time he got his head down for some sleep. But Liz was too stirred up to stop now. She really wanted to tell Jim this. It was clearly important to her. His resistance weakened. She went on:

'I don't remember the journey out of Gulhapur. It was the afternoon. It must have been bumpy, dusty, hot. But I don't remember. I remember feeling very still. I was scared, but I had the feeling that sooner or later it must come to this. I would have to put my fate in His Hands some time. And I had chosen to do so now. You see I was stuck. I couldn't go back to how it was before "The Family" and somehow I couldn't go forward either, to the wedding. You know? So I had to do it. I had to surrender to His judgement.

'I was on the edge of the world, really, fearing and longing for the moment of surrender. And I remember that as the bus approached the village, I became so aware of the pitiful fragility of my ... self. I felt as though a word, a look, a breath could cause my spirit to explode and scatter to the four winds. You see, *I* might be confused, but *He* knew me as I was ... am. And He could damn or save me as he chose. Think what you like but I believed this and I still do. I mean, if I'm doubting Father, I don't doubt *Him*. I knew I loved God. I still do. But was that enough? Or would He turn me away?

'I remember the dust as the bus swerved into the village square, near the shrine, and I think there were chickens scattering and squawking. But all that seemed part of another world and only half impressed itself on me.

It was an ordinary, quite poor village. Men, women and children looked at us pilgrims curiously. I can see them now, down the blinkering tunnel of the sari I'd pulled forward round my face. There seemed to be a lot of jostling and chattering and I remember I was feeling very weak. I was suffering from shock, I think. I'd not eaten or drunk anything since the day before, and it was hot.

'I tripped on the baked clods of earth as the gabbling guide led us to the shrine. Yes, I was in a state of shock! I felt a bit like the sacrificial victim led to the altar really. Still, I was alive and "with it" enough to notice the casual attitude of the Indians to the sacred site. It suggested a degree of familiarity with the God which I envied, and, I suppose because of my Church of England conditioning, abhorred. I tried to silence this inner conflict as we approached the little square immediately before the temple, rebuking myself and wondering if I should copy the casual Indians doing whatever they did. But it wouldn't have been right. I was me, conditioning and all. The artificial had no place here. I pulled my sari further forward, as someone was chosen to go in with the priest and put a garland round the shoulders of the God.

'Someone clean, I thought. Not me. Because I was not clean. I was filth. And I felt a pang of envy for that clean, pure soul who had been chosen to decorate the stone swayambhu that was God's emanation on earth. *I* would have liked to place the garland round His neck. But I was *not* clean. I could not have been chosen. It wouldn't have been right. I swallowed my hurt. Many of the pilgrims were praying. But my throat was dry and I felt on the edge of tears, so I couldn't speak, even if I'd known all the words of the Hindu prayers, which I didn't. So I just prayed, silently, 'Please help me. Help me.' And the words of the Nirvignamastu passed through my mind as I moved forward with the rest towards the temple.

SumukaschAikadantascha Kapilo Gajakarnakah
Lambodarscha Vikato Vignanasho Ganadhipa
DoomraketurGanadyaksho Bhalachandro Gajananah.

Dwadshaitani namaniyah pathet shrunu yadapi
Vidyarambhe vivahesha praveshe nirgame tatha
Sangrame sankate chaiwa vighnastasye na jayate.

'I was kept waiting at the gates. They were only letting us through in small groups. I panicked. So! The time inside was limited! "What will be, will be," I told myself and moved forward with the next group. Now I could see inside. The stone was polished red; with cum cum powder, I supposed. There was the garland round His neck. And He sat, crouched almost, on a marble dais, offerings at His Feet. The wall behind was lined with silver paper and shone. But the greatest light shone from His Forehead. I waited. My turn would come. Then, as worshippers got to their feet and moved out, I was admitted into the shrine.

'I slid inside and I suppose I must have knelt and done obeisance. All I remember is sitting cross-legged in the shadow at one side. I suppose I looked up at Him from time to time, but mostly my eyes were closed. There was a feeling of depth in that place. It was like being at the bottom of a deep well, out of the normal run of time. And, in the silence, the God was listening. I confessed the sins of my fathers, asking forgiveness for them, Jane and Robert, and for the incest they had committed, and which had stained all the rest of their family for generations to come. I asked forgiveness for myself, that whatever karma had caused my birth into such a family might be forgiven, too. I don't know what else I prayed for. But after a while, there seemed no point in saying any more. He knew. I could only *be* there, before Him, hiding nothing, surrendering to His mercy. And as I sat, I felt that the whole temple had become Ganesha; that he had taken me into Himself. I was inside Him. And His compassion and tenderness surrounded and overwhelmed me. He loved me. And oh God, how I loved Him! And I rested in Him there for a while, as all around me, worshippers came in and out like the ebb and flow of a river. And then the moment came when I too rose, bowed and left the shrine.

'Outside in the sunlight, faces were pale, deeply moved. I hid mine and waited quietly to get back on the bus to Gulhapur. I can't put into words what really happened. But the earth itself trembled under me, and my body, already weak, felt transparent. But I wasn't finished yet. He hadn't finished. Not yet. And whatever happens to me now, I know He is with me, in me, round me. He knows my pain, my darkness, my grief, and has taken it into Him. He'll help me to bear it. And somehow, I'll have the strength to continue with my life.'

She had him below the neck. He didn't like it. He had decided that everything she had experienced in India was pure hogwash. But somehow, she had gotten under his skin, reviving a deeper instinct, reminding him of something he once knew. Bridling with irritation, he listened as artificially seeped, like a leaking sewer, back into her voice.

'Bhanamurti was fretting when I got back to the street of the haberdashers,' she said, blithely unaware of the change in Jim. 'I think he was upset after seeing Sushena and took it out on me a bit, which is understandable. And I was very late. He drove hell for leather back to the village, his face dark like a thundercloud and when he got there, he just unloaded me like a piece of baggage. Everybody crowded round for their bits and pieces, and it was only afterwards I realised I'd forgotten to order the most important item of all, the mangalsutra for my wedding. I felt so guilty! But when I told Nathan, his face beamed with joy, though he wouldn't tell me why. I must have looked puzzled or something. Anyway, he put his hand on my shoulder and murmured into my ear:

'"I just want you to know, dear, I can wait."

'"What for?" I asked.

'"You," he said. "Don't be afraid I'll make demands." He looked extremely embarrassed and he said ...'

Jim moved suddenly. Liz jumped and flushed with sudden embarrassment. His body was taut. She sensed it and was afraid. She felt as though he was going to hit her. She couldn't look at him. She passed her hand across her forehead and looked up at the ceiling, feeling somehow disorientated. The fog horn blew again. This time she heard it. She was in Shields and it was autumn. She shivered and pulled her cardi closer round her shoulders. The atmosphere was tense. She didn't dare go on with her story. Had she made herself vulnerable by revealing too much? Would he take advantage of her, seeking to destroy the one thing she knew she could trust, her faith in Father? Jim got up with deliberate slowness and walked towards the window. He looked out across the grey rooftops, into the mist. There were no lights anywhere. It was as though he and Liz were alone in the world; their room an oasis of light in the darkness. More than twenty years had passed since she'd gone, like a bullet from a gun, careering round the world, God knew where; leaving him! More than twenty years! Why the hell did she have to come back now?

'I don't know if I want to hear any more,' he said coldly.

'Why not?'

He flared with sudden anger. 'This Nathan ...!'

She thought he was jealous, and despised him for it. Wasn't she giving him the chance to understand and break free of her? She spoke patiently, as to a child:

'You don't understand,' she told him. 'It's about you. The rest of it, I mean. Not Nathan. Not really. It's about you. I wanted you to know the truth. But I was afraid to tell you. I'm sorry.' Jim turned from the window to watch Liz's back. She was crouched on the other side of the bed, staring apologetically at the floor. So, she thought he was jealous, did she? The rage inside him flared. How could he possibly be jealous? What was there to be jealous of? What had Nathan got? An empty shell! A robot! A lobotomised moron! A criminal with no sense of moral responsibility! And her ability to love had been cut clean away. *That's* why he was angry! He wanted to cry and scream and tear her limb from limb for having let them do it to her! She was a precious being once! He had loved her! But, hurrying to soothe his feelings, she blundered into his anger.

'Nathan said, "I know about the other man." And I said, "What other man"? And he said, "The American."' Suddenly Liz turned and looked straight at Jim. He fought an instinct to flinch, to hide his anger. But shocked by the violence in his eyes, she hurried on with her explanation. 'He said, "Father told me you loved someone before you came to us." But I hadn't told anyone about you. Not anyone. Not even Paula. All the same, he knew. Father. He knew! He knows everything, you see. He hears your thoughts, and tunes into your dreams at night. I know he does. I've had proof of it, often. And he knew about you.'

Jim felt his flesh creep. The filth was contagious, then. Following her own interpretation of Jim's state of mind, Liz saw disbelief following jealousy and started backing up her case. 'He can hear your thoughts, Jim! Honestly! That first time I saw him, in India, there was a whole roomful of people, all sitting cross-legged before him, and he said something about how Westerners were too ego-oriented. He said we should learn to give and give. And I thought, hold on a minute, sometimes people take advantage of you, think you're a soft touch. And he gave a sort of sideways look in my direction, and he said, "Of course sometimes, people might want to take advantage of you. And that's not a good thing. But mostly you should learn to give." He had answered me without my having said a word. And I realised suddenly, sitting there, that not only could he hear my thoughts, but he could hear the thoughts of everyone in that room, all at once, and not only the people in that room, but everyone in the whole world! Jim, only God can do that!'

And then Jim let rip. 'Crap!' His voice cracked like a whip. 'There's nothing special about hearing thoughts! A lot of people can! You don't even have to be God realised to do it!'

'I don't just mean telepathy ...' she objected, shakily.

'I know you don't,' Jim snapped. He snorted, 'So is this what your belief in him hangs on? That he can hear your thoughts? Because if it is a lot of people could claim to be God!'

Liz was visibly shaken. She knew Jim had had experiences with the Hopi Indians. His stepmother was a Hopi and magic sprang naturally out of the vast mesas of Arizona and New Mexico where he'd spent his childhood. It was in his blood. Suddenly she felt very small. How could she have failed to take account of his knowledge? How could she have been so arrogant?

'So, you do believe he knows everything?' she asked timidly.

'There's a big gap between picking things up by listening at keyholes and tapping phones, and having a cosmic understanding of the entire universe!' he shouted. She shrivelled. And now he was feeling sorry for her. How did she do it? How was this damned woman able to get through his armour? His rage trembled on the edge of pity, but falling into the mould of tutor with stupid student, he was saved from the ultimate abandonment to compassion. He came to the bed and sat, back to her, on the opposite side. He couldn't bring himself to sit beside her.

'What did you say to Nathan?' he asked in his professional voice.

'I told him it was a long time ago ...' Liz's voice trailed then picked up again, fortified by some detail which bolstered her failing faith. 'It was funny. It was soon after that I missed my watch. I'd begun thinking, you see. I knew I shouldn't, but I did. About Paula, I mean. And Billy, and ... Anyway, I'd begun to think maybe everything had been exaggerated and people were getting hysterical and she hadn't really done that much wrong. And then I missed my watch!' Liz turned and saw Jim's back. She wanted to speak directly to him, but she couldn't. The position was too uncomfortable anyway. And then the fog horn blew again, and the moment had gone. She turned back to look at the lino on the floor.

'My father'd given me that watch, when I got into "The Slade". I didn't have much. Paula knew how much

it meant to me. I mean I gave up almost all my possessions when I went into the ashram; but not the watch.
Well, you've got to have something to check the time,
haven't you? So I kept it. And now it'd gone missing,
like so many things. I searched high and low. And
before long I knew, I just knew Paula was behind it.
She'd made it disappear. It was *her* fault. Or was Father
teaching me a lesson, for doubting his judgement?
Because, you see, I had. He'd said Paula was evil, and
I'd doubted it. And now my watch was lost. I got scared.
I mean, people *can* influence events. There are people
who spread bad luck and there are poltergeists and so
on. You do have to be careful.'

Then her voice started losing strength again. Jim's
presence had grown in the room. It threatened her;
made it all seem so far away, so unreal compared with
him and his anger. 'Well,' she went on reluctantly, 'there
was no sign of my watch for a couple of days, and then I
was summoned to see Father. I was nervous. I always
was on the rare occasions I got anywhere near him. But
Nathan was there, and so, to my surprise, were
Bhanamurti and Sushena, his daughter. Sushena was
white as a sheet. She was sitting cross-legged on the
ground at Father's feet and he was fondling her with his
hand.

'"Poor child," he was saying as I crept in and bowed.
"But I *had* to take you away from her. She would have
killed you. Do you know that?" Sushena looked startled,
afraid. She looked at her father but Bhanamurti was
inspecting the ground at his feet. "Because of the
money," Father explained. "She was after your father's
money and she didn't want you to get it. Poor child!
How you have suffered!" Then Sushena began to look
sorry for herself and started crying.

'"Come!" the guru ordered me to sit beside her,
facing him, then he turned to Sushena again. "You
should let her know what you think of her now," he said.

"You should write your stepmother a letter. Then she'll know what she is, and she won't dare to bother you or your father ever again! You must do it. You know she'll have her claws in you otherwise! You know what she wants? To drag you down to hell!"

'Now the poor child was really frightened and started howling loudly. I made the mistake of taking her in my arms. "Elizabeth will tell you!" Father waved his hand in my direction. "She will tell you what an evil woman your stepmother is. She hates you for being so pretty. Do you know that? I think if I hadn't stepped in she'd have ended up poisoning you! Tell her, Elizabeth!" My lips moved, but I couldn't get anything out. I didn't know *what* to say. But his eyes were fixed on me, and I had to say something.

'"She seemed so very fond of Sushena," I said. The guru's eyes narrowed. It felt like lasers slicing through the layers of my being, right through me, to the core. I looked away. But it made no difference.

'"Seemed!" Father snatched at the word victoriously. "You see? Your stepmother *pretended* to love you and your father for her own ends," he told the little girl. "She's a witch!" Now Sushena was howling quite un-controllably. The guru held out his hands to her, and her father propelled her towards him. He took her and held her gently, stroking her hair, speaking in soothing murmurs, "but you're alright with Father. You know that. Nothing to be afraid of now. Why, I am stronger than anyone or anything. And I'm protecting you. *I* won't let her hurt you." The crying slowly stopped and the child was transferred back to her real father. She looked up at him and said quietly:

"You won't see her again, will you Daddy?" Bhanamurti's pale lips were trembling as he promised he wouldn't.

'Then they went, leaving Nathan and me alone with Father. He seemed to have gone into a deep trance of some sort. I tried to go into meditation but found it difficult. Even when his eyes are closed you still feel as though they're watching you from every corner of the room. Then suddenly his eyes sprang open and he spoke:

"I think, Elizabeth, you had better help her write the letter." He meant I should help Sushena write the letter to her stepmother, the one he was on about, you know? Telling her how evil she was. Well, I've no idea how I reacted. There's a sort of blank in my memory. It was like I'd gone onto automatic pilot. I think I sort of nodded and made agreeing sort of noises, while inside, I was ..." She shook her head and tried again, "It was like being struck by lightning!" she whispered. "I felt thrown out of time, caught in a sort of blinding light that left my brain completely blank." She was close to tears. Sitting with his back to her, Jim's nerves pricked, sensing the moment of truth; the moment when Liz couldn't hide her doubts from herself any more. Though doubtless she would try. She must not lose faith. For if she lost faith her life would end. 'If anyone else had asked me to do such a thing,' she blurted out, 'I'd have thought them criminals, but Father's incapable of doing wrong. If he tells a lie it becomes a truth because he's said it. So he can do anything. Well, he's God, isn't he? Only ...' panic coursed through her, 'I never thought he'd do a thing like that! I mean, maybe I'm too conditioned by Christianity or something, but I can't believe in a God who's a jealous God! And if He is like that then I don't want to know Him!' she cried. Then the lights went out. She moaned in terror. Jim threw himself across the bed and sat by her, holding her.

'It's just a fuse gone,' he said as calmly as he could. 'The wiring in the house is very old. I'd left the heaters on, to dry the place out a bit; probably overloaded the system.' Liz shook her head. She knew better. It was a warning. The light flickered and came back on.

'Don't let it throw you!' Jim urged. But Liz was cold with certainty.

'That was Father. He's playing games with me to teach me a lesson. He does that. He was doing it to me then.' Her pace gathered speed as though she was afraid she'd be cut off before she'd said it all.

'I don't know,' she said. 'Looking back, it's like a moment caught in a photograph. You know, where you don't recognise yourself. Anyway, the next thing, Father was smiling broadly at me, and pulling a box out from under his shawl.

'I think you will need one of these,' he said, opening the box to reveal a mangalsutra. You know, the wedding necklace. He knew about that, too. He'd probably made me forget to buy it, just so he could give me one. He's in my head. He organises me from inside. He can do what he likes with me. Anyway, I blushed and accepted the gift, muttering about his extreme generosity and his wisdom and Nathan was overjoyed. He was near to tears actually. Of course he'd known, but ... you know, I think he was getting fond of me. Yes. I think he was.'

Liz shivered and pulled the duvet round her. 'He'll be waiting for me now,' she said. The fog horn blew outside. Jim was very still. His heart was racing but he was cold as ice. Liz continued speaking, faster still. 'The mangalsutra was made of gold. Indian gold. Very high quality. Neither Nathan nor I could have afforded it. Father had given me something before. Most of the women had some beads or other round their necks that he'd given them for services rendered. In fact I had mine on.'

And she had them on now. They were still there, the tangible link between herself and her guru; the sutra that bound them. Involuntarily she raised her hand to feel the shape of the beads under her dress. 'Yes, I think he *was* playing games with me, to see how surrendered I was, and how much he could do with me, when I was

67

Nathan's wife. I think I must have passed the tests, too. I told myself not to think, that if it was God's will I marry Nathan, then I would marry him and serve our master forever and never question anything. It seemed to satisfy him.' Her hand dropped from the beads and grasped the other as though for comfort.

'This child. Sushena.' She knew Jim was looking at her and she strained to see him through the gloom.

'I couldn't do it,' she confessed. 'I tried. I went to see her with Bhanamurti and I sat beside her, and I just made some excuse and said I'd come back later. Bhanamurti was very upset, I think. Poor man. God knows what he was going through. But as I was leaving, he suddenly remembered something, and he felt in his pocket and brought out my watch. The clasp had snapped and it'd fallen off in the car. But I was suspicious. It's ridiculous, isn't it? I mean I can see how you'd see it. Paula'd disappeared from the scene long before, and she couldn't have taken it. Yet it passed through my mind that maybe Bhanamurti was covering for her. I can't have been thinking rationally. Actually, I was trying not to think at all. But ... this thing with Sushena. It broke my heart. It did really. I couldn't do it to the child. I couldn't do it to Paula. No matter what she'd done, she hadn't deserved this. Sinners can be saved, can't they? They can be saved? I couldn't condemn Paula! Anyway who was I? And why did Father want to destroy her? Why? I couldn't take it. I couldn't take the suffering. I mean, it could have been me!'

Liz was sobbing violently. Jim got up and walked round to her side of the bed. He let his hand rest on hers. Jumping at his icy touch, she pulled the duvet round him, too.

'You're freezing,' she said, 'Come on. Get warm.' He let her do it, because there were no sexual undertones to her behaviour. She was like a sister. And it was warm under the duvet. He was glad of it when all was said and done. 'Oh Jim, I was so confused,' she explained as though he hadn't guessed. 'I think I hoped Father would enlighten me. You know? Help me to understand and accept. I prayed for that. But he didn't. So I tried not to think of what was happening to Paula. I knew she'd gone away, but I didn't know where. I still don't know. I wonder where she is?' Liz swallowed a sob. 'You see I think a lot of this sort of thing had been going on, all the time, but like most devotees I didn't know about it, you see? I mean most of them just follow their own noses and do what they're told and get on with it. I mean, I did. You're told not to think or to gossip and to take attention away from negative people. So you do, you see. No. I'm not being honest. I knew things went on. But I blinded myself to them. I didn't want to know. That's the truth. I didn't want to know. But this time I'd no choice. My nose had been positively rubbed in it. And it was hard to accept that what had been done to Paula had been for her own good. I had always liked her. She had been like a sister to me. And now I'll never see her again.'

She was thinking about Paula. She cared about her friend. So, Jim thought, she did have some love left in her then. She was not completely lobotomised. But she was very uncomfortable. Was it the stirrings of conscience? He was surprised to feel glad for her. She was like a wayward student come back to the fold. Actually, Liz was thinking about Paula's family. Her parents were in the States, but she had an aunt in England. Would *she* know where Paula was? But no. Liz didn't want to be involved. She didn't dare.

'Anyway,' she went on, 'before I saw Bhanamurti again, something happened. I was grinding spices in the back garden when Jeanne came out to me waving a piece of paper in her hand. She held it before me like a palm she was about to spread at my feet.

'A letter. For you,' she announced and laid it

ceremoniously in my spicy hands. I rubbed my hands on my sari and looked at the envelope. It was from Dad. It felt very funny, looking down at his handwriting. Even funnier to think he'd written that letter in London, a week or so before. I mean, to me, he was part of another life. Why, I didn't even know if he was still alive. But I could remember his face so clearly and looking at his handwriting I suddenly wanted to cry. I didn't want Jeanne to see, so I just said I had to finish my work and the letter could wait. Jeanne was very disappointed, I could see that. And I must say I wasn't sorry I'd miffed her. She always wants to be in on everything! Anyway she went off in a huff and as soon as she was out of the way, I opened the letter. It was weird. Dad didn't say a word about himself. It was just: your Auntie Evie has died and you've inherited part of her estate and if you'd like to claim it, you'd better get yourself up to Shields and contact this solicitor. Then he gave the address and telephone number and that was it. Honestly I didn't know what to make of it. I mean he didn't even say how he was or anything. And it was dated over a week ago. The funeral would be over. There was no point going back. But as I sat looking at the page on my lap, it somehow "meant".'

Jim cringed. Liz noticed and tried to explain: 'I mean, it was like when the dove brought back the olive branch and Noah knew it was a sign from God that the waters were receding. It was like that.'

Jim's face was blank. She turned away and, after a slight hesitation, dived back into her story. 'Anyway, I looked at this page on my lap and I thought, well, there's no harm showing it to Nathan, is there? And "The Family" could use the money if there is any. No point looking gift horses in the mouth. So, at lunch time when the men came round for their food, I managed to get him away from the group and showed him the letter. He looked at it as though he didn't understand, then said he'd show it to Father and pocketed it. It was odd how I felt about that. I didn't like the letter being taken out of my hands like that. I thought I'd never see it again. And actually I *haven't* seen it since. Not that it really matters. Anyway, Father asked to see me straight away. He was very keen on this letter. I said I didn't want to go back to England; I didn't want to go out into the world, leave "the Family" and him and so on, no matter for how short a time. But he pooh poohed all that. He said the money was a sign from heaven. It showed how different I was from Paula. She was cursed and I was blessed. I should be glad. Anyway, he told me I shouldn't be selfish and I should think of "The Family" and all my brothers and sisters. They needed the money, if I didn't! Actually he positively ordered me to go home and collect.

'But first there were the weddings to get through. I don't know. I did enjoy the build-up really. There was a happy atmosphere in the ashram. Everybody teased everybody else; even Jeanne. And there was mounting excitement as new partners were constantly being announced and having to suddenly prepare themselves for the feast. We ended up with about thirty couples, I think. All ages. Of course it wasn't legal. It was a "religious" wedding, you know? A "Family" affair; no outsiders. The legal thing's supposed to follow later.'

'After the various divorces, I suppose,' Jim said. Elizabeth glanced at him, took in the remark and ploughed on.

'Anyway, the night before the ceremony, all the brides slept, cheek by jowl on the meditation room floor. One of the brides snored and somebody else had a cough, so I didn't sleep very well. And when I woke I felt really grey; not bridelike at all. We were meditating at five a.m., meditating or queuing to use the loo and bathrooms. Actually, a lot of people meditated in the queue. We all wanted to be as lovely as possible. The bridegrooms had slept outside in the garden. Except Nathan, of course. He'd slept in Father's anteroom. And then some young female devotees came into the meditation room with cups of tea for the brides, and a lot of henna paste to paint symbols on our hands and feet. Oh yes, and on our foreheads, too. Mine hasn't washed off yet. Look.'

Jim looked and saw the fading patterns on Liz's hands and head. If he had been wondering how much of this was true, here was proof. The brownish marks made his flesh creep. The whole thing was feeling more and more sinister. 'And then we all had to get into our wedding saris and jewellery and so on.' Liz spoke dreamily like one in a trance. 'All the saris were white, like Western wedding dresses. Which is odd, because in India, white's the colour of sannyasa, you know? Celibate renunciation? It was really difficult, because we were all so crowded, but everybody helped each other dress, then medallions on gilt chains were handed round. Each bride had to wear one. On one side was a picture of Father and on the other a sun and a moon to represent the bride and groom.

'And then the buses arrived. The men got in one, the women in the other, segregated. The men were all dressed in dark suits. They had medallions too. We were all absolutely silent, by the way, as the bus hurtled to the hall they'd booked for the occasion. I think some of the women were praying. I know I was. Of course the wedding ceremonies are completely secret. Only those taking part are allowed into the hall and no-one's supposed to say a word about what goes on. It's all secret, you see, Jim. Everything. All I've told you. You know, I'm breaking a vow by telling you this.'

Liz paused, expecting the light to cut out again. When it didn't, she let out a sigh of relief and went on, 'Maybe I'm meant to tell you!' She smiled at the happy thought. He shivered. 'Anyway, when we arrived at the hall, we were herded into lines, men one side, women the other, each man opposite his betrothed. Someone came down the line giving out posies. Each bride carried one, each bride, each posy identical. No-one was allowed to feel special. Why should they, when the marriage was meant only to progress spiritual evolution for the good of "The Family"? I mean it's not a personal ego trip. Being "in love" is frowned on because, well, because it's just illusion, isn't it? I mean, there's no such thing, it's just self-deceiving. And marriage is more than that. I mean the Jews consider it important for the community, don't they? And it is! The individual's just a cog in the wheel.' Liz was staring at Jim, willing him to respond. After a while he shifted slightly, pulling the duvet closer and said:

'So that's what you believe, is it? I mean you believe you, as you, don't actually matter? Because if you do that means me as me doesn't matter either, and the whole community's made up of yous and mes, as I see it. But still, if that's what you believe ...' He sounded sullen. Liz's eyes dulled. She tried to explain:

'You see, we're all working towards the new world, Jim. A world in which everyone lives in harmony.' Jim began singing a sixties tune, chuckling wickedly, and Elizabeth turned on him briskly. 'You're just a cynic! I mean, what's wrong with harmony?'

'Depends what it's based on,' he commented.

'It's based on the subjugation of the individual ego,' she told him earnestly. 'It's ego which gets in the way all the time. I mean, it's beautiful, once you stop thinking ... thought comes from the ego, you know? And you *can* stop thinking through meditation. You forget about "I" and it's a relief really to be ... well, Father said we should be like a beehive, workers with only one thing in mind, the future good of the commune.'

'Who's the queen bee?' Jim asked.

'He is, of course.'

'And when the workers have outlived their usefulness, the old queen kills them, right?'

There was a long pause. Liz took a deep breath and replied: 'Yes. That has to be accepted. We live and die for the community. For "The Family". Nothing else matters.'

'When did you last paint anything?' Jim asked out of the blue. A pained look crossed her face. She shook her head. 'Come on. Tell me. How long is it?'

'I don't know.' She was near to tears again. 'Painting's too individualistic. It made me egotistical,' she said. 'I had to stop.'

'They were afraid of your creativity,' he told her.

'Don't be stupid. They were *releasing* my creativity!'

'How? By grinding spices? Not to mention your spirit!' Jim sighed. He was beginning to feel very tired. But he had to at least try and get his point home. 'Art has to be practised. You know that. Through art truth emerges. Always has done since the world began. True creativity is a door of the soul.'

'It's just words!' she shouted.

'Alright. Alright,' Jim sighed. 'Go on. Tell me about this wonderful wedding.' Liz heard the irony and chose to ignore it. She was tired too; too tired to argue. She wondered whether to go on with her story, but it was like she'd set the ball rolling and now it would roll on till it reached the bottom of the hill and then she would see where she'd landed. Somehow she couldn't stop herself.

'Well, we were standing,' she went on. 'We'd been standing a long time. I remember swaying a bit. I was exhausted. My head swam. Actually I felt sick. I remember that. Oh yes, and I wanted to go to the loo. Such low thoughts! You see how much I was centred on myself? On my own egotistical needs? I wondered if I could last the ceremony, actually. I knew it went on for hours and there was no escape. Anyway, suddenly there was a flurry. It seemed to pass down the line and on.

Someone blew a horn. I jumped. It upset me. I broke out in a sweat and wondered how the other brides were feeling. And then the line started moving forwards into the hall, and we were guided into three long rows of couples. There was an empty throne on the dais, with flowers and incense and so on, and we stood again for a long long time, waiting, standing where we were. Father was doing it on purpose of course, to make sure we all got through the physical discomforts early so our minds would be clear for the spiritual experience ahead. I remember the flowers smelt very sweet and I tried to concentrate on them instead of how I felt.

'And other things. Paula for instance. I remember a sudden feeling of panic when I thought she'd been through this same ceremony only a year before. And I wondered if I would be where she was next year. But, of course, that's one of the tricks of the negative, you know? It makes you see yourself in a negative light, then it draws you like a magnet; a sort of self-fulfilling prophecy, you know? Anyway, I tried very hard not to think about Paula, but just concentrate on feeling grateful to Father for deigning to marry me to his favourite son.

'Dear Nathan: he looked so sweet. But of course I wasn't supposed to think about *him* either. Not as an individual anyway. So I tried simply to clear my mind of everything. Then several horns blew and everyone grew very still as Father swept into the hall, up the stairs and onto the dais. We were all looking up at him. He had ten helpers with him. Jeanne was amongst them. They all stood on the stairs, graded according to seniority. Of course normally Nathan would have been there, but he was one of the bridegrooms so he wasn't. And they stood there, looking down on us all as Father raised his hands and gestured us to sit.

'My legs didn't want to bend into the lotus after standing all that time. And it was difficult in a stiff

75

ceremonial sari, covered in jewellery. But we were all in the same boat. So, with a bit of struggling we got to the floor and somehow settled. And then Father spoke for a long time on the subject of marriage and the duties of a husband and wife. He told us it was a great occasion. The bonding of a couple and the renewal of vows to "The Family" was a kind of rebirth, and from that day on we would share, not only our wedding anniversaries, but also the same birthday. And then, we all stood, repeating the vows, to dedicate our lives, our wealth and our talents to the service of "The Family"; to be faithful to one another until Father decreed otherwise; to bring up our children in "The Way", remembering they are not our children but Father's children; to help one another in our spiritual evolution, so that through our growth the new world would come on earth; to be always faithful to Father, recognising that all things come from him and through him and must go back to him; and of course ... we all vowed secrecy.'

'Why the secrecy?' Jim interrupted. 'If it's for the good of the world and so on, what's the need for it? I should think you'd all be dying to spread the word abroad!'

'Oh we do!' Liz assured him. 'Jeanne teaches all over the world. She's a master of "The Way". I told you that.'

'But she doesn't teach *everything*,' Jim said, pointedly.

'No. But that's not because there's anything shameful to hide! It's to do with power; spiritual power. Some things lose their power when spoken of. They are occult, which means hidden, veiled, kept sacred ... secret. It's almost the same word, sacred and secret. It's all to do with respect and reverence. Anyway, Father said we shouldn't cast pearls before swine. It wasn't good for the swine. They'd only eat them and get indigestion.' Jim burst out laughing.

'He's got a "way" with words, I'll say that for him,' he said. He was fascinated in spite of himself.

'Yes,' Elizabeth nodded eagerly. 'He's very clever.'

'I noticed.' Jim wasn't laughing. She turned away from his penetrating eyes and took refuge in her story.

'Anyway, after we'd made our vows the rituals started. I really can't tell you about those. I'm afraid you'll damage yourself by saying disrespectful things about them.' Jim grimaced. 'But anyway, at the end, each couple had to go up onto the dais and kneel before Father for his blessing. He put his finger on our foreheads and gave us new names. Mine's "Pragya". You see it was a rebirth. Nathan and I had been made one whole person, and so we were new, like a new-born baby.'

'I see! So you were Pragya "a" and he was Pragya "b" I suppose,' Jim laughed. Liz was hurt.

'No! We had different names,' she said primly.

'Doesn't seem logical,' Jim mocked. 'I mean, if you were two halves of the same person!'

'Why are you so bitter, Jim?' Liz accused. 'Are you jealous? Is that it?' She saw hatred cross his face and wished she hadn't said it. He hated her. Becuse of what she'd done to him, Jim really hated her. And he used to love her ... once. For a moment she realised she had lost everything. They stared at one another for a long moment, then she turned sadly away. After a while, Jim spoke.

'No. I'm not jealous,' he said. And now she wanted to know why not. But didn't dare ask.

'Well, to cut a long story short ...'

'Oh, don't do that.' He spoke with irony. 'You were just getting to the interesting bit.'

'What?'

'I suppose this marriage did have its physical side, or were you supposed to create children by making spiritual signs to one another?'

'Don't be stupid.'

'Sorry. I'm just an ignorant ...' Jim took a deep breath and then said, genuinely, 'Sorry.'

'You *are* jealous.'

'Oh get on with it!' he snapped. His head was muddled by the maze of tricks she had drawn him through. He hardly knew which way he was pointing and he was tired, bloody tired!

'Well, after that,' she went on, 'when we all had our new names and everything, we all sang praises to Father. And then there was a concert. The ceremony had taken all day. I was exhausted by the evening and so was Nathan, I think. But do you know, it's amazing, I didn't need the loo once! You know? It's really a miracle!'

'Sure!' Jim mocked.

'Well! Anyway,' she continued primly, 'to get onto the interesting bit, as you call it. All the couples had been allocated rooms at an hotel. And yes, we *were* supposed to consummate the marriages, since you ask! Only Nathan ... well, he is a nice man, Jim. Really, he is. He knew I needed time and he didn't want to force me, you know? So he said he'd wait, and I slept on the bed while he slept on the floor, like a real gentleman. And he didn't tell anybody either. And next morning at breakfast there were the usual sort of Western cracks, and the brides blushed and the men blushed, too, and we did, I mean Nathan and me, just like the rest as though we had ... well ... you know. I wondered how many of the others had chickened out, too. I bet there were a few. Anyway, I was very grateful to Nathan. I still am. And it was very brave of him, you know. Because he knew I was going back to England ...'

'This Father of yours believed the marriage had been consummated?' Jim asked slowly.

'I suppose so.' Liz paused to consider. 'I mean, nobody told him otherwise and it was expected and Nathan was a senior devotee, so, yes, I suppose so. I suppose if Father had asked him directly he wouldn't have lied to him, but ... he did lie to the others!'

'Good for Nathan,' Jim said drily. Liz was feeling very uncomfortable. She pushed the duvet away and hitched up onto the bed, crossing her legs in meditation posture. Any minute, Jim thought, she's going to close her eyes and shut me out. His urge was to hold on, like a mountaineer with a rope. It was a mental challenge to keep her hanging on there, to not let her go.

'You'd been in India a long time,' he encouraged. Liz said nothing. She closed her eyes and started humming her mantra. Jim sighed. For two pins he'd get up off this bed and sod off downstairs for a cup of coffee. He was sick to his eyeballs with her and 'Father' and the whole nauseating lot of them. But why was he so upset about it? He wasn't jealous. How could you be jealous of a pair of zombies getting hitched? It was like a drama played out in the lunatic asylum. Except, it wasn't. He felt his heart shift. This 'Father' knew about *him*. So he was involved, whether he liked it or not. By loving Liz, as he had done in the past, he had given her the key to his psyche. She had kept it, and when she opened her doors to this guru and let him into her mind, she had given him power over Jim too. So it *was* contagious. It was a sort of psychic AIDS, only more disgusting. Yes, he *had* to get through to her. Had to get her through it, somehow! For his own sake!

He looked at her hands, the red diagrams still visible, though fading. This wedding business had actually happened. And so recently. A week ago? It was incredible. His eyes rose to her face. Her eyes were screwed up tight, as though shutting out the world. She was probably trying not to think. He almost laughed. And all the time she kept on humming this mantra. What for? Was it some sort of cutting out device like they use to jam radio waves? Was she jamming him? What would happen if he touched her? She'd probably die of shock, have a heart attack or something. He blew gently against her ear. She flinched, and slowly opened her eyes, rubbing the place where his breath had fallen.

'What is it?' she said in a very high and mighty voice.

'I'm sorry.' He managed to look contrite. 'I want you to finish your story.'

'My story won't finish till life's end,' she said haughtily.

'Well, alright, the story up to now.' He acquiesced.

'Where had I got to?' Her voice was dreamy. She'd drifted off to never never land in the interval.

'You and Nathan hadn't consummated your marriage,' he prompted.

'Oh.' She drew herself up as though inhaling the prana of life and said:

'I'll only go on if you promise me you'll be more respectful. I'm saying this for your own good.'

'I promise.' He crossed his heart.

'You don't need to go in for any of that superstition, surely?' she sneered. Jim opened his hands and let them fall to his side. Then he waited and, finally, she went on.

'Of course the arrangements for my departure had been started the moment I'd left Father's room. I mean, before the wedding. I must admit, to my shame, I felt lightheaded as I came down the stairs after he'd told me. There was definitely, and yes, I must admit it, a sense of release. But, of course, I was scared too! I hadn't been in the outside world, apart from Gulhapur and one or two other small Indian towns, for so many years. I'd got to be like a village girl terrified of going to the big city! And it was all to happen so soon! Nathan was put in charge of the travel arrangements so I didn't have much to worry about except that my passport was out of date, which was a problem. I mean I hadn't been out of India for so long. Actually in human terms, I suppose I was an illegal immigrant, of a sort. But, anyway, Nathan had to take my passport and birth certificate and so on to Bombay to sort out the passport business for me.

'My ticket was bought for me by "The Family". I think they must have pulled a few strings to get me my passport. I mean, "The Family" does have connections in high places. Well it would, wouldn't it? It's going to rule the world.' The laughter which had been bubbling up in Jim surfaced. 'Don't you dare laugh!' she yelled. He feigned a coughing fit. 'You're not laughing, then. Well, I hope not. Because you shouldn't. Only a fool would laugh. Once a majority of people have let Father into their minds ...' Jim suddenly lost the urge to laugh. He felt sick. Liz took in more prana and exhaled slowly. She looked peaceful, as though giving up responsibility and free will was the ultimate relief. And, Jim realised with pity, for those in pain it surely must be. But Liz was talking again:

'Of course I'd had my packing to do. Not that I had much, especially Western things ...'

'Why Western things?' Jim asked curiously. 'Why aren't you wearing your sari now?' Liz smiled as to a child.

'This isn't some regimented cult you know, Jim. We don't wear uniforms. In India we wear saris, of course, like everyone. But in the West ... well, there are hundreds and thousands of us walking the streets, blending with the crowd, undetectable. We look exactly the same as everyone else. Except, of course, we're not. *We* carry the divine message in our souls, and we transmit it, like a pulse growing louder and louder till one day, every pulse will beat to the same rhythm and Father will rule the world.' Jim shuddered.

'I see.'

'You could tune your pulse to ours, just like that.' She clicked her fingers.

'How would I do it?' he asked with real interest. At once, Liz rose and went to her travel bag. She was rummaging in the bottom. Then she found what she was looking for. Reverently, she drew out a folded frame, opened it, and revealed a photograph of her guru. She showed it to Jim, then put it on the beside table.

'I need a candle,' she said and was going to get one. But Jim stopped her.

'Not yet,' he said, feigning a smile. 'I'm not ready. Perhaps later.' Disappointed, Liz dropped the candle idea and came back to sit beside him on the edge of the bed. She was stiff, tense. Jim glanced at the photograph. The bright eagle eyes of the guru seemed to be watching them. He didn't like it. It made him want to puke. He got up and turned the photograph over.

'You don't want him to know you're telling me his secrets, do you?' he said cleverly.

'Oh no!' Suddenly Liz looked afraid. Jim dropped his hand onto hers and held it. She was freezing cold. He felt her forehead. It was hot. But she shook him off. 'Don't!' she said in fright, as though he was contaminating her with his touch.

'You were packing,' he reminded her. 'To come to England.'

'Packing. Yes.' Liz looked vague, like a wild pony, abandoned on the moors, the weather closing in. She looked round for support. Then she closed her eyes, screwing them tight and breathing deeply. When she opened them again, her eyes were bright, glinting in the electric light from the bedside lamp. 'He said I was filth. And I am, aren't I? I'm proving it now by telling you all this.' She looked directly at Jim. He looked back, not knowing what to say. She might take off in any direction. But he needn't have worried. She pulled herself up, then galloped on with her story.

'Yes, I was packing. I had a few Western things left. I knew they'd be ridiculously old-fashioned, but I packed them anyway and I packed a few saris and shawls as well. I don't know why. They're so easy to wear, you know? Once you get used to them. So practical.' She glanced at her small travelling bag. 'Bhanamurti and Nathan went to the airport with me. I was excited, like a little girl, and they laughed at me, teasing me and saying I'd never come back, I'd get corrupted by Western thinking and so on.' She had tears in her eyes.

'Of course they knew I wouldn't. They'd seen how shocked I was when we got to Bombay! We'd had a meal in a hotel there, and I'd seen this woman, this Indian woman, in a sari, and it was falling off her shoulder, so wantonly and she had on high heels, would you believe? I was really shocked! I thought how decadent she looked and what an affront it was to Indian womanhood. Well it is! She let the side down. I mean, I was more Indian than she was! I was really shocked! Anyway, I'd been in "The Family" for as long as any of them and ... well, anyway, I wouldn't desert! But Nathan was nervous. I could feel it. I suppose he would have felt better if we'd ... if we'd ... consummated the marriage. Oh, he is so kind. So brave! I think he must really love me. He asked me to write every day. And I did. I have written three times. But not today. Not yesterday either. He'll be anxious. Poor Nathan.'

'You were at the airport.'

She drew herself out of a faltering, creeping paralysis, and went on: 'Yes. It was weird waving goodbye to them, to India. I felt so alone. But I was going on a mission. I had to be brave. So I waved back cheerfully and got on the plane, and ... when I landed in England I felt really depressed. Everyone looked so pinched and mean and pale. They were fighting each other for trollies in the luggage hall. Really, England needs "The Way" more than anywhere. It's so trapped, so insular. The inner release experienced by each devotee could be the release of this whole country. But it needs more of us, Jim, if we're going to do it. Father can't do it on his own. We're like transmitters, you see. We're his satellites. The more of us there are, the stronger the transmissions, until one day, there'll be an end to war and crime and hate and poverty, too, and peace and harmony will rule the world.' Liz was glowing. She looked down on Jim with a huge smile. He felt as though she was going to eat him.

'You're spinning me a line. Know that?' was all he said. The smile crashed like a plane. But she pulled herself together quickly.

'It's alright, Jim. I forgive you,' she said. 'I realise it's your unhappiness speaking. You're a slave to your own past, your karma, your conditioning. It encloses you like an egg encloses the baby chick. You have to break free, like I have. That's why I've been telling you all this.' Jim said nothing, then finally he asked:

'Tell me honestly, are you happy, Liz?'

'Of course!' she replied joyously, 'as long as I don't think!' She shared a laugh with him. Then, with smile fixed, he said:

'You're still spinning a line.' And she closed up.

'You don't deserve it,' she told him angrily. 'I mean, I should have known I was wasting my time. Father told us not to cast pearls before swine.' She got up and quickly folded the photograph, thrusting it into the safety of her bag. He watched her nervously. What could he say? But she hadn't finished. 'You're too American, that's your problem. Like Paula. She couldn't free herself; not properly. Her conditioning dragged her down. In the end it drags all of us down, that's why we had to let her go. I'm glad I ran out on you. You'd have dragged me right down, Jim.' She shook her head and surveyed him with distaste. 'It's because you were brought up in the "Dream Factory", you see. Hollywood and all that. You can't tell the difference between illusion and reality.'

'*I* can't?!' he yelled.

'Yes,' she replied patiently. 'The spiritual dimension is the only reality. All this ... flesh, things, the life we lead, is all illusion. You have to give that up before you can see the truth.'

'I wasn't brought up in the "Dream Factory",' Jim said. Liz wavered, as she remembered.

'Oh yes,' she said. 'You were brought up by the Hopi

84

Indians, weren't you? Now they knew a lot about spiritual power!'

'I know,' Jim replied. 'In the war, the Koreans tried to brainwash *me*! We're all brainwashed. Every one of us from birth. It's nothing new. The difference is I know it. And I can still sense who I am at the centre of it all. Who are you?'

Liz gaped. It was as though he'd pressed her to the rim of the Grand Canyon and she'd looked down into the chasm and found nothing. But she recovered quickly.

'I'm nothing,' she said. 'I am a vessel to contain the divine will.'

'That's okay, I suppose, if you're sure it *is* the divine. But you're still spinning a line. Only this time it's to yourself.' She was pale and near to tears. Or, Jim wondered, was she angry? She maybe thought he was just being thick. Maybe he was. Maybe all this was just beyond his simple, unevolved understanding. He had at least to pretend to make a few concessions if he was going to hang on in there. And that story of hers about Chintamani had really got through to him. In all the crap, it shone like a gem. Risking exposure, he dared to mention it.

'Look,' he said, hoarsely, 'I don't say that some of what you've experienced wasn't real. That time you went to the shrine ...' Liz's eyes softened, as she remembered. 'That was real. I mean I could feel you really had got in touch with something there. But, I mean, that was you and ... well, God, wasn't it? It didn't have anything to do with this "Father" of yours?' Liz thought for a minute, then said:

'Father is all the aspects in one. In worshipping him you worship all the deities of all the religions. And in worshipping them, you worship Him, you see?'

'Crap,' said Jim. He got up, yawned, and his bones cracked as he stretched. 'I'm going to hit the sack. I'm

85

tired. You better get your letter written to your new husband.' Then he left the room. And Liz heard the fog horns blow.

Bedded down on the sofa in Eve's old sitting room, Jim thought about the alien upstairs. Had he really been in love with that ... that zombie? That vampire? Dear God, he'd almost married her. What an escape! If he'd only known, he would have been thanking his lucky stars all these years. He laughed out loud. 'I'll say it now. Thank you, Liz, for walking out on me. You did me a real favour.' He laughed again. Unbelievable! First she emasculates you then she tries to recruit you. Incredible! Fascinating! Was that how they got *her*? It was like ... like being fascinated by a snake before the kill. Deadly. They paralyse you then suck the soul clean out of you. Vampires.

He stopped laughing and punched the ancient cushions. Dust flew out. He flopped back, pushing against them, reshaping them with his shoulders. He couldn't get comfortable. He was hot and itching all over. He scratched under his arm. What was she doing up there now? Chanting mantras? Not that he cared! Just a waste of a good bed, that's all. Mantras. Self-hypnosis. Silly cow! He scratched again. Why the hell did he bother? Was she worth it? No! She'd made her bed, let her lie on it. He turned abruptly as though to surprise the cushions, took them by the scruff of the neck and shook them hard before flopping back against them, as uncomfortable as before. Hell! He was breathing hard. He ought to relax. But he was smarting. She had bested him, Jim Ridley, Cambridge scholar, and almost had his brain running round in circles.

'The Way'. Hah! She was caught in 'The Way' now alright. Couldn't see any way out. Well, she might not be able to, but he could. Sleep. At last. He yawned and switched off the light and immediately saw her again:

86

that Korean kid, Kim; in the seersucker pyjamas. Damn it! Wouldn't let him go. 'You get killed ...' And that interfering nun at the orphanage.

'When the war's over, who knows, he might take you back to America with him!' Why'd she have to say that to the poor kid? Her words came back like an accusation from the past. Hell, that kid had nothing to do with him. Nothing! So, why did he keep seeing her eyes, pleading with him not to go? Why'd he have to suffer for other folks' kids? He had one of his own. Not that it felt like it. Helen was always Louise's kid, really. Independent, wayward, always going off at a tangent just to see how people reacted. Hard to guide a kid like that. Hard to relate to. Got to learn from her own bitter experience. Most likely go the way of her mother. Not a constant thought in her head.

Flighty, Eve called her. Maybe that's what Jim'd liked about her, Louise's very instability was attractive. Jim would never have got into the scrapes he did when he was young, not without her, anyway. Did he have his youth vicariously through his wife? Did he? And then he just grew up and left her behind. He'd closed the door on her and walked on along the corridor. He'd used her. No wonder she called him an arrogant, self-centred bastard! She knew he didn't care about her, or Helen. And she was right. He didn't. But then they weren't real to him, so they left him cold. But then most things left him cold. Except that kid: Kim. She'd got through alright.

Damn Liz for bringing her back. He'd left her behind, in more ways than one. Why'd he do it? At the time, he didn't want to get in too deep. Looking back, he saw his whole life had been a lone walk down a corridor. Now and then a door'd opened and he'd been invited in, and he'd had the choice to enter a world or not. The people in it believed in their world entirely. For them there was no other. They were locked in that room. But not him.

He'd been born a white man on a ranch in New Mexico. He had a bit of Hispanic blood, from his grandmother, but he was mostly white. And then, just after he was born, his ma had died, and he'd been nursed by a Hopi Indian. And the Indian invited him into her world, and he'd gone along with her, running the Indian side along with the white raising his pa insisted on. And none of it was real. He was just play-acting through life. Right up to the Initiation. Because, in the Grand Canyon, something happened to him.

Jim shot off the sofa and switched on the light. He had to tell Liz. Pulling on a sweater he ran upstairs. He stopped at the top, hearing the sound of repeated mantra. His heart sank. He was going to walk away. But this was important, so he changed his mind and propelled himself towards her door, purposely noisy. The mantras stopped. He put his hand on the knob and turned it and when the door opened, she was sitting cross-legged on the bed, head turned towards him.

'I've got to tell you something,' he said.

'Now? I was meditating.'

'Now,' he insisted.

'Actually,' she demurred, 'I don't feel too good. I got the flash, but, I don't know, I've got a pain in my head and I feel sick. Do you think it's because I broke my vow of secrecy? I've betrayed him. I have. I've betrayed Father!'

'Cut the crap and listen to me!' But she wouldn't.

'He said we had to meditate at a certain time, all together, so he can put his attention on us. He knows everything. He knows what I've done. I'm being punished.'

'Listen.' She stopped talking and, trembling, looked at him. 'Just tell him to sod off,' he told her. Liz's mouth fell open and a squeak came out. But he didn't give her time to expand on it, he just launched into what he had to say. 'That experience you had with Chintamani; that

88

was real. Now you've got to hang onto that. That was you plugging into something primeval, cosmic if you like, it's only words, but it *was* real. And it was good; healthy.

'You see, it wasn't the same, but it was like what happened to me in the Canyon. The Grand Canyon. I was on an initiation test. The Hopi Indians. You know? I'd been walking barefoot for days, living on nothing but what my bow and arrow could kill. I'd walked all the way down the Canyon. It was like being in an isolation unit. There was me and the Canyon and that was it. Apart from a few snakes and game. The idea was to get to the far end, past the Bright Angel Trail, collect the salt, then go all the way back and deliver the salt to the priest. Then I'd be initiated. I'd be a fully-fledged member of the Clan. But ... well, I guess I was half starved, I'd been half frozen and ... then there was this massive storm. The noise burst your eardrums, and it shook the earth. Shook me! Lightning flashed, boomeranging from side to side of the Canyon like a laser show. Amazing colours, red, purple, green, flashed out of the stone, rising miles high on either side of me. And I was trapped between them, terrified out of my head. And you know, the rocks, Temple of Vishnu, Shiva Temple and so on, seemed to be rising out of the shifting gorge, and it felt like being at the beginning of time or the end of it and it really didn't matter which. The North Rim seemed to be on fire. And I was whipped raw by the rain. You know? I felt like I was being stripped. And at the end of it, everything had been torn clean away from me. All the myths, all the ideas, all the emotion had gone. The very act of initiation that should have bound me to the Hopi had torn me from them.

'And yet, I wasn't really a white man, either. I was ... naked. Like Adam before he got drawn into believing in anything. And you know, I told Eve about it. And she thought I meant I didn't believe in the Hopi thing any

89

more. And she just didn't get it, you know? It wasn't like that. The Hopi myth is as real as any of the others. They're all real. Every one of them. It's just I didn't belong in anyone's myths any more. Not white, not Indian, not Catholic, not Jew not ... not any. I was just ... a man. I didn't go back to the Hopis. I turned off the trail and went up to the rim at Bright Angel and when I got there, I just threw the salt back into the Canyon.'

Liz was agitated, trying to speak. Jim paused to let her.

'In India, salt's the traditional offering to the guru. Did you know that?' she said. She was shivering. 'You threw the salt back in his face!' She spoke as if it was the ultimate crime. Jim laughed. What he was about to say was the most obvious thing in the world.

'You don't need a guru! I mean when you've plugged into the mains, why do you want to bother with an adapter? See? I plugged into the mains in the Canyon. You plugged in with Chintamani. We don't need gurus any more. They only get in the way.' Liz was silent. He'd sprained her mind and it wouldn't work any more. 'What happened to me in the Canyon is the only real thing that ever happened in my whole life. Apart from ...' He was going to say, 'Kim', and surprised himself by almost saying, 'loving you', but stopped himself in time. There was no way he was taking responsibility for her. He'd never taken responsibility for anyone in his life. Not even in retrospect. 'Just don't let fear make you cling to what you've grown out of, that's all,' he said.

'I haven't grown out of "The Family"!' Elizabeth retorted. 'It's the ultimate. It's God's Kingdom on earth. How *can* you grow out of it? Jim, you are thick!'

'If God's infinite,' Jim said slyly, 'how can an incarnate being be the ultimate? An incarnate being is finite. By definition, not God. The same goes for God's Kingdom on earth. There *is* no ultimate, not till the end of time!'

'That's a brain teaser,' Liz said, shaking her head. 'You've got me so I can't think!'

'That should make you happy!' Pleased with himself, he laughed. Then *she* laughed, actually laughed, then she stopped laughing and looked terrified. 'If only I could stop the voice!' she wailed.

'What voice?' he asked. 'What's it telling you?'

'It's telling me I'm filth. I'm a turd under the foot of The Father, and I am for even listening to you!'

'Probably him speaking.'

'But it's true.'

'That you're a turd?'

'Yes!'

'Why? Who says?'

'I do!'

'Then you're crazy.' He bit his tongue. He shouldn't have said that.

'I'm the result of an act of incest. I'm a walking blasphemy!' she insisted.

'Look. Okay,' he agreed. 'Most myths say incest is a sin. Most. Not all! Suppose it's true. Are you sure about this incest business? I mean are you sure it really happened?'

'Eve told me so. Why should she lie?'

'I'd want tangible proof if I was you.' He shrugged, then yawned. 'I'm bushed,' he said.

'So am I,' she sighed, 'but I can't sleep.'

'Jet lag?'

'Yes,' she agreed, then added, 'and anyway they're all awake in India. I can't sleep while they're awake. I mean I'm part of them.'

'Ah yes. A drone in the hive. I remember. Well goodnight, drone. See you in the morning.'

'You blasphemous ... ooh!'

Liz woke at one in the afternoon. The seagulls were screeching fit to waken the dead outside her window. It took her a while to remember where she was. Then she got up and looked at her clothes folded neatly over the back of the chair; such awkward garments! Reluctantly she went to put them on but stood looking at them instead. So many bits and pieces. The underpinnings of the Western image. Still, when in Rome . . . She put them on, brushed her hair back into a band, and went down to the kitchen.

Jim was reading a book. He was so engrossed in it he didn't hear her come in. Mildly irritated, she looked at the stove, saw that it was gas, went over to it and put the kettle on. She was gasping for a cup of tea. As she struck the match, he looked up, momentarily.

'Afternoon,' he said.

'Hi,' she answered. She was going to ask if he'd slept well, but he'd already gone back to his book. He wore glasses now, she observed. She filled the kettle at the tap. Actually she was beginning to find him rather annoying. Why was he ignoring her? Who did he think he was? Hah! Why should she care? It was just as well she had walked out on him all those years ago, blasphemous, shallow intellectual that he was! She banged the kettle down on the stove and told herself to be more detached. Anyway, she was filth. Her very interest in him proved she was. So why should he be interested in her? *And* she was a married woman. She put a teabag in a cup and looked for something to eat. Cereal, she thought. Everybody eats cereal. She started looking in the cupboards, banging the doors one after the other.

'Is there anything to eat?' she asked finally. Jim looked up, startled.

'What?'

'Is there anything to eat?'

'Oh. Some bacon in the fridge. Don't know how old it is.'

'Yuk!'

'Ah yes.' He sighed and put down his book. 'I

remember how I felt when I got back from Korea. Didn't want anything but rice. Wonder if they've got any?' He got up and started looking in the cupboards, too. 'Instant whip,' he said, holding up a packet.

'I don't want rice, anyway!' she objected.

'Oh. Fine. What *do* you want?' Liz thought for a minute, then said:

'Cereal.'

'Great. I think there's some of that.' He pulled out a packet of something with honey on. Liz started drooling.

'Ooh!' she said. 'You know, I like Indian food. I do really. But curried cornflakes for breakfast? I never got used to that!' He smiled and she poured her cornflakes, then realised there was no milk. Her disappointment was acute. He laughed at her.

'We could go out shopping,' he offered.

'I'm not going to *live* here!' she protested. 'I mean I'm not moving in! I'm just here for a few days, to dispose of the place. You know?'

'Ah,' he said and took off his glasses.

'What do you mean, "Ah"?' The kettle started whistling and she poured the water onto the teabag.

'Making me one?' he asked. Annoyed, but not prepared to say anything, Liz got another teabag and put it into a cup. Then she poured water over that, too, and handed the cup to him. He didn't bother to say thank you.

'What do you mean, "Ah"?' she asked again.

'Just we'll have to discuss it. That's all.'

'Oh. I see.' Liz sighed. 'The trustees have the last word.'

'Yes.'

'So you're not going to let me sell the place?'

'Maybe. Depends what you want to do with the proceeds.' Suddenly Liz realised what it was all about. How slow she'd been! Of course. It was a plot to stop her giving her money to 'The Family'.

'God, I'm thick!' she said angrily. Then, 'Bloody Eve!'

'Don't they frown on swearing in this cult of yours?' Jim asked.

'Oh shut up! And it isn't a cult!'

'Sorry.' He watched her for a moment, puffing and blowing out her fury, then said:

'Give it a while. Don't make up your mind too quickly. You need a break. So do I. As a matter of fact, I'm taking one.' She looked at him sharply.

'What are you suggesting?' she snapped.

'Why don't we go for a walk?' He took her long, suspicious stare without flinching. She knew that he knew that she knew that he'd meant more than just going for a walk. Or, at least she thought she did, he did. Oh hell! What *was* he going to say last night, 'the only real thing that happened to me, apart from ...' What? Her? She let it rest. She had to. She couldn't get her mind round it. The seagulls were screeching outside. There was nothing to eat in the house. They might as well go out.

'Okay,' she agreed. 'But I must write to Nathan when we get back.'

The road to the sea was shorter than either of them remembered, and the dunes seemed to have disappeared. There'd been some rumour about lorries coming in the middle of the night and carting off the sand to make cement. Nobody knew if it was true or not. Anyway, the sea was still there. Nobody could do very much about that. It still came in and went out according to its own nature. It still made waves, and it was still good to look at, no matter what a chemical analysis might bring up. They walked along the prom, breathing in familiar smells and thinking but not saying how warm it was for the time of year.

The fog had disappeared through the night and the horizon was clear. Too clear. There weren't many big ships going up the Tyne these days. Not many fishing boats, either. The river had been developed for tourists instead. 'Catherine Cookson Country', and 'Land of the prince Bishops', the signposts announced. The place had become another myth. People lived on myths one way or another. Anyway, it fed a few bellies! Liz's stomach was rumbling.

'Fish and chips?' Jim asked.

'Yuk,' Liz answered.

'Curry?'

'No, thanks.' She hesitated, then said, 'Know what I'd really like?'

'No idea. What?'

'I'd like to try one of those American hamburger places. You know?'

'Who doesn't?'

'Actually,' she admitted, 'I already did try one. In Bombay.' Jim laughed.

'They've got one in Moscow, too. Let's see if there's one in Shields!' So they turned away from the sea into the town, catching the trolley bus up King Street.

Liz's head turned as they passed the Memorial Lifeboat.

'I remember that,' she said. 'There's been a few heroes from round here. A few myths maybe!' Her eyes twinkled. He obliged her by laughing, then asked:

'You're not really a Geordie, are you?'

'Well ... I wasn't born here,' Liz answered, 'but I went to school here, you know.'

'You sound defensive. As though you *want* to belong,' he told her.

'I suppose I do.' She shrugged. 'I want to belong somewhere, anyway. And my family comes from here. Well, half of my family.'

'I thought your "Family" was in India now.' He was twisting the knife. Liz said nothing. She was looking out of the bus window. Then her eyes lit up. She'd seen the hamburger sign. She shouted and they shot off the bus into the restaurant.

'Seriously,' she said, as she dug into a double-decker burger. 'Seriously, Jim, you don't want to give me problems over the house, now do you?' Jim shook his head but managed to look non-committal. 'I mean, it's going to be a bit difficult for me if you won't let me sell it and realise the profits and so on.' Jim said nothing. He sucked noisily on the straw. He'd finished his shake and was wondering about getting another. 'I mean, if I have to go back empty-handed ...' Jim raised his eyebrows.

'Surely that won't matter?' he feigned surprise. 'They're spiritual people! Surely they're not into materialism?'

'Of course not! But I'll have failed them, won't I?'

'So you *would* hand the money over, eh?' Liz said nothing. She sighed and he shook his head, saying, 'Eve didn't want that.'

'The dead have no right to interfere with the living!'

'Tell that to your great-grandparents,' he sniped. For the second time since her return Liz's brain went into paralysis. Jim was amused and pained by the ease with which Liz could be manipulated. The Koreans would have had her in the palm of their hands, a commie in no time.

'You're a bastard,' she said.

'You're not the first to have observed that,' he answered. 'Anyway. You only said that because you can't cope.'

'Smug bastard.'

'Oh dear,' he laughed. 'Now that *is* hard!'

'What am I going to say to Nathan?' she pushed.

'Nothing,' he evaded.

'I've got to say something!'

'Why?'

'He's my husband, for God's sake!'

'Is he?' Jim let the question sink in, then added another, 'I mean it wasn't exactly legal this so-called wedding, was it?'

'Not in the eyes of man,' she admitted. He almost laughed, but stopped himself in time.

'And, actually, he's already married,' he rubbed in. Then hastily, before *she* said it, he added, 'Only in the eyes of man, of course.' Liz said nothing. 'Alright.' He took a deep breath and tried another tack. 'Were you telling me the truth when you said you and this Nathan hadn't consummated your ... "marriage"?' Liz nodded. He waited. She looked directly at him and said:

'I was telling you the truth.'

'Fine.' He was pleased. 'In that case, you're not actually married in any sense at all, are you? I mean, not finally, irrevocably married, are you?' Liz said nothing.

'It's only a formality,' she said, at last.

'Formalities can be very useful,' he observed. 'All I'm saying is, give yourself time, Liz. Get used to it over here. Then, if you still want to go back ...'

'Of course I want to go back!'

'But last night you were telling me you didn't believe in "The Family" any more!'

'I never said any such thing!' She was shocked.

'Alright. Not in so many words. But ... ' What was the point of discussing semantics when there were more useful arguments at his disposal? 'Paula. This friend of yours,' he began. Liz's eyes clouded. 'And the kid. What was she called?'

'Sushena.'

'Are you telling me what's being done to them is right?' he asked. She shook her head.

'I don't know. I don't know what to think. Father sees everything. I don't. I've got to accept that what he's doing's right.'

'They cooked the books, Liz,' he said. She looked at him sharply, then looked away again, as though looking for escape.

'Maybe Jeanne did ...' she said. 'I could accept that. I mean I could believe her doing it. But ...' She took a

97

deep breath and her face lit up. 'Or maybe it's all a test for *me*!' Now she was overjoyed. 'Maybe I'm meant to prove Paula's innocence, and expose the conspiracy, Jeanne's conspiracy! Maybe that's what Father wants me to do! He did say the battle was hotting up. You know, light against dark.'

'Ah.' Jim blew down his straw. 'So now Jeanne's the enemy in the camp, is she?'

'Well, she might be! I mean, it would explain things, wouldn't it? Otherwise, I don't understand Father doing such a thing. I mean, he's God. He's beyond conspiracies and lies and fabrication of evidence and that sort of thing. He wouldn't dirty his hands with it. I mean it's a terrible thought, God cooking the books! No. It must be Jeanne. Subtly, Jeanne is trying to overthrow "The Family". Yes! That's it!'

Jim drew in a slow breath and let it out in a long whistle. She looked at him, eyes aglow. He said nothing, but she saw his eyes were sad. He looked away. She had a long way to go and he wasn't sure she was going to make it. Still, the twinkle returned, it sure was going to be interesting watching the struggle!

'You see, Jim,' she tried to persuade him, 'Father loves all of us. He loves Paula and he loves me and he loves Sushena. Actually he loves you, too. In some way what he's doing is for our good. You'll see. He'll turn it all round, if I play my part right.' Jim got up and threw the litter into the bin. Then he looked out of the window at the blue sky and the seagulls swooping down from grey rooftops, scavengers in the town.

'Just give it time,' he said. He held out his hand to help her from her seat, but she ignored it and passed him, going straight out into the street.

'I don't know if that was lunch or breakfast or supper,' she laughed. She was better now. She had convinced herself everything was alright. She would write home to Nathan and explain it all to him.

★

Back in Fowler Street, armed with a bottle of milk and some ready dinners, they settled down for the evening. It felt like they were laying in for a siege, but the besiegers and the besieged were one. Liz was bubbly and happy, more like she used to be. She'd taken it into her head to turn the house over and was going in and out of every room, seeing what there was. She rifled the bureau in the office, looking through paper after paper. He wondered if she was looking for evidence of her great-grandparents' transgression. If so, she didn't find any. But she'd found the statue of Ganesha. It was in a wardrobe on the first floor.

She got Jim to help put it in the corridor where she could see it. It seemed to please her; or maybe placate her would be a better way of putting it. And outside, in the yard, she'd found some geraniums, dying, in pots. She'd picked a flower and put it on the floor in front of the statue, as a sort of offering.

'Ganesha didn't turn me away,' she said. 'He's with me. I know that at least.' Jim nodded and made some tea. Well, she could be right, at that. Then each turned to sorting out their individual affairs. Liz was writing her letter. Jim, watching her, wondered what to do about Cambridge. He was due a sabbatical. It had been urged upon him by the Master who had seen his waning enthusiasm for academia.

'Go and get yourself an injection of something stimulating, Ridley!' he'd exhorted him. 'Come back with some fire in your belly!' We're all fading into Misses Havershams here! Especially you!'

Jim hadn't been too keen on the idea. On the other hand, he hadn't been too keen on going back for the next trimester, either. He'd dried up. He had nothing new to say. He was descending to the realms of pedantry, a boring footnote in the book of academic life.

So he had been non-committal. But would the Master still let him go?

There'd been some blurb about a seminar somewhere. It'd sounded interesting. Jim started rummaging in his briefcase. A glossy brochure slipped out into his hand. ALTERNATIVE ENERGY RESOURCES, it announced. Where was the venue? Erice, Sicily. 'Ideal conference centre', it said. There was a letter, too. Rummaging again, he found it. It was from the Energy Commission in Geneva. E.E.C. funded. They'd be delighted if he would speak on the subject of geothermal developments. He looked up and found Liz staring at him curiously.

'Ever been to Sicily?' he asked. She shook her head.

'Isn't that where Mount Etna is?'

'Yes!' he replied, pleased. After all, volcanoes are sources of geothermal energy and it was as good an excuse as you could get to go on a paid holiday.

'Why?' she asked, suspiciously.

'Oh. Nothing,' he said, folding the letter. 'Just, I'm off there for a seminar. Thought I might extend the trip. Treat myself to a vacation.' He stopped, as though he'd had a sudden thought. 'You wouldn't like to come with me, would you? Keep me company?' She gaped. It was an outrageous suggestion. And yet, her instinct told her to jump at it. 'No funny business' he assured her. 'Separate rooms.' Then he smiled, and said, 'We could stop off at Venice on the way home.'

'Venice!' she enthused. 'All those lovely paintings! Do you think I could?'

'Why not?'

'I haven't got any money.'

'It's alright. You can pay me back out of the sale of the house.' He winked and she laughed. Then she hesitated, wondering if she dared. But she wasn't doing anything wrong, was she?

'Look,' he said, as a final offering, 'I'll talk to the

solicitor about selling the house, if you like. Then we can go away and leave him to sort things out.'

'Oh,' she said. Suddenly she didn't know if she felt happy or sad. She looked round the tatty old sitting room.

'It's funny. You know I'm more attached to this place than I thought.'

'So you won't sell it?'

'I didn't say that,' she corrected quickly. She looked down at her writing pad. 'I've tried to explain to Nathan about the trust. I've said I'm trying to persuade the trustees to let me have the money. I mean, it's not my fault if you're all playing games with me, is it?'

'No.' She folded the paper and slipped it into an envelope. Then she looked at the sealed letter.

'I keep thinking about Paula.' She looked up suddenly and asked, 'Do you think I should try and contact her? Well ... her family maybe, just to see if she's alright?' Jim said nothing. 'I could try her aunt. She lives in Devon.'

'Are you up to it?' he asked at last.

'I don't know.' She shivered. 'I'm scared.'

'Would you like me to find out for you?' She stared at him, nodded slowly, then:

'Only I don't know her aunt's surname,' she sighed. He watched relief and hopelessness chase one another across her face. Even here she was in conflict.

'I'll book the flights,' he said, closing his briefcase.

'Flights?' she asked, vacantly.

'To Sicily,' he reminded her. She looked confused.

'When for?' she asked.

'End of October.'

'But that's ages away. I might not still be here!'

'You don't want to go back to India empty-handed, do you?' he pushed gently.

'No. But ...' Then her eyes narrowed. 'You're trapping me aren't you?' He sighed and shrugged. She was right. He was. He was trying to stop her going back into that room. And yet to her, that room was the only real world. What right had he?

'I'm sorry,' he said. 'Cards on the table. Of course you must make up your own mind what you do. It's your life. Only I can't let you give away your inheritance to "The Family". I've got a duty to Eve.' She was fingering the letter to Nathan.

'I'm tired,' she said, absently tearing the corner of the envelope. Then, suddenly realising what she was doing, she slapped her hand down on the table. 'What have you done to me?' she shouted at him.

'Me?' He was genuinely taken aback.

'You're trying to drag me down to your level.'

'Oh God, here we go again. Go to bed. Get some sleep. Meditate. Do what the hell you like!' He banged out of the room. And then she was alone. And he was alone, out in the corridor, wondering what it was he'd left unsaid. Abruptly, he opened the door. She was staring at him from her seat at the table.

'Whatever you do don't meditate when this guru of yours told you to,' Jim told her. 'Meditate any other time. But not then.' He closed the door again. He hadn't meant to say that. He'd thought he was going to tell her he wasn't just playing games with her; that he cared. But what he'd said was probably more use. He was still standing there, minutes later, when he heard an unconvinced humming sound coming from inside the room. He checked his watch. It was very early in the morning in India; peak tuning-in time for yogis. He decided to go out for a walk.

The pub was welcoming and warm. The Master was in when he phoned and gave his blessing to the sabbatical.

'You sound relieved,' Jim complained.

'I already have a locum,' the Master said. 'Have a nice time. And do try to come back with something interesting.' So, all he had to do was to send off his acceptance of the conference invitation, and that he would do tomorrow. Pronto! His step was light as he walked back down the street to the house. But, as he took out his keys, something made him look up. He saw a dark shape against the upstairs window. He stood back so he could see better, and there was Liz, a darker silhouette in the dark window, struggling with the sash. She was trying to open it. He shouted up to her, but she didn't hear. What in God's name was she trying to do?

Instinctively, Jim wrenched open the door and bounded up the stairs, hurling himself along the corridor and into the room. Liz was deaf to everything, heaving and straining, desperate to shift the window. He came up behind her and she screamed with shock as his body touched hers.

'Hey! It's okay. It's okay. I'm not going to hurt you.' He felt he had to shout to get through to her. But she retreated from him. He could see it in her eyes. Who was behind those eyes? Who was it, staring wildly out at him? She was like a wild animal caught in a trap, terrified out of her life! Suddenly she put her hands on her ears and screamed:

'Shut up! Shut up! Shut up! Please, oh please, shut up!' He covered her hands with his. She felt him, warm, and it seemed to reassure her a little. Her shoulders relaxed, though her face was still screwed up tight and her breaths were coming in short, panicky gasps. He wrenched her hands away from her ears, and held her arms to her sides.

'Who are you telling to shut up?' he asked loudly and slowly.

'The voices,' she whispered in terror.

'What voices? What do they sound like?'

'I don't know,' she said. 'Maybe my own? I don't know. It might be a man.'

'And what's it saying?' he shouted.

'It told me to destroy myself. It told me I was filth, and didn't deserve to live. It told me I had betrayed him.'

'Father?' he asked. She nodded dumbly. Tears stung her eyes but wouldn't fall. She spoke with terror.

'They know I've told you about "The Family". They know I've betrayed them.'

'Who is "they"?'

'The voices.'

'There's more than one?'

'I think so. Yes. Yes. I don't know. Yes. More than one. Male. Female. They talk in low tones. At first you think it's you thinking. Then suddenly you start hearing them, louder and clearer. And you know it isn't you.'

'So it isn't your voice?' he urged.

'No. I don't think so.' Her eyes widened in horror. 'It must be demons! I'm possessed by demons,' she whispered. He took her in his arms. And, not knowing what she was doing, she let him. A sob wrenched itself up from her guts.

'I wanted to throw myself out of the window,' she howled.

'Why? Did the voices tell you to?' He was gently rocking her to and fro, her body leaning against his.

'No. They said, "see if you can fly". They said, "If you can fly, God will forgive you."' Jim shivered. In the darkness he could believe anything. 'I told you I was filth.' Her voice was growing stronger with growing conviction. 'I'm no good to you, Jim. I did you a favour when I walked out. Why did Eve want to go dragging us back together again? She shouldn't have done it! She knew what was wrong with me!'

'Shh. Shh.' He tried to soothe her, but couldn't think of any words. And she clung to him, not thinking, not feeling, just because he was there. Slowly the experience sank into history and she grew calmer. She shivered.

'Do you think I'm mad?' she asked fearfully. Jim drew in a long, deep breath, then said:

'No. But I think someone's trying to *drive* you mad.'

He became aware of a strange warmth, that in those

moments had been born in him. It grew and spread and moved him with an overwhelming compassion. He wanted to cry. And he wondered if he had ever loved anyone before in his entire life; because he had never loved as he did now. If this was love. He tried to pull himself together for her sake. God knew where her mind was taking her.

'Have the voices stopped?' he asked. She listened, then nodded and said:

'They're there though, listening to us. They're waiting. I don't know what for. I'm scared.' She looked up at him in the darkness. The whites of her eyes glowed. He urged her away from the window. 'They don't like you,' she said with sudden decision.

'No,' he answered. 'I don't suppose they do.' He drew her from the darkened room into the lighted corridor, and there she stood, petrified, staring at the statue of Ganesha.

'*He* hasn't rejected you,' Jim said. 'Hang on to that!' She gave a jerky little nod and hiccoughed. Then she laughed at herself. She wouldn't have a scotch. She didn't drink. Hadn't drunk for years. He didn't know what else to give her. Aspirins wouldn't be a lot of good! Maybe some food? With gentle pressure he guided her into the warm kitchen and sat her down. She kept looking at him. Sometimes her eyes were suspicious, sometimes they were trusting. But now she came to think about it, she was definitely hungry. He put the ready dinners in the oven and they sat, waiting for them to heat.

'I've got to go back,' she said.

'Where?' he asked.

'To "The Family".' He sighed, pulling his hands over his face. Suddenly he felt very tired. He fought desperately to think of a ploy to keep her.

'Let me try and find out about Paula,' he said, at last. Then she started crying. She shook her head hopelessly.

'No,' she said in a voice that would brook no argument. 'I've got to go back.'

After a silent dinner, Liz fell asleep, exhausted. Jim sat on, watching her. He was all wrung out, but he couldn't sleep. He felt nervous, jumpy. He didn't know what to do next. He cried a little. He didn't know why exactly, he only knew he needed to. Looking back, he realised he hadn't loved her before; before she'd run off, that is. He'd *wanted* her. He'd *needed* what she had to offer. She would have made him happy alright. But he hadn't loved her. The only person he had loved before had been Kim. The memory of the kid's face struck into him like a dagger. Why hadn't he gone back for her? Hadn't he been man enough?

Liz stirred uneasily. He watched her, hoping she wouldn't wake. She needed sleep. But she just sighed and settled back again. He sighed with relief, knowing that if she'd wakened he wouldn't have been ready for her. *He* needed space, too.

Jim fell asleep in his chair. He was cold when he woke at dawn to the now familiar sound of screeching gulls. Liz was still sleeping. He stretched, easing out his muscles, then got up to make some coffee. He had that letter to write. He checked the invitation again, then put the kettle on and rubbed his hands. The season had changed abruptly. Heat had given way to a damp chill. He looked out of the window at the watery light that played on rooftops and echoed the sky in the window panes and in the puddles in the back lane. And his heart felt lighter. He didn't know why. But he thought, 'It'll be okay.' For no reason at all, he just thought it and accepted it gratefully, like an unexpected gift.

When she woke and saw him, standing at the window, she thought how beautiful he was. The light caught him and, unobserved, his features were calm and sensitive. She would have liked to draw him like that; in pastels, soft and light to catch his spirit. Her face grew tender and happiness played on her lips. She was remembering how it was. They really had something going for them once. She had given herself to him and he had given her joy. What did he say? 'The only real thing that ever happened to me, apart from ...' What?

'Jim ...' He jumped and turned.

'Hi.'

'Hi,' she said. 'What did you mean the other night?'

'When?'

'When you said, what happened to you in the Canyon was the only real thing that ever happened to you, apart from ... what? What else was there?'

'Kim,' he replied immediately. Her expression was blank.

'What?' she asked. But he'd said it so quickly, she believed him. 'Who's Kim?' she asked.

'A little girl. Korean. She was an orphan. She was real.'

'Oh.' She tried to hide her disappointment. He tried not to see it. Then the flash seared her brain, and she gasped as the voice spoke.

'Leave him,' it commanded. 'You'll drag him down to hell.' She cried out. He rushed from the window towards her and tried to hold onto her. But she was fighting him, screaming.

'No. No. Don't touch me. Don't touch me!' He didn't understand. He thought she didn't want him. And when she realised it, she thought it was better that way and didn't enlighten him. So when they had breakfast, they were far apart.

'Planning on doing anything today?' he asked. She shook her head. 'Thought I'd go into Newcastle.'

'Oh?' She pretended lack of interest, but her voice had tightened with fear.

'Want to come?' he asked. She looked at him, paralysed. To go or not to go? 'We could try out the metro,' he said. 'I've never been on it. Have you?' She shook her head.

'It's all changed so much,' she said for want of something to say. Then, suddenly, he changed his mind and put her off.

'Of course I've got a lot to do. You might get bored. Perhaps it'd be better if you *didn't* come.' His face had closed. She was disappointed and a band began to tighten round her chest. Was he going to leave her alone here forever? Go back to Cambridge? This very day? She fought down the desire to ask. It was selfish of her to want to keep him. Better for him, and her too probably, if he just went. But he saw her pain and reached out to touch her. 'Anything you'd like me to bring back?' he asked. Tears welled up spontaneously. He was so kind. She wiped under her eyes with her fingers.

'I'll go in with you another day. If I may,' she said. 'I need some space just now.' Then she smiled up at him brightly. He nodded.

'Sure.' He was on his way out. Then, with sudden panic, he turned to reassure himself she was still there. Suppose she took it into her head to up and off back to India? Did he dare leave her? It was her turn to put him right.

'I'll do some shopping,' she said, 'locally. For supper.' But he thought he saw deceit in her eyes. What was she planning? He steeled himself against her, smiled, and with a wave Jim went.

It was impossible to meditate. But there were other things she must do. For instance, she had to see the solicitor. So, Liz bathed and dressed carefully, combing her long hair smooth and plaiting it behind her head. Then she inspected herself in the mirror. It was a novel experience. She wasn't used to mirrors. She had a small pocket job in her bag, but there weren't any in the ashram and she'd avoided looking at herself in the airport cloakrooms. But here, now, she looked, and in the morning light a withered spinster looked back at her. She had grown plain and old. And yet, she reminded herself, she wasn't quite past bearing children ... had things been different. Sadness invaded her, then suspicion. Was that why Nathan had held back from her? Had Father told him they were not to have a physical union? Was theirs to be a purely spiritual affair? Was Nathan afraid of contamination through sex as if she had AIDS or something?

Why, oh why did her life have to be like this? She remembered the joy with Jim. The woman in the mirror was about to cry, but Elizabeth, the devotee, told her not to be so sorry for herself. 'Such base feelings you had for that man! You have to rise above them!' she told her. 'You're privileged! Father has chosen you to be his child. So it's hard. So what? You'll be saved. And what you're doing helps others. These are the latter days, when the great battle between good and evil is at its height. Will you desert your Father now? Will you swing the balance by reverting to the side of darkness? Your sins must be purged through fire!'

She could hear Jeanne's searing voice as she chided Paula, after Bhanamurti's letter. Paula. It had been alright up until Paula. She hadn't doubted anything until Paula. She'd been shaken by the news she was to be married, alright, but she hadn't doubted, had she? No. She hadn't doubted till that moment Paula had looked at her in Father's room. Then something had passed from Paula into her, like a dart into her heart; a fatal wound. The armour of her faith had been breached. And now this man, this Jim Ridley like a ghost from the past had followed the dart's path through the chink, into her heart. It was Paula's fault. Paula! The unconscious evil in her polluted everything! And now, how could Elizabeth ever cleanse herself?

A ringing noise crept into her consciousness like a

sound from another world, and Liz stood, in confusion, listening to it. Then she recognised it as the telephone. Her first instinct was to rush to it. But she didn't know where it was. Her second instinct was to hide from it. Who knew she was here? And then she realised that only Nathan, Jeanne and Father knew. Or perhaps it wasn't really a telephone? Perhaps it was a supernatural sound; Father warning her again, to be careful, reminding her that he could hear her thoughts, and knew that because of Paula she was at risk. But it kept on ringing. Her heart was jumping all over the place. But if there *was* a telephone, a *real* telephone, then she had to find it.

She rushed, trembling, from room to room, then stopped in the corridor, listening. If there was a real telephone in the house, then it would probably be in the sitting room. She rushed into the room but didn't find it. It kept on ringing. It sounded far away. Perhaps it was an illusion after all? Then she remembered the office and ran down the corridor, skipping the steps, into the room, and there it was on the desk. Gingerly, she picked up the receiver.

'Hello, is that Miss Strachan?' Liz had no breath to answer 'Hello? Hello? Is anybody there?' The voice waited. Liz coughed, then spoke in a hoarse whisper.

'Er, yes. Who is that, please?'

'Platt and Burdon. Solicitors. We wondered if there was anything you needed, Miss Strachan?'

'Anything I needed?' Liz echoed. Then quickly, realising she sounded stupid, she added, 'No thank you. How very kind of you.'

'Well, if there is . . .'

'Thank you. I'm fine. Goodbye.' She put the receiver down. Only afterwards did she remember she'd been getting ready to go out and see the solicitors. She would look stupid if she rang back now to tell him. Her behaviour reflected on "The Family". She must pull herself together or he would think they were all a lot of freaks! But she couldn't just walk in on the solicitor either, could she? Not after he'd phoned. He'd wonder why she hadn't said. It would look even more stupid. What was she to do? Then the phone rang again. Liz jumped. She picked up the receiver, expecting somehow it would be the solicitor again.

'Hello ...?' The voice was distant. Indian. 'Hello? Can I speak to Elizabeth Strachan, please?' it said.

'Yes. Who is it?' Liz asked.

'Bhanamurti. How are you, Elizabeth?'

'I'm fine!' She managed to sound as though she was.

'Good. I'm glad to hear it,' said Bhanamurti. 'Nathan's here. He wants to speak to you. But first I want to ask you something.'

'What is it?'

'It's difficult.' At once Liz knew it was about Paula. Her flesh crept. Bhanamurti didn't want her to do anything, did he? 'Father has found another wife for me,' he said, apologetically. Automatically, Liz offered her congratulations. 'It was most unexpected. Anyway, I need to start my divorce. The bride's parents won't let her marry me till the papers are through. They're very proper people from Nassik, you see. And Paula's disappeared. We think she might be in England at her auntie's.'

'Oh?'

'Will you check it out for me please? You don't have to see her, just find out if she's there and I'll get my solicitor to write to her. You don't have to be involved,' Bhanamurti persuaded.

'That's a relief,' she answered.

'Shall I give you the address of the auntie?'

'Okay.'

'It's Mrs Cook, 5 Pekham Cottages, Otterburn, Devon. I haven't got the telephone number.' Liz was rummaging for a pen among the papers on the desk. Finally she found one but dropped the phone. Bhanamurti thought the line had gone dead and started shouting, 'Hello. Hello,' down the line. Then she heard him say to someone, 'I think the line's gone dead.' But Liz grabbed the receiver again and panted into it:

'It's okay I'm here. I dropped the phone, that's all. I was looking for a pen. Tell me the address again.' Bhanamurti repeated it, said goodbye, and Nathan was on the line.

'Hello darling,' he said. He sounded glad to hear her.

'Hello, darling,' she answered.

'How's it going?' he asked. He meant the inheritance.

'Well, there's a problem,' she said apologetically. 'I've written you a letter, but of course you won't have got it yet. You see, the house has been left to me in trust. I can't sell it without the permission of the trustees.'

Nathan sighed. 'That's a shame,' he said grimly. 'Father's planning a lecture tour this winter. We need the money to pay for the trip and the halls and everything.'

'Well it might take some time to come through,' Liz explained helplessly. She sensed his panic and understood it. If Father was displeased with her she'd be in trouble, and then where would *he* be? Wifeless in no time! 'I'm going to see the solicitor again today,' she said as if to prove her willingness for things to work out in Father's favour.

'Meditate before you go,' he urged her. Meditation was the open sesame to any barrier.

'Yes, I will,' Liz replied. There was a silence. Elizabeth filled it in. 'Bhanamurti's so surrendered,' she said. 'I do admire him.'

'An example to the rest of us,' agreed Nathan. Then suddenly, as though bothered by something, he asked, 'Are you alright?' His voice was sharp and put her on her guard.

'Yes,' she answered. 'Why?'

'You feel . . . your vibes are confused.'

'Oh? Probably jet lag,' she lied.

112

'Yes. Better get some sleep before you see the solicitor.' Another silence. Nathan coughed. 'Do you miss me?' he asked in a small voice.

'Yes. Do you miss me?'

'Very much,' he said. 'Come back soon.'

'Yes. I will. Bye, Nathan.'

'Bye.'

Liz stood by the telephone, shivering. They all seemed so far away. And where was she? It felt like nowhere; it felt as though she'd slipped through some hole in the three worlds and ended up floating round the void. She was lost and Nathan had noticed. He'd felt the difference in her. Yes. He knew she was in trouble. Oh, why were they putting so much onto her? First the money, and now Paula! And Father was doing a lecture tour this winter. She *must* do her best to help. Where was he going? America probably. 'The Way' had a big following in the States, in spite of Paula's article. Yes, Paula had been a journalist once; small time, small town. Was that why they'd gone for her? Were they afraid she'd blow the whistle on them? But she would never've done that. She believed totally in Father. Liz resolutely put the thought out of her mind, dismissing all doubt. 'Don't think!' Father had warned them, 'It only gets you into trouble!' and he was right. Anyway, she didn't *want* to think about it. It was none of her business in the first place.

Her eye sought escape and fell on the painting over the mantelpiece: so outdated; so self-conscious. She wouldn't paint like that now. She walked up to it and stood staring up at the hard lines of primary colour. There was no light there. That was what was missing. Her hand rose to touch the canvas. She'd forgotten how to use a paintbrush. If she was to do anything now, and it was a big 'if', she'd want to try some other medium. Maybe pastels? She remembered Jim's face at the window. Light.

Her meditation was good. She hadn't used the picture, but had lit her candle and sat cross-legged, eyes closed, the way she liked it most. She concentrated on the silence. Slowly her mind stopped swinging to and fro and became still. There were no voices. None at all, thank God. Jim's face lit up at the window floated up out of her unconscious. She smiled, eyes still closed. Then she fell asleep.

When she woke, Jim was home. He had hurried back, afraid of what he might find. He looked in the sitting room first and when she wasn't there he checked the kitchen. The fridge was empty. So she hadn't been shopping. Then he went out into the corridor and noticed the office door was open. So he walked quickly to it, and once through the door saw the telephone off the hook. He put the receiver back and saw the note. Who was Mrs Cook? Then he ran upstairs to Liz's room and was relieved to find her crashed out on the bed. He touched her, as though to reassure himself she was really there. She was freezing cold. He put the duvet over her and went down to make some tea. They would have to eat out tonight.

Liz came round at eight o'clock. It was almost dark. She felt the weight of the duvet and realised Jim had put it there. He was so kind. She flung it off and slipping out of bed, ran downstairs, still in stocking feet.

'Hi,' she greeted him from the door. He looked up from his paper and smiled.

'Hi. Feel better?' She nodded. 'Good!'

'Had a good day?' she asked.

'Yeah. Not bad. Got what I wanted!' She grinned back at him. But the smile lay like plaster over a cracked wall, uneasily. She wondered what he was thinking. She soon knew. 'Anything happened while I was out?' he asked. He sounded like Nathan on the phone, 'Are you alright?' She shrugged.

'Not really, no.'

'Phone was off the hook.'

'Was it?' She was puzzled. Obviously she hadn't realised she'd left it off. Well, that was a relief. But who had she been talking to? He was watching her hard. 'The solicitor phoned,' she said. He was still watching. She squirmed. Then her resistance broke. 'There was a call from India,' she confessed.

'Who?' he asked.

'Bhanamurti. Nathan came on, too.'

'Checking up on you? Or the money?'

'Do you have to be so cynical?' she objected.

'Sorry.'

'I don't think I should tell you.'

'Who's Mrs Cook?' he asked.

'What?'

'Who's Mrs Cook?'

'Paula's aunt,' she replied. Liz stared at him, wondering if some telepathic magic had told him her name. 'Bhanamurti wants me to check her out. See if Paula's there. He's suing for divorce.'

'Nice,' said Jim. 'So. They've got you doing their dirty work now.'

'Someone's got to do it.' She sat and tried the teapot. It was empty. She started crying. 'I can't face it, Jim.'

'I did offer,' he reminded her. She wondered whether to accept, then said:

'I can't face Paula. She's a source of evil, Jim. My life's gone wrong ever since she looked at me in Father's room. It's her fault. And I'm not strong enough to cope with it.'

'I see,' he said. 'Okay. I'll check her out for you, if you like.' At least Liz'd come clean. She hadn't tried to hide the truth or use him either. Basically, she was an honest soul. And she, so relieved not to have to speak to Paula, fought down the impulse to jump up and kiss him, inclining her head graciously instead.

'Shall I make some tea?' she offered.

'Sure.' He flung down his paper and went out to the office. Liz stood, listening. She heard his steps turn at the office door and the door close softly behind him. Then she heard the faint 'ting' as he picked up the receiver. Was he going to phone her now? She drew a circle round herself to prevent the evil coming down the phone at her and put on the kettle.

He was a long time. The tea was made and the cups were out. She sat, tense, at the table, waiting. Then she heard him coming back along the corridor. When he entered the room, his face was grave. She looked at him for a long time. He cleared his throat as he sat down and she asked him if he'd like some tea. He nodded without looking at her. She poured him a cup and slid the cup along to him. He took it and drank. He was staring at the table.

'Are you going to tell me?' she asked at last.

'I don't think your Bhanamurti's going to be *able* to sue for divorce,' he said.

'Why not? Won't she give him one? The nasty-minded ...!'

'Paula's in a psychiatric hospital. Seems she's convinced she's evil.' And now he looked at Liz. She was white. The words reverberated through her system, hollow, terrible. Paula was in a psychiatric hospital. She couldn't believe it, yet his shocked face told her it was true. She shook her head.

'Paula's not mad,' she said. 'She wasn't, anyway.' Her agony expressed itself in a long, low wail. 'What have they done to her?' she wept. 'Oh my God! It's cruel. It's so cruel. It can't be right.' She looked at him, desperately. 'It can't be right, can it?' He looked back, but didn't say anything. 'God's good. He loves us. He isn't cruel, like this! Christ said God was love!' He rose and went behind her, circling her in his arms, holding her while her body convulsed with sobs. 'That poor little kid!' she cried. 'What's going to happen to Billy and Sushena?' Jim thought about the kids. They had one hope: their father. But he was in the cult.

'It's up to their father,' he said. 'I mean their real father. Though maybe Paula's family'll do something ... I don't know. They're all too shocked right now.' Silence contained them like a bright light. Both were too dazed to speak. 'There's an organisation looks into cults ...'

'"The Family" isn't a cult!' she shouted.

'Then it looks very like one!' he said. She couldn't answer. It was true. And if it was true, then who and what was Father? She became more frightened than before. To deny Father was the ultimate sin. She couldn't go against him. He'd said, once, "Those who are not for me are against me and if they are against me I will drag them down to hell." And then, she thought, how could he drag them down to hell unless he was there already? And her thought stopped. She was standing on the edge of the known world. But she couldn't jump. She pulled back from the precipice and tried to explain the problem away.

'Paula was a journalist once. Father had to destroy her before she destroyed "The Family".'

'Ah. The end justifies the means,' said Jim.

'Yes,' said Liz, but didn't really believe it.

'If your guru's God, what's he worried about a small-time journalist for? He can do anything he likes! He can put the clock back and make it so she never came into "The Family", anything! He doesn't *have* to destroy her!'

'Don't!' Liz pleaded. 'Don't make me think! I mustn't think.' Jim said nothing. 'Father's going on a lecture tour,' she said, clinging to the practical as to a lifebelt. 'He needs the money.'

'Too bad,' said Jim. 'Look, tell them the trustees won't play.' He saw her terror and added, 'It's not your fault. They can't blame you.'

'They will, Jim. Somehow. They'll say it didn't work

117

out because I didn't want it to. Something in my unconscious was working against it.'

'In that case, good for your unconscious!'

'You don't understand, do you? Jim, this is real!'

'I know it is,' he said seriously. 'There's a woman in a lunatic asylum because of it.'

Liz moaned, rhythmically rocking from side to side. 'I must not sympathise with the negative,' she told herself. He was horrified. It was as though she was voluntarily reinforcing the brainwashing herself by creating a barrier to the truth. But perhaps Paula could get through to her.

'Seems Paula won't talk to anyone,' he said. 'She's in a never never land. No man's land rather. No-one can reach her.' Liz understood at once.

'She doesn't belong in "The Family" and she doesn't belong in the world,' she explained simply. Jim pushed it further.

'She *could* belong in the world,' he said, '*if* she rejected the judgement this guru's made on her!'

'Rejecting Father is rejecting God! She would be committing herself to hell. She'd be damned!'

'She's damned already, according to him!' Jim commented in exasperation. 'Might as well plunge in! Come on, the water's lovely!' There was cold amusement in his eyes. Liz couldn't understand it. Looking at him now, she wondered, was he a demon too? Was he beckoning her down to hell? She edged back from him. Had he stirred her carnal feelings on purpose? If so, he was playing on her weakness and she must turn her back on him. Watching her face, Jim saw her mind turn. Trust turned to hate and suspicion. What was she thinking?

Liz was thinking, 'Because of the sins of my fathers, lust is my weakness and through lust this man has drawn me away from my Father and "The Way". Yes. Paula made the chink, and he passed through it. He is the enemy.'

He asked, 'What would you like to eat tonight?' She shrugged.

'Chinese?'

'If you like.'

'Good. Get your coat on. You can pay me back when the house is sold.'

She thought, 'He's playing games with me. He thinks he can manipulate me how he likes, just because he's a clever Cambridge intellectual. Well, I'll teach him. I'll slip away. Where to? I can't go back to India without the inheritance. I'd be disgraced. No. Somehow I've got to play him along and get my own way. I must do it, for my Father's sake.'

He didn't know how to help her any more. She'd gone from him. It crossed his mind maybe he should call in a doctor. But look what had happened to Paula! No, doctors don't understand this sort of thing. A priest maybe? He toyed with the idea over sweet and sour chicken in the 'Canton Kitchen'. It would have to be the right priest, of course. Not just any priest. But would she talk to one? Not very likely. He tried another tack. What was the hold this Father of hers had over her? Wasn't it the incest? Wasn't it belief in her own lack of grace, if you like, that had sent her into his clutches? Her own lack had made her dependent on another who claimed to have grace to spare. Yes, it was the incest, or at least, her belief in it. The sins of the fathers made their presence felt in some peculiar ways alright.

Maybe he should try to find out more about these ancestors of hers. What were they called? Jane and Robert. Yes. Maybe he should find out about them. Hell, every family had its skeletons in the closet! And if everyone who had incest in the family was damned, then there would be precious few of us left! Suddenly the restaurant door opened and Liz jumped. Her face'd gone white. Nerves like piano wires, he observed. He watched her hand shake as she tackled the rice. And she knew he was watching her. She was having trouble with the fork. It wasn't *just* that her hand was shaking, it was because she wasn't used to forks; she was used to eating with her fingers. Everyone did in India.

Suddenly it occurred to her to wonder, was eating with Jim a sin? She could never claim him as a brother. After all, she had slept with him, years ago. And she remembered it. It aroused feelings in her; low feelings. After all, it wasn't something she could forget easily. It wasn't something she'd done often, with other men. In fact, there hadn't been other men; only Jim; ever. And now she was married to Nathan; though she didn't love him and they hadn't ... Of course she'd grow to love him. Eventually. She liked him. She admired him. But she didn't really know Nathan and he certainly didn't know her.

Jim knew her. She looked up at him suddenly and found his eyes on her. He looked away. She didn't know *him* though. Not any more. He was a closed book to her now. Her mind turned over the difference between the Jim she knew once and the Jim she didn't know now. What had happened to him in the last twenty years? A disappointing marriage; a failure to communicate with his child; a waning interest in his work. It looked as though he'd slowly withdrawn from life into a sort of isolation. She observed his face, curiously. It was still, impassive. What was he thinking? Hard to tell. He looked up unexpectedly and, catching one another's eye, they smiled then bent to their food again. She felt caught out, showing an interest in him. Her pulse raced. She was blushing. This was ridiculous. She was behaving like a silly teenager in love. She wasn't a teenager *or* in love! 'And anyway,' she thought, 'Love's just illusion. It's just heightened sexual awareness, isn't it?' Anyway, whatever it was, she was very aware of him now. She pulled her knees away from his. He shuffled under the table. Both were intent on their food. Then he chuckled.

'What is it?' she asked, surprised.

'I feel so young tonight,' he said.

'Funny,' she replied. 'So do I.' Both found that extraordinarily amusing. They exchanged a slow shake of the head, as though each should know better, and smiling, they got back to the serious business of eating.

The next day, the solicitor was not available. He was in court. Liz was restive.

'Do some drawing,' Jim suggested. 'Pass the time.' Liz behaved as though he'd suggested a striptease. 'Please yourself,' he said with some irritation, and left her to it. Liz *wanted* to paint, or draw, or something like that. But she didn't dare. She would merely be indulging her ego. It would be idiosyncratic behaviour! Anyway, what was there to paint? If only Jim would sit for her ... she'd love to draw his face. But it was no use. Anyway, it would be asking for trouble and she knew it. It was no good reviving memories. No good at all. She sighed and doodled on a piece of paper Jim had left behind. She was drawing a tree. Its roots went deep and its trunk was huge and strong, sinewy, and its branches spread far and wide. It was a tortured tree. Its muscles twined and fought like serpents and when she'd finished it, she wept. There was no peace; certainly not in this house. How could there be? This was a house of sin. Its walls had seen incest. Abruptly, she threw on her mac and left, seeking a church. There was one up the road, up the hill. She remembered it was rather big. She turned to go that way, then stopped and turned round, heading towards the town. There she found a Catholic church, but the doors were closed. Anyway, what was the point? For as she turned back towards the house, she knew she was finished.

She had fallen in love.

Jim was apparently unconcerned. He looked up as she popped her head round the kitchen door.

'Had a nice walk?' he asked.

'Yes,' she said. 'It's a lovely day.'

'Mmm,' he answered. 'What about a trip out? Go up the coast somewhere? Or ... I don't know, how about Durham?'

'Sounds nice,' she said, thinking frivolously. 'If I'm finished I might as well enjoy it!'

'Have you ever seen the Cathedral?' he asked. 'It's really lovely!'

The light sparkled on the river. A perfect day for boating. She observed how Jim's face reflected the pale watery light as she lay back and he rowed. One hand trailing in the cool water, she watched the light play on his features. Such beauty. He smiled at her, and she smiled back and the voice said:

'You are unclean. You must leave him.' Such nightmare.

She said: 'We should have brought a picnic!'

He agreed, then said perhaps they would find a nice place for lunch. And the voice said:

'Give him up. He will be damned because of you.'

'Happy?' he asked. And she smiled and nodded, thinking how well he looked. He suited happiness. He deserved to be happy. He was a good man. And the voice said:

'He will suffer because of you.'

'You alright?' he asked, watching her intently. She nodded. But her smile was strained.

'You?' she asked.

'Never better,' he answered. And he looked so well, so fit! And the voice said:

'You will make him ill. Through you disease will enter into his soul.' Her mouth distorted with misery.

'What is it?' he asked.

'Nothing.' She dried the dampness round her eyes. Another boat was passing them, heading down river.

The people inside were looking. Jim waited, waving back as the people waved at them.

'What is it?' he asked again when the boat had passed.

'I'm bad for you. You should have nothing to do with me.'

'Who says?'

She didn't answer. But he knew. 'Tell the voices to sod off,' he said. She was alarmed at the idea. Suppose it was Father's voice? 'Try it,' he insisted, 'after me.' And he shouted, 'Sod off!' The people in the boat that had just passed turned and looked at them in surprise. They had seemed such a nice couple.

'Sod off!' she yelled back hoarsely. It was magic. The voices stopped. Then suddenly, a terrible pain plunged through her brain. When it stopped, she was reeling, holding her head. He watched her helplessly. Then it came again in her left side, plunging through her like a spear. She cried out. Then, when it was over, she said:

'The voices didn't like that much.' She began to laugh. His mouth was hanging open. 'I feel sick,' she said and retched violently over the side of the boat. '.'m sorry.' She was wiping her mouth on his handkerchief, 'And it's such a lovely day, too!'

She felt a little shaky afterwards. The voices were there. She could feel them, but they weren't saying anything. They were waiting to see what she would do next. Her legs shook as Jim pulled her from the boat onto dry land. Then as they went into the coffee shop they started up again, whispering as though afraid Jim might hear. It was a garbled message, mostly about filth. She trembled as she sat, sipping her coffee, hoping she wouldn't throw it up all over Jim. But Jim was pretty philosophical at the prospect.

As a lad, back home in New Mexico, he'd seen magic in practice. There was still a tradition of it in the pueblos. Whether it'd emerged from the native Indian or incoming Hispanic influence, was hard to tell. Anyway, it was like someone was sticking pins in her. Only it was more subtle than that. It used a more sophisticated technique; like they didn't need pins any more. A sick thought was enough. Thoughts took wings, demonic missiles programmed to home in on the target and destroy. But perhaps there was an antidote? Jim put his right hand flat against her left, and held it on the table. He closed his eyes and sent his love flooding into her tortured system.

'That's lovely.' She sighed with relief. 'Thank you.' He opened his eyes and smiled at her. 'What did you do?'

'I sent you nice thoughts,' he said.

'You're crazy,' she answered. 'Either that or I am.' She looked at him. He looked back.

'Who cares?' he asked.

Liz took a deep breath and prepared to enter the Cathedral. She hadn't been inside a church for twenty years. How would it feel? Was she doing right in going inside at all? Father didn't like churches. He said they were full of demons from things like the Inquisition and materialistic attitudes and so on. She was taking her eternal life in her hands. On the other hand, suppose *she* was the demon? Would Christ revile her? To her combined relief and disappointment, they were stopped at the Cathedral doors. A service was about to start. Immediately Liz fell into a mental spin, 'It's a sign. I am a demon. Christ condemns me!' But she couldn't tell whether she'd sinned in following Father or sinned in doubting him. Only she definitely knew she was a sinner. After all, she was the product of an incestuous union. Jim told her she wasn't sure of anything and if they'd had any sense they'd have checked the service times beforehand.

He drew her into the small chapel at the back where they looked down on the tomb of the Venerable Bede. Then, like good tourists, they sat listening to the choir beyond the chapel doors. If she had been expecting a sign from heaven, then she was disappointed. The journey home passed in a state of calm.

The telephone was ringing when they got in. They looked at each other.

'Shall I answer it?' Jim asked. Then she realised it was probably the solicitor and picked up the receiver herself. It wasn't the solicitor. It was Nathan. He spoke with authority.

'Elizabeth,' he said, 'I have to tell you, our Father is very worried about you.' Her heart yo-yoed.

'Oh,' she answered.

'What *are* you doing?' Nathan asked anxiously.

'Nothing. I'm trying to sort out the inheritance,' she said.

'Are you meditating?' he probed.

'When I get the chance,' Liz said defensively.

'You *must* meditate. Get out Father's picture, light a candle and sit in front of it now!'

'I ...' She was about to say, 'I can't. There's someone here.' But instinct told her not to. 'Alright,' she said. 'I will.'

'I hope so. For *your* sake!' There was threat in the air. 'Have you found out where Paula is?' This was one question she *could* answer.

'Yes. She's in a psychiatric hospital. Apparently she's very ill. Not in her own mind, Nathan. Bhanamurti's going to have to wait for his divorce.'

'I see.' Nathan's voice was terse. 'What did you say to her? Or did you speak to her aunt?'

'Her aunt. And I said as little as possible,' Liz answered truthfully.

'Good.' Nathan sighed. 'What *have* you been doing? I've been with Father for hours.' Liz was trembling.

'Why? What did he say?'

'Not much. Just ... "Elizabeth had better watch her

step." And when I tried to find out what he meant, he just said, "She's heading for trouble."'

'Well, I can't think why.' Her voice was unnaturally high.

'Someone's coming. I've got to go.' Nathan rang off abruptly. He must have been using the phone in Father's house. He had been trying to warn her. It was kind of him. It showed he cared. She put the receiver down and leant on it for support.

'What now?' Jim asked. At first she couldn't speak.

'He knows,' she said at last.

'Who?'

Jim came up behind her, and laid his hands on her shoulders but she shrugged him off.

'Father. He knows.' There was no need to ask what. Father knew everything. 'I'm scared,' she whispered into the darkness.

She tried to meditate with the picture, but after a few moments she had to put it away. She felt sick. She closed the frame and slipped it into a drawer then, taking a deep breath, she shut her eyes and tried again. But her head was full of light. It was as though someone had switched a light on inside her head. It frightened her. She opened her eyes again. It was actually darker with them open. What was happening to her? Again she tried closing them. And she saw light. She prayed to God to help her. Then, remembering Ganesha, she asked him to remove the obstacle. There was a sudden flash behind her eyes and the voices were there. She heard them whispering; she ignored them; she didn't want to know what they were saying. There was a terrible pain in her side. But the light slowly faded to normal and soon she was seeing dark red behind her eyes as she usually did. Sweat was pouring off her, but she sighed with relief.

When her brain was still and she was listening to the silence, she would ask the question 'Who is he?' and if he was God, then she would ask forgiveness and if he

126

was not ... horror, hell, where should she turn? To Christ? The pain was suddenly so severe that she screamed and held onto her head.

Jim rushed into the room. He didn't know how to help her. Unless ... well, it had worked before! He closed his eyes, mustering all his strength and visualised his love as golden light and with it he drew a golden circle all around her. And inside the circle she became lighter and lighter. She stopped screaming. The pain ebbed away. She was crying now, and he sat on the bed beside her, holding her.

'I think ...' he said slowly, 'you're going through a kind of withdrawal. Like drugs. You know? All the poisons that man's put into your brain are coming out.' She hid her head in his chest. 'Hey, it's alright. It will be anyway. I'll see you through it. I promise I'll see you through it.' But she fought him off, tormented by the voices.

'Suppose they're right? Suppose I am evil? Suppose I drag you down to hell, too? I can't bear it. I've hurt you enough. I can't bear to think I'd hurt you any more. I can't bear it.'

'You aren't evil, Liz,' Jim said kindly. 'You're what God made you.'

'Then why did he make me this way?' she cried, shaking her head in disbelief. 'Why did he make me Liz Strachan? Why not somebody else with a normal life? You know, I don't believe my life! It can't be true! I mean, is this really my life?'

'No. It isn't your life,' Jim said, heart racing. 'And what you're living through isn't true. It's only true as long as you believe it is. He only has power over you because you believe in him. You let him in, and now he's sucked your powers from you and is using them against you. Take away your commitment to him and he's got no hold over you; no power over you, nothing! You've got to believe in *yourself*!'

'But what am I, Jim? Look at me. What am I?' He held her very close. His warmth soothed and reassured her. Then he asked her where the pain was. 'Almost everywhere,' she said. She felt so sick, she told him. He didn't tell her she smelt of it; that she positively reeked of vomit. It was as though someone had spilt a bucketful all over her. It made him want to retch. This guru had created a myth around himself, but the myth was a sick lie and though the belief of his devotees brought the lie into reality, they stank of it. Evil incarnates.

But Liz, though she believed, though she had helped make the lie real, she was not sick. She was not evil. He felt that with all his heart. If it was so, the contact with evil wouldn't be giving her such pain. And she was in agony. Was he strong enough? Could he heal her? He rubbed and soothed the pain away as best he could. And when she said she felt easier but her head swam, he told her to lie down and get some sleep. But she was afraid to sleep alone. So he dragged the single bed in from the next room and, chaste as a knight, lay down to sleep some two feet away from her. Then he put out the light. There was silence for a moment as their eyes got used to the dim moonlight that crept in from the dormer window. Then she said:

'Are you still there?'

He reached out his hand and she felt him touch the bedclothes, so she put out her hand, too, and they held on until she fell asleep.

When Jim woke, it was very hot. He was stifling. He threw back the bedclothes, gasping for breath. He heard Liz panting.

'What is it?' he asked.

'Flames,' she said. 'Can't you see them?' Jim looked at the walls. He saw darkness. 'Can you?'

'No,' he said. 'But it is very hot.'

'The walls are covered in flames,' she said, 'all around

us. Is someone's house on fire?' She got out of bed and
went to the window, expecting to see the sky ablaze. But
there was nothing. The grey rooftops reflected the pale
starlight. The flames weren't real. She must have been
dreaming. She turned, expecting to see a dark room. But
the flames were still there. The walls were dancing with
them.

'Oh God. I'm in hell. I'm in hell!' she moaned. She
was burning. She crossed to his bed. She wanted to
touch him, to be with him, but didn't dare. Her evil
touch would hurt him. And she didn't want to hurt him.
So she stood in the middle of the room, swaying, head
spinning, as slowly, the flames died. Then she started
breathing again in the cooling air, and she sat on the
edge of her bed, wrung out.

'A nightmare?' he asked. She nodded.

'I was asleep. In a huge sort of hall. There were no
windows. There were marble pillars. Like a mausoleum.
I was lying on a sort of slab, on a dais. And you ...
somebody ... actually I don't know if it was you or not,
but a man anyway was lying on the slab at my left,
about two feet away from me. And he was asleep, his
hands crossed on his breast. And a creature, muscled
like a hideous dwarf appeared, holding a sharp dagger in
his hand and he was trying to make a hole in ... in the
man. Was it Nathan? I don't know. It might have been.
I don't know. But ... he was trying to put something in
... in the foot. In the heel. And I shouted but the man
didn't wake up. Yes it was Nathan. Nathan. He was
sleeping like the dead, in a sort of coma. I got off the
slab. It was like a tomb. Yes, we were lying there like a
knight and his lady, on their tombs. Anyway, I reached
for a scimitar and I started hacking away at the thing's
shoulder, trying to hack its arm off so it couldn't hurt
him any more ...' She started crying. 'Then I woke up
and the room was on fire. I was lying two feet away from
you and you were asleep and there were flames dancing

129

all round the walls!' She wept, moaning, 'I'm in hell.'

Jim said nothing for some time. He had felt the heat. He had smelt vomit. So he wasn't going to say she'd had a nightmare and just imagined she saw the flames. That wasn't good enough. But he didn't know what else to say. Finally, he advised her:

'Don't jump to any conclusions. Wait and see. The meaning will become clear eventually.' She nodded obediently and let him tuck her in. But as he drew away, she held onto his hand. Her eyes were black with fear.

'I ...' she whispered, as though afraid someone would hear, 'Love you ... love you ... love you ...' Her thoughts echoed from the walls of the room.

'What?' he asked gently. In the end, she couldn't risk even Jim knowing.

'Nothing.'

'Don't give up,' he whispered, and pulling his hand away, went back to bed. Liz lay for some time, wide awake, stiff with shock. She was caught between the extremes of heaven and hell, but was unable to tell which was which or in which of them she belonged. How she wished she had never left earth.

She was beginning to look ill. She was pale, even thinner than before and her nerves were close to breaking point. But as the days went on, the onslaught continued. Pain and torment ceased neither night nor day. And now the voices were telling her:

'You should kill yourself. It's the only way out. If you love him, you'll do away with yourself. Destroy the evil in you! Throw yourself out of the window! Cut your wrists.' A variety of suicide methods were suggested. And in the circumstances the idea of leaving life was tempting. But while Jim continued sleeping in her room, thank God, there were no more nightmares.

Before sleep, like a child, she prayed to Christ to watch over her and, bathed in the glaring light behind her eyes, she drifted into a fitful sleep. Now it was when she woke she entered the nightmare world. Waking was nightmare. Sleep was forgetting. Yes, suicide was attractive. But what was the use? When she died, she wouldn't die. She would live on, in certain hell. Better face it now. Better get through it and, please God, be done with it. But Jim was in danger.

She talked to him, trying to send him away. She pleaded with him. She told him Father would curse him. Or, if not him, *she* would drag him down to hell. One way or another he was in mortal danger. But he wouldn't go. It was his free will, he told her, to decide for himself. She couldn't force him into anything. And she had to accept that.

'God gave us free will,' Jim said. And the voice said:

'With God there is no free will!' And then she knew the voice was lying.

But where did the voice come from?

Then a letter came. It was postmarked 'Devon'; Paula's aunt. They were trying to get Paula's child back, but had run into problems. Bhanamurti had been told to put the children into the hands of his first wife's family. The guru had seen the Indian family and told them what a depraved and wicked person Paula was. He had shown them a letter written by Sushena herself, in which the child had written an account of cruelties inflicted on her by her stepmother. Fabricated evidence. Who had told the child to write such a thing? Who had helped her? Father? Jeanne? Or others? Who were these self-righteous people who believed God had chosen them to protect someone else's children? And what lies were they telling them? God help them!

Was the voice Liz heard the same voice that was telling lies to the children? Then, whose was it? Liz was in agony over Billy. But Paula was ill, and Bhanamurti was the legal father. He had the right to do as he pleased and, until Paula recovered, there was precious little any of them could do about it.

'I'd like to help Paula.' Liz said. But she knew she wasn't strong enough. She had yet to find her own way out.

Now, on the rare occasions when the phone rang, they both jumped. But Liz always ran to take it. She didn't want Nathan to know about Jim. If he knew, he would tell Father and she had to protect Jim from that. So when Nathan finally called again, one Sunday morning, it was Liz who answered. He asked how the legal business was going re the house. He asked if she'd heard from Paula's aunt. Then he asked her if she was lonely. She must surely be missing 'The Family'.

To Jim, waiting in the sitting room, it seemed they'd been talking for ages. He was jumpy. Something was up. He felt it in his bones. He picked up the paper, hoping to distract himself and, turning to the back page, spotted an advert. 'The Sublime Father' was making a lecture tour and would be speaking in London on the following dates: October 23rd, 26th and 31st. It was already the 18th. He looked up and saw the sky through the window. They *had* to get away. But how was he going to persuade her? And what were they talking about on that damned telephone?

'Father told me we should have our legal marriage in London,' Nathan was saying. 'So can I rely on you to get the papers sorted out?'

'Yes. Of course.' Liz answered as if in a dream.

'Then, you have to come back with me,' he said.

'But the inheritance ...?'

'Never mind that,' Nathan commanded. 'The trustees'll get tired eventually, then you'll have the money anyway. Leave it now.'

'Yes, Nathan,' she said obediently.

'I'll be staying with Father at the Savoy Hotel, so you'd better go down to the London ashram. You'll need an address to get the licence, anyway.'

'Oh yes. Thank you, Nathan,' she said brightly.

132

'I can't wait to see you,' he said. There was genuine longing in his voice. 'Then we can be truly married at last.'

'I can hardly believe it,' she answered.

'Father works everything out eventually.' He sounded very content. 'Won't be long now.'

'No,' she replied weakly. 'See you in London!'

Liz was dazed by the news. She wandered back into the sitting room and, in answer to Jim's inquiring eyes, shook her head. She sat, speechless. A few weeks ago she would have been ecstatic at Nathan's news! But now ... Jim was looking at her. She supposed he wanted her to tell him about the call. But she couldn't face it, so she turned to say so, and saw he was holding the paper out to her. She took it, puzzled, glanced at the page and saw the advert. So, it was true. And she'd thought Father was going to America! Neither of them said anything. Better not. They were learning discretion.

'I'm going to Sicily,' he said at last. 'You know, the conference.' She managed a smile.

'Great. When?'

'End of the month.'

'I see.'

He smiled and she thought, 'He needn't look so happy about it!' But then, why shouldn't he? Life with her wasn't exactly a picnic. She could hardly blame him if he was looking forward to going away. But his smile was mysterious, as though he had something up his sleeve. Was she being thick? Or ... her pulse raced ... was he going to take her with him, after all? She didn't dare ask. She looked at him, but he only said:

'Like to come into Newcastle with me?'

'Yes. Why?' she asked.

'You need some new clothes!' he laughed.

'But I haven't any money.'

'I'll do a deal with you,' he said. She looked at him curiously. 'I'll lend you the money ...'

'Against the sale of the house,' they both said together.

'Exactly.' He smiled. 'On one condition.' Her face grew serious as she waited to hear it. 'I want you to take those beads off ...' Her hand jumped to her throat to cover them protectively, '... and throw them in the rubbish bin.' She stared at him. He watched her. He knew what they meant to her. They were a gift from Father. They tied her to him. She sat transfixed for some time. Then she whispered:

'I can't.'

'You must,' he insisted. 'This is something you have to do for yourself.' Her hand clutched at the beads. She supposed she could take them off, temporarily, just to see what it felt like. That couldn't do any harm. Could it? She licked her dry lips, took a deep breath and lifted the beads over her head. Then she laid them on the coffee table in front of her and looked at them.

'Do I *have* to throw them out?' she asked. He didn't say anything. She knew. She put her hand out and felt warmth emanating from them. When she touched them, she expected to feel something ... she didn't know what. But they were just warm from her own warm flesh. They were just ordinary beads, after all.

She picked them up and walked out of the room with them. But as she walked along the corridor the pain started. She walked on, past the office, down the stairs, and as she walked through the back of the house out into the yard where the bins were, the pain boomer-anged through her head. Well, this was it. Was the pain telling her she was doing wrong? Or was the pain trying to stop her doing right? She stood for some time in front of the bins. Then, quickly, before she could stop herself, she took the top off one of them, threw the beads amongst the potato peelings and discarded containers and banged the lid back on, tight. She stood trembling. The pain stopped. She went inside, weak at the knees, and made a cup of tea.

Going to Newcastle with Jim felt like playing truant. She enjoyed the metro ride and Newcastle was buzzing with life. Jim took her into a big store and got out his credit card. But there was so much choice! She didn't know where to start! She fumbled through a rail of skirts. Jim groaned and taking her hand, pulled her away from the middle-aged collections of day dresses and separates and into the noisy boutique where the young shopped. Liz giggled and shook her head. She couldn't wear that! Could she? Jim nodded. Good God, she thought, he means it! So she started looking through the rails.

Jim directed her to a rack of trousers and sweatshirts. Liz's face dropped. She looked at him with pleading eyes. But he meant it, alright. So she gulped and took a few items to try on. And there were no cubicles! She felt exposed, embarrassed. The need for new underclothes was reinforced. But when she saw herself in the mirror in the trousers and the shirt, she saw the point.

It was amazing. She looked like a different person! 'I see,' she told her reflection. 'Camouflage!' Then, together, she and Jim bought their way through the underclothes, the anoraks, the sexy frocks, the high heels, the tracksuits, the trainers, the lot. And when they'd finished, they bought a large suitcase.

'You're going on holiday,' he said and winked. She smiled gleefully. She was right. He *was* taking her with him. But he hadn't finished yet. After a late lunch he took her up to the top floor, thrust her into the beauty salon and said to the girl on reception:

'Cut her hair ... dye it, the works! And ... put some make-up on her!' The girl thought he was crazy and referred to Liz. Liz shrugged.

'Do as he says,' she said.

'Chauvinist pig,' the receptionist muttered to Jim's departing back and ushered Liz into the salon.

Liz shut her eyes tight when the scissors started

snipping at her long hair. But with each snip came a sense of relief. So she opened her eyes to watch what was happening to her in the mirror. It was like magic. She watched entranced as the hair dryer got to work, lifting Liz's hair, adding bounce, and the red sheen which emerged as it dried was really rather fetching. She smiled at herself, then at the girl.

'It's nice,' she said.

'We aim to please,' the girl answered and took her to the counter where Jim was waiting for her, the bill paid. She smiled confidently at him. But he just stared and stared at her. Her confidence waned. He shook himself.

'Very nice!' he told her, 'You look twenty years younger.' And then she understood. He had seen her as the young Liz again.

'What've you been doing?' she asked as she put on her anorak.

'Called in at the travel agent,' he said. 'Brought forward the flight. We'll have time for a few days in Taormina before the conference. We both deserve a holiday!' She smiled. He was doing it for her. He wanted to get her out of the way before they came.

'Come on.' He took her arm and escorted her from the salon. 'Let's get you into some of that new gear.'

As they travelled home on the metro, Liz chattered away blissfully unaware of the man eavesdropping behind them.

'If I'm evil,' she explained to Jim, 'then I always was evil. I mean, it's nothing new. I was evil when Father engaged me to Nathan. I was evil when I was born! So what's new? And if I'm evil, then I belong in hell. So I might as well hold my nose and jump in. In any case if "The Family's" heaven, I don't like it very much!' Jim laughed.

'That's the first sensible thing you've said in twenty

years!' he told her. The man behind looked as though he'd swallowed his tonsils. Had the Martians landed? Shaking his head, he watched them get off the train. But Liz didn't notice or care. She was too full of her big discovery. She had been living on the wrong side of the mirror! All she'd needed was the courage to jump right through it to the other side! She was lucky. Jim was there to catch her. Poor Paula had nobody; nobody who understood, anyway. So she got stuck in the middle of the mirror, unable to jump either way! That was her no-man's land.

They picked up fish and chips on the way from the station and ate them in the taxi. The driver wasn't too pleased, but cheered up when they offered him some. And catching sight of Jim planting a kiss on Liz's cheek as they entered the house, he decided yuppies weren't so bad after all.

To all appearances, Jim and Liz were like everybody else.

The kiss took Liz by surprise. She flushed to her red roots and Jim apologised.

'You look so cheeky with the new hair,' he excused himself.

'You're the one that's cheeky!' she complained. Then, she pecked him on his cheek. But when she looked at him afterwards, she saw how hungry he was and looked away, embarrassed.

'Oh, get 'em off!' he said, pushing her into the house.

She enjoyed throwing her clothes in the bin. But she couldn't throw absolutely everything away, and hung onto a shawl. She felt naked without all that hair! She kept touching the back of her head and it felt strange. But it did look nice, she had to admit it. She was standing in front of the mirror, inspecting the new image, when the phone rang. Jim was already in the office. It was 24th October. Her heart stood still. She could hear Jim's voice on the phone. She went in to join him, heart pounding. He was putting the receiver back as she entered the office. He was very pale.

'Wrong number,' he said. Then he took the receiver off the hook and laid it on the desk. She nodded slowly.

There was no time to lose. They were packed the next morning, and after debating whether or not to tell the solicitor where they were going, they decided against it. Suppose, having been unable to raise Liz either at the house or the ashram, Nathan was to phone him? Their cover would be blown, so they locked up the house and left silently in the early morning, catching a cab *en route* to the station.

They were in London by mid-afternoon. Their flight was the next day. Liz was in a state of nerves and Jim wasn't much better. They'd checked into separate rooms at a cheap hotel in Earl's Court. But if they wanted to eat, they had to go out. Liz insisted they look for a takeaway, so they ventured onto the streets, feeling like criminals at large. There were posters advertising the lecture tour everywhere. On every other corner they were surprised by yet another photograph of the 'Sublime Father'. It really felt like Big Brother was watching them. Liz knew, too, that devotees would have come in their thousands to support him and as she had said, they looked like everyone else. But the rhythm they pulsed as they walked down the street was different, was contagious. Only the sensitive knew when they had been invaded and they didn't know what to do about it. At the corner of the tube station, Liz gasped and fled into a doorway.

'I thought ...' she peered out nervously. 'I thought I saw Nathan!'

'And is it?' Jim asked, searching the crowd on the street. She shook her head. 'This is ridiculous.' He didn't know whether to be angry or to laugh. 'We'll end up as paranoid as they are! Come on! There's a good Greek restaurant round the corner. Let's go and eat there.' Liz bit her lip. She'd feel safer in their room. But she was glad Jim wasn't afraid. Or at least, if he was, he wasn't going to let them get him down!

PART TWO

They were sitting in the Gods, high up in the auditorium of the Greek theatre. Before them, row upon row of empty seats descended like a stone staircase to the pits and the stage beyond. Pillars supported the backdrop of blue sea and the smoking crater of snow-capped Etna. She was telling him the story of her family.

'In the beginning Jane Ridley had two brothers and a sister. The youngest was Josh. He stowed away to sea. Actually, Jim, he's your great-grandfather or something. Anyway he went to America to found your side of the family.' Jim picked up a stray twig and began drawing his family tree in the sand at their feet. 'Her other brother, Robert, and her sister, I think she was called Fanny, were both older than Jane. Well, Fanny's neither here nor there. She married a pilot and died of drink or something. I remember Aunt Frances used to say that by all accounts she was a bad lot and never did have much going for her. But Robert and Jane, the middle two, were artistic, intelligent people and, so Frances said, very fond of one another – too fond of one another by all accounts ...'

'Yes. You're right. Joshua Ridley *was* my great-grandfather,' Jim interrupted. Glancing briefly at his diagram, Liz resumed her story.

'Well ...' she said, 'when she was still just a young girl, Jane got a job in George Beattie's flower shop in Fowler Street. He was Mayor of Shields at the time and a big noise in the town. He was married, of course, and not for the first time, either. Apparently he was quite a lad. Anyway, after Jane had been there for a bit, Mrs Beattie died, and George started courting Jane. He must have been quite a bit older than her, and I bet she was really innocent, too. Anyway, she ended up marrying him. Meanwhile, the brother, Robert, had gone abroad. I don't know much about him. I think he must have been a bit of an adventurer.'

'Like Jason and the Argonauts?' Jim suggested.

'Oh, I don't think there were any argonauts,' Liz retorted. 'I think he went on his own.' Jim smiled, a little too glibly for Liz's comfort and gazed with interest into the wings, where some tourists were gathering. 'Anyway, it seems Jane and George were very happy to start with and they had children and so on. First there was Ellen, who was Eve's grandma, then Maisie. She never married. Then, catastrophe! Jane found out George was having an affair with another woman and she hit the roof. Well, it so happened that Robert had come home for a spell about that time, and ... something happened.' Liz gave a dramatic pause. The tourists had entered the amphitheatre and were now crossing the stage – a long line of tiny figures. Their leader raised a hand, bringing them to a halt, and started reading aloud from a guide book. Contemplating the attentive Japanese, Jim was amused at their incongruity, dressed in neat jeans and jumpers, cameras slung over their shoulders.

'Exactly what that something was ...' Liz persisted, 'is a bit of a mystery, but one thing's for sure. It changed the course of family history.' Jim dragged his attention away from the Japanese.

'A mystery?' he said raising his eyebrows. 'And were there any clues to this mystery?'

'Of course! Listen, will you!'

'Sorry.'

'What we know for definite is this: Robert was staying with his sister in the house in Fowler Street. My house.

And one night, hoping to cheer her up, I suppose, he took her out to the circus. George was elsewhere; probably with his mistress. We don't know what happened at the circus, but, when George came home he found Jane alone and in a state. Robert had scarpered, she'd lost her engagement ring, and to crown it all there was money missing from the till. Anyway, that's what Eve told me. And she'd got it from her mother and stepfather, Jack, who was well in with George. Anyway, according to Eve something then happened between George and Jane. They hadn't been having ... "relations" as they called them in those days, and when he came home that night to find things as they were, well he saw red, and he attacked her. Raped, her, to be more precise.

'The next day, the pair of them put it about that Robert had stolen the money from the shop and run off with it, so he was in disgrace and must never be allowed to darken the doors at Fowler Street again. But that was just a cover up. Or at least ...'

'That's what Eve said,' Jim filled in for her.

'Yes. And Jack, Eve's stepfather. He thought so, too. George liked him. He confided in Jack. In fact Jack was there when George finally died, years later. He heard his dying words ... but I'm getting ahead of myself. Well, as a result of that night, Jane and George had a third child. She was called Hester; my grandmother.

'Hester was always a problem. You know how she ended up? Cut her own throat in the asylum!'

Liz shivered and Jim remembered a day in New Mexico when Eve had got the news. It had shaken her to the core. But Liz had already gone on to the next generation. 'Faster than Genesis,' Jim thought.

'And my mother wasn't a lot better. She was crazy. She had several breakdowns. I know Dad was really relieved when she died. "Good thing too," he said, "put her and everybody else out of their misery." Fifteen years

145

ago nearly. It was the last letter Dad wrote to me, till this time of course, about Eve.' Liz sighed. 'Poor Mam. What an epitaph, "put her out of her misery". And all her problems went back to Hester. Apparently, George was always against Hester marrying and having children. He seemed to think she was cursed in some way. She certainly behaved as though she was. And Jane herself was never the same after the "fateful night". She ended up throwing herself under a horse-drawn carriage eventually! Now why was that? There's got to be some reason why a perfectly sane and normal family suddenly goes berserk, hasn't there?'

Suddenly the chorus of Japanese tourists broke out in a loud, wailing gabble. They were standing centre-stage, looking directly out into the auditorium; testing the acoustics, no doubt. When they'd finished, Jim clapped obligingly. The tourists bowed, laughing and waving at him, before going off, stage left, to explore the pits.

'Anyway,' Liz continued, 'it seems Hester bore a grudge against her father. All her life he treated her as though she was filth, till eventually she cracked, and murdered him. Did you know we had a murderer in the family?' Jim looked bemused, then said, philosophically:

'Well, there's murder and murder, isn't there?'

'What do you mean?' she asked. He didn't say anything, but she knew. There were murderers of souls.

'What happened?' he prompted her. 'I suppose she had to stand trial?'

'No. She wasn't considered sane enough. Actually, it was then she was carted off to the asylum. But, and this is the interesting part, Jack was there to hear George's last words. You know, after she'd poisoned him. He must've told Jack what had happened that night – between Jane and Robert. He must have done! Jack always behaved as though he was "in" on the story! Looking back I can see that. Anyway, George's last words were, "Shadow of the Elephant". It was a clue and a warning at the same time.

'Jack knew a lot about a lot of things. He knew Jane had been sent that statue of Ganesha from India. You know, the one we've still got up at the house. Or was it Ellen? I can't remember. Anyway, one of them. Ganesha, the elephant-headed god of innocence. Chintamani. By saying there was a shadow, George was telling Jack there'd been some transgression against innocence.'

'There was!' Jim cried. 'Your grandma killed her father!'

'No. Before that. Eve believed, like Jack, and George himself, that the night Robert took his sister to the circus, they came home and committed incest. Then, realising what he'd done, Robert ran away, leaving Jane to bear their child! There's your shadow!'

The chorus of Japanese passed across the stage again, chattering as they went. Liz broke off, impatient for them to go. But one of their number, dislocating himself from the rest, walked to the middle of the stage and bowed. Then he stood up very straight and surveying the auditorium, declaimed:

> *'Our revels now are ended. These our actors,*
> *As I foretold you, were all spirits, and*
> *Like the baseless fabric of this vision,*
> *The cloud capp'd towers, the gorgeous palaces,*
> *The solemn temples, the great globe itself*
> *Yes, all which it inherit, shall dissolve,*
> *And like this insubstantial pageant faded,*
> *Leave not a rack behind. We are such stuff*
> *As dreams are made on; and our little life*
> *Is rounded with a sleep.'*

When he had finished he bowed stiffly. The tourists waiting in the wings broke into tumultuous applause and he walked off, to collapse in giggles in the wings.

'You see?' Jim said. 'It's only a story.'

'But it must be true!' Liz insisted, as they walked later in the English garden. Jim was surveying the smoking volcano on the other side of the bay. He shrugged.

'What does it matter?' he asked. But Liz was upset.

'It's my inheritance,' she said.

'Isn't it time you forgave your ancestors?' Jim was standing under a summer house and looked up to see a canopy of jasmine flowering overhead. It smelt heavenly. He smiled and pointed up at it. Liz looked and nodded. Yes, it was very nice. It was a lovely garden and she would have liked to enjoy it, but the story wasn't finished yet and, unlike Jim, she was part of it! She couldn't relax and just forget. Not yet. Not even to please him!

After all, *they* hadn't forgotten her; that other 'Family'. They knew about her past. She'd gone to them to escape from her inheritance and now that she'd turned her back on them, too, they pursued her like the furies over land and sea.

She felt Nathan's discovery of her desertion: panic, followed by fear; anger, followed by pain. Her soul had mirrored all the progressions of his feelings. Then sharper pain had followed. Father had been told. His anger scorched her head, and filled her throat with dust. If she had thought she could get away from them just by escaping to Sicily, she was wrong. She had tried to evade her destiny by putting herself under Father's powerful protection; and whatever he was, he was certainly powerful. He had given her something real. Her health had improved, her nerves had grown stronger, she hadn't gone mad. She'd been freed of all the family burdens because of him. And now she'd turned her back on her guru, had she brought not only his wrath down on her head but also that of the cheated fates? What had she done?

She couldn't go back. She looked over the wall down

to the sea, far below. There was no escape. Raising her eyes, she saw the volcano. It might erupt any time, spewing its guts over the countryside, spilling lava into the towns. And, from where she was standing, she'd get a ringside seat. She must not go mad.

'I'd like to take a closer look at it,' Jim said, coming up behind her. 'Volcanoes create an energy field; a dynamic. This island's alive with it.'

'Isn't it dangerous?' Liz asked.

'I like living dangerously,' Jim laughed.

'No, you don't,' Liz cut in bitterly, 'you just like watching.'

That night, Liz slept fitfully. It was dark and hot with the shutters closed. She got up and tried to open them, but they were stuck fast. So she lay back again, breathing slowly to keep cool, listening to the distant sound of cars, struggling up the hairpins to Taormina, then revving desperately through the little streets in search of a parking place.

Then, when at last she drifted into sleep, her unconscious spewed up wild, violent dreams, terrifying images of demons, horsemen and blood. She woke in a sweat, more tired than before, suffocating in the dark heat. Then, exhausted, she slept again.

In the other bed, Jim listened. Her breathing was becoming more and more distressed. What was she dreaming? He didn't dream much, or if he did, didn't remember. He had successfully turned his back on most of his traumas; apart from Kim, of course ... Damn! Why had he let her into his consciousness? Now he wouldn't get her out again till morning! Liz was moaning. Her dream was gathering pace. He supposed she would have liked him to creep in beside her and comfort her. But he was tired. He wanted to sleep. And anyway, like the lady said, he just liked watching. Why should he get involved? He felt trapped in this dark, stifling room

149

with Liz! He threw back the coverlet, exposing his bare torso. It didn't help much. The air lay heavily on his skin, like air that had been breathed too often and lost its vigour. He'd give anything to get out.

He stared through the darkness to the darker shape of the door in the corner. He could go. He could quietly put on his clothes, open the door and leave. Nothing to stop him. Those little noises of hers irritated him beyond belief. Perhaps a shower would help. Bed creaking, he slipped past the restless dreamer and escaped into the bathroom, where he bathed in rivers of tepid water.

She was ashamed. She had been found out. She was a lecher, an adulteress. But she was no Mary Magdalen. Christ would not hear her screams and come to save and canonise her. For she had lost faith. She had turned against the herd and there it was, gathering in restless groups, Paula at the head of them, a stone in her hand. And a voice cried out, 'Pray to have faith in me.' Father's voice! But she would not pray for that! She could not. A cold hand gripped her heart. Terrified, she prayed to wake up instead. And as she fell through the flames and chaos God said, 'The Lord thy God is a jealous God!' She jerked awake, the words echoing in her ears as though borne on a gushing river. 'The Lord thy God is a vengeful God!' And sweating, she woke into nightmare, knowing her dream was blasphemy.

This place under the volcano had spewed her up into another dimension of hell. Which was reality? This or her dream? She must not go mad.

It was strangely light. She could see suitcases on top of the cupboard; Jim's and hers. She turned, looking for him in the other bed. He wasn't there. Perhaps he'd gone. Perhaps she'd driven him away. Perhaps he'd never existed! But ... she looked again at the suitcases ... And now she saw the light was coming from under the bathroom door. He was having a shower. She sighed with relief. That was what had wakened her, the rushing water! 'The Lord Thy God is a jealous God.' She must take hold of herself or they really would drive her mad.

She heard Jim turn off the shower and shake the gurgling water out of his mouth. It was silent outside; middle of the night; no cars now. They were quite alone, he in one room, she in another. And now he was cleaning his teeth. She listened eagerly to the banal sounds of brushing and gargling and found them comforting. He was really there, behind that door, standing in the light before the bathroom mirror. She would like to be able to get up, suddenly open the door and make him jump. Then he'd laugh and she'd laugh like a normal couple. But a barrier divided them. She was in one world, he another, and she could no more open the bathroom door to say boo than she could fly. This was not the holiday she had hoped for.

The door opened. She glanced away from the shock of light, but he saw her face glistening with sweat and knew she was awake.

'Sorry. Did I wake you?'

'No,' she said.

He put out the bathroom light and felt his way back to bed, bumping the furniture as he went.

'Were you dreaming?' he asked.

'Why?'

'You were making little noises.'

'Oh.' He could tell from her voice she was embarrassed. 'I think telling you about Jane and Robert stirred things up.'

'Ah,' he said. 'Bad dreams, then?'

'Yes.'

He sighed. She held her breath, wishing he would comfort her. But he seemed far away, on another planet. Well, he was lucky, damn him! Would the morning never come? There was silence, as each stared blindly at the dark ceiling. They had reached a stalemate in their relationship.

The next day, they took off along the Catania road in a hire car, heading for Etna. Smoke billowed across the road as they turned onto the trail that would take them up the mountainside. The leaves were yellow, dropping lazily from the trees. Shepherds were driving their herds down the slopes into lower pastures for the winter. You could hear their bells clanging spasmodically in the distance. It was cold, and as they climbed, drifts of snow materialised behind rocks along the sides of the road and finally, as the scenery turned to white, it started snowing in earnest. Jim sighed.

'We're nearly there,' he said, 'but I can't see any guides wanting to take us up to the crater in this.' He pulled up in the park where the road ended. There was a shop. It was closed, but there were several hotels and at least one of the cafés was open. They got out of the car into the bitter cold. Liz shivered as she looked up the mountain.

Somewhere up there through the mist, a blazing crater was hurling sulphurous smoke into the scorching air; the summit, veiled by falling snow; ice and fire. 'The Lord thy God is a jealous God.' She must not go mad. Stamping their feet, they looked round for signs of life. There were a couple of cars and a van in the parking lot, but no other tourists. They made their way to the café and, glad to be back in the warmth, ordered coffee, consoling themselves by looking at the exhibits: a photograph of the hotel during the last eruption, surrounded by fiery lava; the collection of volcanic stones.

He tried to tell her what they all were, but he could tell she wasn't really interested. Too absorbed in herself, he thought. Then the coffee arrived and they sat by a window to drink it. Here they were again, cut off from the rest of humanity, marooned, this time by ice and snow. At least, Liz thought, they had each other. Or did they? Who was she fooling? He'd let her down! He wasn't the support and comfort she'd hoped. And Jim's drawn expression was clear indication of discontent. Then suddenly she saw it, the way his face was lit by the snow outside.

'Have you got a pencil on you?' she asked suddenly. He searched and pulled out a biro.

'That do?'

'Thanks.' She took it and opened out her paper napkin. 'Just stay exactly as you are,' she said and began drawing. His smile spread. Her gaze rested on his face. 'You're very difficult,' she said. 'Elusive in fact.'

'Sorry.'

'It's alright.' Tracing the line of his cheekbones, she came to his eyes. But they evaded her. Yes, he was elusive. He had thick armour and he hid far, far behind it. One day she would like to catch the sparkle in his eyes, or that trusting deep compassion which he sometimes showed her; sometimes; not today. Not yesterday. Not here in Taormina. Still, no-one else saw it. No-one else had ever seen it, she thought. It was her privilege. She quickly rounded off the sketch and showed it to him. 'It's only a quickie of course,' she said apologetically.

'Very good,' he commented with surprise.

'I've not drawn anything in years!'

'No. It's good.' Then, 'Do I really look that old?' he asked. She grinned and was about to say, 'Ancient, in fact ageless; that's why you're so hard to draw.' But that would be betraying herself. He would laugh at her. She took refuge in her craft.

'It needs highlights,' she said, looking at the picture again with disappointment. 'I wish I had some pastels.'

He was pleased. This was progress! At least they'd got something out of the trip! And then there was the excitement of the drive back. Would they make it? Or would they get stuck on the mountainside, in a drift of snow? He drove recklessly down, zig-zagging below the snow line till soon they were on their way back to their little town on the clifftop. The excitement had been short-lived. All in all, the trip had been a let-down. As at Durham Cathedral, they'd been turned away, empty-handed.

She knew he was feeling irritable by the way he kept flicking the air in front of him, as though he could dispel Etna's smoke with a wave of the hand. Somehow she felt it was her fault, this cloud that had descended not only on the road, but on their holiday. Was she hampering his style? He was a geophysicist; he would surely have preferred someone more knowledgeable to accompany him on his ascent of Etna? She knew she should have shown more interest in the stones, but how could she? It was as thought he was deliberately ignoring her mental state.

Her mind was in a blind panic! She couldn't just turn it on, be a barrel of laughs, just like that, could she? She sighed, then immediately wished she hadn't as she sensed rather than saw the scowl that crossed his face. And yet this man had connived and bullied to get her to agree to this trip! He knew the state she was in! So what was he expecting of her that he wasn't getting? Sex? Was that all she was to him? Her prim expression reflected back at her from the windscreen. She looked away. It was hypocritical to keep herself from Jim when she would have given herself to Nathan without a thought (had he insisted).

And she didn't love Nathan. He didn't love her, either! He enclosed her like an iron maiden, stabbing her with his anger and resentment, while Jeanne sent clouds of poison that made her vomit. And then there was Paula. She made Liz feel dizzy whenever she thought of her, not to mention the children ... all the children of all the devotees. What would become of them? Little satellites of the guru, transmitting the noxious signals of their master over the air waves, spreading them like a mental disease? And what would become of her, Liz, if the onslaught of hatred continued? Since her betrayal, they had laid siege against her, bombarding her with hatred and curses. 'The Lord thy God is a jealous God.' Yes, and he wasn't showing any signs of saving her right now. Saving her from what? Who? Father? Suppose God *was* Father. No! She must not go through all that again! She could not go back. She had gone through the mirror and now was in heaven or hell and either way they would kill her in the end. And maybe ... she glanced at Jim. Her bitterness turned to an aching love. Was it any wonder she wasn't the life and soul?

'I'm sorry,' she said. But her tone was resentful.

'Oh shut up,' he responded. 'I'm sick of hearing you say "I'm sorry". If you ask me ...' he changed gear abruptly as they started to climb, 'saying you're sorry is an excuse for not changing.'

'Changing?' she asked furiously.

'Changing the way you think! I mean, coming away with me was an ideal opportunity, wasn't it? But I don't know why I bothered. You think about them all the time, don't you?'

'Who?'

'The Family.'

'No. I don't.'

'Yes, you do! I've seen you, gasping with pain, suddenly touching your head or your stomach, being sick.'

'It's them who's transmitting! I'm on the *receiving* end!'

'If you didn't think about them they wouldn't be able to get through to you!'

'Fat lot you know about it! Do you think I like being in pain all the time?' Jim was silent, his lips tight, eyes

155

fixed on the smoky road. 'Your little ploy of changing my image didn't work very well, did it? They can still identify me! No trouble! The missiles still home in on me with amazing accuracy!'

'Stop being a drama queen.'

'I am not being a drama queen!' she yelled.

'You think being sensitive makes you special, don't you?' For a second, Liz was thrown. He felt a heel for saying it. It was below the belt. He was right, of course. And yet she'd give anything not to be. And to be fair, she suffered in silence, never said she was in pain. He glanced at her, almost contrite, but her eyes were closed against him. He supposed she was saying that damned mantra again!

How dare he! She always had been too apologetic. That was her trouble. That's why she'd run away to 'The Family' in the first place; felt she was 'unworthy'! And yet she wasn't a complete no no! She'd done things others hadn't! She'd learnt things few people ever learnt! She had overcome her inheritance. Her eyes sprang open. She had powers, if she only had the confidence to use them. Staring at the smoke, she commanded it to clear. Immediately the car drove out of the smoke. Liz laughed out loud. Of course it was probably just a coincidence. . . .

'What're you laughing at?' Jim asked.

'Nothing,' she said airily. Jim was angry. So, she was shutting him out again! Some mumbo jumbo no doubt. And she thought herself so bloody superior! Well sod her! She deserved to suffer! Suddenly, Liz cried out, her hand on her chest, eyes black with pain. Jim paled. Had he done that? Oh my God, she was drawing him in deeper and deeper! Before long she'd have him in a strait-jacket!

And if he was against her, how could she go on in this living hell? She was finished.

'He sees through you,' the voice said. 'You shouldn't

have told him about the incest. He doesn't love you. How could he?'

'You don't care about me.' Liz told Jim.

'Bollocks,' he answered.

'He knows you're filth!' the voice said. 'He's making use of you. You're a sex object, that's all.'

'It's sex, isn't it? That's what you're after. That's why you invited me here.'

'If it was, I'd be very disappointed,' Jim answered.

'He's after your money.'

'Don't worry. I'll pay you back for the trip. As soon as the house is sold.'

'Hah!'

'He wants you to leave. You could catch a plane tomorrow and be out of here in no time.'

'I'll get a plane home.'

'What?!'

'It's what you want, isn't it?'

As the car zig-zagged furiously up the cliff, Liz cried. What had happened to them?

Too early to eat, too late to check out planes at the tourist office, Jim and Liz wandered aimlessly through the streets, gazing forlornly at the colourful display of marzipan fruits and little cakes that tempted from shop windows, glowing gem-like in the gathering gloom.

Then the street lights flickered on, casting a shadowy glow on the lanes and the steep stairways to undiscovered alleys, the little town a maze of delights. The locals began to appear, opening cafés, the jewellers' and antique shops for evening trade. Sociably they greeted one another and chatted on street corners, nodding like the flowers in the hanging baskets, casting speculative glances at the passing couple. Then, when the strangers didn't respond, they shrugged philosophically. They were probably in love or out of love or one of those things and not in a mood to spend, poor souls. But their troubles would no doubt pass as all things passed. And they returned to the important business of gossip, smiling more like Greeks than Sicilians, relaxed and homely as the starlings that roosted in the rooftops.

Slowly the place began to work its gentle magic. A fresh breeze revived Jim and Liz as they wandered into the square. It drew them to the wall, where they found themselves looking down onto a moonlit sea. Each recognised the romance and beauty of the night and each felt sad, knowing it was wasted on them. Suddenly, Liz became uncomfortably aware that while she had been angry, her pain had ceased; and she knew the voices had got the better of her. They had tried to get between her and Jim and they had succeeded. Dear God, they had burrowed deep to become part of her. For a while they had even controlled her! But she wouldn't have it! She would fight them every inch of the way! She leant over the parapet to relieve the jerk of pain that stabbed her left side, and looked up at the rainbow aureole of the moon. No, she would not let them win.

'Are you cold?' he asked.

'Yes. I am. It's so beautiful here, I hate to leave, but, we'll catch our deaths if we stay.'

'Let's go and eat.'

Wandering down through dark alleys they inspected the restaurants and cafés that had remained open so late into the season. By silent consent they avoided the noisy tourist traps and found themselves in a back street, skirting a badly parked car to slide through the door of a homely café. They were the first customers of the evening; perhaps the only ones. The patron's family descended on them joyfully, recommending local specialities and, unresisting, Jim and Liz allowed themselves to be guided. They started with soup. The patron, his wife and two children stood watching from the kitchen door as they swallowed the first piece of squid, trailing in the delicate broth. They performed the

158

required 'mmming' and 'aahing', till, satisfied, the patron shooed the family out into the kitchen to prepare the next course. Then the café was silent. Liz had an urge to talk. There were drawings on the walls. She gabbled on about them. But he wasn't listening. He was deep in his own thoughts . . .

'Kim, Kim? Are you trying to tell me something? Is that it? You're probably happily married with kids of your own and haven't given me a thought for years! Thing is, it isn't you who missed out, it's me. Didn't want to get involved. Didn't want to get dragged into anything. Yeah. Probably married and with kids. Teaching school. Movie star! Who knows? Unless . . . no . . . she wouldn't be dead. Bastards couldn't have got her in the orphanage! Got others. Why not her? Don't want to know. Daren't risk seeing her as a corpse, finished; locked her into an eternity of a single memory, "Jim get killed!"

'Either her or me. Crazy thoughts. What does it matter? All the same in a thousand years. But not to her. Not to me. Not to Liz. All that incest crap. All that mumbo jumbo. Crap. Got her cornered, though. Got her in chains. Open the door for her and she still can't walk out. Needs somebody to cut through it all. Me? You're crazy. Never get involved. Never? Shut up, Kim. Okay, so I love Liz! So what? She's an independent being, got to sort out her own mess. And yes, she gets me, right in the cardiac region. She's like a dull ache in there, throbbing. Look at her! So fragile, so vulnerable. She's almost finished. So what if she did get herself into this mess? So what? What am I? A man or a mouse? And she was right about the sex. I had hoped . . . Well you can always hope, can't you? Not that that was all I wanted. But it was part of it. I'm a man. And she's very fanciable with that short hair bobbing round her head, that little mouth nervously twitching, waiting to be kissed. God, she's still gabbling on about those damn

159

pictures and here comes the little boy to clear away our plates. What a miserable kid. Does he ever smile?'

'*Bene?*' the little boy asked solemnly.

'*Si, bene, grazie, Benissimo!*' Jim kissed his fingers. The boy grinned suddenly and ran off into the kitchen, dropping a plate. Jim caught Liz's eye and they laughed, sharing their smile afterwards with the mother, who came in to lay their places for the second course. And now she was gabbling on in Italian, probably about the little boy. The little girl was peering round the door, eyeing them. The father must've been cooking the dinner. They heard him say something to the little girl and she came back in, shyly, some books under her arm. Still eyeing them, she sidled into a seat at a corner table and spread her books out. The mother finished laying, turned and saw her. She raised her arm in objection, letting forth a tirade of abuse. The girl looked sulky and said something about 'Papa', and 'Papa' shouted from the kitchen. Mama shrugged and ruffled her daughter's hair on the way out. The girl watched till her mother had disappeared into the kitchen, then she turned to the foreigners and beamed.

'Homework,' Liz said, smiling at the girl sympathetically.

'Yes,' Jim answered. 'Same the whole world over.' A final shout from the kitchen and the girl bent her eyes to her books. Then it was silent again.

He hadn't been listening to her. She might as well have been talking to the wall. Well, she hadn't shown much interest in his stones, had she? She sighed, and said nothing.

But what are the chains that bind her? Only her belief in this incest thing. Suppose he was to do something about it? What? Find out if it was true. What if it *was* true? Better not interfere. Much too dangerous. It was her life. Why didn't she sleep with him? Was it this Nathan guy? Did she still feel married to him in some way? Didn't she fancy him? Or was she just scared? She'd not done it in a long time. Maybe not since....

He had a strangely speculative look in his eye. Like those shopkeepers, she thought. She blushed and didn't know why. He was a funny man; she knew he wanted it and yet he hadn't made a single pass at her since they came away together. Of course she was glad, but, she couldn't help wondering why. Had she put him off? Why wasn't she willing to commit herself? *Because he wasn't!* came the answer clear as a bell.

The kitchen door swung open. Mama came in bearing plates of fish and steaming veg.

'*Specialida locale!*' She announced with a flourish.

'I wonder if it's safe,' Liz whispered.

'What?'

'The fish. You know what the Mediterranean's like.'

'*They* look healthy enough.'

They glanced at the watching group: the Mama, standing over them, hands on her hips, the patron and his son eyeballing from the door, the little girl darting surreptitious glances from under long lashes, as she bent over her work. There was nothing for it. And it smelt wonderful. So the performance of 'mmms' and 'aahhs' was repeated till, placated, the family retreated once again.

'There's one thing. We know it's been freshly cooked,' Jim said. Liz laughed and ate. It was very good.

'She looks gorgeous when she laughs. Needs more meat on her though. Probably lived on rice all those years.'

'Eat up,' he said.

'You betcha,' she answered, grinning.

'She's okay. Got a sense of humour. But buried, maybe. Still, not her fault. If I'd followed her out to India ... me? What am I thinking? I've never gone out of my way to do anything for anybody in the whole of my life. Hell! Is that true? Apart from Kim? Is it really true? Am I such a selfish bastard? And doing something for somebody doesn't necessarily mean you have to get involved. Suppose I . . .

'Would you like me to go to India for you?' Liz swallowed a courgette the wrong way and started choking. Immediately four pairs of eyes were on them. Jim thumped her on the back and she made a grab for the water, spluttering fish and veg over the table.

'Sorry,' she wheezed at the Mama. The Mama muttered something darkly and retreated with her son and husband behind the door. The little girl gazed at them thoughtfully. Liz smiled at her, to prove she wasn't going to die, and the girl resumed her work. Liz blew her nose. Her mascara was running. 'Sorry,' she said to Jim. He didn't react.

'Would you like me to find out more about Jane and Robert?' he repeated. Liz gulped down more water.

'How?' she asked.

'Didn't Robert end up in India?'

'Yes,' Liz whispered, then gabbled on, 'do you know, a funny thing, Jack apparently bumped into one of Robert's sons in the trenches. In the first war. Eve said he killed him!'

'Why? Was he German?'

'No. He was fighting on our side. He'd joined up in India. Mind you, I don't know if it's true.'

'Well, if Robert had one son, maybe he had others. Anyway, it must be possible to trace the family.' Liz was silent. 'If you want me to.' Suddenly she knew she was afraid of knowing.

'I thought you said it was only a story?' she reminded him.

'. . . if *you* still believe in it . . .'

'I don't think I could go back to India,' she said.

'I wasn't suggesting it,' he answered. 'I'd go alone. We'd find a safe place for you somewhere, till I got back, hopefully with the required information. Did they, or didn't they? Tarrah!' She waited for his awkward display of bad taste to end, then whispered, seriously:

'You'd do this for me?'

'I just thought maybe if you knew for certain one way or another you'd be better able to put it behind you.'

'Maybe I would,' she replied. They ate silently, not tasting the food. To his alarm tears were dripping down her nose, dribbling over her lips, and finally splashing onto the plate.

'What's wrong now?' he asked with some irritation.

'I ... Nothing,' she answered. 'It's just ...' she hiccuped, 'you're nice. That's all.' He reached for her hand across the table and, as he squeezed it and she squeezed back, four pairs of eyes were watching them.

The next morning, paying their final visit to the English Garden, Liz stepped in and out of the criss-cross shadows made by the sunshine through the trellised wall.

'Kids' game,' Jim objected.

'Step on a crack and you go to hell!' Liz laughed. She was full of the joys this morning.

'Stupid game,' he said sourly.

'Why are you always saying I'm stupid?' Liz objected. 'Just because I didn't finish college, just because you're a Cambridge bigwig, doesn't mean I'm stupid and you're not!'

'True,' he agreed. 'But it's certainly a clue.'

'You arrogant bastard!' She glared at him across the distant backcloth of smoking Etna. 'I suppose this is because you didn't make it with me last night, is it?'

'I didn't want it.'

'Oh no?' she challenged. 'I'm not so stupid as you seem to think!'

'You were stupid enough to get yourself caught out by a spiritual con artist, weren't you?! I mean, how could you get taken in by all that crap?'

'I'm sorry if I've given the impression it's all crap! It

163

isn't though! If it was, people wouldn't be drawn to it! I got real things out of it. There is a real spiritual energy and it can move mountains. I've felt it. Jim, people these days are looking for so much more than the churches can give them. They're looking for God, union, oneness, nirvana, whatever you want to call it, but they want to get somewhere spiritually. They want to learn, so they look for a master to teach them. I could tell you a thing or two about spiritual power ...'

'Eve!' He had stopped her in mid-flow. She stared at him, in astonishment.

'I think you're confusing me with somebody else,' she said coldly.

'No. I'm not.'

'You called me Eve!' she objected.

'Sure.'

'What did you mean by it?'

I wasn't talking about your "aunt" Eve,' he sneered.

'Well then what *are* you talking about?'

'You. As Adam's tempter. Well this time, I'm not nibbling. The tree of knowledge, my love, is not the tree of life.'

'What?'

'Byron. Probably the only sensible thing the stupid berk ever said.

"Sorrow is knowledge: they who know the most
Must mourn the deepest o'er the fatal truth,
The tree of Knowledge is not that of Life."'

Liz stared at him. 'How do you know Byron?' she asked.

'Went out with an English major for a while. Called Patsy Fortismere. She was into poetry. She was a walking quotation mark. I don't know if she ever said an original thing. I mean even if she wanted the bathroom, she'd quote poetry at you. "Too much of water hast thou, poor Ophelia", she'd say and then she'd tell you it was from *Hamlet* and swan off to the Ladies'. She was pretty stupid, too.'

'Of course! She was a woman!' Liz shouted.

'Sure.'

'Oooh!!!' Suddenly she laughed. 'What did she say when she came back?'

'"For this relief much thanks." That was Shakespeare as well.'

Laughing, they made their way under the heady, scented jasmine, back to the car. They'd finished with Taormina. It had nearly finished them.

There was more snow on the mountains, as they drove silently through the jagged peaks, eagles encircling them. The roads were empty. Only the odd local car, driven by necessity, made its way on chained tyres down the hairpin bends and through the passes. The towns and villages perched on craggy tops as though grown out of the rock and, like the inhabitants, were almost invisible. The atmosphere was one of desperation, of outlaws driven into hiding, telling the kind of story that begins, 'It was a dark and stormy night ...' It was a terrain of the extreme and Jim and Liz empathised with it.

High up in a place exposed to the bleak beauty of the mountains they stopped for a lunch of mortadella and soft cheese on bread, all washed down with the wonderful thick peach juice of the island. The taste made them think of summer. Then the spot must have been filled with tourists, but now it was deserted. Just as well; desperate for a pee, Liz flung open the car door. The chill went straight through her as she surveyed the surrounding area. There wasn't a bush in sight. Silence filled the air. It was almost tangible.

'Crouch beside the car,' Jim suggested. Liz took one last look round and started pulling up her anorak. Then came the unmistakeable sound of a car engine. She froze. The car rounded the mountainside and stopped, facing them.

'Damn,' she said, looking round for another spot. There was nothing for it. Ambling, like a woman bent on a nature trail, Liz crossed the road, walking away from the two cars. She was aiming for a little gulley where a stream had carved a niche between the rocks. There she'd be screened from both cars. At last! Sighing with relief, she raised her anorak once more. Then it started again. The car drove slowly past, an entire gaping family inside, looking first at her, then at Jim in the car perched on the edge of the road. Why didn't they just bugger off? she thought with anguish. Pretending to inspect the stones, she waited. But the car pulled up again, also waiting and watching. Resigned, Liz trudged back and told Jim to start the engine.

'Did you have your pee?' he asked. She shook her head and glanced out of the window at the company.

'They think we've broken down.' Jim laughed and started the engine. He turned the car round, and the good samaritans drove off, satisfied. 'Thank God,' Liz said. She wrenched open the door, leapt out and crouched quickly, her moan of delight filling the air and making Jim think of Patsy Fortismere.

The mountainous hinterland of Taormina finally took them north, to the motoroad. It was late and Erice was still a long way off, so they decided to bed down for the night in Cefalu. Most of the hotels were beyond the town, on the beach road. Most were closed. But one vast complex had remained open.

It was in the charge of an attractive young woman, who, taking pity on them gave them the keys to a luxurious room with, she said, a good view of the dramatic outline of Cefalu further along the sands. They might like to visit the town later, as the hotel restaurant was closed.

Jim's stomach was rumbling as they trudged through deep carpets down empty corridors to the door with their number on it. She was right. It was a nice room.

They stood on the balcony looking at the advertised view: Cefalu cramped under the cliff, its towering cathedral standing like King Canute against the tide. The late sun glanced on its towers for a brief instant, then left them in shadow. The beach itself was pale and empty. They tried to imagine what the place was like in high season, the sands crowded, the hotel full, the restaurants open. They ate some souvenir crystallised orange and wandered out, collecting pumice stones on the beach.

It was then it came in. Liz felt it approaching like a thick dark cloud and, as it hit her, she reeled. Her stomach turned. She retched and cried out to the four corners:

'Who *is* this?'

Fed up, Jim waited for her to sort it out. He was tired of all this, tired of the attacks that came unexpectedly like witches on invisible broomsticks. Liz had curled up on the sand. She felt weak, dizzy. Her eyes were closed. She was trying to identify the invader.

'It's Nathan,' she gasped. 'He's doing something wrong. Something against me.'

'Tell him to sod off,' Jim snapped.

'*You* tell him!' she snapped back. Then, 'Please don't let's fight. That's what they want. Divide and rule.'

Jim sighed. 'Sorry,' he said. He sat beside her on the cold sand, playing with a pumice while she retched convulsively.

'Whatever has he done?' she gasped.

'Soon know,' Jim answered, 'once we're back.' Liz grew silent. She hadn't looked so far ahead. It frightened her.

'What are you going to do?' she asked. 'I mean after the holiday?'

'I don't know.' Jim hurled the pumice along the beach and watched a stray dog run after it. 'Depends.'

'On what?' He shrugged. 'Did you mean it about going to India?'

168

'Sure. Shall we go find something to eat or are you going to throw up all night?'

'The worst's over,' she said. Then, as they walked along the sands to Cefalu, she added, 'Or is it still to come?'

Palermo gave Liz a headache, so they skirted the town on the motoroad and kept on for Erice. Both were exhausted; she from pain, he from the relentless interfering presence of 'The Family'. He'd be glad when he could escape into the conference hall!

'Where is it?' she asked, searching the horizon as they followed the signs from Trapani.

'Straight up,' Jim answered.

It was like climbing through a hole in the sky; the last refuge. The triangular fortress of Erice, perched miles high on the tip of a rock, had given sanctuary to the Knights Templars when there was no place left to go, and had resisted all comers. Car engines burned when they reached the summit, and the smell of rubber pervaded the maze of narrow streets as cars went round in circles looking for somewhere to stop. Lanterns shone on the street corners, highlighting the cobbled alleys, walled in, windowless, doors barred. The whole town was turned in on itself, Arab style. Life was enclosed as if in purdah, enjoyed in private in tiny garden courtyards behind thick, eyeless walls.

Blankly the patron gave them the key to their room and left them to carry up their own bags. It was an old house. Its roots went deep down into the rock of history and gave the place strength. It was full, because of the conference, but very quiet. Unconsciously people talked in low voices, averting their eyes from one another as though afraid to break some secret spell. Closing the door of their room, Jim and Liz put down their bags and collapsed on the bed. They lay still for a while, digesting the unfamiliar atmosphere.

169

'There's something missing,' Liz said eventually. Jim turned to look at her. There were tears glistening in the corners of her eyes.

'What?' he asked.

'They've stopped bothering me,' she said. He turned back to looking at the ceiling.

'Thank God for that,' he said. She started giggling and slowly he joined in.

The restaurant was expensive and cold which, perhaps, accounted for its emptiness. Oil paintings hung on the walls and antiques lined the corridors. The dinner service was of bone china and the silver was genuine. A log fire blazed tantalisingly some distance from their table. A German (was he here for the conference?) ate alone at the other side of the room. The ceiling was high as a barn and was hung with chandeliers. Neither Jim nor Liz said much. The psychic silence, if welcome and extremely pleasant, was nevertheless eerie. They really had escaped through a hole in the sky; a sort of Bermuda Triangle. No-one could find them there. To all intents and purposes, they had disappeared from the face of the earth. Relaxed at last, both felt the weight of tiredness creep up on them and went early to bed, where they slept a long and dreamless sleep.

Liz accompanied Jim to the conference centre the following morning. Like everything else, it was well camouflaged – a church restored to the original outside, but modernised inside to luxurious business standards. It seemed Erice was often host to conventions of one sort or another. Reluctantly, Liz left him introducing himself to the other delegates around the waiting coffee cups then, ignoring her map, she wandered into the maze of narrow streets.

Punic, Roman, Norman and Baroque were blended by stone and lichen into pleasing harmony. Discreet, the cafés and restaurants hid themselves, while the bank and town hall melted into the walls.

Were there any shops, or had she missed them? There weren't many people about, and those who were passed unobtrusively. She really was alone at last! No voices to torment her, no poison darts invading her, no clouds of darkness to send her brain spinning. It was strange. She wasn't used to being just herself, without those alien forces to grapple with.

Coming suddenly to one side of the town, she leant over the castle walls and saw, as from a plane, the earth beneath. What merciful hand had guided her and Jim to this spot? She breathed deeply, looking from earth to sky and thanked God for it. Here, free from external interference she would be able to orientate, to see clearly what she was, good or evil. Circling the town, she reached the lower gate, where her steps turned, leading her up the hill to the Cathedral. Many a beleaguered knight had climbed these cobbled streets before her, passing through the ancient portal to pray for protection inside its sheltering walls. She pushed the wooden door and entered.

It was a simple church, whose soaring arches lifted the spirit and the eyes high over the altar where a golden light seemed to radiate from the stone and fill the space above her head. It was very peaceful. 'The Lord thy God is a jealous God'. But not here. Here there was no judgement. Not yet. Something held it in abeyance; even for those who had tasted of the tree of knowledge. Liz slid down the aisle and sat in a pew.

A priest was there in the choir stall, talking in low tones to a young man. He glanced up as she sat and then, ignoring her, continued his conversation. She was free to let her thoughts wander in this House of God which neither welcomed her nor turned her away.

What, if anything, did it have to say to her? 'Thou shalt not take the name of the Lord Thy God in vain'. As a child she'd thought that meant not saying 'damn' and 'blast' and so on. But now ...? Had she not committed other blasphemies? Had she not idolised The Father? On the other hand if he was God's messenger, she had blasphemed by denying him. What a predicament, to be done for either way! 'Thou shalt not tempt the Lord Thy God'. She had certainly done that by tasting of the tree, and sorrow had been her reward; pain and sorrow. Better forget all she'd ever learnt. What good had it done her to aspire to spiritual heights? How arrogant she'd been! But having learnt, how could she now forget? Tears stung her eyes. The light sparkled in them, blinding her, as she looked up into the golden haze and half saw the dove that hovered high over the altar. She wiped the tears and looked harder. It *was* a dove; God's harbinger of peace. It summed up the whole town. Suddenly the young man left. The priest stayed on, watching her. He made a move, as if to approach her, and she fled.

She was suspended by a thread. Judgement was withheld ... temporarily. She would not go to hell ... yet. In need of a bracer, she sought a coffee bar and found one through an inconspicuous door in a side street.

It was a long narrow room with a shop counter down one side and a bar at the far end. Sitting at the bar she ordered an espresso. It was served her, as ever, in total silence.

Suddenly she was aware of a strange sensation, something cold sucking the back of her head. She looked up straight into the eyes of Christ. Clear and uncritical they were gazing at her from a coloured print, pinned to the wall. Mildly shaken, she dragged her eyes away and drank her coffee. Automatically she repeated in her head, 'Our Father ...'

She finished the coffee, paid and left the café, glancing back momentarily at the poster. She was very tired. It wasn't lunchtime, yet she needed to sleep. She went back to the hotel and lay down on the freshly made bed.

She was still repeating ... 'Forgive us our trespasses as we forgive them'. Forgive ... and forget? But she was not forgiven. Not yet. Christ's clear eyes were still considering her and judgement had not yet been made. Christ who held the keys to the gates of heaven and hell might yet decide against her.

Suddenly her heart was aching. She hadn't meant to do any wrong! All she'd wanted was to be one with God. Wouldn't he forgive her her mistakes? She slipped into an uneasy sleep in which she saw herself as Magdalen, and woke knowing she had blasphemed. Still she was not judged, but she knew the thread she hung by was very fine indeed.

She had missed lunch and emerged to find the town shut up for its siesta. Only the conference centre was open for business. Was Jim enjoying himself? She hoped so. She walked past the converted church and on to the town square, her stomach rumbling. Finding a little shop she bought some bread and cheese and took them to the Balio Gardens, where Venus' fountain splashed and the stray cats gathered to share her meal. She enjoyed their society. The gang had its hierarchy, the young kittens were indulged and allowed to tease their elders playfully. The warlords had first choice of the best morsels. The queens rounded up their young, fought off the greedy toms and all, warily trusting, circled her round and round, mewing for more, long after she'd finished.

She felt lightheaded and lighthearted, almost happy. Suspension of judgement was not so bad. If only she knew where to go next ...

In the evening, Jim returned, bright-eyed and stimulated from the day's encounters. He didn't mind her silence. He chattered on about the earth's resources and the ozone layer and she listened, remembering her own previous interest. In another life, before India, she had been CND, anti-nuclear, and would have been

Greenpeace, too, if she'd heard of it. Thank goodness some people had been working on saving the earth while she'd been disappearing up herself, she thought. She felt humble before Jim's enthusiastic involvement. She felt shut out. Eventually, seeing her sad eyes, Jim paused and said:

'And what have you been doing with yourself?' She didn't know what to say. She shook her head.

'Wandering around,' she said, and told him how she'd shared her lunch with some cats. She gave an entertaining account of their antics, embroidering to please him. She was rewarded by his warmth and comfort and when they went to bed, she nestled in beside him, feeling safer in his arms.

When she woke he was up already, working on his address. She eyed him from the bed.

'Can I come and hear you?' she asked. He sighed, considering the matter.

'I don't know. It would be a bit of a palaver getting you in ...'

'Oh. Well. Never mind.'

'I'll try if you like.'

'No no. It's alright.' Obviously he didn't want her there. They ate breakfast together and, as on the previous day, she escorted him to the conference centre.

'Good luck!' she shouted after him. He turned and smiled, waving back at her, before being swamped by the Japanese delegation who carried him along with them to the church doors. For one crazy moment, she wondered if they were the same Japanese they'd seen in Taormina, but the thought was driven off by an attack of panic as Jim disappeared from sight and the long, lonely day stretched ahead of her. She stayed for a while, guessing at the nationality of the various groups who followed in later, then turned away, nursing an ache in her heart.

Grey streets led from one to another, taking her round

in circles. She was back at the church. He was inside, perhaps even now making his address to the conference with no more thought of her than as if she had never existed. He was good at shutting things out. She wished he would teach her the knack. She turned away and walked on. Of course, she thought, this was merely temporary. He would be back that evening, and at night they would curl up together as they had done the night before. There would be many nights of comfort. How many?

She had stopped walking and was standing staring at the bell tower by the Church of St Giuliano. She was remembering his body curled around her back, warming her, his arm holding her. They had fitted together like pieces in a puzzle and she had glowed from the sensation of completeness. Such a precious thing, she feared to lose it. Was it merely the magic of Erice? Would it be different tonight? What would happen when he went to India? Dear God, suppose he met 'The Family'. Suppose they drew him in, as they'd drawn her, turning him against her? She couldn't bear it. She couldn't possibly bear it. She would die, go mad! Why, he was her anchor and her strength. He alone preserved her from a living hell. Without him, there was chaos; with him was life, love.

Suddenly the bell started clanging. She looked up at the bell tower. For a second she stood, head ringing, not a clue where she was. Then, looking down she saw across the road where a door stood open, revealing a baby's cradle, rocking, rocking. She took a step towards it, then a shadowy face came between, peering at her, shutting out the cradle, shutting the door and she was left, forlorn. The ache in her heart turned to a piercing grief.

She stood in the piazza, sobbing, calling the cruelty that has derived her womb fulfilment. This was not fair. This had been below the belt. It had risen up like a bolt from the blue to shake her at the roots. Drying her tears, she retreated from the bells and made her way to the quiet familiarity of the gardens. Would her child have been any worse than anyone else's? She would never know. Unless Jim was to give the lie to this story of incest? For a moment, her heart leapt at the possibility. But suppose, instead, he discovered that she really was descended from Jane and Robert. Could she possibly bear his disgust? Better he didn't go! Better she never knew! She was too old for children now. His love for her was enough. She would hang onto that. If he loved her. What if he didn't?

But another fear rushed in on the heels of the first. *If they let her!* Father had powers, she was only too aware of them, and his curse was very effective. Hadn't she exhausted herself in the struggle to fend off his ill-wishing? 'If you're not with me you're against me, and if you're against me I'll drag you down to hell!' Suppose he bent his thought against Jim? Would he be able to defend himself, or would some fatal 'accident' befall him? Were her prayers enough to keep him safe? Why, she was not saved herself let alone able to save others! Leaning against the fountain of Venus she rocked herself in a misery of fear. Loving him, how could she possibly bear to lose him? No. Better not risk it. She would settle for Jim, as long as God allowed it.

Her mind made up, Liz was calm again. It was almost noon and the shops would soon be closing. The cats, gathering round the garden urns, were mewing hopefully. So she hurried off to her little grocer's and bought lunch.

On her way back, Liz noticed a small art gallery. She hadn't seen it before. According to the poster outside, it was currently holding an exhibition of local artists. It was closed now, but opened again from 4 to 8 p.m. She resolved to have a look at it later and meanwhile hurried on to feed the cats. They greeted her like an old friend.

As she watched them eat, she felt a momentary pang

of guilt. She knew this was plain self-indulgence, for the following day the cats would look for her in vain. Or perhaps, she consoled herself, there were others like her to take pity on them. She hoped so. She had brought them a feast today: bread, cold meats and real cat biscuits. There was plenty for everybody, and the threatening howls and whines soon gave way to little chirrups and mews as the skirmishing ceased. She enjoyed watching them, and though most of them made off as soon as their stomachs were filled, the odd one or two hung around, rubbing against her legs. Quelling fears of rabies she bent to stroke them and was rewarded by their gentle purring. But even the need for love was soon assuaged and she was left alone to study her map. She ought to take in some sights before the gallery opened. She had plenty of time. Perhaps the castle?

It was closed, of course, but it didn't really matter. The whole point of the place was the extraordinary view it commanded. In ancient times, the castle had been the abode of Venus' priestesses, who kept a close watch on passing ships in the far distant bay below. The sailors had been their most frequent customers, though it was a wonder they had any energy left for sexual antics after climbing the precipitous rock to reach them. The Normans and the Spaniards had held the place since, a Christian fortress against the infidel. How many people had found their last refuge there? There was no way out but up into the rich, turquoise-blue sky. Such finality ought to make her afraid, but it didn't. Instead it gave her a sense of freedom. Hurrying back towards the gallery, Liz was stopped again, this time by a little shop whose window displayed a few discreet souvenirs, pictures and postcards of the town.

Suddenly, longing to buy them, she went inside and discovered the town's art shop. It had everything, from easels down to HB pencils. Her heart beat faster as she inspected the quality of the paper. Subtle shades gave

177

background to softest, smoothest pastels which, dusting the surface, caught the light, transforming paper into the luminosity of sky and shining sea.

Like a child in Santa's Grotto she could no more resist such treasures than fly to the moon! She emerged, face glowing, laden with parcels and without a single post-card. Well, she could make her own record of the place! How much longer were they going to be there? One more day if she could persuade Jim to stay? Why had she wasted so much time!

Hurrying back to the hotel, she passed the gallery. She hesitated outside, then ducked under the low doorway into the shadowy interior. Glancing quickly through she saw many pictures of the town in all its moods, but none of them evoked the magic of the place as she'd known it. They were recognisable in material terms but not in those of the spirit. Surely she could do better?

Inspired, she swept from the rooms, catching sight of a poster by the door. She did a double take. It was in English! An advertisement for an exhibition at the Royal Academy in London; Monet, the series paintings. It was on until the 9th of December. Perhaps she and Jim could see it when they got back!

Suddenly, going back seemed possible. There would be life after Erice. She and Jim were inseparable, she could see that. All her visions of the future included him. She would go to art classes. She would use Jim as a model! He mustn't go to India. What would she do without him? For Liz, playing happily with colour and texture, the hours before Jim's return passed quickly, the griefs of the morning forgotten.

Jim burst in, eyes glistening, full of his own success. His address had been well received, so well that he had been invited by the Australian delegation to attend a conference there next month! He had never been to Australia! It'd be great! Feeling just a little like a punch bag, Liz smiled her congratulations. It was wonderful, if it was what he wanted. At last Jim heard the reservation in her voice.

'I'm sorry I can't ask you to come,' he said.

'It'd be too expensive,' she agreed. 'We've already spent a lot of the house money and there's got to be something left to live on.' Jim's face took on a wary look. They hadn't spoken of the house since leaving England. The whole complicated business had yet to be thrashed out. But not now. He was too tired and she looked strained.

'One good thing,' he consoled her, 'I'll be able to break my journey one way. I could stop off in India.' Liz's jaw dropped.

'Oh,' she fluttered, 'you're still thinking of going, then?'

'Sure. Don't you want me to?'

'Well,' she began, 'I've been thinking ...' she couldn't look at him, 'I really don't see the point.'

'You don't see the point?' Jim shouted.

'There's no need to yell!' Glancing up at him, then away again she said unhappily, 'I'd've thought you'd be glad I wasn't bothered any more ... I've put it all behind me. It's only a story. You said so yourself!' Jim wasn't taken in.

'Crap. What's really bugging you?'

Dismayed, Liz felt her fragile world of a few hours crumble. She bit her lip and shook her head. Jim sighed and sat beside her on the bed, prepared to coax the truth out of her. Then, for the first time, he noticed she'd been drawing. She'd done an atmospheric pastel of a street in the town; one of those where the sky seems to meet the road, on the very edge of the rock. What an insensitive bastard he'd been, coming in so full of himself when here she'd been, taking a giant leap for mankind!

'Hey!' He picked up the half-finished sheet, 'you've started work again!'

'... Just experimental,' she demurred, 'trying to get

the feel of it. I've never worked in pastels before.'

'You should take some art classes when you get back.' Liz noted the singular 'you'.

'Yes,' she replied hoarsely, 'I was thinking that myself.' Nervously, she cleared the frog from her throat. She was falling off the edge of the world and Jim wasn't even trying to hold onto her; hadn't even noticed. She tried not to cry. She'd done too much crying.

'Now tell me why you don't want me to go to India,' Jim asked quietly.

'I was scared,' she admitted. 'I was afraid of losing you.'

'How can you lose me?' Jim reasoned, 'you don't own me.'

'Of course not! I didn't mean ...'

'Yes, you did.' Liz took a deep breath and let it out very slowly.

'Yes I did,' she admitted. 'I'm scared of what might happen, to come between us. I mean, so much could happen. Especially if you went to India ... Would you get in touch with "The Family?"' Jim stared in disbelief.

'Am I crazy?'

'*They* might try and get in touch with *you*.'

'How could they? They won't even know I'm there!'

'How can you be sure of that? He can read our thoughts!' Jim was unimpressed. 'Alright, you might bump into someone, and ... you don't know them, you don't know how persuasive they are. They twist everything. They can end up making you believe black's white and day's night and the moon's made of green cheese, if they want!'

'I've noticed,' he said wryly.

'Suppose they told you things about me ...?'

'What could they say?'

'Lies. To turn you against me!'

'I wouldn't listen.'

'They'd make you.'

'The Koreans didn't manage, why should they?' His pale eyes witnessed her every wriggling attempt to avoid coming to the point. It was the one thing that her honest nature didn't want to face. But she must.

'What about this incest thing?' she blurted at him. At last, he thought. 'Suppose it's true?'

'Suppose it is,' he said carefully, 'would you be able to cope with it?' Unable to answer, she threw the question back at him.

'Would you?'

'Stop trying to project your own fears onto me, Liz!'

His anger silenced her. He was beside himself. For the first time in his life Jim had been prepared to risk involvement. He had been ready to launch himself into action on her behalf, like a knight to the rescue. And now she wanted to deny him, as though he wasn't a man at all, never had been, never would be, his humanity fading into ghostliness because he had never really lived. Frustration tore at him. She ought to release his powers and instead she was binding him in chains. He began walking to and fro in the restricted space of the room. Suddenly he stopped, and, looking directly at her, said,

'This is hopeless!' Liz shook her head miserably. What had she done?

'I'm sorry,' she said. 'I've loused it up, haven't I?' Now she could see the morning's panic for what it was and felt more and more ashamed. 'I'm really sorry. I've been using you like a life-belt. Or a lucky charm or something. And it's all wrong, I know. You'll laugh, but you've no idea how scared I am of losing you ... for completely selfish reasons. I mean I feel pretty safe here, but once we've left the protection of this place, I know I'll die a thousand deaths every time you say goodbye to me, wondering if you'll get knocked down in the street or your plane will crash or you'll fall ill, and ... it's not just I'll feel it'll be my fault, rightly or wrongly, but I'll be completely lost without you. That's the truth. And it's no good. I know it's not. It's no good.'

The shock of what seemed to have happened suddenly but had been creeping on them for a long time, stunned them both into silence. Liz was pale. The day's hope drained into desolation. With terrifying clarity she now saw that while Erice had sheltered her from the evils without, it had revealed the evils within. The only problems she had to face here were her own. And it was no good using Jim as an excuse to postpone the evil day, she would have to face herself sooner or later. Because, meanwhile, what would she be doing to Jim?

She looked at him, his face grey, morosely staring at his shoes. He'd been so happy when he came in. She couldn't do it to him. She touched his hand. He turned to her, eyes full of betrayal. She flinched when she saw, nearly giving in to tears, but forced herself to say in a voice that was almost steady:

'Jim, I think maybe we'd both be better off alone.' The silence swallowed what was left of her mind. She was vacant of thought or emotion. Jim shifted and sighed.

'Yeah,' he agreed. 'I've not exactly been fair to you either, have I? I've had you all tied up ... and who am I to say how you should run your life?' He sucked on his teeth, then said, 'I won't stand in the way of your selling the house. I mean, you can do what you like with it.'

'Thanks,' she answered automatically. 'I'll pay you back when ...'

'Sure ...' He stood, absently looking round the room, wondering whether he should pack his bags. The cue seemed to have come and gone. Liz also stood, politely, like a hostess with an unwilling guest.

'Me too,' she said. 'I mean, I really hope you'll be happy, Jim.' A pair of lemons, they hovered, not knowing what to do next. Then his hand reached out and touched hers, and her fingers responded, reassuring, warm, and he took her hand and somehow she had moved towards him and he to her and, touching, they embraced, tears wetting one anothers' cheeks.

'I love you,' he said.

'I love you too,' she said. 'I haven't dared say before.'

They made love for the first time, fearing it was the last, but knowing it couldn't be. It was too natural, too generous, too kind a love to be anything but forever.

Both were shaken. Their joy, so suddenly, so unexpectedly released, was threatened beforehand. They protected it in the armour of silence, and holding onto one anothers' hands, they ventured out to eat that night. But where to go? Intrigued by a restaurant sign which led into a garden, they followed a trail down winding paths, under an archway, along an alley, through a gate, onto a lawn and on the verge of giving up, they saw beyond, the curtained windows of a restaurant glowing dimly in the darkness.

At last, they thought, food, warmth and welcome! But an unsmiling woman admitted them to a huge and empty room where the only sound was the crackling of logs in the distant grate. Then, having presented them with menus, she wandered off. They shivered, wondering why among so many empty tables they had been shown to one so far from the fire. When she turned up again, they ordered, and the woman went off to cook for them. Evidently it was a one-woman show. Jim and Liz looked at one another and grinned. They didn't dare say anything for fear of being heard, but their eyes said, 'Isn't it a funny world?' They entwined their legs under the table, as much to keep warm as to be friendly, and they were relieved when a group came in from the conference, talking noisily. Jim greeted them, but seeing he had company, they politely chose a separate table. Liz eyed them curiously. The woman was American and strident, one of the others was clearly East European, perhaps Czech? They were talking shop.

'Better them than me,' Jim chuckled. Reassured, Liz relaxed. Instead of invading their privacy, the presence of the other group protected them by distracting the hostess. So, they were free to enjoy the comradely silence, the hot food, and knee covertly nuzzling knee, reminder of the world to which, fed and watered, they would soon be able to return.

Liz was smiling when, hand in hand, they left the restaurant and made their thankful way back home. Home was their room. It embraced them on entering as though it remembered the afternoon, and they came to life again in its fold, making love, affectionately, playfully, as natural mates.

They slept well, Jim not dreaming at all and Liz in technicolour. She had entered her picture. The grey street had become a corridor, door opening off at either side. She kept trying them. The first contained her mother and behind her the crinolined and whiskered figures of her ancestors. Her mother screamed her name and made a grab for her, catching at her skirt. The second revealed India, women in saris, incense, and Nathan at the door, hands stretched out to drag her in. But hurrying past, she opened a third door. This time Jim came out, leaving behind a Red Indian smoking his peace pipe. Jim smiled at Liz and took her hand, urging her up the corridor. But she looked back and, terrified, saw a thousand writhing hands snaking from the open doors, seeking a hold on her. Afraid, she turned to Jim, but he was just a ghost in the corridor, and as they passed, another door sprang open. Inside was a cradle with a baby, rocking, rocking. The baby was crying, but as Liz's hands reached out to take it, Jim tore her away again. Where was he taking her? With his ghostly hand he was speeding her faster and faster past all the unopened doors, to the end of the corridor where the wall had grown a new door, half open. She tried to see what was beyond it, but all she could see was blue sky and scudding clouds. Was she to step off into empty space? Was that it? Moaning in terror, she was pulled towards the door. A blast of air rushed past her and she stepped out....

Waking, she found Jim's naked body lying beside her. It was warm and solid, and he murmured pleasantly when she touched his flesh. Where were they going, she and her mate? God knew. They couldn't stay in Erice forever. She sighed, dreading the exit from its protecting walls, the descent back to earth. Would they be waiting for her, like wolves howling round the base of a tree? Would their hands reach out to take her? Sensing her distress even in his sleep, Jim turned towards her, one arm shielding her. She lay still, comforted by the warmth of his breath on her cheek and listened, as his steady breathing exhorted her to sleep. She would need all her strength for tomorrow. She snuggled in beside him and, still sleeping, he accommodated her, offering his shoulder as a cushion for her head.

As they descended the winding path their antennae quivered, searching for sign of the enemy. But the expected cacophony of demons was mercifully absent. They drove on, heading south to Agrigento, hardly able to believe their luck. What had happened? Having lost them, had they panicked, careering off in all directions? It certainly felt like it. They laughed quietly and said little. They had learnt discretion. It was better to avoid giving off signals that might lead to their discovery. They passed a quiet night at Agrigento, content to see the Valley of the Temples from the road, and drove overland the next morning to Catania and the airport.

They held hands on the plane, hardly daring to breathe for fear of attracting attention. But, changing at Rome, they found themselves still unmolested, and they homed in on Venice. They could hardly believe their luck. 'I must not think,' Liz told herself as they descended to earth. For once the directive was very much to the point. But in any case thinking was difficult. It was hard to orientate as they found themselves whisked off the earth into a new element almost as soon as they had landed.

Under cover of a grey mist that confused sea and sky, the water taxi drove them the back way into Venice. Entering the maze of canals, they slipped into the life of the city unnoticed and unremarked. The transition from craft to hotel was made swiftly, the unsmiling commissionaire ushering them inside even as the craft turned and disappeared from the empty landing stage. They could hardly believe they were safely in Venice. But, looking up at the ornate glass chandelier they suspected it. The gilt-framed pictures on the walls suggested it and the sound of lapping water that filtered through the blinds affirmed it. They stood for a moment, taking in the new situation and sighed.

'God, I'm tired!' Jim said.

'You drove one hell of a long way this morning,' Liz reminded him.

'Bed looks nice.' Liz thought the same, but they were also very hungry. 'Quick spaghetti?' he asked. She nodded, and wresting her umbrella from deep inside her case, they ventured into the town.

It was raining like it rains in the North of England, a fine drizzle that soaks you as soon as look at it. It was like being in limbo. But at least they were together. And Jim and Liz hung onto one another, huddling under their one umbrella, sorry for the lonely straggled cat that hovered round the hotel door. They stopped to talk to it until the commissionaire came out and chased it away. It looked half starved. Liz thought of her cats in the Balio Gardens and hoped someone was looking after them.

She shivered and hurried on after Jim, round the corner and up the little alleys, over tiny bridges till the empty streets gave away to crowded thoroughfares. Dazed and jostled they found themselves among the tourists and the vultures that fed off them. This was no good. They'd never find anywhere to eat here. So they escaped back into the unfrequented side streets and joined the Venetians at an Italian take-out where pizza and spaghetti vied with chicken and steak on the menu, all served up with friendly banter and a clean serviette.

This was more like it. Standing against the wall, they ate, watching the workers order and eat, watching the T.V. screen in the corner. When they'd had enough, they wrapped the leftovers in paper for the cat and took off, braver for food, returning to the hotel by St Mark's and the waterfront. All romantic ideas of drifting in gondolas faded as they observed the seasick passengers and the desperate gondoliers, struggling against the tide to keep their crafts from disappearing into the fog.

'Nice to see the place out of season,' Liz remarked.

'Not so much romantic as rheumatic,' Jim chuckled, nursing the warm pizza for the cat.

But the cat was nowhere to be seen. Reluctantly they left their offering by a pillar, the last known feline checkpoint.

'I hope the commissionaire hasn't seen us,' Liz whispered as they slipped into the hotel. And when, surprisingly, he greeted them, smiling, they jumped guiltily. But they needn't have worried.

'I have booked you a free trip to Murano in the morning,' he beamed. Liz and Jim looked at him blankly. His brow creased with irritation. 'Most famous island in the lagoon. Famous for glassworks. You like it.'

'Oh,' Jim said. 'Thanks a lot.'

As they fled through the hall towards the lift, the commissionaire called after them:

'Taxi collect you at 9.30 in the morning. Sharp!'

They waved and smiled as the lift doors closed, then collapsed giggling in the corner.

'Do we have to go?' Liz asked as she studied the guide book.

'Why not?' Jim asked.

'It's just there's a few places I'd really like to see. The Accademia for a start, then there's the Guggenheim collection and this church, the Frari.'

'We've got the whole weekend,' Jim replied, yawning. 'Come to bed.'

Next morning, promptly at 9.30 a.m., the water taxi arrived to whisk them away. The driver was unusually chatty and insisted on pointing out places of interest through the light veil of water which still hung over the lagoon. He explained that whatever they bought at Murano would be free of tax. They could even arrange shipping. Jim and Liz looked steadfastly ahead through the spattered windows, their hearts sinking faster than Venice itself. What had they let themselves in for? Arriving at Murano, they were given the million dollar treatment, a quick look at someone blowing the fluted glass tubes that went into the same ornate chandeliers that graced their hotel room, onto an historical collection of glass, and then to the showrooms. The lurking sense of being mistaken for someone else – a millionaire for example – now crystallised into certainty. They hardly dared admire the exhibits for fear their praise would be taken for a firm order.

'Imagine that in Fowler Street,' Liz whispered in Jim's ear, as they gazed on the ruby-faceted goblets that glowed gem-like from the illuminated table.

'Have we enough money for a paperweight?' Jim muttered. Liz shook her head.

'Not at that price!' she hissed.

'Well, look around,' Jim implored her, 'I've a feeling we're going to have to buy something if we ever want to get out of here!'

They went back through the showrooms. It was all

quite impossible. Their host's smile had become more and more fixed. Finally, losing patience, he directed them to the final stage of their tour. And here at last Jim saw their way out. 'Like these beads?' he asked.

'Nice,' Liz replied, fingering the gorgeously coloured glass.

'How much?' Jim asked.

'900,000 *lire*, *signori*.' The host replied much too quickly. Liz gasped. 'I can do them for 750,0000, special prize for the lovely lady,' he added with a sigh.

'Done,' Jim answered, getting out his wallet. They were ushered quickly out of the factory and informed where they could wait for a bus.

'Do you like your prize?' Jim asked, as the water bus speeded away from the jetty. Liz laughed and nodded. She was enjoying this. At the various stops, normal working people clambered in and out, mildly curious of the foreigners, but not that curious. Liz smiled at a baby, and wondered what a soldier was doing on board, what work that woman did, or whether she was merely going shopping. It was the same the world over, on an Indian bus, or the Geordie metro, Liz felt at home. Here she could almost pretend to be normal. When finally they arrived back at St Mark's, they grabbed a quick hamburger before setting out on a serious bit of tourism. Now at last she would see her pictures.

Liz gave way when Jim asked to see the Doge's Palace first. One side of it was covered in scaffolding, giving the impression that if they didn't get in quick it wouldn't be there to see for very much longer. An edge of the terrace had collapsed already and they teetered over the waving mosaic, dismayed at the extent of the damage. Liz was a little bored. Somehow, she felt it wasn't what she'd come to Venice for. Uneasily she wondered what she'd expected and forced herself to concentrate like Jim, on the guided tour. He was just like he'd been with those volcanic rocks. It was quite annoying, how, in a sea of uncertainty, he could inspect the various species of fish. When, at last, the tour was finished, it was tea time, and both being tired they wandered back to the hotel. Limbo was exhausting.

'That's the church where Vivaldi used to be a violin teacher,' Jim read from the guide book.

'The Pieta,' Liz read over his shoulder. 'It's got a Tiepolo on the ceiling.'

'And it's having a concert tonight!' Jim squinted at the poster. 'The Tallis Singers. Singing Palestrina!'

'But they're English!' Liz complained.

'It'd be lovely!'

'Alright, I suppose so,' Liz agreed. She waited while he went inside for the tickets, and pondered on the dangerously leaning tower she had seen from one of the inlets further along the front. Was she losing her sense of reality or were these people purposely blinding themselves to the stones crashing around their ears? Life must go on; the show must go on; business as usual. The routine of daily life had a hypnotic effect which was catching. One might even fool oneself into thinking everything was alright. A Martian might look on planet Earth in the same way, wondering how humanity could ignore the hole in the ozone layer, or the invasion of the human psyche by an alien virus. Was that what Jim was trying to do? Uneasily, Liz watched him return, knowing that in this limbo, fate had something in store for them.

Later, as they sat on the hard seats in a cold draught listening to heavenly music, Liz surveyed the 'Triumph of Faith' painted on the ceiling, the wedding cake decor, the inscrutable faces of the scattered few who formed the audience. The English voices joined hearts and soul to lift even their spirits, till the joy of giving and receiving floated tangibly on the air and performers and audience were one. It was as though God Himself was listening. If, Liz thought, out of nothing, such miracles can still happen, then all is not yet lost. Faith fortified, Jim and

Liz retired to sleep in an internal silence, too deep for any invader to disturb.

Next morning, Liz knew she wanted to go to the Frari.

'I must see the Titians!' she insisted.

'I know, dear,' Jim prevaricated, 'but, I mean, there's this Guggenheim place and the Rialto Bridge and so many other things. Besides, it's Sunday! You can't crash in on a church service! Remember what happened at Durham.'

Liz sighed and tried to be patient. They took a water bus to the Guggenheim and inspected the Magrittes, the Warhols, the Bacons, all the trendies of the twentieth century. They left them cold.

Liz used the lavatory and they wandered out again. They walked the streets aimlessly, marvelling at the abundance of fur coats (hadn't they heard of animal rights?) brought out of mothballs for the Sunday display, and wondering where to go next. There were so many churches, so many little turnings and bridges. Liz was feeling very tired. Ahead of them a huge brick building loomed. It didn't look like anything very much.

'Shall we go in?' she asked. Jim shrugged his acquiescence. They were surprised by a turnpike at the entrance. You had to pay to enter a church? They paid and went in. Glancing at the pamphlet they had been given at the ticket office, they realised suddenly that this was in fact the Frari, Titian's church!

'Well,' Jim laughed, 'you got your wish!'

But Liz wasn't looking at paintings. Something was drawing her. It was on the far side of the church. Looking, she saw a simple statue of the Virgin, candles flickering in front of it. She started walking towards it. She felt excited as though something was going to happen. It was getting colder. Her pulse was racing. She stood before it and was immediately embraced by a whirlwind of freezing air. She gasped.

'Jim,' she called quietly. 'Come here.' Jim came and

stood beside her. 'Can you feel it?'

He nodded. He was holding his hands out, feeling the sparkling vibrations as they whirled around them. She was there. Mary, the Virgin, was there.

This was why they had come to Venice. This was it. And now Liz didn't know what to ask, to pray for, or to say. Her heart was bursting with gratitude. All she could think was:

'Please forgive me everything.'

Immediately, a voice, young and lovely, called out to her, 'Of course I forgive you everything! I love you!'

With a surge of unbelievable relief, Liz sobbed. She could hardly bear the love that was flowing out to her. It opened her wounded heart, pouring into every crevice, till she was flooded with it, floating on a sea of love. There had been no questions asked, no criticisms, no punishment, nothing. There was nothing else to say. Except thank you.

Trembling, Liz went forward to light a candle. Jim lit one, too. There was so much she wanted to ask, but it had been pre-empted. She had been told she was loved and forgiven. That was all there was to it. Nothing more was required. Jim started to drift away. She wanted to stay, but felt she should follow him, and perhaps she should, anyway. Reluctantly she left the statue, walking with Jim down the church, but the voice pursued her, like a bird on the wing, urgently repeating over and over again:

'I love you! I love you!'

Pale with joy, shaking, they waited for the water bus.

'You felt it, didn't you?' she asked. Jim nodded.

'Yes,' he answered. 'No matter what we've done, no matter how far things have gone, she forgives everybody everything, without question, without criticism, without judgement.'

'Yes,' Liz wiped the flowing tears from her cheeks. 'I've never felt anything like that before. Never.'

'So, you see,' Jim said, taking her hand, 'there's hope.'

PART THREE

PART THREE

... I knew Nathan had done something. I felt it on the beach at Cefalu. I think that to wish evil on anyone, no matter what they've done, has to be wrong. It means you're allying yourself with the forces of darkness. Nathan had become dark. Poor Nathan. When I think of the things he said, I still want to cry. I went through a kind of marriage service with him and even if the marriage was never consummated, it still gives him a kind of power over me. So his letter's had its effect. Do you want to know what he said? Shall I write it down for you? If I don't you mightn't realise how terrible it was. You might think I was just hurt because he rejected me, hurt pride and so on. As if I had much pride left! Well, hold your breath....

Bombay, 30th October 1990

Elizabeth,
With this letter I put you from me eternally. You are the issue of lust. Your flesh is putrid with corruption. I thank God I abstained from you. Father must have been looking after me or you would have had me in your coil and dragged me down with you. You are the most subtle kind of devil, appearing so sweet and sincere, when all the time you're undermining God's divine plan and corrupting his children. I was shown some of your early paintings and drawings. They betrayed your true nature. They are sheer pornography. What kind of mind could produce such filth? Father stopped you painting, but now I hear you're drawing pictures which will corrupt the innocence of anyone who looks on them! Father has said you will drag thousands down to

hell if you continue to express this base side of yourself. You should stop painting! No doubt you are inspired by the promiscuous relationships you are indulging in. As for your work against The Family, I hardly know what to say. How could you use our Father as you have? It is devilish to take the divine powers he gives so freely, only to use them against him, to bring down the kingdom of heaven, undoing all his work. You deserve to burn in eternal agony for what you've done. I pray for it, with all my heart. You won't hear from me again. I have to go away because of you, to cleanse myself. I exhort you to fall at Father's feet and pray for forgiveness. Though how he can ever forgive you is beyond me. May you rot in hell,
Nathan.

God, I hated writing that. It brought all the horrors back. It's like falling into a black hole and being spun round and round till you don't know which way is out. And the worst of it is knowing that maybe they're right. I am the issue of lust. And yet, rationally, I know a lot of what he says just doesn't make sense. I honestly don't see I've painted anything even remotely pornographic! I mean, an artist's got to be like a mirror, reflecting reality. So I paint what I see as truthfully as I can. That's all. I think maybe dirt, like beauty, is in the eye of the beholder!

And as for my using powers against The Family, well all I've ever tried to do is defend myself against the poison they keep transmitting! Am I not allowed to defend myself? And what work? What am I supposed to be doing against them? I've got a funny feeling I've not heard the last of this. My heart really sinks sometimes when I think what they might be plotting.

I'll never forget how it felt when we landed back in England. I know you didn't say much, but I'm sure you felt it, didn't you? Your face was grim, I know that. I'd never felt anything so sinister. It was as though they were waiting for us; like they'd met the plane; invisible but so present you could almost feel their breath hot on the

196

back of your neck. I know it terrified me. I wanted to turn back, get the next plane out. But my legs felt like lead and I was exhausted, as though I was dying. It's what they want. I feel it. I mean they want me to die; or go mad like poor Paula. But don't worry. They won't succeed, no matter how hard they try.

It's funny, I find it easier to write things down than talk about them. So I hope you don't mind me chuntering on like this. Anyway, it makes me feel as though you're still around and that's nice. Dear Jim, I miss you so much! At the airport I had this terrible feeling I might never see you again. That's why I was so funny. You were going clean out of my world, like a man going up in a space rocket. Bye bye.

God, I don't know how I managed to let you go at all. I miss you so much. I miss your sense of humour. I miss your gentle voice. I miss your strength, your stillness. And now you've gone I know how much you shielded me, just by being there. Oh no, I'm crying! These pages will be unreadable. But I can't write them out again. I just can't.

On a more practical level, the solicitor has put the house on the market. It won't fetch as much as we hoped but I don't want to hang on till the market picks up. What do you think? Also, I forced myself to do some drawing today. (Wasn't I brave?) My subject was surely beyond reproach! (Still life with carrot and chrysanthemum). Though I daresay they'd make something of it! I love you very much and I'm longing to hear your voice. I'm well in spite of everything. Enjoy Australia. Your own Lizzie.

The wet pavements reflected the sunshine, so that she walked through pools of light to the pillar box. When she got there, she looked at the black gaping slit and dropped the envelope in. She heard it fall to the bottom and stood looking at the hole. When you thought about it, everything was an act of faith, even sending a letter. She looked up. A funeral procession was going by. She looked away again quickly. Yes, in spite of all they threw at her, she would have faith. Head down she made for the shops — everyday acts kept her sane — then back to the house. It was coming in dark. She closed the curtains, remembering how last night someone had looked in. She had felt the presence and dropped her dinner on the floor. She must shut out the evil. No matter the kitchen was on the first floor. Her Peeping Tom was not made of flesh and blood. Her hand was shaking. She opened a can of beans and put some bread under the grill to toast. Then she put on the radio to stop herself thinking.

Uluru, November

Darling Liz,

At last I've got a moment to write. I had a good flight, and the Ozzies have been very hospitable, but I was absolutely shattered to begin with and didn't take too much in. They're really hot on the green issue in this part of the world. There's a strong aboriginal input here, too. Well we are on their land, more or less, right beside Ayers Rock. Matter of fact, I keep thinking about how the aboriginal attitude to the earth is like the Hopi Indians'. The earth's alive for them and has to be revered, so its magic works for humanity, not against us. I think I might go into that for my address.

The Polynesians took me for a typical Yankee and had a go at me about the American burning of chemical weapons in the Pacific as though it was all my fault. But they cooled off a bit when I told them I represented Cambridge University! There's a lot of press interest here, too. Lot of questions about what a war in the Gulf would mean to the environment. All in all it's pretty busy, and I don't get much time for myself, so forgive me if my letter's a bit short and sweet....

★

Watching television, Liz heard the banging. She turned down the sound and listened. It was coming from the kitchen. She got up slowly and walked through. The washing machine was jumping all over the floor; uneven load? She switched it off and stood waiting for the time catch to clear. She looked round uneasily. The empty house was not empty. But the evil was centred in the kitchen, where she felt a lurking presence. She jumped when the catch clicked. She must keep hold of herself. She bent to release it and checked the washing. There was nothing wrong with it. She started the machine again. It jumped, then settled down. She stood for a moment, staring into the corners by the cupboards, under the fridge, behind the door.

'Sod off!' she hissed.

There was a smell of gas. She checked the taps on the stove. They were all off. Everything was fine. She made for the kitchen door and a loud crash made her turn with a scream. A glass vase had fallen off the shelf. She cleared the mess and put salt down. She must keep her wits about her.

Uluru

Got your letter today, Were you funny at the airport? I didn't notice. I noticed your nose was cold and you needed to use your hanky. That's all. So don't get paranoid. As for Nathan's *billet doux*, you know as well as I do it's a load of crap. I know it's easy to say when it's not you who's being got at but it is all the same. By the way, may I ask whether the carrot is complete or diced, as it makes some difference to the phallic content of your piece? I have nothing to suggest re the chrysanthemum. I'm glad the house is on the market. If you take my advice you'll let the solicitor deal with it and get the hell out of there. The bastards know where you are and will practise all kinds of psychic terrorism to wear you down; so play foxy. How about paying your father a visit? He

seemed a nice enough old guy. Let me know what you decide. I'll be here till the 20th or thereabouts. I've got to go now. There's a man waiting for me. By the way, I suppose I should tell you my wife's suing me for divorce. Wants to get married again. Think I should let her? Don't let the bastards get you down!
Love, Jim.
P.S. Think seriously about going to your father's.

The other delegates were assembling in their glad rags. But Jim was in his jeans. The black face watched him hand over a letter at reception, then guided him out to the pickup. Curious eyes watched them go.

'You didn't say where you were going,' the guide said. Jim shook his head. 'Good. White men don't understand.' The guide let in the clutch and the pickup rocked off the road into the bush.

She had given up drawing and was doing the ironing. But the pressure on her head was still growing. Something was pushing her down, weighing her down into the floor. Her legs shook. She felt sick. This was getting to be a habit. It always came in at the same time, between three and four in the afternoon, when the pain flashed through her skull. Then, repeating the pattern of the day before, her heart was squeezed until there was a tight band around her chest and she was struggling for breath. There was no doubt there was an intelligence behind it; a malign intelligence. Someone, somewhere was deliberately trying to destroy her.

She made for the sofa and lay down, screwing up her courage to work on the attack. Who was it? But she couldn't concentrate, couldn't think. There was only one thing she could do. Summoning up all her energies she threw up a shield. She imagined it to be made of steel, shining, bright like a mirror. The pain vanished. Lifting her mind to the level of the shield she felt the incoming weapons exploding against it like fireworks, bouncing back whence they came. She laughed out loud. it was like *Star Wars*! Only this was real. 'Well,' she thought, 'Let them take some of their own medicine!'

In the firelight, the leathery old face watched Jim smoke.

'He knows the old ways,' the guide said. 'If you'd heard him speak ...' The old man raised his hand. He nodded. Then slowly he smiled. It was like the sun coming up. Jim smiled back.

'We understand each other,' the old man said.

Bare feet put out the fire. Darkness returned. The guide led Jim back to the pickup.

'By the way, my wife's suing me for divorce! By the way!' Bloody hell, what was the so-and-so playing at? Liz kicked the easel. 'By the way, my wife! By the way'! Liz let forth a blood-curdling yell and went out for a walk.

Uluru Centre was coming into view. They were almost back in the twentieth century. It was quite a culture shock. Jim squawked as the pickup jolted back onto the road. His guide laughed.

'Too much for you?' he asked. Jim shook his head.

'Not so different from New Mexico! My folks've got a ranch! Wanted to dig for uranium long time back. Wouldn't let them!'

'Good for you!' his guide said. 'Now I know why my grandfather likes you!' Jim was elated. It was a funny feeling, like he'd come home; like he'd tied up the two sides of himself. White man and Indian had fused and released in him an undreamt of energy. He felt he could topple mountains and fly through the clouds. He was the energy of the volcano and the speed of the laser. He was potent as the seed, pushing its head through the concrete jungle. 'Liz! Liz!' He grinned at the Rock,

201

glowing red in the morning light. 'I love you!'

It was like a star bursting on her head, showering her with tiny drops of joy that made her laugh out loud.

'You bastard, Jim!' She laughed at the waves and the gulls and the dog running across the sands. 'I love you, too!'

Entering the Centre, Jim felt her like a glow round his heart. He booked himself in for an extra couple of days and went to bed.

It was after three. Liz put down her pastels cautiously and started for home. It was strangely silent as she walked along the cliff top, well away from the edge, trusting to nothing. As she walked, she pondered on her father. Jim was right. Her dad was old now; it was time she made her peace. She could at least try to explain things. Understanding often lessens the hurt. And she had hurt him. She must have, poor old ... Suddenly, as though her own thoughts had projected the image, a funeral car passed by her in the street. She looked away from it and told herself it meant nothing.

She was afraid of her father dying. That was all. This was her last chance to make their worlds touch, before she lost him forever. Her tread became more urgent, and she was almost home before she realised it was half past four and nothing had happened. She smiled as she let herself into the house. They hadn't liked their own medicine!

Fowler Street, November 18th

Dear Jim,

Are you having me on? Of course you should let the poor cow get married again! Honestly, you are a pig! It's a good job I love you! Which reminds me, what were you doing yesterday? I know something happened and it felt very nice at this end! It was late afternoon here, so you work out when it was.

By the way, I've taken your advice. I think it *would* be a good idea to get out of here. In fact I tried to ring Dad this afternoon. I left a message on his answering machine. God knows where he is! Gallivanting, I expect. He used to be quite a ball of energy when Myra was alive. Do you remember Dad's 'fancy woman'? She was marvellous. Poor Dad. I hope he hasn't changed. Wittering again. Sorry. News is what you want. I did a nice pastel of Marsden Rock today. I thought I'd do a Monet on it and paint the same thing in different lights. It's very Bel'Isle! I'd never realised how beautiful it was here. You have to look at things with new eyes all the time, or you miss out. You see what your brain tells you, not what's there. Oh, pastels are wonderful! But my drawing technique needs brushing up. Myra used to work for the council. I wonder if Dad's got any contacts. He might get me on a course. Do you know, I'm really looking forward to seeing him again....

To celebrate, Liz put a chicken in the oven. She was singing as she prepared the veg, listening for the telephone. Then she made herself a coffee and whiled away an hour, checking the telly programmes. Television was still a miracle to her, a new toy. How things had changed in her absence! She remembered the black and white programmes so well; Andy Pandy, that sort of thing. She looked up. Was that the telephone? It might be her Dad! Or, better still, Jim! She ran down the corridor to the office and picked up the receiver. She was panting as she spoke joyfully down the line,

'Hello? Hello?' The distant crackling faded. 'Hello? Can you hear me?' she shouted. The line went dead. Liz turned cold. She was shaking as she walked back into the kitchen. 'Fools rush in ...' They were changing their attack.

As it went dark, Liz turned on all the lights. She could smell the chicken. It was good. She would have liked company. She should contact the family, *her* family, Os and Mary Jean. Os was Eve's brother. He and his wife used to help Eve run the school. But whenever she thought about getting in touch, something always stopped her. Perhaps she just wasn't ready for them. They weren't ready for her come to that! *They* hadn't made contact, had they?

She went into the kitchen and checked the chicken. Its skin was bubbling, crisp and brown. It smelt wonderful. She took it out and laid it in its dish on the draining board while she saw to the gravy. She heard a sound, like something slipping, and turning, she saw the plate jump, throwing the chicken into the air. Instinctively, she reached out to catch it. The plate smashed on the floor. Failing to catch the chicken it fell, sliding everywhere. Caught off balance, Liz slipped, landing painfully, her back wrenched. She screamed with pain.

'Bastards!' she cried. No. She didn't hear laughter. That was not laughter. She must not go mad. She got up, slowly, carefully, rubbing her back, and salvaged the meat. Then she cleaned the floor three times to remove every vestige of fat. You could eat off that floor. Her back hurt like hell. Bastards! She served up her dinner and ate. 'Let them drool!' she thought.

The Rock looked nearer than it was. Leaving the pickup behind, they went on foot as the sun downed. It grew colder and colder. Jim zipped up his anorak. His guide stopped, turning at the unexpected noise and put his finger to his lips. Then he went on again, deliberately choosing his way, following signs Jim never saw. Had he lost his old skills? Now and then he looked up. Was the aborigine using the stars to guide him? Probably. But the configurations were different here; unfamiliar. They twinkled in the vast sky, clusters, shapes that had guided men for aeons. Were they really there? Or was it just the light he saw, transmitted thousands of years ago, to reach him only now, the source long since dead. Stars, mere rays of light, determining the fate of man! How long ago had all that was happening now been predicted?

The guide stopped. Jim halted behind him and felt rather than saw the snake that crossed their path. Hesitating, the guide went on. But the snake was still with them.

'Don't be scared,' whispered the aborigine. Jim smiled in the darkness. Hadn't he carried the snake in his mouth, and sat deep in the kiva with it nestling in his lap? Wasn't he a member of the Snake Clan? And now the snake was taking him home.

Liz tried her father again. The answering machine was still on and she began to be afraid he was away. Suppose he was? What would she do? Where would she go? Suddenly she was very anxious to be clear of the house. But she must not be afraid. If she transmitted fear they would home in on it. There must be no gap in her armour. But her back hurt. Every movement was agony. She lay on the floor for a while, her legs up on a chair. It relieved the spasm and she felt a little better. The house was very quiet, listening. She must put on the armour of silence. Her thought must be still. But the pain had exhausted her. Her resources were low. She switched on the television and sat soaking up whatever it offered. The voices were company and the flickering images filled her mind, making it easier not to think. She began to relax.

Suddenly the lights went out and the screen faded. She must not be afraid. This had happened before. They were just putting on the frighteners. 'Psychic terrorism' Jim called it. She opened the curtains to let in the moonlight, then found the cupboard where the candles were kept. The matches, she knew, were by the stove. She felt her way down the corridor and into the kitchen. There was a strong smell of gas. . . .

It was the coldest, darkest part of the night. Jim was aware of presences around him. Invisible, the guardians of The Rock crowded in as they neared Uluru, watching, waiting, ready to strike. But the snake would be there before them. For it knew Jim and would test his mastery.

And Jim had not forgotten its teaching. No dark thought entered his mind and they passed on safely, looking to neither left nor right. They were very close. He could feel stirrings under his feet and his skin prickled with the static in the air. The guide made a last stop, lighting a small fire to warm some tea. Jim sat and watched the sparks rise into the sky like a swarm of fireflies. Fascinated, his eyes travelled from them up to the stars. They had wheeled round now and were in a new configuration. They twinkled brightly in the clear atmosphere. Yes, the star might be dead but its light carried on, like the dark rays of the fallen angel.

His evil still existed. It was still boomeranging round the universe two thousand years after the source had been dealt with; seeking to invade and control sympathetic souls, attacking the rest with disease and ill fortune and always seeking a new source to energise and focus it. The poison cloud that had risen like a tidal wave to meet Jim and Liz at Heathrow was focussed evil. And now it was turned on Liz. . . .

She picked up the matches and backed out of the kitchen, closing the door behind her. She was standing in the corridor. A faint light described the open doors that came off the narrow passage. One by one she shut them and stood in total darkness. Ganesha faced her from the other end of the corridor. Ganesha, guardian of the gates of hell. She took out a match to light the candle. . . .

The guide leapt back, dislodging the fire with his foot, sending sparks flying into the air.

'Watch out!' He aimed a stone.

'Leave it!' Jim whispered urgently.

As the snake lunged, he hurled his thought through the sparks, high into the heavens. . . .

'Nirvighnamastu, Ganesha!' She struck the match. . . .

The snake curled round his ankle, and settled to sleep.

Breathing deeply, Liz put down the flickering candle and eased herself to the floor to rest her back. She felt as though she'd been run over by a steamroller. The smell of gas was gone. But the attack wasn't over yet. She felt it creeping in. She threw up a shield. But it crept under it. She built a wall. But it tunnelled beneath. She withdrew into a globe, but it seeped through the glass. She drew a circle, but it was already inside. The stench of vomit rose up around her.

'You are filth. You can smell yourself? You stink! Can you see yourself? You are green, gangrenous with the sins of your fathers. Corruption eats at your soul. You are the incarnation of lust . . .'

'Hail Mary, full of grace, the Lord is with Thee. Blessed are Thou among women . . .'

The voice sucked itself into oblivion. There was silence. Liz eased herself from the floor. But her back shrieked with pain.

'Jesus!' she screamed, closing her eyes, and saw light. Her head was full of light, flashing light. She opened her eyes again. She could still see the light on the rims of her eyes, even as she peered into the darkness. She crawled towards the statue of Ganesha. Her stomach was heaving. She vomited on the floor and tasted blood. She

was in agony,. But she must not faint. She must not die
...

   'Pray for us sinners ...'

Intent on The Rock, Jim urged on the pace. The rim was
bright with gold; The Rock dark as blood. The trembling
under the earth had turned to mighty thunder as though
a regiment of horsemen galloped beneath his feet. But
they didn't pass. They kept on drumming. And as they
drummed, gravity grew stronger, drawing him down to
the earth, making it harder and harder to walk. But he
must reach The Rock. Dragged onto his knees, he
crawled. His hands and legs trembled. Those who look
on God, die. He closed his eyes. He touched The Rock.
The thunder entered him. This was the power that
created the earth and it would destroy it, too. God giveth
and God taketh away; not nuclear bombs; not a hole in
the sky. For all those things there's hope of reprieve. But
this ...! Restrained for ages, the power was awaiting the
day when it would be unleashed.

   'Thine is the Kingdom,' Jim whispered, 'the Power
and the Glory. Lord let us into Thy Kingdom.' But what
if, when it came, it destroyed them ... for ever and ever
...?

Her head was spinning. She must not faint! Her spine
screeched with pain. They were burning her throat. She
would choke, coughing on the dust!

   'Chintamani, my brother, help me!!!'

Jim's eyes sprang open.

   'Through Jesus Christ our Lord ...'

   He threw a shield across the sky. It hurtled through
time and space and sliced into the darkness.

It had stopped. They had gone. The air grew lighter over
her head and her mind floated up with it. She sobbed

208

with relief, repeating 'thank you, thank you' over and over again.

Next morning, Liz locked up the house and dropped the key in at the solicitor's.

'Get rid of the contents, too. All I want's that statue. The Indian one of the elephant-headed God. Perhaps you could arrange for it to be sent on?' Mr Platt nodded and murmured something about an address. 'I'll be with my father,' she told him, 'but if anyone asks, you don't know where I am.' Then she caught the train to London.

That afternoon, an Indian man in a grey suit appeared in Fowler Street. He looked up and down the row before knocking at the door of number eighteen. There was no answer. Peering through the dusty windows, he could see the bare boards of the downstairs room. It was empty. He stood back, looking at the derelict exterior. The guttering had gone and the wall was green where rain had poured into the wall, rotting the sill of the window beneath. He knocked again, harder. The sound echoed hollowly through the house, rousing the neighbour who flung open her sash window and leaned out, craning her neck into the street below.

'If you want the Indian takeaway it's round the corner, in Everley Street!' she told him angrily. The window slammed shut. For a few moments the Indian looked up at her, still mouthing insults behind the glass. Then he tried again, hammering on the door. The sash slid up again with a bang.

'What do you want to go making a racket like that for?' she asked in injured tones. 'My man's on nights, you know!'

'I'm sorry.' The man bowed apologetically. 'I was not aware of that. I was looking for the lady of the house.' The woman laughed harshly.

'Well you'll have to look damn hard then!'

'Why?' he asked. 'Has she gone?'

209

'I'd say! To a better place than you're likely to go to, disturbing folk like that!'

'Perhaps you could tell me where?'

'Can you not get it into your thick skull, man? She's dead!' The window slammed shut with the force of the guillotine.

Jim was holed up in a condominium overlooking Sydney Harbour. He was waiting for a flight. His Ozzie host pressed him to stay on for a while.

'At least see the Dolphinarium!' he remonstrated. 'You can't come all this way and not see that!' Jim laughed, but he was anxious. He hadn't been able to raise Liz on the phone. He toured the old town, even took a ride round the bay, but as soon as the seat came up he was on his way to the airport. It was a last minute cancellation and they had to step on it.

'More like a Pom than a Yank!' The Ozzie groused as he drove him. 'I bet you what you like, there's a Sheila at the bottom of this, you tight-lipped bastard. Am I right?' Jim grinned and, too late for normal check in, took his host's grudging handshake before entering passport control. The Ozzie looked up to check the flight time. 'Delhi?' He opened his mouth to call him back, but Jim had vanished.

Putney, November

Dear Jim,

Well, here I am. I must say, Dad was very surprised to see me. I'd left a message on his machine but he hadn't got back to me so I just turned up on his doorstep so to speak. Long lost daughter etc! I'd hurt my back and hobbled in like Long John Silver. I must have looked like death. I know I felt like it. Anyway, it took some of the awkwardness out of the situation. I mean it's difficult to ask searching questions of anybody who's flat on their back on your kitchen floor with their legs waving in the air! I told him I'd skidded on some fat, which was true. I'd dropped a chicken actually, but that's a long story. Anyway, he said:

'There's been a call for you.' I must have looked blank, because he said, 'From your solicitor. A Mr Platt.' Then he handed me the message. I didn't have my glasses on. They were in my handbag, and it was too much trouble to get up and fetch them, so I just squinted at it from where I was, holding it at arm's length. Dad was watching me like a hawk. He hadn't offered me a cup of tea or anything, you know. Anyway, finally I made it out. The solicitor said a man had called at the office asking after me. He was a well-spoken Indian, middle-aged, clean-shaven, in a grey suit. Well, my head immediately started spinning. I was feeling terrible. Actually I don't know how I made it to the house. I remember I put my hand to my head and groaned and Dad said:

'Is there something wrong?' I laughed, thinking he meant my back, then realised he meant the message. And I muttered something about not wanting them to find me. He said, 'Who?' He knew very well, but he was playing what you'd call 'foxy'.

'The Family,' I said.

'You mean that cult?' I managed not to rise to it. I just nodded and he asked, 'Why? What've you done?'

I said:

'Nothing! They just won't leave me alone!' Then the penny must have dropped, because his whole face started beaming.

'Have you left them then?' he asked.

'Yes,' I said.

'Well,' he answered, 'it's the first sensible thing you've done in years!' I said something about not rubbing it in and would it be too much to ask if he made a cup of tea. He said, no it wouldn't and while he was waiting for the kettle, and I groaned a lot, he looked up the number of

211

this marvellous chiropractor he knows. Apparently he got housemaid's knee very badly after Myra died and this man worked miracles on him. Anyway, he phoned him up and asked if I could get round to the surgery. And I thought, well, I got here, didn't I? So we had our cup of tea ...

Well when I say we had it, Dad had his and I spilled most of mine down the front of my frock. Have you ever tried drinking scalding hot tea flat on your back? Then Dad helped me up, looked out his stick and off we hobbled. When we got to the surgery, Mr Lal Sen (he turned out to be Indian, isn't it a small world?), asked me to lie flat on my stomach. Well, I tried. I screamed the place down as well. Then he said, he didn't know how I'd walked into the surgery in the first place and he couldn't do anything till the inflammation went down, so I had to lie flat on my back with frozen peas pressed against the sore bit for a few days.

So here I am, in my Dad's spare room, flat on my back. And the peas have been in and out of the freezer so often, they smell. Dad's having to nurse me twenty-four hours a day! I can't go to the loo without him. And the bastard's enjoying every minute of it! Do you know, when he'd got me into bed and tucked me in, he looked down on me and he said:

'For years I've dreamt of having you in my power so I could tell you what I think of you! And now I've got my wish!'

The bastard! Still, you've got to laugh. He's turned out to be a good cook. I get boiled egg and marmite soldiers for breakfast. I feel like I'm five years old. If I didn't hurt so much I'd enjoy it. By the way, I asked him to ring up the solicitor and thank him and tell him for God's sake not to let on to anybody where I am! And he did. When he came back to tell me he'd done it, he was rubbing his hands together with undisguised glee. I thought he was going to let rip at me then and there, but he didn't. He got this mellow look on his face and his eyes went watery, and he said:

'I suppose that American bloke sorted you out, did he?'

I didn't like the way he put it but I wasn't in a position to argue so I just said:

'Yes.' And he said:

'He's a better man than I am, Gunga Din!' I gather he likes you. Anyway, after that he hovered about a bit, obviously winding himself up to say something else, and finally he came out with it. 'Are you and him getting back together then?' I told him I didn't even know where you were, but you were probably in India by now! He went pale at that. But it shut him up, anyway. The painkillers are giving me wind. It's awful. It's making me very irritable, the whole thing. And Dad *is* being good. Honestly. He isn't asking about 'The Family' or what happened or anything. I dread being thought well enough for a heart to heart. Though I know it's got to come! Oh well, roll on Thursday. The chiropractor's coming!

P.S. I hope you can read this. It's very difficult trying to write when you're lying on your back.

Thursday

An attack came in yesterday evening. It had me awake most of the night. I started feeling really sad. No, more than sad, I felt grief-stricken. And I was full of foreboding. I didn't know why. I thought maybe everything was catching up with me. You know? I mean I keep seeing funerals and wreaths and things all the time and it gets you down. I mean I know it's what they want, to get me down, I mean, but all the same. I kept hearing that voice telling me I'd go to hell and you would, too, and then I started worrying about you and where you were and what you were doing and, before I knew it, I was crying my eyes out. I couldn't help it. Dad was getting really worried. Then I traced the whole damn thing back to Bhanamurti. He was broadcasting distress signals! (Though why I should feel it, I don't know!)

Anyway, once I'd sorted that out, the attack changed to chest pain and I was sick. Dad thought I was going down with flu on top of everything and blamed a long-term diet of rice and chapatis. But I knew better. I wish I could tell him. I wish I could just explain what the pains are. But how can I? One thing I now know is that it was Bhanamurti who turned up at the solicitors. I wish I knew what he wanted, though. I expect it's something about Paula. Poor Bhanamurti. No wonder he's in a state. He adored her. I keep thinking about Paula and the baby and Sushena and wonder how they are. Especially the baby. I mean it was given into my care, however temporarily. Poor little blighter. What a start in life! Anyway, I'm not well enough to do anything about them just now!

The chiropractor came this morning and clunked my back. Apparently it's a disc. He says I'll be hopping about in a few days. I hope he doesn't mean that literally!

Anyway, I'd better stop waffling and get this off, so you know where I am. I'm assuming *you're* at the hotel in Delhi by now ... and even as I write it I know you are. You give me such a good feeling, like a fountain coming out of my head and falling all round me. What's happened to you? I love you. I pray for you all the time. I hope you feel my love coming your way.
Your own Lizzie.

Soon after his arrival in Delhi, Jim telephoned the house. The wife answered. Her husband was not in. He was of course at the waterworks. But he was expecting to hear from his American cousin and would be glad to receive him at his home at four o'clock. Jim had the rest of the day to kill. He got a taxi into the city, looking for a suitable gift for his hosts. But the anarchy of klaxons and bicycle bells gave him a headache. He was almost run over by a man with three passengers, pyramid-style, on his motor bike and he was angry. He realised he hadn't yet got over the flight. So he went back to the hotel and, asking the man on reception to find him something, he went up to his room to sleep.

He was awakened at 3 p.m. by a telephone call. Mr Ridley was in reception. For a second, Jim wondered what the hell was going on, then he remembered his date for tea.

'Okay,' he said, 'Tell him I'll be down!' Dressing quickly, Jim ran down the marble staircase into the grand reception area. It was like a ballroom. Looking lost, in the corner, a small, anxious-looking man in a brown suit was waiting. He glanced up as Jim approached and tried to smile. Jim extended a hand, the Indian bowed. Jim retracted the hand, bowed and the Indian extended his hand. They laughed awkwardly.

'Mr Ridley, I presume!' The Indian, trying hard, flashed a smile. Jim smiled back and nodded.

'The name's Jim,' he said.

'And I'm Prem.' Prem hesitated, then gabbled on, 'Look, I am sorry my wife was so inhospitable. When she phoned me I told her she should have arranged for me to pick you up. You are a stranger in this place. How will you find your way about? The taxi drivers charge ridiculous prices!'

'Not at all,' Jim replied graciously. 'I should have invited you to tea here. And since you are here, why don't you be my guest?' At that moment the receptionist interrupted them by handing Jim a package. Jim glanced at it, puzzled, then remembered his present.

'Oh no. I can't do that,' Prem said. 'I haven't brought you anything.'

'That's alright!' Jim gave him the package. 'I've got something for you!'

'Then you *must* have tea at my place!' Prem insisted, giving the package back. Worn down by politeness, Jim allowed himself to be driven off into the suburbs, horn blaring, to a street where the bungalows became shabbier and smaller the further they went.

Mrs Ridley opened the door to them. She was very flustered. She led Jim into the tiny sitting room where everything, though shabby, was spotless. There were pictures of Hindu Gods on the walls. Jim recognised Ganesha. There was a tinsel garland round the frame and the atmosphere was full of incense.

'Ganesha,' Jim remarked, looking at the picture. Prem beamed. His wife said something enthusiastic in Hindi and sat Jim down. She was wearing her best sari and had laid the tea table with a china tea service in his honour.

'I am very shy,' she apologised. 'I've never asked an American to tea before.' Then Jim offered his present and she opened it. Apparently sweetmeats were the perfect offering. Prem insisted on arranging them himself, choosing the best plate for the purpose, then he offered them to Jim. When Jim took one, the pattern of sweets was adjusted to cover the gap and placed decoratively on the table.

'Aren't you going to have one yourself?' Jim asked. Prem laughed and waved the sweets away, glancing at his wife. She immediately began pouring the tea. Her husband watched her, a nerve twitching in his cheek. Politely ignoring this, Jim asked about the waterworks. This gave rise to a polite but animated discussion about the merits of Delhi water. It lasted through the first cup of tea. Then Prem asked about Jim's work and Jim was wondering how on earth he was going to broach the subject he'd actually come about, when Mrs Ridley left the room to refill the tea pot. Immediately Prem cleared his throat and asked in a hushed voice:

'How did you find me?'

'The High Commission.'

'It's because I work for a Government Department.' Prem spoke as though his discovery was a punishment for holding high office. 'You said in your letter you wanted to know about the family?' he asked.

'Sure,' Jim replied, smiling encouragingly. 'You know we share the same ancestors!'

'I realise that.' Prem frowned. Jim shifted uneasily. It wasn't going to be easy to ask if his grandfather had committed incest!

'But ...?' he encouraged.

'It's not something I'm particularly proud of. That's all.'

'Why not?' Jim persisted.

'Not everybody thinks being white's the bees knees!' Prem glared at his guest. 'I mean it's alright for you. You're American. But I'm an Indian! Lucky for me my skin's so dark! Most people never suspect.'

'But, the name?' Jim asked, amazed.

'I know,' Prem agreed uncomfortably. 'It is a problem. My wife thinks I should change it, by deed poll. But ...' he shook his head, 'God gave me a white name. So, what to do? Better stick with it, I suppose!'

'I see.' Jim lay back, surveying the lump of misery before him. 'I was hoping you'd help me research into our mutual background ...'

'I'm sorry. I have no interest in doing so. None at all.'

Jim was phased. He'd expected it to be difficult, but he hadn't expected a complete stone wall.

'But you knew I was looking into the family tree. I told you that much in my letter! So why did you agree to see me?' he asked.

'One must be hospitable!' the Indian replied, astonished at the question.

'Look, Prem, you're my only lead!' Jim pleaded. 'I don't know of any other Ridleys in India!'

'There aren't many of us left,' Prem said grudgingly.

'Only me. And my younger brother.' Hope dawned.

'Where is he?' Jim asked.

'God knows! Went off to Kuwait to make his fortune. You know what they're doing to foreigners out there?' Jim was silent. He'd seen Indian refugees on T.V., stuck in the Jordanian desert, with nothing but the clothes they stood in. 'There's only us two ... and my sister.' Jim glanced up. 'Nandini!' It was clear he despised her. 'She's a doctor. Lives in Kashmir. She might talk to you. She's *very* liberal! Full of all that melting pot sixties rubbish. You know the Beatles?' Jim nodded and Prem sank into a deeper gloom. Tentatively, Jim prodded him out of it.

'Can you give me her address?' he asked. 'Maybe a telephone number?' Prem wrote it down and Jim rose to leave just as Mrs Ridley re-entered with the replenished pot.

'You must not go so soon!' she wailed.

'She is right,' Prem insisted. 'You must stay a while longer. You've had nothing to eat.' He pushed the plate of sweets at him. Jim smiled and shook his head. But Prem looked insulted, so Jim gave in and put out his hand to take one, as Prem turned, removing the plate. Plate and hand collided. The plate fell on the floor and smashed. Torn between the carpet and the urgent need to be hospitable, Prem was unable to prevent Jim's escape and he backed out, apologising profusely.

When he finally got back to the hotel, having walked for miles and taken a taxi which, as predicted, cost a fortune, it was late enough to try England. Jim dialled Liz's number. There was no reply. He had already decided that in this eventuality he would try the solicitor. He rang Platt and Burdon.

'I'm sorry. I'm under instruction not to divulge the whereabouts of my client,' Mr Platt said. Jim reminded him that he was a trustee of Miss Strachan's inheritance. But it made no difference. Another stone wall. He looked at his piece of paper. He picked up the phone again and dialled the number in Kashmir. By a miracle, it answered.

'I wish to speak to Dr Nandini Ridley,' he said.

'Speaking.'

Putney, Saturday

Dear Jim,

Where are you? Why don't you write? Are you okay? The solicitor said you'd phoned. The bloody fool should have told you where I was. Come to that, he should have asked where *you* were! I could kill him! There is such a thing as being too much of a stickler! Have you had my letters? Honestly, I feel cut off from the world in Dad's spare room. It's beginning to get me down. I'm completely at his mercy. He keeps on and on about how the Conservatives have ruined local government, he forgets to buy the books I want, and last night he actually gave me spaghetti bolognaise for supper! Can you imagine anything more cruel? You try eating spaghetti on your back! You winda the pasta rounda the fork, then, holding the plate under the chin to catcha the drips, quickly droppa the fork into the mouth. Unfortunately, as the forka drop, the spaghetti unwind and slappa you acrossa the face. I swear he did it on purpose! I laid into him about it afterwards and he promised to make it up to me by getting me a ticket for the Monet Exhibition. It closes in less than a week! I hope Mr Lal Sen lets me get up in time!'

Dad came in just then, wanting 'our chat'. And I was just beginning to like the old so and so! He'd been to the library for me and got this book out, *Jung and the Eastern Religions*. (As if I hadn't had enough!) Still, he meant well. He wanted to know why I'd joined 'that stupid cult'. I tried to tell him there was something real in it. You know? A spiritual truth. I mean, he wasn't always an atheist. I thought he'd at least go along with that.

219

But he's never meditated, so it's pretty difficult for him to understand something like spiritual energy that you can plug into and when you do you start getting sensitive and feeling things. I mean, I can feel my spiritual centres, chakras and so on. But when I told him he just asked if they'd had us on drugs! So I tried explaining how thought's real and whatever you think has its effect. I mean everybody's affected, it's just I know I am, because I feel it.

Like when he came in the other day. He'd got me a bunch of flowers, the old so-and-so. And I felt this sparkle coming up the stairs towards me. Lovely. That was his love for me I was feeling and it really lifted me. But, there's the other side. I tried to tell him what a lie, a spiteful thought or a bit of old-fashioned ill-wishing does to me, that I feel it, as pain. I think he took it in. I mean he believed I felt it, but he just said, 'You'll get over it.' He thinks it's my imagination playing tricks on me, all part of the brainwashing.

Sometimes I wish it was. I mean, I wish he was right, that it'd pass and I'd be accepted back into the human race again. It's a barrier between me and everyone else. I'm not living in the same world. I'm caught somewhere between heaven and hell and the worst of it is, I can't share my experience. Not even with my own Dad. Dear old thing, he looked so bemused. I know he wants to help, but he just can't take this in. Maybe he doesn't want to. Well, I shouldn't wish it on him, should I? It's no joke being condemned to feel the suffering and sins of others. In fact it's bloody painful! When he got up to go he had a lost look on his face, like a little boy, and I couldn't bear it. I wanted to bridge the gap between us and be like I used to be with him, when I was little, before I knew too much. I pulled him back and hugged him. I told him I wasn't mad and I wasn't going to end up like my mother, and I was crying and going on about how I loved him and everything. And he did his best. He told me he loved me, too, and everything would be alright, but the poor sod looked more worried than ever! Whatever did he do to deserve me? (Marry my mother, I suppose.)

Anyway, I shouldn't be sorry for him. His re-entry into Eden will be easier than mine. I know too much. Mind you, it's useful sometimes. I'm forewarned about trouble! Speaking of which, I've heard nothing from Bhanamurti, except over the air waves. Jeanne's been coming in pretty strongly, too. I wonder what they're up to? I'm scared. But I daren't tell Dad. He'd have me in a straitjacket as soon as vote Labour! Thank God you understand. I think I'd go mad if I couldn't talk to someone. I mean, whatever Father is, he's got powers alright. Real ones. I hope you're taking care. Ring soon. Or write. I love you, Your own Lizzie.

Dal Lake, Kashmir
December

Darling Lizzie,

Wish you were here! It's the perfect honeymoon spot. I have a room at the back of a houseboat with my own bathroom. The john looks out onto the lake and the steam from the bath brings out the scent of cedar. The entire boat's made of the stuff. It's quite heady. You can smell it, lying in bed, very soothing. Makes me quite sleepy! Usually the lake's alive with tourists, but for one thing the riots have kept people away, and for another it's winter and bloody cold here, (quite a shock after Delhi) so there's a lot of boats free. Prem's sister rents this one from the father of one of her students. (Apparently he's got a fleet of them.) Nancy's a doctor of economics at the university and we get on like a house on fire. She's a complete contrast to her brother. When she met me at Srinagar airport, she threw a garland of marigolds round my neck. She was really pleased to see me! She asked how on earth I'd tracked her down. When I told her her brother had given me her address, she said: 'Prem? How is the old stuffed shirt?' I was very relieved I can tell you. Because there was no way I was going to get anything out of him. To be honest, you'd hardly think they came from the same family. Nancy's pale, almost white, and Prem's dark. She says Prem thinks she's sold out because she wears skirts. (He still calls her Nandini.) He says she's denying the Indian in her. I don't. I think it's him, denying the white in himself! He's the one who's got himself into a knot. She's positively dynamic! She got me and my luggage safely stowed on a shikara in no time, and even handed me a hot water bottle for the journey across the lake! There's already been snow here. It's a bit like Austria really, except somehow, you know you're on the edge of the Himalayas. You can see them, from the houseboat. They form a sort of backcloth to the lake, white with snow. In summer it must be wonderful with the lotuses and waterlilies in full bloom! Paradise! Though, as Nancy hasn't ceased telling me, the people are poor and live a hard life. She's into the fight for an independent Kashmir.

Nancy says she wants me to meet some people, so she's asked a colleague round for dinner tonight. He's the Professor of Philosophy, and as I'm feeling pretty bushed I'm just hoping the conversation won't get too heavy! There's some wonderful smells coming from the kitchen I must say. I can hardly wait! I'm starving! I'll write a bit more later. I've just felt my chin. I need a shave. Love, Jim.

Liz dreamt the corridor dream again. Only this time different doors were open. Her father was in one of the rooms with Myra. They were holding placards and Liz was right behind them in her black polo neck with the CND badge on it. Her hair was backcombed into a fright. She went up to her father and, smiling, he put his arm round her. Then they both turned to look at Liz in the corridor and slowly the door closed. But Jim was there. Less of a ghost now, he had form and colour. His hand was warm as he held hers, urging her to the end of the passage where an open door let in a stream of light. It was dazzling. Shading her eyes, she tried to see beyond, but could not. The open door was drawing her towards it. A blast of air rushed past her and she stepped out into the light. . . .

Professor Sethi chewed slowly. The candle flames lengthened.

'Why this interest in the past?' he asked. 'You're an evolved soul. You should know better than to take an interest in such humdrum tales of family jealousy and petty larceny.' He threw down his chicken leg in disgust. 'Who cares?' he asked.

'It's not me', Jim answered. He pushed the remainder of his supper away, defeated. Nancy laughed and passed him the fruit bowl.

'Then who?' the Professor asked.

Jim picked up a fig and started peeling it. 'An Englishwoman called Elizabeth Strachan. She believes herself to be third generation in direct descent from an incestuous union.' Nancy choked on her chicken.

'My great-grandfather?' she asked. 'Robert? With whom?'

'His sister, Jane.'

'Good God! It's a new one on me!'

'The other story, about the theft, was only a cover-up.'

The Professor wiped his mouth on his napkin. 'You have proof of this?' Jim shook his head.

'That's why I've come here. We looked high and low back in England. There's nothing. No documentary evidence, I mean. Only the story as passed down from generation to generation. I thought there might be something here. Maybe some of Robert's papers? I don't

223

know.' Nancy drank a glassful of water and licked her lips.

'Well! If there's anything at all, Prem's got it. He kept all that sort of rubbish. I never cared about it.' She screwed up her eyes thoughtfully. 'I wonder if there is and he's read it. I wonder if that's why he's so set against his white inheritance.'

'But what I don't understand,' the Professor said, 'is why it matters! Do you want to marry this girl?'

'Maybe. But, it's not that. It's her. How she feels about herself,' Jim explained.

'What makes her think it's true?' Nancy asked.

'It accounts for a lot of things. Her mother and grandmother both went crazy. Jane committed suicide. Did you know that? And anyway, her guru told her it was true.' Now they had come to it.

'Her guru? Which guru?' Professor Sethi asked.

'Calls himself "Father".'

'Which "father"? There are so many!'

'His organisation's called "The Family".'

'Ah.' The Professor nodded.

'She thinks he's God. Or she used to, until she discovered he was plotting against people and cooking the books.'

'Hah! How can he be God? He's not even God realised!'

'How do you know?'

'Read the Gita. Krishna didn't involve himself in the battle. And he didn't judge. Each side played its part. You see, Westerners often get into trouble when they turn to the east. They're used to God being one. Easy. But in India we are more subtle, more complex. We can accept that everything comes from God. Brahma, He created it all; including the devil. Yes! The devil's part of God, too! He plays his part in the world. He fights in the battle, just as God meant him to. And when it's all over? Well done. You played your part well. No good Arjuna being surprised to find his enemy in heaven with him. There are no sides. Not really. And if your guru gets involved in the fighting, gets his hands dirty, then you know he is not God! He is merely one of the participants in the drama!

'And here's the point. The devil has powers, has he not? God gave him them. Yes, his powers are divine. That's why we Indians play it very cagey when we come across all these gurus. We respect their powers. We know they are real. But we don't think of them as God. He might be alright. He might be a saint. He might even be realised. But you Westerners can't differentiate, you see.

'You are so naive. You fall down before this guru, that guru, and you worship him. But who is he really? His powers might be divine, he might be able to give *you* powers! But who is he? And what does he want of you? Better be careful. Fools rush in ...'

Nancy left the table to make the tea. Jim was staring at the opened fig. Without looking up, he said slowly:

'Is it wrong to have powers?'

'How can it be wrong? It is. *You* have them. I know. Just don't go thinking you are God. Don't set yourself up as a guru! Your powers come from God. Be ready to give them back to him. Be a simple man.'

'It was over before it even started, wasn't it? Before Adam bit into the apple.'

The Professor laughed. 'Do you still care about this family drama of yours?' he asked.

'The story must be played out,' Jim replied. The Professor smiled.

'Touché!'

Jim was standing on the verandah of the houseboat, looking out onto the lake. The sun was coming up and a morning star shone crystal-clear in the pale sky. He saw the distant hills, with their gardens, 'Shalimar', darling of the moghuls, the pale outline of Srinagar, the house-boats on the lake, the shikaras, the islands of lily leaves shimmering, half created by the watery light, a still translucent world ...

Liz was sitting in front of 'The Water Lily Pond' at the Royal Academy. Heady with the perfume of the foyer lilies, she had entered a sensational world. Ignited by the fire of 'Haystacks' at sunset, pierced by the incandescent 'Poplars on the River Epte', dematerialised by 'Rouen Cathedral', she had floated into the spaces of light between the lily pads and found peace. Monet had not painted the objects but their creation by light. In the end, there was nothing but light. No wonder he was blinded, dazzled by his own vision of the truth. Who would not be a painter and spend his life simply seeing, and seeing, hold the vision in a drop of paint? She would! Oh yes, she would! Leaving the gallery she wandered, dazed, into the London afternoon.

A falcon flew up into the sun and, glancing up, Jim realised the day had begun. He took a cup of tea into his room, and finished his letter to Liz. It was fine for him, looking on from a great height, but Liz was still playing her part. And when, at last, they knew the truth, would she be hurt by it? An open wound lets in infection and they would take every advantage. He must warn her. 'The Family' hadn't finished with her yet. If he could only be like the falcon, and carry her up to the light, far above the battle ... He wrote:
    '... the only danger is to get involved in the story. Don't go believing it's real, Liz, or you'll be in trouble. Whatever the outcome, just accept it and know it'll be alright. It'll all be the same in a thousand years....'

Days later, she was walking from Putney Bridge to the house. She had overdone it, of course, and now her thigh

226

and hip were in spasm. She stopped on the bridge, leaning against the side, and as the pain eased she noticed how the sparkling winter sky had dissolved into the river. She tried to think how Monet would have painted it. Or, more important, how would she?

Her father was lucky to live here. He'd moved when Myra had died and found a modern house, clean and easy to run, with a garage on the ground floor. She had never really liked modern houses and was surprised to find she liked this one. Perhaps it was because it was so near the Thames. She set off again, slowly, painfully making her way along the riverside.

She looked with curiosity at the people. A group of boy scouts was taking a canoe out. They hesitated on the brink, glancing over to a small crowd that was gathering on the mud. There was something in the water. A dog barked excitedly, running in and out between their legs as a man wearing oilskins pulled in . . . a body.

Liz turned her head away. Too late; she had seen it. If it wasn't funerals, it was something similar. She was bombarded with images of death. Shaken, she struggled on. She must not let them wear her down! Why had they such power over her? More to the point, why oh why hadn't she got a taxi from the station as she had done when she'd gone to the Academy? She felt sick and was sweating from the increasing agony of her leg. To think a few nerves could cause so much trouble! Damn that chicken! And she was still some distance from the house. She had to traverse the gardens to reach it.

As she turned towards the gate she thought for a fleeting moment she was going to faint. The sky seemed to grow darker and her balance wavered. She was tired unto death. She could hear children laughing as she entered the garden. Their au pairs brought them to play on the swings while they chatted away in Swedish, French and Spanish on the park seats. The thought of those seats flooded Liz with longing. She had to sit down.

There was a bench just beyond the sheltering privet on the corner. She knew it well. Her father often sat there to do his crossword. She struggled towards it, and as she rounded the hedge, saw Bhanamurti sitting there.

She reeled. Her instinct was to run. But she couldn't. So she stood, swaying helplessly before the paralysed man. Good manners battled with his hatred. He could see that any moment the woman's knees would buckle and she would fall to the ground. He should be glad God had dealt with her this way. She should suffer for what she'd done. But being a well-brought-up Indian, he rose, in spite of himself and, taking her gently by the arm, guided Liz to the seat. As she struggled desperately to collect herself, Bhanamurti waited, his face grey under his dark brown skin.

'How did you find me?' she asked at last.

'It wasn't difficult. When I missed you at your house in South Shields, I contacted India. Father still had the letter. The Putney address was on it.' He folded his hands in his lap. 'He wants to see you,' he said. Liz's heart jumped.

'Who does?'

'Father.'

'Is he in England?'

'No. He's gone back to India.'

'Was his tour successful?'

'What do you care?'

'Not much. Why does he want to see me?'

'To help you. He knows your soul is in peril. He is kind. He loves you. He is so sad because you're hurting yourself.'

'Hurting *myself*? How?'

'With this vindictive campaign of yours. You know you can never hurt Father. He is beyond hurt.'

'What campaign? What are you talking about?'

'Don't even try to hide what you're doing. Father sees

everything!' He waggled his eyebrows meaningfully. Liz couldn't help laughing.

'Bhanamurti, you sweet loony, I really haven't got a clue what you're on about.' It was extraordinary how innocent she looked. Bhanamurti stared at her in wonder. Thank heaven he had been told the truth in advance or he might have been taken in by her.

'Father said you were very cunning. Now I see he was right as always. You have lost your battle against evil.' Bhanamurti sighed, genuinely sad. 'I don't suppose you even know what you're saying. The demons from your family's past control you too completely.' Liz licked her lips because they were dry. She swallowed hard. 'If I'd only known what was going on.' He shook his head sorrowfully. 'I blame myself, not you, for what happened to Paula,' he added smugly. 'I am a senior devotee. I should have seen the dangers.' Liz was puzzled.

'Why should you blame me anyway?' she asked. 'What happened to Paula had nothing to do with me!'

'You corrupted her, Liz. Please don't lie. We know you were in league together.'

'This is such amazing crap!'

Bhanamurti snapped back, 'Control your demons before me, Elizabeth! Their language betrays them. They have brought you to the level of the gutter!'

Liz stared at the man beside her. He wasn't Bhanamurti. Or, if he was, his brain had been rewired. He was like a robot, programmed. If she wanted to get to the bottom of this she had to forget the human being she thought she once knew. Her voice took on a hard edge.

'Bhanamurti, what am I supposed to have done?' He looked at her in disgust. She tried again. 'Okay. You think demons have blinded me and I don't know what I'm doing, so hadn't you better tell me?' This Bhanamurti could accept. And anyway, he wanted to talk about it; he wanted to see her reaction. The indictment slipped out pat.

'You helped Paula steal Father's property and money, as part of a conspiracy to discredit "The Family".' He might have added, 'So there!' Liz's brain whirled. Where to begin?

'Steal what?' she asked. 'Are you by any chance talking about that goblet?'

'Among other things, yes.'

'Come off it, Bhanamurti. Paula didn't steal that goblet any more than I did! Anyway, while we're on the subject, I didn't realise it was Father's private property in the first place. I thought we'd bought that goblet for ceremonial purposes. And as for the funds, they don't belong to Father either. It's our money. My money, some of it. It's meant for "Family" purposes not his private use.'

'This is the attitude that led you to steal. You should remember, whatever we have, Father gave us.'

'How very convenient for him!'

Bhanamurti hissed. He glared at her. He would not hear such blasphemy.

'You know Father wants nothing for himself. Everything we give, not that we *can* give him anything,' he added hastily and in some confusion, 'because of course everything's his in the first place. So whatever we give is already his.' Liz waited patiently for Bhanamurti to repair his mental short circuit. 'Anyway, through his goodness, we are to be blessed with new ashrams, schools, a whole village, where "The Family" can live together free from the negative influences of others. The Kingdom of heaven on earth; God's elect living in perfect harmony.'

Liz sighed. She had heard it all before, and believed it. There was no point in arguing.

'Look, Bhanamurti,' she said, 'whatever Father wants to do with the money is neither here nor there.' Bhanamurti opened his mouth to object but Liz ploughed on. 'The point is, if money's gone from the funds, it's got nothing to do with me. And if you ask me it's got nothing to do with Paula, either. Jeanne's the only one who had access to the books. Jeanne and Father. So, if anybody's been fiddling the books it's them. Good God, man, don't you realise? They tampered with the accounts in an attempt to discredit your wife! They were afraid she'd go to the newspapers, so they tried to destroy her. And they succeeded. She believes she's evil! Well, she can't go to the newspapers when she's holed up in a psychiatric unit, can she?' Bhanamurti's face expressed shock.

'You'll stoop to anything, won't you?' he spat. 'You are the one who destroyed my wife! You corrupted her! And now you're using her to hide behind, while you pursue your conspiracies against us.'

'What conspiracies? Bhanamurti, this is lunatic! If anybody's been conspiring it's Jeanne and Father against me and Paula!' Bhanamurti took a deep breath and spoke in a cold steady voice.

'Think carefully, Elizabeth,' he said, 'before continuing with what you are doing. You are not the only one who will suffer. Great Britain itself will be in terrible trouble for insulting Father. Your own family. The innocent children you come in contact with ...' On cue the children in the gardens laughed. 'The Gods will punish everyone. Heaven knows what calamities will fall down on your heads.'

'Bhanamurti, will you please tell me what I'm supposed to be doing? Remember *I* don't know. The demons are doing it.'

'I can almost feel sorry for you, Elizabeth. They have complete control of your subconscious. They must have to have led you into the ultimate sin, accusing Father of your own crime.'

Liz gasped, 'Father's been accused of a crime?'

Bhanamurti pursed his lips with distaste. The words that he was about to utter were bitter gall to him.

'They have asked for the books,' he said with great

231

dignity. 'They are going through them with a fine tooth comb. I hope you're happy.'

'Excuse me, but who's going through the books?' Liz asked.

'Lawyers, accountants.' Bhanamurti bit his lips, then added reluctantly, 'customs officials.' His bitterness turned immediately to anger. He rounded on Liz with sudden vehemence. 'Paula's wealthy family started them off, as you well know!'

'How would I know?' Liz objected. 'I haven't been in touch with them! Well, not since you asked me to find out where Paula was. And I didn't even speak to them then. Not personally. I couldn't face it. I asked a friend to ring her aunt for me.' She looked at Bhanamurti. His eyes were sunken, unseeing. 'Why did Paula's family start off this ... investigation?' she asked. 'Are they trying to get the children back?' Bhanamurti nodded.

'It's all so terrible. I feel to blame for what's happening to Father. I feel so guilty!' Bhanamurti started crying. 'But, he said it wouldn't go to court! They wouldn't dare contest for custody. Our case rested on Paula's being criminally insane. She *is* unfit to look after the children!'

'She is now!' Liz bit her tongue to stop her anger. She didn't want to block Bhanamurti in mid-flow. But it would have been difficult. The damn had been breached.

'You see,' he went on, 'there were some political changes and the police started to investigate what Paula'd done. I don't know why. We hadn't brought charges of theft or anything. She's lucky Father is so forgiving. But anyway, they didn't stop at investigating Paula, they looked through *everything* and then the customs got interested.' Liz laughed.

'Oh dear, it's all rather backfired on you, hasn't it?'

'How can you laugh? It could look very bad for Father. They're saying he had been creaming off the funds and putting the money in a Swiss bank account.

They say he encouraged smuggling; jewellery, antiques and so on. He hasn't been paying tax on his earnings as a guru! Imagine! Earnings? Do gurus earn anything? They have even used the word "extortion"! Imagine! Everything we give to Father, we give from our hearts. Gladly! And why? Because he knows best how to use it! I have seen the plans for the village. They are wonderful! But now it is all in jeopardy. The books are such a mess ...! It makes things look bad. Paula's fault of course. Now they're *all* on our backs: builders, garage repair people, they all want their bills paid. We shall go bankrupt to top everything.'

'Paula *didn't* fiddle the books, Bhanamurti! Jeanne's the only one who could have done *that*! Why don't you take a look at them for yourself! See if it's her writing! I bet it is! Mind you,' Liz shrugged, 'Father probably told her to do it. They were really gunning for Paula.'

'If this reaches the newspapers ...' Distressed, Bhanamurti turned to her. 'Please, Elizabeth, I beg you ...I know you're the one behind this, I know you've egged on Paula's family and told them things about "The Family", please tell them to stop the investigation. Paula isn't fit to have the children in any case! And I stand to lose my job!' Liz roared with fury:

'You stand to lose your job? Paula's in a psychiatric unit and you've all tried pretty hard to put me in there with her! Why the hell should I care about your bloody job?' Bhanamurti wrung his hands in anguish.

'You conspired with Paula!' he wailed desperately.

'When? How?' Liz insisted. 'From what I hear Paula isn't *compos mentis*. How am I supposed to have conspired with her?' Sure of himself, Bhanamurti came in quickly.

'Before she went mad. Before she left India. Nathan told me all about it, how you pleaded with him to leave the room when he took the baby to her to be fed. That's when you and she laid your plans.' Liz let out a hollow laugh.

'All Paula cared about was her child, you bastard. She was in a terrible state. She couldn't have laid a plan to save her life. And as for me having the power to stop the investigation, I don't know what you think I am, but I didn't start it and I certainly can't stop it.' Bhanamurti howled so loudly the children in the playground stopped laughing. Was there a werewolf in the vicinity?

'You are a devil!' he screamed. 'You turn everything on its head. So cunning you are. So powerful. You set yourself against the Kingdom of God to bring it down.'

Liz made one last attempt. 'Bhanamurti, "The Family's" brought all this down on its own head. It's no good looking for a scapegoat. I'm not the devil incarnate bent on the destruction of you lunatic lot. Face it! You have been hoist with your own petard. They that live by the sword shall die by the sword. I haven't done a thing!' She shouted in his face. Bhanamurti blinked. For one brief second he believed her. The ensuing confusion broke his overloaded mind.

'We're all finished,' he said crying. He rose from the seat.

'How is Paula?' Liz asked, before he should pass out of her reach. Bhanamurti turned to her, a blank expression on his face.

'I don't know anyone by that name,' he said and left.

Liz vomited in the rhododendron bushes. She tried to stagger on to the house, but feeling faint had to sit again. One of the au pairs, quietly rocking a baby near the swings, took pity on her and came up to ask if she was alright. Liz could hardly speak. There were tears in her eyes and she was shaking. The girl was anxiously wondering what to do, when she had an idea.

'I know what you need!' she said. 'The English swear by tea! I have some in my flask. My lady makes it for me. I shall get you a cup. Will you hold the baby, please?' She planted the sleeping infant in Liz's arms. Immediately it woke and screamed. Liz cried out and thrust the child back at her, getting to her feet and staggering away, well away from the screaming infant. At the gate, she looked back. The au pair was jiggling the still crying baby up and down, while its little brother, returned from the swings, stood looking at the disappearing cripple, wondering what on earth she had done.

Liz's father was out. Thank God, she thought, for small mercies. She leant on the balustrade, sobbing. The baby's scream echoed in her ears. It was her fault. It must be. The child had reacted as if she'd burnt it. She remembered the flames that surrounded her when she woke after the dream; the dream where she had fought the demon. She had thought she was saving Nathan from it, but was the demon in fact herself? The baby knew. The innocent child had recognised her for what she was, a lost soul, possessed by the evil of her ancestors! And the evil burnt, corrupted the very souls of those with whom she came in contact. Everything Bhanamurti had said was true. She was finished. Might as well end it now. Her head had sunk low. She was looking at the bottom stair. There was a letter there. It was an air mail letter. She wiped her tears away and bent to pick it up. It was from India, from Jim! She hugged it to her chest, crying out, 'Please God, let it be good news! Let it not be true! Free me from the burden of my ancestors!' Shaking, she looked at the envelope again. Dare she open it? Not here, where her father might come in and find her. She put the letter in her pocket and looked up the impossible stairs. She started climbing. But her hip was agony and pain shot up her back. She got down on her knees and crawled.

It was snowing in the foothills. Jim's guide, though just ahead, was barely visible in the growing darkness and the ponies were slipping underfoot. They would be lucky to make the next hill station. It was bitterly cold. His backside ached from the bumping trot; he was used to bigger horses! But Jim was smiling, relieved to have time off from the dual pressures of travel and responsibility.

It had been Nancy's suggestion. He was looking grey, she said. He had come all this way, he should see something of the place. Why didn't he just take off and leave it to her? *She* would talk to Prem. So, reassuring himself it was not a cop out, and that Nancy had a better chance of winkling what he wanted out of her tight-arsed brother than himself, Jim took his chance and went.

He hadn't realised he was so wound up; not till he hit the air. And then, taking in deep breaths of the stuff as they rode through the afternoon, he began to relax, his mind melting like the snow on the pony's back. Though tired, his energies were released. It was like he'd felt after meeting the aborigines; on top of the world; well, almost. He let out a holler of joy. Astonished, the guide looked back. He shouted and pointed on ahead. Jim could just make out the dim lights of a low wooden building; the hill station. The guide dug in his heels and urged his pony forward, believing the American was desperate for his 'hot toddy'.

Earlier in the day another boy had gone up ahead of them to prepare supper and the kettle was boiling when they arrived. All they had to do was pour the water onto the lemon and sugar in the cup, then add the scotch. (Nancy had told them how to make it.) Proudly they presented it to Jim, who took it gladly, warming his hands on the cup as he sat in the window, watching the snow fall.

He remembered Etna; how he and Liz had sat in the café with their coffee and she'd got all excited about the light and the snow ... Jim's chest tightened. Every second the dull ache was getting stronger. He put his hand over the pain to soothe it. The guides watched him anxiously. He wasn't going to die on them, was he? He breathed slowly, concentrating his mind. He had been thinking of Liz when it started. Immediately the pain

236

hardened to a fist in his heart and a gripping band encaged him. He gasped. What in God's name had happened to her? He closed his eyes, nurturing the seed of love in his heart and letting it grow till the bands of pain had loosened. Then he sent it out, seeking her, to comfort her in her distress.

Liz was lying on the floor, the letter open beside her. She was rigid with pain and shock. Over and over, she repeated Jim's words, '... Don't go believing it's real, Liz, or you'll be in trouble. Whatever the outcome, just accept it and know it'll be alright. It'll all be the same in a thousand years ...' Slowly she became aware of something lifting her, like a light shining in her heart.

'Is there a telephone?' Jim asked.

'Telephone?' The guides looked at him as if he was crazy.

'No telephone?'

'No telephone.'

'Can we go back?' Jim asked.

'Go back?' The guide asked.

'Yes,' Jim answered. 'To Srinagar.'

'Srinagar?'

'Yes.'

'Definitely not!' the guide told him. 'Morning! If we are lucky!' Jim shrugged. Well, you can only ask. The guides started gabbling among themselves. It was clear what they thought; Western people were crazy. They dragged you out in the snow to the back of beyond and then they wanted to make telephone calls. Why couldn't they be like everyone else and telephone before they came out? Better still, not come out at all! Absolutely and completely crazy! Jim smiled. He didn't blame them. Though they had none of them expected it to snow like this. He made amends by helping them bed down the ponies for the night, then sat to eat with them before a roaring fire.

★

Liz's father came home to find his daughter had relapsed. He phoned Mr Lal Sen, who came round and ministered to her. It was very odd; a strange case; even overdoing it shouldn't bring on pain like this. He didn't know what to make of it. He was very sorry. He would not charge for the visit.

'You mustn't take it personally, Mr Lal Sen,' Liz pleaded. 'It isn't your fault.' But he would not be comforted. He showed Liz's father how to relieve spasms and left, a disappointed man. Back in bed, Liz was her father's captive once again. Her eyes closed against him as he hovered by the door, offering tea, painkillers, frozen peas. All she wanted was to be left alone. But he was restive, anxious. He had something on his mind. He came to sit on the bed beside her.

'Liz ...?' he said tentatively. Her eyes opened. Her voice was weary.

'Yes?'

'That letter.' He glanced at the chest of drawers where the thin blue envelope lay open. 'I couldn't help seeing it was from India.'

'It was from Jim,' she reassured him quickly, hoping that would be an end to it. But he was still not satisfied.

'What's he doing in India?' he asked. Liz sighed. What could she tell him?

'It's nothing to do with "The Family", if that's what you're thinking,' she said.

'I'm glad to hear it,' he answered with obvious relief. 'Look, Liz, I wouldn't poke my nose in but, well, a man came this morning, while you were out ... an Indian man. He was asking for you.'

'I'm sorry, Dad. They shouldn't involve you.'

'He was one of them yogis, wasn't he?' Liz nodded. 'Did you know he was coming?'

'No.'

'Well, I sent him away. Told him not to come back if

238

he knew what was good for him. Maybe I shouldn't've. But ...'

'I saw him in the gardens on my way back.'

Her voice was heavy with pain. She was exhausted. This was his daughter, his only child. So, she had rejected him, so she had called another man 'father'; he still loved the silly bitch, didn't he? He couldn't help himself! And here she was, the spark extinguished, white hairs in the brown, her youth and talents stolen. How could they do it to her? By Christ he could murder the bastards! And the worst of it was he was so helpless. Stupid old man, he hadn't even succeeded in keeping that fool of an Indian from her. When she opened her eyes, Liz saw tears streaming down her father's face. He wiped them away quickly, but not quickly enough. Her hand reached out to him.

'I'm sorry, Dad,' she said. 'I'm sorry I hurt you. But don't worry. They'll never get me back again. Never. If I hadn't finished with them, they've finished with me. They think I'm a devil ...' she convulsed with sobs.

Her father took her in his arms and held her, rocking her like a baby, telling her over and over again she was the most beautiful girl in the whole wide world.

Jim missed the hot water bottle as the shikara picked its way through the ice to the houseboat. There were no lights on and the place was freezing cold. Nancy had not expected him back so soon. But the boy would tell her and she would be there to rescue him before long. Meanwhile, unable to fathom the boiler, Jim lit the lamps and put the kettle on the stove. At least he could make some tea. He closed his eyes and inhaled the perfume of the cedar; balm to the soul. He rubbed his chest, still aching, but duller now. Liz was recovering from whatever it was had happened to her. But she seemed very tired. It was as though she'd been run over by a steamroller.

Had he been selfish going off into the hills, leaving her alone? He hadn't heard from her in a long time. He didn't even know for sure where she was. With her father? The real one, he hoped. Imbued with a sense of urgency he awaited Nancy's return. The sooner he had that information she was digging out for him and got it back to England, the better!

Nancy dashed in just over an hour later, rubbing her hands against the cold.

'I hear it snowed a little!' she laughed. Jim laughed back, glad to see her, and helped unload her shopping from the shikara.

'Did you get anywhere with Prem?' he asked.

'Prem?' she seemed surprised.

'Yes. You said you were going to phone him, twist his arm for me.' She stared at him, as though she didn't know what he was talking about, then pushed past into the boat. He pursued her inside, urgent for news. 'You know, Robert's papers and so on? You said you'd phone.'

'Help me with this, will you?' She was unpacking the food. He groaned with delight at the sight of fresh saffron and almonds amongst the general abundance. Evidently they were going to have a feast tonight.

'You know, Jim,' Nancy said, as he helped her chop the onions, 'you and I are kindred spirits!'

'You feel that too?' he asked, pleased.

'Sure!' she cried. 'We have the same priorities in life! Our stomachs . . .!' Jim was taken aback.

'Stomachs?' he objected. 'Really?' She nodded slowly. 'I didn't know. I always thought I was . . .'

'Above that sort of thing?' Nancy's eyes twinkled. Jim laughed.

'Okay. Yes. Yes, I did.'

'We have something else in common,' she cajoled.

'What's that?' he asked, resigned to her teasing.

'We're apt to get a little bit above ourselves.'

240

Jim felt the hairs prick on the back of his neck. What the hell was she on about? Had he put his foot in it somehow?

'What do you mean?' he asked.

'I didn't like what you said about "twisting" Prem's arm.'

'I'm sorry. I didn't mean to offend you.'

'He is my brother, you know. One has to have respect. I couldn't possibly twist his arm, as you put it.'

'Of course not. I'm really sorry I said that. Please forgive me.'

'Okay. I forgive you.' She laughed and threw the onions into the frying pan. Panic rising, Jim watched her stir the spices into the ghee.

'But, without wanting to sound pushy ... you are going to help me, Nancy, aren't you?' he asked.

'All in good time,' she replied, smiling. 'Rome wasn't built in a day!'

'It's just I've got this feeling, Nancy. I've got to get back. There's something wrong.'

'If there's something wrong, then now is not the moment to introduce a new element into the situation. Better leave it till things calm down. You must learn to be patient, Jim!'

'Liz needs to know!'

'Maybe like a hole in the head,' Nancy replied. 'Anyway, I can't ask Prem just like that. I will have to choose my moment. It will take time.' Jim couldn't hide his disappointment. 'Look at it this way,' she argued, 'I haven't phoned Prem. Not yet. So it must be for the best. That must be how it's meant to be.' He sighed with frustration. 'Now, Jim, don't be angry. What's the point? Things have a way of timing *themselves*. They *can't* always just work out at the drop of a hat, just because you want them to! You will get what you need when you need it and not before.' Jim stared at her. He shook his head, smiling in spite of himself.

'You sound like an Indian,' he said.

'I *am* an Indian,' she answered. 'And we can run rings round you Westerners!'

'I'm an Indian, too,' he told her. 'A red Indian. And don't you forget it.'

'Pax!' Nancy cried. 'Let us agree we're both hybrids and be done with it!' They laughed and spent a happy evening comparing their experiences of Cambridge and the L.S.E.

Jeanne had started transmitting. It started within hours of the meeting with Bhanamurti. Had he phoned her in India? Or was she in England? Suppose she too came to the house? She was worse than Bhanamurti, both more powerful and more sinister. The very thought of her made Liz's head reel. And then a feeling of weakness invaded her, like a poison, creeping slowly through her limbs.

'It's the painkillers,' her father told her. But Liz knew it was not. It was Jeanne. She had come out of hiding and was now mounting a personal attack. There was no doubt it was her. But why, Liz couldn't tell. She hadn't done anything to her. She posed her no threat. The worst of it was, Liz seemed to have no defences against her. She was worn out, her concentration nil, her powers exhausted. She needed to sleep. 'It'll all be the same in a thousand years ...' Well then, what was the point? She drifted off into an uneasy slumber ...

... She was held in a great spider's web, with a big fat spider at the centre of it. And she could do nothing as, paralysed, she watched the spider suck the life out of the other living prey around her, victims like herself, half alive, half conscious of what was being done to them. If only she could move! If only she could hide! If only she couldn't see the agony of the other flies. But then it was her turn. The spider teetered towards her along the invisible threads. It put out its proboscis and thrust it at her ...

She woke, screaming. Her father didn't hear her. He was watching football on T.V. and the crowd was roaring. It was just as well. She couldn't bear his pain as well as her own. But she was afraid. For as her mind refocussed its perception from dream to reality, she felt a presence in the room; a malign presence. She drew in her breath slowly. She must not be afraid.

'Leave me alone!' she hissed into the darkness. 'Bugger off!' She felt the presence rise from the end of the bed and, spreading its wings, cover her. She turned quickly to put on the light, and wrenched her spine. She cried out in agony. She was shaking, sweating. The sweat smelt bad. Was she so very sick? Carefully, deliberately, she turned herself again and laid her spine flat on the hard bed. Breathing slowly, she instructed her muscles to relax. It was still there, lurking behind the light, invisible to the naked eye. 'In the name of Jesus Christ ...' she whispered.

The spiteful knife went in. She gasped with the pain. Why did they hate her so much? 'Sweet Jesus, take the pain away ...' For a second, it went, but then came again more vicious than before. She lay back, helpless, wishing she could dream that other dream, and step off into empty space, because she didn't think she could bear this agony much longer ...

Putney, December 15th

Dear Jim,

I got your letter yesterday. It came in the nick of time, I can tell you. I was about to go under! But when you think, 'It'll all be the same in a thousand years ...' Well, what the hell! So thank you for that.

I bumped into Bhanamurti yesterday. Dad'd sent him off with a flea in his ear and he was lying in wait for me, in the gardens. You'd have laughed yourself silly! 'The Family's' got itself into trouble. There's been a change of mayor and our old friend's gone, so now the local police have got free rein to investigate. Apparently Paula's folks lit the fuse. (I didn't know Father had a Swiss Bank Account!) Anyway, no wonder I've been getting flak in over the air waves! The loonies have been blaming *me* for it all! (Well, it's always easier to blame someone else than to blame yourself, isn't it?)

You see, Father can't do any wrong, because he's God (and it he does, it immediately becomes right because he can do anything, get your brain round that one!), so someone else had to be at the bottom of it, plotting and scheming to make it *look* bad for him, poor innocent man. And guess who's been chosen as prime scapegoat! Well, I suppose I should be flattered. Apparently I'm a really powerful demon and spend all my time scheming to bring about the overthrow of 'The Family'! What imaginations people have!

Actually, seeing Bhanamurti was all a bit traumatic. Well, I say 'a bit', actually it was very traumatic. It set off my back again. So, here I am once more, in bed and at Dad's mercy! The pain's excruciating!

On the plus side, I went to the Monet exhibition which was truly magic! I tried to write and tell you what it was like but I couldn't, so I'm sending you some post-cards instead. Much better to look at them than read my idiot wanderings. Also, Dad's been sounding out the local art colleges for me. He thinks he can get me into a life class starting in January. So, cross your fingers, I might be shut away for hours drawing naked young men! Are you jealous? I hope Bhanamurti and company don't get wind of my activities or they'll mark it up as more proof of my disgustingly promiscuous nature! (Weren't Adam and Eve naked ...? Before they ate of the famous tree, of course!) Speaking of which, any news of my ancestors?

London's completely taken up with Christmas. The radio's all Christmassy songs and the lights are on and Dad's writing mounds of Christmas cards. He seems to know a lot of people. I asked him for some money so I can get him a present. I'll pay him back out of the sale of the house! Ha ha! (Will it *ever* sell?) What would *you* like? Will you be back for Christmas? Dad's told me to ask you here. He's really keen on you and me getting together. So am I, actually. Hope you still feel the same way. God, it nearly *is* Christmas! I'd better stop waffling and get this off or you won't get it in time! I love you, love you, love you! Your own, Lizzie. xxx

Out of politeness, Prem met Jim at Delhi airport, and out of politeness, Jim allowed Prem to show him the sights. A stiff formality characterised their exchanges but the more each wanted to be shot of the other, the more pressing the host became. Jim voiced his concern for Prem's job at the Waterworks. Surely Delhi's water could not do without his constant and expert attention? With the air of a martyr, Prem assured Jim that Delhi water would get a bad press no matter what he did. No-one ever appreciated his efforts. A programme of sight-seeing had been arranged and Jim had better resign himself to it.

It was particularly galling because he was under strict instructions from Nancy to say nothing about Robert's papers. She insisted he leave it to her. Jim's job was therefore restricted to oiling the wheels with the ghee of protocol. It was the toughest assignment of his life. He had no talent for it, no experience of it, and no stomach for it. But, for Liz's sake, he gritted his teeth and performed his duty. If he wanted to bring home the bacon, he really had no choice. And her letters (which had finally caught up with him at the hotel) hadn't given him too much to worry about.

He had read them in sequence. She was painting.

Good. She'd hurt her back? Bad. But it was good again that she was with her father. He was obviously doing his best to look after her and Jim laughed at the story of the spaghetti. As for the attacks, he'd known about that. He'd felt it happening, so it wasn't exactly news. And from what she said it wasn't as bad as he'd feared. Perhaps he'd been worrying himself unnecessarily. Of course it was worrying. Bhanamurti turning up like that. Was that why the solicitor wouldn't tell him where Liz was? That was good. She was being protected. She was bound to be anxious of course, but now her father knew the score (he was glad they'd made it up), he would look after her. All in all the letters put his mind at rest and he went out to do his duty by 'The Red Fort' with an easy conscience.

Explaining the trick, Prem advised Jim not to throw his money away on the levitating beggars. Better spend it on the *son et lumiere*, he said. But when, after a thorough daytime exploration of the famous fortress, they returned to sit in it all evening, Prem again insisted on paying. Oppressed by his cousin's generosity, Jim sat wrapped in shawls against the cold as Shah Jehan's horsemen galloped from tannoy to tannoy and the lights flashed.

It was an excellent show and, had he been a more experienced tourist, Jim would probably have enjoyed it. However he praised the fights and the splendid costumes. He judged the sound effects to be riveting, and having been forced back to Prem's bungalow for supper, it was early morning before Jim was at last allowed to retire. Exhausted, he sank into a hot tub. He wondered what time it was in London. Morning, he decided, but still too early to phone. He closed his eyes for a second and fell asleep in the water.

Jim woke feeling very cold. He emptied the bath and refilled it. His skin felt like wallpaper. Then he dried himself and got into bed. At last! Sleep! The telephone woke him an hour later. It was Prem. He was downstairs in the hotel lobby. Jim got up, dressed and packed a small bag. Prem greeted him brightly.

'Good sleep?' he asked.

'Wonderful,' Jim answered. The irony was lost on Prem.

'Better eat some breakfast,' he said, 'I'll have some with you, then we must be on the road!' They ate in the hotel restaurant, whose decor of medieval knights and hunting scenes seemed faintly inappropriate. And then, as the light came up over Delhi, they joined the blaring horns jamming up the streets.

Jim stayed awake, feeling he had to keep an eye on Prem's driving. He did offer to do some himself, but Prem would have none of it. He was his guest, he should relax and enjoy himself. Jim tried hard to relax as Prem raced buses with bald tyres, daring death by overtaking them on bends at breakneck speed, his hand hard on the horn. The little shrine on the dashboard, Ganesha with plastic flowers, was their only insurance against this suicidal madness. Prem was deeply religious. The lorry in front bore the legend, 'Close your eyes and pray.' Jim hoped against hope Prem wouldn't follow its advice. However he had little option but to follow it himself. Against all the odds, he dozed off. When he woke, they were far out into the desert. The light was stark. Vultures homed in on a dead bullock at the roadside. They tore at its flesh or watched from the bare branches of a tree, beaks like witches' noses, feathers like witches' hair. Poverty cried from the tiny villages, joy from the mouths of children, already at work, herding the bullocks down to the dam.

'They have only a well for water!' Prem told him, putting on his sunglasses. 'My wife comes from one of these villages. Very simple lady. She is very proud of her husband! He has given her water from a tap!' His teeth bared into a smile.

'You're a lucky man,' Jim remarked. 'Have you any

children?' Prem's face darkened. He shook his head.

'Haven't you noticed how clean the house is!' he asked. 'My wife spends all her time cleaning. She is very houseproud. It takes her mind off things, I suppose.'

Jim searched for a means of bringing back Prem's smile. 'Then it's just as well she *has* got water on tap,' he said. Prem laughed and, taking both hands off the wheel, wagged his finger at him.

'But the water is not good in Delhi. Soon we'll be in Agra. Then you'll see the difference. They have good water there!'

'I'll look forward to it,' Jim responded good-humouredly.

It tasted like bleach and it was at Agra Jim got his Delhi belly. Tripping around the town in a rickshaw was torture. He sent Liz a card and hoped it would reach her before Christmas. 'The Taj is magical. The most beautiful thing I ever saw. I love you, Jim.' At Jaipur, Jim shopped for Christmas. He bought Prem's wife a bracelet. Prem was thrilled. It was gold with emeralds. He bought Prem a mascot to hang on his watch. That was gold, too, and imprinted with the swastika, symbol of Ganesha.

'I have to get back for Christmas,' Jim told him as he accepted his thanks. 'So I'll have to go soon.'

'I understand,' Prem said, taking his hands. 'It's a traditional festival. You should be with your family at such a time.'

'I am with my family,' Jim reminded him. Prem was very touched. As he rushed his guest through the desert ruins of Fatehpur Sikri, he began talking about coming to England. Did he mean it, Jim wondered? He couldn't tell. However, he made encouraging noises about showing him the Tower of London and Buckingham Palace and by the time he was eating his last meal at the bungalow in Delhi, Prem and his wife were moist of eye and wishing they had had him to stay.

'Hotels are all very well, but a man needs a home,' Mrs Ridley stated. 'We should find him a wife,' she told her husband.

'I've found one already,' Jim said. His hosts were up in arms.

'But you didn't tell us!' they shouted at once. 'When are you getting married?'

'Soon, I hope.' Jim smiled sheepishly. He didn't feel he could mention the divorce.

'We must definitely send him a present,' Mrs Ridley announced. 'What would you like most in the world?'

Jim glanced at Prem, who looked away. Had Nancy spoken to him? For two pins, Jim would tell him. But the hostess rattled on:

'We could take it over when we visit in the spring!' Her eyes were alight at the prospect. But already Prem had cooled. His look was evasive.

'Perhaps,' he said.

Liz was in the bath when Jim phoned. Pinching her father's bathrobe, she dripped her way to the phone.

'Where are you?'

'Delhi.'

'I've missed you.'

'Me too.'

'I love you.'

'Yes.'

'What do you mean, "yes"?'

'I mean, I love you too.'

'Oh Jim ...' Then tears.

'I'm coming back.'

'When!?'

'Tomorrow. I'll be with you by evening.'

'Christmas Eve! Oh!' She called to her father. 'He'll be here for Christmas!' Then back to the phone. 'I love you.'

'You said. Meet me at Heathrow?'

'Yes. You're not stopping in Kuwait or anywhere are you?'

'You're crazy! No. Cairo.'

'Thank God. What time?'

'Cairo?'

'No! Heathrow, you loony!'

'Ten past five. Air Egypt. Better check it's on time before you set out.'

'I will. I love you.'

'I know!'

'Love me?'

'Are you still as disgracefully lustful as you were?'

Liz giggled. 'Yes! At least where you're concerned.'

'That's alright then.'

'Ooh.'

'Ooh.'

'See you tomorrow ...' Then before he could put the phone down, 'What do you want for Christmas?'

'Can't you guess?'

His low chuckle sent her into raptures of delight. 'He's coming home!' She leapt joyously upon her smiling father, then suddenly cringed with pain. 'I shouldn't have done that,' she said, as he helped her to a chair. 'Oh dear, I hope he won't be disappointed.'

Prem and his wife had come to see him off. They were both very sorry to see him go.

'You know, Jim, I didn't like you at first,' Prem said. 'Frankly, I thought you were very arrogant. I hope you don't mind me telling you this.'

'Not at all,' Jim answered. 'You'll be surprised to know your sister agrees with you.'

'Prem and Nancy agree?' Mrs Ridley asked, round-eyed. Jim laughed and nodded. 'Wonders will never cease!' she said, twinkling. 'Anyway, I think they're both wrong. He's very nice.'

'Thank you,' Jim bowed. Embarrassed, Prem's head inclined to one side, then to the other, then he said:

'What I want to say, if I can get the chance,' he glared at his wife, 'is that I like you now!'

'That's alright then.' Jim smiled.

'Perhaps blood is thicker than water after all!'

Jim saw that Prem's eyes were troubled as he said this. He shook hands with him, bowed again to his wife, and turned to go. He looked back to wave at the departure gate. They were standing side by side, unsmiling, sad. He had grown quite fond of them.

'Thanks for everything!' he called.

'You're welcome!' they called back. And he was gone.

PART FOUR

The nights were getting lighter. Curves of light defined the young man who was the focus of concentration. He was a soft, shy being, vulnerable.

'Stay exactly as you are, please.' Donald snapped on the lights. 'Now, draw him again. Fifteen minutes. Okay Martin?' The model grunted his compliance. Liz turned the page and stared at him, transformed by the harsh light into an angular youth with sharp, even, aggressive features. She worked quickly. Donald was doing his rounds. He would be with her shortly. She wanted to have something for him.

'You've got the pelvis slightly wrong, I think.' The teacher was peering over her shoulder. 'Look at the chair behind him and trace the line down. It's not quite straight.' Liz traced the line. He was right. It wasn't. The pelvis twisted slightly, so slightly, you hardly noticed. But it made all the difference to the whole. Donald nodded slowly. 'Apart from that it's really very good, Liz. You're coming on well.' She could hardly believe her ears. It couldn't be true. She looked for faults.

'Have I got the proportions right? I was a bit worried I'd done a bit of an El Greco on him. You know, elongated him a bit.' Donald tested the lines with his pencil.

'No, it's fine. You've got him very well. He *is* rather long and thin.'

'Thanks, Donald.' Liz tried to sound as though the praise had not gone to her head. 'I'll have another go at the pelvis.' The model didn't blink an eyelash and Donald moved off to look at the next student's work. Liz stuck out her tongue to concentrate, sketched in the new line, rubbed out the old, then smiled. Good old Donald. It really wasn't at all bad now. Even she was pleased. She glanced at the clock. It was almost time. Five minutes to finish off and ...

'Don't forget to leave something for the model,' Donald reminded them.

Going home, Liz allowed herself to bask in Donald's praise. Her face glowed in the dismal bus and she felt like a girl again. It was as though total immersion in form and light had restored her youth. It was all coming back to her, the joy, the excitement, the commitment, just as it had been during her time at the Slade, all those years ago!

All those years lost! But were they? Perhaps 'The Family' was something she'd had to go through. Certainly the experience had changed her. It had unravelled her complexities and made her compassionate, ready to appreciate what was good in life. People were kinder than she'd remembered, nature more poignantly beautiful. Life itself was so precious! Against a background of darkness she was able to see more clearly. This gave a new authority to her work, and expressed itself equally in her attitude to life, which was not surprising, because for Liz, art was life and life was art ... and Jim.

Returning home, she passed the huge carving of Ganesha in the hall. It had finally arrived in February, with a letter of apology from the solicitor. He had forgotten about it, till a couple from Gateshead had raised his hopes about the house. (Would it *ever* sell?) The false alarm had at least got Platt moving! The statue looked strangely at home in the entrance hall of her father's town house.

'Tea?' he called from the back kitchen.

'Not half!' Liz yelled. She threw her anorak and scarf over the banisters, and went through.

'Jim phoned.'

'Oh, good!' she smiled as she took her mug. 'Is he coming down this weekend?'

'He said he wondered if you'd like to go up there.'

'Cambridge? Okay. Would you mind?'

'I'll survive,' her father replied dryly.

'I could take him that picture. If it's back from the framers'.' Her father pulled a face.

'Hah! I just had the bill from the last time!'

'Don't worry, Dad. I'll pay you back out of the sale of the house.' He gave her a dirty look. 'Alright, out of the sale of my pictures.' She opened her drawing book and showed him her latest effort.

'No comment.'

'Have faith!'

He sighed and said, 'I do, I do!' He was putting a roast in the oven.

'Someone coming?' Liz asked.

'Mmm. Boris.'

Liz nodded. She liked Boris. He was a plain-clothes priest and had served with Henry Strachan in the fire service during the war. He was semi-retired now and attached to some sort of centre in Birmingham. But if he was in town, he always called in on Henry for a game of monopoly and a feed up. He was a dab hand at York-shire puddings, too.

'Boris Hubbard's Yorkshires are legendary,' Liz's Dad told her, and he left the making of them entirely to him.

There was time for a lie down before supper. Liz trailed wearily up the stairs and flopped on her bed. Life would be so good, if they'd only leave her alone. Who was it this time? Nathan? Jeanne? She'd almost got used to their broadcasts. Every day something came in and often through the night, too. Then she would wake feeling exhausted and wonder why she couldn't raise the energy to get out of bed. But she wouldn't give in to it. She'd think, 'No, this isn't me. This is nothing to do

257

with me. This is somebody else's pain I'm feeling.' And as soon as she thought it, the attack became more tangible as though it had been exposed. And soon, by putting her attention on possible sources, she was able to pin it down still further to a transmission from Bhanamurti, Nathan or more often Jeanne, or even Father himself. Apparently he was not above a bit of negative projection either! And it wasn't only 'the Family'.

When the Gulf War started, she'd felt it. She had gone icy cold and started shaking. 'It's started!' she told her father. And it had, an hour later. One way or another, she could hardly call her life her own these days. She had tried to shut out the war. It was too painful. But it wasn't so easy to shut out 'the Family'.

She yawned. Perhaps if she ignored it; a sleep might help. She closed her eyes. But her head was heavy, muzzy with the promise of more to come. It was no good; someone, somewhere was confused, worried, and blaming Liz. She would have to deal with it. She opened her eyes and searched for the source. Not Bhanamurti. Not Nathan. Jeanne? Her stomach convulsed. She shot off the bed and ran to the loo. God, what was wrong with the woman? Why couldn't she leave Liz alone!?

Downstairs in the kitchen, Henry Strachan heard his daughter, singing under the shower.

'One fine day you'll sod off, all you nasty bastards and leave me alone, and I won't give ... won't give a sodding monkey's, because you're all bloody loony clones! One fine day ...' He shook his head. He hoped she would finish before Boris arrived. He was broadminded but, well, you've got to respect the cloth, haven't you?

Liz was back in the bedroom when she felt him coming. His signature tune was quite different from Jim's. She could feel Jim as soon as he'd entered her three-mile radius. She'd worked it out. She would feel this icy tingle start up on the top of her head and it got stronger and stronger the nearer he came. He made her shiver! Ooh, he was gorgeous! Boris, however, preceded himself with a soft twinkle, just like 'Twinkle twinkle little star . . .'

What a gentle man he was! She started humming the tune, smiling softly to herself. Well there had to be some compensation for getting in all the dross. Her receivers picked up some lovely messages on the air waves, like Boris now. He really did love everybody. Not that you would think it when you watched him amassing his hotels and houses, she thought, as they entered the second hour of the game.

'Mayfair!' he shouted as Liz's ship landed. 'You owe me . . .'

'She'll pay you when she sells her house!' Henry winked at his daughter, who laughed back.

'No joy?' Boris asked. Liz shook her head.

'I sometimes think Father's put the fluence on it.'

'Mmm.' Boris stroked his bare chin. 'He's not as powerful as all that, you know.' He shook the dice and threw a double. He moved the top hat to a home square and shook again. 'His days are definitely numbered.' He shook a six and a four. He moved the top hat, took his salary and arrived on Henry's station. He paid up without complaint.

'How numbered?' Liz asked.

'Revelations. 12. "The devil is come down unto you, having great wrath, because he knoweth that he hath but a short time." Your guru and his kind were predicted by Christ,' Boris told her. '"For there shall arise false Christs and false prophets, and shall show great signs and wonders; insomuch that, if it were possible, they shall deceive the very elect." Matthew 24. But you should look at "Revelations", if you've got the bottle. It's *very* interesting.'

'My so-called guru said *I* was the devil,' Liz said quietly.

'He would. Diversionary tactics. But you don't have to

accept his judgement anyway. You're a beautiful person, Elizabeth; honest, compassionate, loving. You never lost your contact with God during all your time with them; because God's inside you. That's what's saved you.'

'Am I saved?' she asked doubtfully.

'Christ saved you two thousand years ago.'

'Then why am I suffering now?'

'Are you suffering, my child?'

'Yes, Father.'

'Then you must pray for those who are making you suffer, including your guru. Forgive them. They're worse off than you.'

'I do, Father. But how can I defend myself against them?'

'There's only one thing you can do. Ask Christ to die for you again.' Liz was aghast. How could she do that? How could she ask Christ to suffer? 'You haven't paid,' he told her. Liz's anguish was only too apparent. 'For landing on Mayfair,' Boris twinkled. She paid. Her father conceded. The twinkle burst forth like the morning star.

'You're a terrible man, Father,' Liz chided in an Irish accent.

'I know,' he laughed. 'But then we're all sinners, aren't we?'

When Jim returned from India, empty-handed, Liz had been disappointed, relieved, frustrated, and amused. In fact, she'd gone through a variety of conflicting reactions. But as time went on and she became stronger, she began to feel the time had come to end the suspense. If she could give the lie to the story, then perhaps 'The Family' would lose its hold on her and life could begin again. There had been talk of Prem coming to England in the spring. Of course the war had put him off. No-one wanted to risk flying anywhere, because of the terrorist threat. But it was now the end of March and the war was

260

over. Couldn't Jim ring him and jog his memory? Clutching her picture on the train to Cambridge, she resolved to twist his arm.

Jim was proud of his college, St Timothy's. Like many Americans, he treasured the ancient traditions, the well-trodden stairs and arching courtyards. He had become expert at punting and put many an undergraduate to shame as he guided the craft smoothly along the backs, bending and stretching like a young man, strong and capable. Liz was proud of him. She glanced at the other boats, wanting them to notice how good he was. He made her feel like a queen. She sighed contentedly and pulled the rug around her. It was still a little chilly.

'Got a title for the book yet?' she asked.

'Yes.' He pushed thoughtfully on the pole then, as the impetus thrust them forward, he pulled it free. 'I thought of calling it "The Dark Energy", but it sounds a bit too New Age.'

'Sounds wonderful to me!'

'Not scientific enough.' The punt was drifting. He dropped the pole back in. 'I guess I've more or less decided on "Natural Patterns of Energy Development".' Liz pulled a face. Jim laughed. 'People will take more notice of it, I promise you!' She had to be satisfied with that. She lay back and dreamt of future days when Jim would be know as 'Ridley', the man who wrote that book. People would flock to hear him and he would have his own programme on Channel 4. She, the artist wife, would of course live in Cambridge with her famous husband. Lost in her projections, she was surprised to find they were back at 'Timothy's'. It was twelve o'clock. They were invited to lunch with the Master. The dream had already begun.

'So what's it about, this book?' the Master asked. 'Sounds vaguely ecological to me.'

'Sure,' Jim said. 'But it's not so much about saving

261

nature, as about allowing nature to do the job of saving herself. I reckon it's time we humans stopped interfering so much.' The Master raised his eyebrows and glanced at his wife. This was novel indeed. 'You see,' Jim went on, 'nature is self-renewing. All we've got to do is be very careful not to interfere with the renewing process by pushing the balance too far, blowing holes in the ozone layer and sucking stratas out from under us ...'

'Sounds like received wisdom to me,' the Master observed, disappointed.

'... because,' Jim went on, 'if we go on doing that sort of thing, sooner or later nature is going to creep up behind us and blow us sky high. Nature abhors a vacuum. If we create one, something will rush to fill it. God knows what it'll be. You see, it's not the ozone layer itself, or pollution or even bombs that'll finish us off. They're only the trigger! It's the unexpected we've got to watch out for. Ancient civilisations have known this since the beginning of time. Look at the aborigines. Look at the Hopi Indians. They know. They worship nature as a living organism. She is our mother. We have to respect her or, at best, she'll withdraw her nurturing spirit from us, leaving us to die of drought and famine, and at worst reverse it, to bring about a cataclysmic disaster of apocalyptic proportions.'

The Master took in a deep breath. Was this physics or anthropology? 'The worst of it is,' Jim continued passionately, 'we can't predict what form that disaster will take. It'll come out of the blue. Like I said, it's the unexpected we've got to watch out for.' The Master coughed lightly.

'So, er, where do Geothermal Studies come into the scheme of things?'

'In future,' Jim explained, 'we're going to have to restrict ourselves to creaming off excess energy, rather than creating it and by doing so creating new problems, as the nuclear, and oil or coal-generated electricity industries tend to do. Where hydro-electricity isn't feasible, geothermal energy is the obvious answer. Master, we are literally sitting on a volcano here. It's time we used it and in using it learned to have a healthy respect for it, too. Or ...' Jim shrugged and dropped his hands on the table. 'Finito.'

'You know, Ridley,' the Master said after a pause, 'you've got a reputation for being a bit on the dry side.' His eyes twinkled. 'I think this should scotch all that!' Everyone laughed. 'That sabbatical of yours certainly put some fire in your belly! Knew it would!' He chortled, rubbing his hands, taking the credit. 'And the students will love it! You'll have them positively flocking to your lectures!'

'I can see Jim on television!' Liz remarked with delight. Jim went cold. 'Oh Eve!' he thought, 'Still tempting Adam!'

'Oh I do agree!' The Master's wife chimed in, gurgling. 'You could become quite a cult figure, Jim!' Liz swallowed hard. She glanced at Jim. He had pulled back from the table.

'I don't want to become some sort of guru!' he objected.

'You may not have any choice, Jim,' The Master sympathised. 'People will make you a guru, whether you like it or not. The world chooses its own masters; creates its own gods and its own monsters; like Saddam Hussein among other less reputable characters! He has become the focus of collective fantasies, hero or villain depending on your point of view. Look, Jim, it doesn't have to go to your head, just so long as you realise *you* don't matter. Intellectual, spiritual, political, even sexual leaders all emerge from the collective unconscious, they simply pop out, its product, if you like!'

'I don't like,' Jim said testily.

'Don't knock it, Jim!' the Master advised. 'If it happens to you, enjoy it! I know I should! It's how stars are made. Look at Marilyn Monroe!'

'Look at what *happened* to her!'

'Don't be a spoilsport, Jim!' The Master touched his arm. 'Good for the college to have a well-known personality on board! Brings in sponsorship!' Liz's dreams sucked out of her, leaving an aching vacuum. And, as nature abhors a vacuum, angry frustration flooded in. Were they to be denied everything then? She stared at Jim across the table. He had withdrawn. His mouth was set. 'Well,' the Master said soothingly, 'let's see if it happens first.'

Later, in Jim's room, he and Liz had their first row.

'You can't not publish, Jim! It's too important! It needs to be said!'

'Then I'll publish anonymously. That way I'll avoid the hype!'

'But then the book won't have any authority! And what about your career? This could make you!'

'Yes! Into a guru apparently!'

'This is ridiculous.'

'Oh I get it. You want me to take the place of your last guru. And I thought you liked me for myself.'

Liz stared at him. That was below the belt. She mustered all her dignity to reply.

'No,' she said, 'I don't want any more gurus, thank you very much. In fact, I don't want to join any kind of bandwagon ever again. I'm a free spirit, like all artists. But I do care about the earth. I love it. I love the trees and the animals and the sea. I even love human beings sometimes. But not when they're bloody-minded like you!'

'Okay. *You* don't want to be tied down. Okay. Why can't you allow *me* the same privilege? To be myself? Is that too much to ask?'

'Yes, Jim. It is. You've got a responsibility! You've got something to say! You've *got* to say it!'

'It's funny, you know,' Jim sighed. 'My book's about a change in human behaviour. It's saying, that instead of feeling we've got to make our mark on the world, in order to prove how great we are, we've got to live invisibly, like the ancient Americans. When they passed on, it was as though they'd never been. That's the accolade.'

'"Leave the bathroom as you found it!"' Liz snorted.

'Yes! We shouldn't feel the need to put our signature on everything.' He pointed his finger at her. 'That goes for my book, too!' There were tears in Liz's eyes. There was a terrible logic to what he was saying. She could see it, but she couldn't accept it.

'Is there to be no satisfaction in this world?' she cried.

Jim shrugged. 'Not if it's your ego that wants satisfying, no.'

'Well,' she snorted. 'You're in a bit of a fix, aren't you, dear?'

'I don't see why,' he replied smugly.

'Don't you? An intelligent man, like you? Tut tut. Let me explain, dear. Either you selfishly live according to your own precepts and don't publish your book, or you do publish, everybody else gets the message and the earth is saved! So, tell me, oh great one, is it more egotistical to publish or not to publish?' Jim gaped.

'You bitch!' Then he laughed in spite of himself, 'Your years in India certainly left their mark!'

They laughed, but the laughter had an edge to it. There was still a rift between them. Liz was edgy, nervous. Jim was resentful. This was where involvement got you. Their lovemaking was wistfully sad. It was as though each was trying to smooth balm onto the wounds they themselves had inflicted, knowing the battle wasn't over yet and there were more wounds to come.

'You can't sail through life without being touched by it,' Liz said. She was looking at the Monet postcards on the wall, the ones she'd sent Jim when he was in India. They'd travelled half way round the world and back again. They'd inspired thoughts of a holiday. It had been planned for early summer. They were to take the car on the ferry, and follow the Monet trail, down to Bel'isle, Vetheuil, the Seine, Giverny. It would be a sort of honeymoon. Now everything was put in doubt.

'I don't see why not,' Jim replied from under the duvet. 'It's suited me very well so far.'

'You can say that again!' Liz flashed. 'You never do anything, do you? You just sit on the fence and let things happen to you! God! I bet if you'd really tried to find me, you could have stopped me going to India all those years ago!' Jim threw the duvet back.

'Oh, I see. It's all my fault now, is it?'

'But you just don't stir yourself, do you?! You just stand back and watch! If I was attacked in the street, you'd just stand by and watch, wouldn't you?!' He threw the duvet off and launched himself into his clothes. 'You couldn't even bring back a few papers from India!'

'Ah! So that's it!' Jim froze her with a look. 'Could you have dealt with it, if I had?' She looked away. 'I did my best, Liz. And when the papers were not forthcoming, I left it in the lap of the Gods. There's a time to act and a time to leave it. It was a time to leave it!'

'It's always a time to leave it where you're concerned!' Liz snapped.

'I thought it was for the best.' He was patently sincere. Liz turned away to hide bitter tears. He finished dressing, then said, 'Look, this isn't getting us anywhere. What do you say we take a rain check on the rest of this weekend? Cool off a bit?' Liz started shaking. She could hardly look at him. He seemed so deadly calm.

'I'm sorry....' she began. Jim butted in:

'Don't say that.' She stared at her shoes, bent to put them on, then finally stood up, unwilling to go.

'Do you like your picture?' she asked. He glanced at the portrait on the wall. His expression softened. 'That's how I really see you,' she said. 'I love you.'

'I know,' he answered and drove her to the station.

Twist his arm? she thought, as the train hurtled through the evening back to London. Some hope! A confusion of emotions surged through her as she walked along the peaceful Thames. And when, unexpectedly, she let herself into the house, looking pale and strained, her father forebore asking questions. He just made her a hot chocolate and settled to watch the football match as planned. She'd talk, if she wanted. But Liz was ashamed. She wasn't without blame. Okay, Jim was an unreasonable, uncompromising bastard. But, all the same, she shouldn't have laid into him like that. Look at all he'd done for her! Why had she shot her mouth off about the papers? What had got into her? She climbed the stairs to her room, crept into bed and put out the light. At least the air waves were clear. The only pain was in her heart.

And she dreamt the corridor dream again. And again the doors opened to different rooms. In the last, she saw herself and Jim, accepted Cambridge noteworthies, happy in the cosy framework of academia. She wanted to go inside. But the ghost closed the door, and when she looked, she realised in panic there were no more doors; only the gaping hole at the end of the corridor! And the ghost had let go of her hand. He had disappeared. Where had he gone? She called out for him. But she was being sucked down the corridor, through the gaping hole, and out into the blue sky ...

She woke, sweating. But she knew what she had to do. She dressed and went out into the early morning. The river was silent, shimmering; the trees, bare or freshly green gleamed in the damp light that hung in the air and sparkled in the grass. She trembled with excitement. She had never been so clear about anything in all her life.

Jim was staring at the flashing light on his computer

screen. He had to make a decision. There was a publication date to meet and the Master breathing down his neck. She was right of course. In a perverse kind of a way (typical of him) it was arrogant to avoid celebrity status. It was a cop out. Leaving his own personal commitment aside, the thing still needed to be said. So, he argued, it was just a kind of a job. And it fell to him. He had to finish the book.

Okay. What then? Suppose the media took it up? Great! It'd get the message across. Suppose people wanted to hear him speak? Well, he was the best person to push the message home! He could always return from the limelight afterwards and, in time, people would forget him. Only the message would remain. The thing was not to take any of it personally. Anyone could be doing the job, it just so happened it was him. That was it. That was how to avoid it going to his head. Just because they called Liz a devil didn't make her one. (Unless she accepted the judgement, which of course she didn't.) And if they called him a guru it wouldn't make him a guru either! The trick was to keep your identity innocent of the projections of others. Do, but don't get involved in the doing. Was that what Sethi meant?

The green light was still flashing. Jim looked away from it to the window. The early light streaming through the glass was pure white. Liz was always on about light. Why had he been so hard on her? Why was he always so hard on those he loved? Take Kim ... come to think he hadn't thought of Kim in a long while. She'd faded out of his consciousness. Had she let him go? Well, he didn't need her to prod him any more, did he. He had Liz! She'd prodded him into life alright!

Suddenly he realised it was no wonder the Koreans hadn't got through to him. He was in a state of mental deadlock at the time. There was no achievement. Nothing to be proud of. He'd been deadlocked for years! And if it hadn't been for Liz he still would be. It was a sobering thought. If it wasn't for her he wouldn't have gone to Oz, wouldn't have written this book. She'd triggered his release. And now ... he got up, went to the cupboard and pulled out a parcel ... he had to trigger hers.

The parcel had arrived the week before. He had meant to give it to her this weekend, and then ... Well, he thought guiltily, maybe it was for the best. Their row had saved her in a way. She couldn't handle bad news. Not yet. Okay, so, in keeping it from her he *had* been motivated by petty spite! He was human, wasn't he? But on reflection, he judged the time wasn't right anyway. He would have to choose the moment carefully. Nancy would have said their row was meant. She could be right at that. The parcel was addressed to him. He opened the padded envelope and drew out the papers. There was a letter from Prem.

Delhi, March 15th

Dear Jim,

I apologise for not having written to you before, but I have been very busy at the Waterworks. We had a crisis here and I am afraid it means I cannot be spared for the trip to England. I am very sorry. My wife also is devastated. In fact, she was so upset she started the spring cleaning early. She found these papers in a cupboard and said she was fed up with them gathering dust. She is quite right. There are far too many papers cluttering up our lives. I never even found the time to do more than glance at them and now I can't be bothered with such things. So, rather than throw them out, I am sending them to you. I believe you said you wanted to see them. If you have changed your mind, don't bother sending them back. As far as I'm concerned it's good riddance to bad rubbish. My wife sends her kind regards. We remember your visit with great pleasure, as does my sister Nandini, who thanks you for the book. As you

know, she is a great fan of Sherlock Holmes. We hope
you will not forget to tell us the date of your wedding so
we can send a nice present. Please present our compli-
ments to the bride.
Kind regards,
Prem.

Jeanne was awake. Liz checked her watch. She could
time Jeanne's movements by her broadcasts. And
judging by her current getting-up time, it looked like she
was in England. She was coming in loud and clear this
morning. Liz retched into the undergrowth and sighed.
What was the matter with the woman? She went home
and made some coffee.

Jim put the letter aside and weighed the papers in his
hand. In a way it was as much his business as hers. They
were his ancestors, too. But did he have the right to read
them before her? He thought not. He felt a shiver of
excitement as he put the papers back in the padded
envelope and closed the cupboard on them. The right
moment ...? Perhaps when he and Liz were on vacation? Their Monet pilgrimage! He looked at Liz's
picture over the fireplace. He hadn't praised it nearly
enough. Typical! And it was good, really good. Jim
Ridley looked down his nose at Jim Ridley. She'd got
him to a 'T'. He smiled a wry smile. What was that she
said about art being a mirror? Did he always look so
superior? And yet the mouth was tenderly drawn, even
compassionate. There was humour in the lines around
the eyes. The body language was gentle. She didn't
think so badly of him, in spite of what she'd said. And
she'd caught the light so it seemed to glow from within
the frame. Now how had she done that? Had she seen it,
or imposed it? He switched off the computer, yawned
and stretched. It was time to make some coffee.

*

270

Liz felt the tingling of icicles on her head and knew Jim was thinking of her. She smiled. So he hadn't gone off her then. She drank her coffee, looking down at the garden. After the shock of ice and snow, spring had come suddenly and, though early, it was already warm as summer. Was it because of the change of climate? The greenhouse effect? It had already begun. Was Jim's warning necessary? Was it too late? A bird flew onto the window ledge and looked in at her. Did it know its world might end? Tears welled up in Liz's eyes. She loved the earth. And yet, Jim was right … What time was it? Half past nine. Would he be up? It was Sunday.

It was flowing again. The green light moved, as Jim's fingers touched the keys, writing with authority and ease. When the telephone rang, he frowned, finished his sentence and picked up the receiver with a churlish:

'Hi. Who's that?'

'Liz.'

'Oh. Morning. How are you?'

'Fine. You?'

'Fine.'

'I rang to say I'm sorry.'

'What for?'

'The book. You were right.'

'Was I?'

'Yes. I was being selfish. You're free to do what you like. You know that.'

'Sure.' Jim stared at the words on the screen. Seeing a clumsy phrase he itched to change it. His finger moved and Liz heard the clicking of the computer keys.

'Are you working?'

'Yeah. Got up early.'

'So did I.'

'Lovely morning.'

'Yes.' She paused, bracing herself to speak. He was staring at the screen. 'I mean it, Jim. You're free, in every way.'

271

'Thanks,' he said, wondering how you spell 'traveler' in English. Did it have one 'l' or two?

'I'm not going to tie you down by hankering after a home, lifestyle, you know, a sort of domestic identity. I don't want to put you into a straitjacket. And I'll kill anybody else who tries to as well! So, if you want to throw up Cambridge and your career and everything, and just take off, it's alright with me. Okay? Jim are you listening?'

'Yeah. Has traveler got one "l" or two?'

'Two. Why? What are you working on?'

'The book.'

'The book?'

'Yeah.'

'You mean *the* book?'

'Yeah.'

'But I thought ...'

'You've got to learn to take things day to day, honey.'

'Yes, dear,' Liz said through clenched teeth.

'Am I really an arrogant bastard?'

'Yes!'

Jim laughed. 'Thought so. Do you still love me?'

'Yes.' Liz sighed. 'Though sometimes I wonder why!'

The following month Jim was hard at it, trying to finish the book. (He wanted it finished before the vacation.) So he stayed in Cambridge and Liz kept out of his way in Putney. She felt nervous, as though something momentous was going to happen. But was that something good or bad? There was no way of knowing.

Perhaps, she reasoned to herself, it was Jim's book. Maybe it was going to make the terrific impact they hoped it would. On the other hand, maybe he was going to have an accident. Or was it her father? He was old. Perhaps he would fall ill, or win the pools (he had a standing entry with Vernons), or win a prize in a Readers' Digest draw! Fear and hope vied with one another in her consciousness, while on a deeper level a battle royal was going on.

At first she had been able to control it. Usually it was one of the 'Family' transmitting hatred, fear, vindictive jealousy, any one of a host of negative emotions. (Usually, but not always, Jeanne, or Father. She always knew who.) By transmitting love, she often neutralised it. If this failed, turning herself into a mirror, she would send back their poisonous darts, 'Return to Sender'.

Sometimes she sensed them weaving the threads of conspiracy like a net around her, and she cut through their entangling mesh with the swords of truth and innocence, before they had entrapped her with their lies and perversions. But when, as often happened, they projected their own sins onto her (as though she could carry the burden of their evil for them), she fell sick. For this was harder to fight. It invaded and weakened her.

Under the onslaught, which let up neither day nor night, a pressure built up all around her. Like a deep sea diver on the ocean bed of resistance, suffering pain in every sinew, every joint, her unconscious self was fighting for its life. And she had no idea why they were doing this to her. Having failed to drive her mad, were they now trying to kill her? For God's sake, why?

Some days, she could hardly walk for pain and her brain had to struggle through misery to function at all. But it was at her life class that it began to be too much. Usually by concentrating on the subject, the pain would at least shift, but this time, she was in such discomfort it brought tears to her eyes and, at the break, she was forced to leave the class.

Donald, who knew of her previous back problems, advised her to have a scotch and lie flat on the floor as soon as she got home. His sympathy impelled her to the bus, but sitting in it, jolted agonisingly from side to side, she began to cry. Her back was hurting alright, but it was a symptom rather than a cause. She knew they were trying to stop her. Stop her doing what? God knew. Somehow she got off the bus at Putney Bridge and, concentrating hard, forced her body home. She felt the twinkling presence of Boris. So, he was visiting! She looked in on them in the sitting room and smiled bleakly. No, she didn't feel in the mood for Monopoly, she had just called in to say hello (before she died!). She made her way slowly up the stairs and lay on the floor of her room. She had tried everything. She had no weapons left. She wished she could pass out, pass away! Anything, to end this pain and misery.

'Hail Mary, full of grace, the Lord is with thee ...' Dear Boris hadn't a clue! What did he know of the invading evil that, like a virus, infiltrated the system and tortured every part till it gave in or died? But she would not give in. They would not control her. She would not become a transmitter of their evil. She would rather die. The pain increased. She began moaning and wept:

'Christ, Christ, please take the pain from me!' The pain covered her like a wave. She felt sick and was close to passing out. 'Christ, please bear the pain for me.' Hot tears stung her face and she retched on the carpet. She felt like death. 'Christ, die for me!'

Her head lightened. There was a sensation like ice on the base of her spine. It spread through her back, as though melting through the sinews, and when it reached her hip it whirled like a wheel and spun out up her side and down her leg, soothing like balm. The nausea was replaced by a sudden headache. The pain shot shafts of splintering light through her brain and a heavy stinging mass hung on the back of her head like a clinging jellyfish.

If Christ had listened to her once ... She had asked Him to die for her. He had made the sacrifice but she hadn't eaten His flesh or drunk His blood. The very idea made her squirm. It was disgusting. It made her a cannibal, the lowest of the low. Never, never had she

understood how anyone could take part in the
Eucharist. How could you claim to love Christ and do
such a thing? But, humbled, she now knew that her love
for Christ was not going to save her, only His love for
her! He was her only hope. It was the bottom line. Only
by eating the sacrifice would she accept it, and if she
didn't accept it, then He had died in vain and she was
finished. She must take the Eucharist.

Closing her eyes she saw the chalice containing
Christ's blood, and she drank with a sense of deep gratitude. Hot and fiery, a shape rose out of her and hung
over her body. She dared not open her eyes. What if
flames encircled her, as before? Hot, silent flames
dancing round her? Wet with sweat, she began shivering.

'Christ, defend me.' She opened her eyes and saw
him, eyes yellow and unblinking, and she knew who he
was. The shivering increased. What weapon had she?
What could she throw at him?

'You're finished!' She told him. 'But you won't finish
me! Christ died for me! I have drunk of his blood!' As
she hurled the word 'blood' in his face, he disappeared.
Where had he gone? Was he an illusion? A phantasm?
A trick of the light? She waited, lying still, breathing
hard. The shivering died. She was very cold. He had
gone. Thank Christ, he had gone. Twisting, she reached
for the duvet and pulled it off the bed. She wrapped it
round her, crying. Now she knew who he was. She
would no longer be deceived. She reached for the bible;
Matthew 24:

'For there shall arise false Christs and false prophets
and shall show great signs and wonders; insomuch that,
if it were possible, they shall deceive the very elect.
Behold I have told you before. Wherefore, if they shall
say unto you, behold, he is in the desert; go not forth;
behold he is in the secret chambers; believe it not.

'For as the lightning cometh out of the east, and

shineth even unto the west; so shall also the coming of the Son of man be.'

How could she have been so stupid? When he comes, no-one's going to miss it! So, 'guru', you know what you can do with your secret mantras! Trembling with elation, Liz eased herself from the floor. The pain had gone. Shouts came from below. Boris was winning the game. She half laughed, half cried as she made her way down to the kitchen for a reviving pot of tea.

The attacks didn't stop. But now Liz had an armour. She knew she was right. She knew Christ had saved her. She knew too that there is a law in the universe, the law of rebound. As a child she had imbued it from Charles Kingsley's *The Water Babies*, through the character of Mrs-Do-as-you-would-be-done-by. She wouldn't wish ill on 'the Family', but if ill befell them they would have brought it on themselves. She fought on. She went to her general drawing class and Donald congratulated her on her miraculous recovery.

'Scotch works wonders,' he winked. She laughed and enjoyed the class. She adored Donald. He was so wonderfully normal! But on her way back home, Liz got a strange feeling. It felt like something creeping up her left side. It squirmed round her kidney and settled in there, making her nauseous. Getting off the bus at Putney, she looked round warily. There was an ache on her right lung. She coughed, then retched. What was going on? She tuned in to her father. His usual light transmission had transformed into a burning heaviness. There was a strong stab of pain in her throat. She coughed again. He was in trouble. Was he ill? She had better hurry. But her instinct told her to be wary.

She took a different route to the house, avoiding the river and the gardens, watching out for signs. When she reached the corner of the street, she looked carefully before turning into it. She must not panic. Whatever had happened, she would have to deal with it, so she must be calm. Was this what she'd felt coming? Was this what her nervousness had meant? As she neared the end of the street, the pain on her lung was suddenly released: it was as though a bubble of cool air had burst inside it.

She paused on the corner, heart racing, legs shaking. It was over, whatever it was. She was too late now. She took a deep breath and turned the corner. She was now parallel with the river. The house was on the right. She walked a few steps towards it, and reeled back as the stench of vomit rose up to meet her. She retched into the grass.

'Are you alright, dear?' the woman across the road called. She was shaking her 'WELCOME' mat out of the front door.

'Yes,' Liz gasped. 'Will be in a minute.'

'Must be that 'flu that's about. Some funny things about these days. You've got to be careful!' She retreated inside her house and closed the door as if to shut out the unseen virus. Very wise, Liz thought.

Gathering herself together she made for her father's door. She was shaking so much, she couldn't find the key. She leaned on the bell. A door banged in the house. Was it her Dad? Or someone else? Please God, let it be her Dad! She heard steps, and with a sigh of relief she recognised her father's light, sharp tread. The door opened stealthily.

'Oh, it's you!' he said. He looked out, to right and left. 'Get inside.' Liz didn't need telling twice. She fell into the house.

'What's happened?'

'What do you mean? Have you seen her?'

'Who?'

'Funny woman, funny accent, short curly hair, looking for you.'

'Jeanne.'

'Didn't give a name. Just a message.'

'What was it?'

'Don't know if I should tell you.'

'Please, Dad!'

'She was one of them wasn't she?' Liz nodded. 'She said, "Tell your daughter she'd better retract her story."'

'What story?'

'That's what I asked. She said she'd had a man following her, a journalist. She thinks it's got something to do with you.'

'Me?'

'Yes. You. Apparently he was from one of the Sunday papers. He was taking her photo in the street.' Liz couldn't help laughing. 'It's no laughing matter!' Henry chastised.

'Dad, I don't know what's going on any more than you do! But, whatever it is, it's got nothing to do with me!'

'She was scared shitless.'

'Good.'

'Especially after I laid into her!' Liz grinned.

'What did you say to her?'

'I wouldn't like to repeat it.' She punched him playfully on the chest as one comrade to another. But Henry wasn't proud of himself. 'Eh, love,' he said, trembling, 'what have you got yourself into?'

'Not into,' Liz corrected him gently, 'out of!'

'Thank Christ!'

'Amen!' Liz kissed him tenderly on the cheek. 'You did well, Dad. Thanks.'

'Aye well, I think I'll just pop round to the newsagents, order a few papers for this coming Sunday, eh? I like a bit of sauce with my bacon!' He made for the door, but his legs buckled. 'On the other hand,' he said, 'I think maybe I'll just have a cup of tea first!'

Jim had finished his book. Exhausted but satisfied, he delivered the manuscript to the publisher on the Friday afternoon and went straight to Putney. He found Henry in quite a state. He'd got it into his head his daughter was going to be in the tabloids. He'd made Liz nervous, too. But how could she be involved? 'The Family' wouldn't dare mention Liz's name because if they did it would backfire on them. The papers would be round like greased lightning offering her thousands upon thousands of pounds for her story!

No, Liz decided, they'd probably got onto Paula's custody case and Jeanne had been trying to stop them publishing. But when Jim returned from the newsagents on Sunday morning, they gasped in astonishment at the headlines: 'The God Flees!' 'What an Unholy Mess!'; and the last and longest article was titled, 'Keeping it in "The Family".' A picture of Father topped the page, devotees crowding round his feet, Bhanamurti clearly visible among them. Taking a deep breath, they read on:

Followers of the man they called 'Father' and thought of as God, were bewildered and dismayed as the police moved in and God moved out, fast, leaving them to tidy up the mess!

And what a mess! Has God really been blackmailing a brothel keeper? No! Surely, that £50,000 donation was a gift from a prominent businessman out of the goodness of his heart! Or that's what they thought when the former mayor of Gulhapur was in power! But a new broom, in the shape of a new mayor has swept out some very murky corners recently.

Police, investigating the affairs of wealthy and much respected businessman, Ranjit Senjali, revealed that Mr Senjali's principal source of income was protection money from brothel keepers! So, it seems pimps and prostitutes have been funding the ambitious plans of the cult to create a 'heaven on earth' in unspoilt countryside close to Gulhapur. And as if that wasn't bad enough, now Senjali claims the money was a blackmail payment to 'Father' who had threatened to expose him if he didn't cough up!

'At the time,' Mr Senjali said, 'I looked on the donation as an insurance against being closed down, but now I see I should never have been asked to pay it.' When he heard of Mr Senjali's

accusation, the new mayor moved in fast. 'The police have been keeping an eye on "The Family's" activities for some time,' he said. 'Minor offences, such as gold and currency smuggling, illegal exportation of antiques, and, on a more serious note, fraudulent misuse of funds had already alerted us to the criminal background of this so-called religious group. These gurus get India a bad name. They should be stopped. Innocent people get enmeshed in their criminal activities and they believe it's all in the interests of heaven. There is a strong business lobby in Gulhapur who would be glad to see the back of "The Family". They do not pay their bills and the village they intend to build on the outskirts of the town poses a threat to the public water supply.

Wandering dazed through the fields, 'Family' members pointed out where God had planned to build their 'Shangri La'. It was to have its own schools, hospitals and ashrams. But was Mr Senjali's 'donation' really intended for this work? The 'Father's' followers point out that building has already begun. But only on the guru's palace! His willing slaves have spent months building this sumptuous home with its marble floors and gold-plated bath taps. (What does a god want with a jacuzzi?) And where has the money come from to pay for all this? Some of it, from the followers themselves who have given all their worldly goods to this guru. The rest, from donations like that of Mr Senjali!

The organisation has branches all over the world, including London. A spokeswoman, pictured here walking down a London street, stated that 'The Family' is not a cult. 'It promotes a relaxed state of being, conducive to good health,' she said to our reporter. 'Everyone would benefit from learning "The Way".' But when asked which 'way' her disappearing guru had gone, she became rather nervous. 'I cannot tell you. I don't know,' she said, and refused to speak to us any more. When pressed, she ran off down the street. We had to take our snapshot on the run! Perhaps she should learn to relax by trying a meditation technique? Word has it that 'Father' has run off with his family ... his real family, that is: brother, sister, mother-in-law and adult children, to South America, where no doubt the Swiss Bank

Account which is rumoured to exist will keep them in the manner they have come to expect. This guru certainly believes in keeping everything in 'the family'!

Liz, Jim and Henry were silent for some time. Jim was thinking of the other monsters thrown up by the collective unconscious. Hitler for instance.

'Seems any charismatic leader can create myth out of lies, when reinforced by popularity,' he said.

'Did you know about any of this?' Henry asked. Liz shook her head.

'I had no idea. And neither would any of the poor sods they interviewed either ... except maybe Jeanne and perhaps one or two others.' Liz was shaking. Her voice broke as she exclaimed, 'And they thought *I* was behind this?'

'I wonder if Boris has seen it!' Henry rose and wandered, dazed, to the door. 'Think I'll give him a bell,' He went out, leaving Jim and Liz alone.

'Well,' Jim said at last, 'lets you off the hook!'

'Does it?' Glancing up, Jim saw she was perplexed. While she believed she was born with a stigma, the cult would still have a hold on her. Perhaps that was why, to her surprise, Liz was feeling sad. 'You know,' she said, 'Father had real powers. He could have used them to do so much good. It's a tragedy!'

'Ah but, where did he get his powers from?' Jim asked. Liz smiled a watery smile.

'I don't want to know,' she said. 'The tree of knowledge etcetera ...' She sighed philosophically. 'I already know more than is good for me. Maybe it's because of the cult I got to be so sensitive. Or perhaps it's a punishment for what I've done, or something to do with my inheritance. I don't know. Anyway, whatever the reason, it looks like I've got to learn to live with pain, haven't I?'

The morning was dazzling. Giddy with light, Liz laughed like a girl, pointing through the window at the rainbows spiralling round the hovercraft. Two, three, four at once encircled them. They leaped and played, darted and arched, accompanying them all the way across the channel. And when, approaching Calais, she and Jim went below to retrieve their car, Liz was so blinded by light she could see only the immaterial shapes of fellow passengers, or the insubstantial curves of vehicles, lined up and ready to go. Her heart lifted as they glided from craft to shore, where the warm sunshine of France greeted them and sent them off down the coast; driving to Dieppe, for coffee, Pourville, Varengeville, Fécamp, then Etretat for a picnic lunch on the cliffs. The light on The Manneporte would have delighted Monet.

'You know,' Liz said, 'this place reminds me of Marsden Rock!' Jim could see what she meant. It was very like Marsden, especially as it was in the old days, when Jane and Robert were alive.

He'd seen early postcards of the beach. But cliffs erode and rocks fall and as time goes on, it gets harder and harder to make out the original structure. 'The north-east light has a more mysterious quality, though,' Liz reflected. 'Like a veil, it masks rather than reveals; no matter what the weather! Here the rock looks totally different, according to the light.' She chewed thoughtfully on her baguette, wondering why her attempts at painting Marsden always left her so dissatisfied.

'I can't catch the spirit of the place!' she said finally. 'It eludes me! I need to see it in this light! Just once!'

'Maybe mystery *is* the spirit of the place?' Jim ventured. 'The North-East's full of stories and legends ... a web of illusion spun round it ... like the Lambton Worm round Penshore Hill!'

'Yes,' Liz replied doubtfully, 'but it's hard to find yourself in an atmosphere of stories and legends.'

'You should have been a miner or a fisherman. You'd have seen things in a different light then!'

'True,' Liz agreed. 'But I wasn't, was I? I was born an artist. And that's not all.' She sighed. 'No, people like me need to get away from it to see things clearly.'

'And, when you can, will you go back?' Liz glanced at Jim, surprised.

'Go back?'

'One day. Why not? You know you love the place. It's home to you. Or at least you'd like it to be.' Liz looked across the shimmering sea. 'Maybe when the house is sold ...?' Jim teased. They laughed. It seemed such an unlikely scenario. 'What are you going to do with the money?' Liz shook her head.

'I don't know,' she said. 'There won't be that much. Maybe enough for a terraced cottage somewhere ...' Her eyes lit up. 'Bamburgh for instance? Oh, I'd love to live at Bamburgh! I could paint that shoreline till I was old, and afterwards! Do you know, when I was young, I used to dream of living in that castle one day!'

'I thought you wanted to get away from stories and legends.' Liz chuckled. For a moment her eyes reflected the rippling light on the sea, then a veil fell in front of them and she said:

'Perhaps if I'd mastered my own past ... it would

make all the difference.' His voice was wistful. 'As it is, I haven't found myself, have I?'

Jim swallowed hard. He had to steady himself to speak.

'I got some papers from India ...' he began. At once there were tears in Liz's eyes. She started shaking. The shock was almost too much to bear.

'Tell me! What do they say?' she asked. She looked all too vulnerable.

'I haven't read them, Liz,' Jim told her and was thankful for it. 'I felt it wasn't my place.' Now he realised it had been an excuse. How could he have told her? She looked away, searching the horizon for strength to cope with whatever fate might throw at her.

'I suppose,' she began, 'I suppose they must have loved one another, in a way.' Her eyes darted to Jim's, pleading for encouragement.

'If you can look at it like that,' he reasoned, 'I don't think it'll do you any harm to know.' Her eyes never left his face. 'I brought the papers with me,' he told her. 'In case the moment came ...' And now it was his turn to plead, 'You won't hold it against me, will you, if the news is bad?' She shook her head quickly and gave a nervous, brittle laugh.

'Just so long as you won't hold it against *me*?'

He took her in his arms and covered her mouth with his. Long and lingering, their kiss reminded her of their lovemaking at Erice. With all the urgency of the first and the last time, it would be with her forever. She was crying as their lips parted.

'I love you,' he said.

'And I love you,' she replied.

'Pax.'

'Pax.'

Gathering their things, they went back to the car. They drove silently on, glancing at Honfleur and Trouville, before making their way downriver to Rouen, where they were to spend the night. After a meal in a side-street café, they went up to their room and Jim produced the documents Prem had sent. Neatly tied with string, they emerged from the padded envelope, a slim bundle which, when untied, revealed an old copy book, a small sheaf of papers and three letters: two without envelopes, one unopened.

Liz put on her glasses and read the postmark. It said 'Bombay' and it was addressed to Mrs G. Beattie, The Florist Shop, 18 Victoria Terrace, Fowler Street, South Shields, County of Durham, England. The address was scored through and the envelope marked, 'Return to Sender'. So, she, or someone, had sent it back! But why? It didn't feel like anything bad! In fact, it felt rather good! Had they got it all wrong?

Surprised and encouraged, Liz searched for dates. The first letter had been written in March 1882. It was from Jane to Robert and it had been very well-thumbed. A newspaper cutting, yellow and fragile, fell from its pages. Liz picked it up and read it. It said:

TO HIS WORSHIP, GEORGE BEATTIE,
MAYOR OF SOUTH SHIELDS, AND TO HIS WIFE,
JANE, NÉE RIDLEY, A GIRL.
THE BOROUGH OFFERS ITS
CONGRATULATIONS AND BEST WISHES
FOR THE FUTURE.

Squinting at the unfamiliar hand, made more obscure by fading ink and stains, Liz read the letter itself. It had a chatty style, containing a frank, lively account of a little girl called Ellen and how she had begged her mother to tell her a story:

'Do you remember the elephant story, Robert? Our Da told us it, when we were kids. It starts, "Once upon a time, there was a little baby elephant ..." Do you remember? It tells how the little elephant, being thirsty,

285

strays from the herd and goes down to the river alone. There it is attacked by a crocodile, and though it fights bravely, its end is near, when, it raises its trunk into the air and it trumpets like billy-o. At once a flash of lightning comes down out of heaven and singes the crocodile's nose. Of course the crocodile lets go and the elephant is saved and its Mam and its Da trumpet their thanks to the God that looks after the elephants. There, I bet you remember it now! You'd have laughed, our Robert, little Ellen couldn't say "elephant", she kept saying "hephalent", "hephalent!" Just like we used to! Nothing changes, does it?

We had some canny times when we were kids, didn't we? We were poor, of course, and we had our troubles. Look at our Fanny! And she doesn't get any better. To be honest I wonder where she gets the money for the drink! I pity poor old Dandy O! So many of us lost now! Dad, Ma Tully, Fanny as well, in a way. And God knows where you are! Your last letter came from Argentina and that was a long while back! Well, I'll send this via the shipping office as usual. I'm enclosing a clipping from the papers. As you'll see you are now the proud uncle of *two* girls. Little Maisie was born a week ago. Fancy the Borough offering its congratulations! Well, I suppose George being Mayor does have *some* compensations! Though sometimes, I wonder. He's always off out somewhere! Still, I shouldn't grumble. He's being especially nice with me while I'm getting over the baby. He's a lovely man. I'm lucky. And he dotes on Maisie, you know. She's really canny! I wish you would come home and see her! I do miss you! Anyway, I'm well and happy, as are George and the bairns. I hope this finds you the same way. Write me a letter soon!

Your everloving sister, Jane.'

So, Robert was away and George and Jane were apparently idyllically happy. Hester, who was the youngest of their children had not yet been born. Liz handed the letter to Jim, and smoothed out the next. There was a long gap. This one was dated, 1888.

Fowler Street

Robert,

I suppose I must thank you for your letter. But I must also tell you that if you dare to come back here and attempt to put 'matters right' with my husband, you will find yourself in deeper water than you expect!

What a pity you ran away in such a panic! It made you look so guilty! And so much more guilty than you think. For your information, George does not believe, as you fear, that in your haste to get away from me, you stole from the till. Because, you see, I told him I had *given* you the money, *and* my engagement ring for good measure! A nice touch, don't you think? But do not think that lets you off the hook! To the contrary, you are no common thief, dear brother! You seduced your sister, not only into giving you her husband's worldly goods (that was nothing), but also of stealing his chattels! Namely his wife! Your sister! Me! Well, you know you intended it. I saw it in your eyes. You enjoyed leading me on, didn't you? You told me you were longing to take me to India with you! You said George didn't know how lucky he was! You said since he had two families, his lady friend's *and* mine, he could surely spare one of them!

You wanted me alright! If it had been the other way round, would it have been different? Was it because it was me that asked and not you? It isn't fair. Just because you're a man, like George, you think you can do what you like! Sail round the world, have affairs with all and sundry and nobody will say a word! While I'm stuck here with nothing! Never been anywhere! Never done anything! When I was young I wanted to go on the stage and you all persuaded me to go into this damned shop!

287

Well, the sickly sweet smell of George's flowers is slowly smothering me. I thought you understood. You certainly sympathised! I am flesh and blood, Robert! I have feelings just the same as you! Women do, you know! Am I supposed to just wither away because George has found somebody else! What's sauce for the gander is sauce for the goose! And serve him right, the lecherous old barkset! I hate him for what he's done to me!

And now you! To back off! To say such vile things of me! How could you? You're all hypocrites, all you men! You wanted me, Robert Ridley, just as much as I wanted you! Well, now you have got your just deserts. And so has George! I have never seen him in such a passion. It is of some consolation to me that he was able to assuage his feelings on my body. It was the first such assault on me in some four years, and it may be the last. However, once is enough, for I find I am pregnant. As a result, George is tortured by doubt, wondering whether the child is his or yours. Such sweet irony, don't you think? So, I have my revenge on him. And on you, too, my hypocritical brother. No man scorns me and gets away with it! My husband has given strict instruction that you are never to darken our doors again, neither must you write to me, nor have any contact with any member of our family. We have washed out hands of you, dear Robert. I am happy to go along with this, because it delights me to tell you that I never want to hear from you again!
Jane Beattie.

Trembling, Liz handed the letter to Jim. She sat, hands clasped, looking at the floor while he read it. Conflicting emotions coursed through her. The brother and sister had not slept together. Hester was not the issue of Jane and Robert, but the legitimate child of the marriage with George. And Liz was free. But the hatred of Jane Beattie, her wounded heart and pride, the spite with which she launched her attack on the men in her life overwhelmed her! Where had all that venom come from? Jim put the letter down and breathed out slowly.

'So,' he said, 'It was all just a story!'

'Yes. But where did it come from? The madness! The suicides!'

'Look at that letter!' Jim said. 'A cold, formal tone one minute, wild with fury the next. It's like two women wrote it! Smacks of schizophrenia!'

'What made her crack? George's infidelity?'

'Why not? She was a talented, passionate woman tied to home and kids with no love, no life of her own! It's driven better women than her crazy!'

'You don't think it might have been inherited?'

'Not necessarily.'

'My grandmother and my mother were both mental!'

'Not surprising is it? George and Jane must both have hated Hester for different reasons! They used her to hurt one another! No wonder she turned out such an oddball! As for your Ma, well, your grandmother gave her one hell of a childhood from what I heard!'

'Dad says Mum was a nervous wreck.'

'Makes sense to me. I always thought that incest story was a bit melodramatic!'

'But what Jane actually did was much worse! It was cruel!'

'George earned it.'

'The children?'

'They suffered. Children do, God help them, and then they pass the suffering on to the next generation and they suffer ...'

'It stops here!' Liz sniffed back her tears. Jim put his hand on hers. It was cold. He held it, warming it for a while.

'Do you think Robert actually stole that money?' Liz asked suddenly.

'I don't know.' Jim considered the circumstances,

then said, 'Sounds like he needed to make a quick getaway to me! And if he didn't have any cash on him, well ... According to her, he wanted to pay George back. So, it was maybe more like borrowing than stealing. And he definitely didn't take her ring! She made that one up all on her own!'

'I can't help feeling sorry for her!' Liz shook her head in stunned amazement. 'She must have gone through hell! I mean, she kept up that story about her and Robert all those years! She took it with her to her grave! How could she do it? Unless she was absolutely consumed with hate!'

'Or unless, by then, she'd persuaded herself the story was true!' Liz stared at him, a glimmer of understanding in her eyes.

'I see.' She nodded slowly. 'For her. Robert's rejection was harder to bear than the stigma of incest.' Liz let out a deep sigh. 'She probably didn't know what the truth was by the time she was finished!'

But there was more. The unopened letter was still waiting to be read, a hundred years after it had been written. Liz's fingers reached for it. A cold wind lifted from the paper to her hand.

'What *is* this?' she gasped. Cautiously, she picked up the letter and broke the seal. She felt as though the top of her head was going to lift right off! Spirals of cold air curled round her as she pulled the pages from the envelope. She was almost crying as she spread them and started to read:

Bombay, January 1889

Dear Jane,

I beg you to forgive me if in any way I led you to believe my loving feelings for you were anything but those of a brother. I was sorry for you and I wanted to help you, if I could, even to taking you and the children to India! But as for wanting to bed you! No! I may be a bit of an adventurer, but I'm not that bad! Jane, your highly strung emotional state has clouded your brain. I blame George for this, not you. I know the woman who tried to persuade me into her bed and who wrote that last letter, forbidding me to come near, is not you, my dear sister. I hope and pray you come to your senses soon. I beg you to tell your husband the truth. He is a good man, in spite of everything and he will forgive you. It may be you and he can still heal the breach between you. But if not you must tell him for the sake of your children, for the sake of the child you are now carrying, and for their children, too! Do not let your grand-children believe they were conceived in sin! Whatever we may be, they surely are innocent! Do not burden them with artificial guilt! I pray, I beseech the God of all Innocence, Lord Ganesha, to bless and protect the generations of your seed to come, that they may not be trammelled by lies, but be guided by the truth within, to know that real love is always innocent! As is my love for you.

Robert.

Handing the letter to Jim, Liz rose and stood listening to the silence. The air was thick with it, like a winter sky before it snows. Then something tells you it's about to happen. Looking up, you see the flakes separating from the clouds to float down to earth. And the laughter of children, rushing out to catch them, lifts the heart till it, too, is floating ... like snowflakes, like feathers on the air. So Liz stood and her heart floated in the silence of the room. Jim put down the letter and looked at her. He was grinning.

'I knew He was with me,' Liz said quietly. 'I knew it.'

Both minds were casting back. Jim was remembering George's words, 'The shadow of the elephant ...'

'The shadow George spoke of was no curse, Liz,' he said.

She shook her head in tearful gratitude. 'No,' she whispered, 'Ganesha's shadow has protected my family for generations. Everybody felt it, but no-one understood! He's been there with us, all the same, standing guard over us, guiding us back to the truth whenever we strayed from it.' Jim was thinking of the statue. Did Robert send it? As though hearing his thought, Liz replied,

'I think that statue was a wedding present for Ellen ... Jane's firstborn! Very appropriate!' Liz's delighted laughter filled the room. 'If we'd only known what it all meant! But, you see, I had to go to India to find Him, didn't I?'

'Looks like it,' Jim said. He was looking at the copybook. 'Come and see this!' Reluctantly, Liz turned back to the material world. The copybook was a kind of journal. It covered Robert's travels for the two years, 1886 and 1887. In it he had recorded the places he'd seen, the people he'd met, his adventures and, alongside, he had illustrated it with pen and ink sketches, watercolours, drawings of all kinds. For a second, Liz was dismayed.

'I didn't know he was an artist! I wondered where I'd ...' she was about to say 'got it from'. Jim put his arm round her and hugged her.

'Look,' he said, 'Robert must have got his talent from somewhere. It didn't start with him! He had the same parents as Jane. Well, the same genes came down to you, but via his sister. She was artistic, too, in her way! She wanted to go on the stage, didn't she! She says so in that letter. Well, her granddaughter, Frances, and *her* daughter, Eve, they both went on the stage! They got the performing genes, you got the arty genes! They're probably a throw back to your great-great-great-great-grandpa or however far back you need to go!' Liz nodded slowly, 'It really is alright, you know,' he told her gently. 'You are allowed to be an artist.' She smiled, shamefaced, and started opening the sheaf of papers. More water colours and sketches fell out onto the bed.

'Aren't I lucky,' she said, 'to have such an inheritance?'

Waking early, they saw the first light on Rouen Cathedral, the spires a vision of brightness, disappearing white into the blue sky, the doorways lit up with gold, the rose window a cavern of blue above. As they stood, watching, the light changed slowly, adding coral to gold, dispelling blue with yellow, the shadows behind transformed with purple.

Seeing this through Monet's eyes, they couldn't wait to see the garden. So, without so much as entering the church, they drove away from the town, along the banks of the Seine to Giverny. The river mirrored the morning, dissolving the trees along its banks, melting colour into colour till there was no colour left, only a blur held in the white of the morning.

Passing through the village, they turned up the hill to the house. There, they followed a dark, winding corridor from the entrance and emerged into the great studio where Monet painted 'The Water Lilies'. The hall was light, but the brilliance of the doors attracted the eye, and Liz was drawn towards them. Dazzling, the light radiated into the room, obscuring the view beyond. And as she walked towards them, Liz recognised the doors of her dream. Blinded, she hesitated for a moment on the threshold, then stepped out into the garden.

Vivid, the colour of wallflowers, tulips, iris, anemones, columbines, lilac and pansies, rioted along the way. The air was aromatic with their blend of perfumes, till, arriving at the lake, they saw the fire of azaleas in the water, and in the depths of green and blue the waterlily leaves newly emerging. White glimmered at the tip of a swelling bud, and a single petal unfurled, pink from another. Raising their eyes, they looked across sky refracted in water to the bridge, where the wisteria was in bloom. It curved like a rainbow over the lake. Their hands reached out and touched.

'I feel so young!' Jim said.

'Yes,' Liz replied, 'I know what you mean. It feels like it's all just beginning ...'

☐	The Turning Tides	Valerie Georgeson	£3.50
☐	Seeds of Love	Valerie Georgeson	£4.99
☐	Whispering Roots	Valerie Georgeson	£4.50
☐	Haunted Tree	Valerie Georgeson	£4.50

Warner Books now offers an exciting range of quality titles by both established and new authors. All of the books in this series are available from:

Little, Brown and Company (UK) Limited,
P.O. Box 11,
Falmouth,
Cornwall TR10 9EN.

Alternatively you may fax your order to the above address.
Fax No. 0326 376423.

Payments can be made as follows: cheque, postal order (payable to Little, Brown and Company) or by credit cards, Visa/Access. Do not send cash or currency. UK customers and B.F.P.O. please allow £1.00 for postage and packing for the first book, plus 50p for the second book, plus 30p for each additional book up to a maximum charge of £3.00 (7 books plus).

Overseas customers including Ireland, please allow £2.00 for the first book plus £1.00 for the second book, plus 50p for each additional book.

NAME (Block Letters) ....

....

ADDRESS ....

....

....

☐ I enclose my remittance for _____

☐ I wish to pay by Access/Visa Card

Number ☐☐☐☐☐☐☐☐☐☐☐☐☐☐☐☐☐☐☐☐

Card Expiry Date ☐☐☐☐